Praise for Lynn Austin

"Austin transports readers into the lives of her characters, plunking them in the middle of a brutal war and giving them a unique take on the traditional World War II tale. Readers won't be able to turn the pages fast enough to find out how Eve and Audrey met and what could have gone so terribly wrong."

LIBRARY JOURNAL, starred review of *If I Were You*

"[A] tantalizing domestic drama. . . . Its message familiar and its world nostalgic and fragile, *If I Were You* looks for answers in changing identities and finds that it's priceless to remain true to oneself."

FOREWORD REVIEWS

"Solid research . . . and detailed descriptions certainly make *If I Were You* a rich and enchanting historical reading experience. Fans of historical fiction and writers such as Jennifer Robson will certainly relish the wonderful story of faith and friendship."

FRESH FICTION

"Lynn is a masterful storyteller. The characters become people you feel like you know and you truly care about. The plot has unexpected turns and keeps you riveted. All while providing encouragement in your faith as you watch the main characters' courage during an extremely difficult time in modern history. 5 out of 5 stars."

ECLA LIBRARIES

"A lovely story, so beautifully told, and with a really good Christian message. . . . I cannot recommend *If I Were You* strongly enough."

CHRISTIAN NOVEL REVIEW

"Lynn Austin is a master at exploring the depths of human relationships. Set against the backdrop of war and its aftermath, *If I Were You* is a beautifully woven page-turner."

SUSAN MEISSNER, bestselling author of *Secrets of a Charmed Life* and *The Last Year of the War*

"I have long enjoyed Lynn Austin's novels, but *If I Were You* resonates above all others. Austin weaves the plot and characters together with sheer perfection, and the ending—oh, pure delight to a reader's heart!"

TAMERA ALEXANDER, bestselling author of *With This Pledge* and *A Note Yet Unsung*

"*If I Were You* is a page-turning, nail-biting, heart-stopping gem of a story. Once again, Lynn Austin has done her homework. Each detail rings true, pulling us into Audrey and Eve's differing worlds of privilege and poverty, while we watch their friendship and their faith in God struggle to survive. I loved traveling along on their journey, with all its unexpected twists and turns, and sighed with satisfaction when I reached the final page. *So* good."

LIZ CURTIS HIGGS, *New York Times* bestselling author of *Mine Is the Night*

"Lynn Austin has long been one of my favorite authors. With an intriguing premise and excellent writing, *If I Were You* is sure to garner accolades and appeal to fans of novels like *The Alice Network* and *The Nightingale*."

JULIE KLASSEN, author of *The Bridge to Belle Island*

"*If I Were You* is an immersive experience, not only into the dangers and deprivations of wartime England, but into the psychological complexities of characters desperate to survive. . . . With her signature attention to detail and unvarnished portrayal of the human heart, Lynn Austin weaves a tale of redemption that bears witness to Christ's power to make all things new."

SHARON GARLOUGH BROWN, author of the Sensible Shoes series and *Shades of Light*

"Lynn Austin's *If I Were You* is a powerful story of heart-wrenching loss, our desperate need to be understood, to forgive and be forgiven, and the loving sacrifice found in true friendship. A compelling read, beautifully written, celebrating the strength of faith and the power of sisterhood."

CATHY GOHLKE, Christy Award–winning author of *The Medallion* and *Night Bird Calling*

"A master at inviting readers onto a journey and sweeping them away with her elegant prose, Lynn Austin once again transports readers back in time to England. *If I Were You* is a beautiful story about courage, relentless love, and the transforming power of forgiveness."

MELANIE DOBSON, award-winning author of *Memories of Glass* and *The Curator's Daughter*

"Lynn Austin's tradition of masterful historical fiction continues in *If I Were You*, an impeccably researched look into the lives of two remarkable women. Her unparalleled skill at evoking the past . . . will appeal to fans of Ariel Lawhon and Lisa Wingate. While longtime fans will appreciate this introspective tale from a writer who deeply feels the nuances of human nature, those uninitiated will immediately recognize why her talented pen has led her to near-legendary status in the realm of inspirational fiction. An unforgettable read."

RACHEL McMILLAN, author of *The London Restoration*

"Lynn Austin knows how to create conflict with her characters. *Par excellence.* Her latest novel is no exception. *If I Were You* tells the story of a *Downton Abbey*–like friendship between Audrey, from the nobility, and Eve, a servant at Audrey's manor house. . . . Bold and brilliant and clever, *If I Were You* will delight Lynn's multitude of fans and garner many new ones."

ELIZABETH MUSSER, author of *When I Close My Eyes*

Also by Lynn Austin

CHASING SHADOWS

LYNN AUSTIN

Tyndale House Publishers
Carol Stream, Illinois

Visit Tyndale online at tyndale.com.

Visit Lynn Austin's website at lynnaustin.org.

TYNDALE and Tyndale's quill logo are registered trademarks of Tyndale House Ministries.

Chasing Shadows

Cover designed by Faceout Studio, Molly von Borstel

Interior designed by Dean H. Renninger

Edited by Kathryn S. Olson

Published in association with the literary agency of Natasha Kern Literary Agency, Inc., P.O. Box 1069, White Salmon, WA 98672.

Scripture quotations are taken from the Holy Bible, *New International Version,*® *NIV.*® Copyright © 1973, 1978, 1984, 2011 by Biblica, Inc.® Used by permission. All rights reserved worldwide.

For information about special discounts for bulk purchases, please contact Tyndale House Publishers at csresponse@tyndale.com, or call 1-855-277-9400.

Library of Congress Cataloging-in-Publication Data
Names: Austin, Lynn N., author.
Title: Chasing shadows / Lynn Austin.
Description: Carol Stream, Illinois : Tyndale House Publishers, [2021]
Identifiers: LCCN 2020051173 (print) | LCCN 2020051174 (ebook) | ISBN 9781496437341 (hardcover) | ISBN 9781496437358 (trade paperback) | ISBN 9781496437365 (kindle edition) | ISBN 9781496437372 (epub) | ISBN 9781496437389 (epub)
Classification: LCC PS3551.U839 C53 2021 (print) | LCC PS3551.U839 (ebook) | DDC 813/.54—dc23
LC record available at https://lccn.loc.gov/2020051173
LC ebook record available at https://lccn.loc.gov/2020051174

Printed in the United States of America

27	26	25	24	23	22	21
7	6	5	4	3	2	1

How could God Himself show truth and love at
the same time in a world like this? By dying.

CORRIE TEN BOOM, *The Hiding Place*

Have mercy on me, my God,
have mercy on me, for in you I take refuge.
I will take refuge in the shadow of your wings
until the disaster has passed.

PSALM 57:1

PROLOGUE

THE NETHERLANDS
MAY 1945

Every sound in the coal-black night seemed magnified as Lena lay awake in bed, waiting. She heard the quiet rustlings of the shadow people as they crept through the darkness downstairs in her farmhouse. The creak of the barn door and whisper of hay as they moved through her barn on this moonless night. The shadow people were also waiting. Did they hate it as much as she did?

The war had taught Lena de Vries to do many things. Hard, impossible things. She had learned to be courageous, propelled by fear and faith. She'd learned to face death, gripping the Savior's hand. But waiting was the hardest lesson of all. Every minute seemed like an hour. Every hour stretched endlessly. The sun stood still in the sky during the day, then took its time dawning after each endless night—like this one. She would find herself hoping against all reason that her husband, Pieter, was alive and would come home and she could hold him in her arms. Or hoping that her daughter Ans and son, Wim, were still alive and would return. She knew that if one of them walked through her door, her joy would swallow up the long months of waiting. If they ever did return.

The past seven days had been the longest week in all of Lena's forty-five years. Spring should be a time of rebirth and hope, but tonight her imagination partnered with fear, squeezing her heart dry, extinguishing hope. She released her breath with a sigh and rolled over in bed, whispering a quiet prayer for Pieter and Ans and Wim. And for all the shadow people who waited in the darkness with her.

Sleep was impossible. She hadn't slept soundly since the Nazis invaded five years ago. She rose from her bed, careful not to awaken her daughters Maaike and Bep, asleep in the bed beside her where Pieter should be. Lena kept her girls close to her side these days. She pulled on a sweater over her nightgown and felt her way downstairs, familiar with every narrow step on the steep, angled stairs. She halted at the bottom. A shadow moved around her kitchen as if searching for something. Her heart leaped.

"Pieter?" she whispered.

The shadow turned. It was Wolf, her contact with the Dutch Resistance. She didn't know his real name. It was safer that way. "Did I wake you?" he whispered. "I'm sorry. I was looking for a pencil. I wanted to leave you a note."

"Do you have news of my husband?"

"No. But I do have good news. Allied troops are in Holland. Canadian tanks have liberated many of our cities. Here's the latest newspaper." He pulled the flimsy underground newssheet from his pocket and handed it to Lena. She glanced at it, then instinctively rolled it up so it would fit inside her bicycle frame. She would hide it there from the Nazis when she delivered it to her cousin in the village.

"But the Allies haven't come this far yet?" she asked.

"Soon. I came to tell you and the others that it won't be long. Maybe even tomorrow."

Two more shadows slipped into the kitchen as Lena and Wolf talked. They left their hiding places only at night and disappeared before dawn. How they must long to feel the sun on their faces again.

"This isn't another false alarm like last fall, is it?" one of the shadows whispered. Lena remembered "Mad Tuesday," when rumors of liberation had swept the country. There had been panic among the Nazis and rejoicing among the Dutch people. Many Nazi occupiers and their collaborators had fled east. When it proved to be a false alarm, they returned. Hope withered.

"This time it's true," Wolf said. "I saw the Canadian tanks myself."

Lena closed her eyes for a moment. Would the waiting truly be over?

"How will we know when it's safe to come out?" the other shadow asked.

"They'll ring the church bells in town. I have to go," Wolf said, backing toward the door. "I need to tell the others."

"Wait," Lena said. "Are you hungry? Have you eaten?" Wolf was shadow-thin. The deep hollows on the planes of his face made him appear skeletal in the darkness. Thousands of people who were trapped in the cities were dying of starvation every day. Cities like Leiden, where Lena's daughter Ans lived.

"You already have so many mouths to feed," Wolf said.

"Then one more won't make a difference." She opened the warming oven above the stove and pulled out a baked potato, wrapped in a cloth to keep it warm, and pushed it into his hands. "I only wish I had more to offer you." The potato was small and shriveled, one of the last few from her depleted root cellar. "Thank you for coming, Wolf. I'll spread the news." He had given Lena hope. And hope would make waiting harder still.

She sat down at the kitchen table with the shadow people after Wolf left, talking about the war and reading the underground newspaper to them while they each ate a potato and some boiled cabbage. She knew only their false names—Max and his wife, Ina—and that they were Jewish. Max forged false ID cards for the Resistance during the night, down in Lena's root cellar.

When it was light enough to see, Lena helped them crawl back into their hiding place behind the piano in her front room. Pieter had boarded up the door to a closet on the other side of the wall as if it had never been there, then built a secret door in the lower panel of their upright piano. The bass keys no longer worked, but the rest of the keys did. Few people knew about the secret place, not even Lena's two younger daughters, or that Max and Ina had lived there for more than a year.

After she'd dressed, Lena put the rest of the baked potatoes and a rind of bread she'd been saving in a basket and carried it through the door that led from the kitchen into the barn. She never knew how many shadows were hiding in her barn or how long they would stay. More hid at the very top of the old windmill that pumped water for their fields. The Resistance would position the windmill blades to signal when it was safe for the shadow people to hide on her farm. Again, it was better for Lena not to know too much. She simply cooked whatever food she had and brought it to them, asking the Lord to multiply it like the loaves and fishes.

Several men of various ages crept out of their hiding places in the barn as Lena sang the hymn that served as a signal. She read Wolf's newspaper to them as they ate. Four of the shadows were in their late teens—her son Wim's age. Others looked like *onderduikers*, ordinary husbands and fathers who'd been forced to "dive under" to avoid being sent to German slave-labor camps. Or they might be railroad workers who'd been ordered by the exiled Dutch government to go on strike to hinder the Nazis. The slender young man with wire-rimmed glasses and ebony hair was undoubtedly Jewish.

"What's the first thing you want to do once the Allies arrive and Holland is free?" she asked.

"Go home" was their unanimous reply. The shadow men talked about things they missed and the food they were hungry for as they finished their bread and potatoes. "I heard that the Allies give out cigarettes," one of them said. "I'd give anything for a smoke."

At dawn, one of the shadows offered to milk Lena's cows for her. "I grew up on a farm in Friesland," he said. "Milking reminds me of home." He stroked the cow's shoulder as if greeting an old friend before straddling the milking stool. "Shall I let them out to graze when I'm finished?" he asked.

"No, they have to stay inside the barn again today. Shrapnel from a stray Nazi rocket killed three cows in a neighboring village."

"Someone might steal them for food too," another shadow said.

"Yes, there is that."

Lena's daughters drank some of the still-warm milk for breakfast. They looked thin and shadowlike too. Wim and Ans had been plump and rosy-cheeked at that age. Before the war. When life was gentle and good. When food was plentiful. "I think we'll take the rest of the milk into town this morning," she told the girls, "and trade it for something."

Bep bounced with excitement at the prospect of a trip into the village. At four years old, she was full of life and energy. "May I wear a bow in my hair?" she asked.

"It isn't Sunday," Maaike replied.

"I know, but may I, Mama?"

"Yes, why not?" Lena brushed Bep's long, dark hair after breakfast and tied a bright bow in it. It fell naturally into thick curls. "Do you want one, too?" she asked Maaike. She shook her head. At eleven years old she was no longer interested in girlish bows. Lena braided Maaike's straw-blonde hair—the same color as her own—into a thick braid that fell nearly to her waist. When it was time to go, Lena fetched her broken-down bicycle from the barn. In peacetime her bicycle would be considered a piece of junk—and it was—but at least the Nazis would deem it not worth confiscating. She lifted Bep onto the handlebars, and Maaike climbed onto the board Pieter had attached to the rear fender. Lena tied the two containers of milk beneath her sweater and apron and set off on the three-mile trip into the village.

The pastures between her farm and the town looked tired and pale this morning, like an invalid who'd lain in bed too long. More fenceposts were missing, and several more trees had disappeared, chopped down for fuel this past winter. They were calling that long, endless season the Hunger Winter. With the railroad workers on strike, food had become so scarce in the cities that starving people had staggered out to Lena's farm from Leiden and Den Haag to beg for food. Her little nation would have much rebuilding to do once the war finally ended. But Lena suspected that the hardest task would be repairing the discord and mistrust among neighbors and even within families. For the past five years, no one had known whom they could trust or who might sell their secrets to the Nazis to feed their starving children. She and Pieter knew when they agreed to hide Jews and *onderduikers* that if they were discovered, they'd be arrested and imprisoned.

Lena was nearly to town when she heard the glorious cacophony of church bells ringing in the distance. She slowed to a halt as joy leaped in her heart. "Listen, girls! Do you hear the bells?"

"But it isn't Sunday, Mama," Bep said.

"I know. It means the Netherlands is free! We're free!" She'd spoken the words but could barely comprehend that they were true.

"Does that mean the Nazis will go away now?" Maaike asked.

"Yes, they'll be gone for good. The Netherlands will be free again!" She couldn't imagine it. Lena wondered if Maaike even remembered a time when Nazi soldiers on roaring motorcycles weren't a common sight. She'd been six years old when they'd invaded the Netherlands. Little Bep had never known freedom at all.

Lena picked up her pace as she pedaled the last mile into town. The village square and the street in front of her father's church were packed with people as if it were Easter Sunday. The church bells clamored so loudly they could probably be heard all the way out to the farm. Lena's friends and neighbors were laughing and embracing each other, their faces streaming with tears. Her cousin Truus pushed through the crowd and hugged Lena tightly, the milk cans clanking as the women rocked in place. "Isn't it wonderful, Lena? We're free! The Nazis are gone at last!"

"And look at all these people who must have been hidden," Lena said when Truus released her again. Crowded among the people she knew were strangers Lena had never seen before. Their milk-white skin and haunted faces told her they were shadow people. "I had no idea so many of them were hiding right here in the village!"

"And do you notice who isn't here?" her cousin asked. "The filthy collaborators have all fled."

"What a relief." Lena wondered if they would face justice for what they'd done. They had much to account for. Lena had known these villagers all her life, had worshiped beside them in church every Sunday, and she knew that the war had brought tragedy into every life, every home. She watched them cheering and hugging each other and asking, "Is it really over? Are they finally gone?" One of the church elders burst into song, and everyone joined in singing the words to the psalm:

"O God, our help in ages past, our hope for years to come,
Our shelter from the stormy blast, and our eternal home."

Lena gripped Bep's hand and wiped tears as she sang. If only Pieter and Papa were here to see this. She needed to hurry home and tell her own shadow people the good news. Max and Ina could come out from behind the piano. The *onderduikers* could go home to their families. Maybe Pieter and Ans and Wim were on their way home right now.

She traded the milk for some cheese and a loaf of bread. "You can carry these for me on the way home," she told her daughters. "There's no need to hide them anymore." Joy and hope warmed her like spring sunshine as she pedaled. The fields looked greener now than they had on the way into town.

"You can come out! It's safe!" she called as she parked her bicycle in the barn. "The Netherlands is free!"

"You're sure?" a voice called.

"Very sure! Quick! Run up to the windmill and tell the others." Lena's daughters hovered close to her as shadows emerged from every corner of the barn. Maaike and Bep would have no idea who these men were. Lena laughed at the girls' astonished expressions and motioned for them to follow her to the kitchen, then into the front room. She bent down and rapped on the lower panel of the piano. "It's safe to come out! The Netherlands is free! We're free!" The girls watched, amazed, as the panel opened and Max and Ina emerged. Lena flung the front door wide for them and said, "Look! It's a glorious day! You can go outside at last!" They moved as if in a dream as they joined the other shadow people outside in the barnyard. Like the villagers, they gazed around in wonder, laughing and rejoicing. Ina dropped to her knees, her face hidden in her hands as she wept. Across the yard, several men stood on the windmill's upper deck, cheering and lifting their faces to the sun. Lena waved to them from her front door. Maaike stood beside her.

"Who are all these people, Mama? What are they doing here?"

"They were hiding from the Nazis. Your papa said they could stay here with us, where it's safe. But they don't need to hide anymore." She looked around for Bep and saw her crouching down to peek beneath the piano.

"Look, Maaike!" Bep said. "There's a little room inside the piano, with blankets and a bookshelf and everything. Come and see!"

As Maaike went over to take a peek, Lena lifted the studio photograph of her family from the top of the piano. It had been taken in 1939 during a trip to Leiden, a year before the Nazi invasion, before any of them ever imagined the war would come to Holland. Lena's oldest daughter, Ans, had been eighteen—so beautiful with her pale-blonde hair and slender frame. Her bold smile and confident stance revealed her strong will. Wim stood beside his sister, already as tall as she was, his fair hair bleached nearly white by the sun. Before the invasion he'd been a curious eleven-year-old who loved to swim in the canals and tease his sisters. The war had forced Wim to become a man before his time. Five-year-old Maaike nestled on Lena's lap, her surprise baby, born when Lena was thirty-four. Lena had convinced her father to pose with them for the portrait, too. Tall and dignified, with a fringe of white hair and a trim white beard and goatee, he stood behind Wim and Ans, every inch the stern pastor. Papa's gray eyes looked pinched behind his wire-rimmed glasses as if he was in pain or had stared at the sun too long. He'd still been grieving the loss of Lena's mother, who'd died a few months earlier. Pieter, the love of Lena's life, stood behind her with his hands resting on her shoulders. How she loved his strong, calloused, sun-browned hands. Would she ever take them in hers again? Out of the six people in the photograph, only Lena and Maaike were safe at home.

Jesus had told His followers, "Anyone who loves their father or mother more than me is not worthy of me; anyone who loves their son or daughter more than me is not worthy of me. Whoever does not take up their cross and follow me is not worthy of me." It was a hard, hard truth, put to the test by the fires of war.

Lena felt a tug on her skirt. Bep looked up at her with a worried expression. "Is Papa going to come home now?" she asked.

"And Wim and Ans, too?" Maaike added.

Lena didn't reply. She didn't know. A tendril of fear sprouted and curled around her heart, and she knew if she allowed it to grow, it would strangle her faith. She used to believe that the enemy of faith was doubt, but she'd learned that faith's destroyer was fear. *"Let your fear drive you into the arms of God,"* her father had said.

"Well, we will hope and pray that they do come home," Lena replied.

"I miss Opa," Maaike said. She was studying the photograph, too.

Lena stroked her daughter's fair hair and thick braid. "So do I."

"Are you crying, Mama?" Bep asked.

Lena brushed away her tears. "Sometimes we cry because we're happy."

"I'm happy, too." Bep wrapped her thin arms around Lena's legs and hugged her tightly. This child was so dear to Lena's heart. She couldn't love Bep more if she had come from her own womb.

But she hadn't.

And now with the liberation, the truth would also come out of hiding, like the shadow people.

CHAPTER 1

Lena didn't want to lose her temper, but her daughter had her close to the edge again. "You simply can't take a train by yourself to a strange city and live there, Ans. It's ridiculous!"

"But I'm tired of being stuck here in this nothing town where everyone knows your business. I can't stand it a minute longer!" Ans was washing dishes, slamming them onto the drainboard to emphasize each word.

"Maybe if you and a group of your friends—"

"They're all happy living here! Rietje and Corrie have *boyfriends*." She said the word as if it disgusted her. "I'd rather be a spinster than marry one of the boys from around here. I would end up being his servant, cooking and cleaning and milking his cows and having countless babies."

Lena stopped wiping the table and faced her daughter. "Is that what you think my life is like? Do you think I'm a servant with no life of my own? That I do nothing but work and have babies?"

"You wanted this life. I don't! I'm tired of smelling manure with every breath I take. Tired of eating in a kitchen that's four feet from the barn."

And tired of church. That was part of her dissatisfaction, too. Lena knew Ans would start complaining about the church next. And she did.

"The church is nothing but a bunch of dull rituals. Do people even believe the words they say and sing every week? The rules the church makes us follow are so old-fashioned! Like the law that says, 'Obey your husband.' The world is a modern place, and—"

"I love your father. It's no hardship at all to work alongside him and do the things that make him happy." Lena couldn't imagine anything better than living with the open fields around her, breathing the aroma of freshly mown hay, and cherishing the seasonal rhythms of land and home. She gave the table a final swipe and tossed the rag into the sink.

"Well, I feel trapped here," Ans said. "I want to live in Leiden."

They never should have traveled there by train that day when they'd had their photograph taken. Ans had loved the city. Lena had hated it. It was too noisy and busy, with cars and bicycles and trains racing past. Lena had felt lost and disoriented among the twisting streets and winding rivers and canals. The houses crowded together like kernels of corn on a cob with no open spaces between them. Ans had declared the city beautiful. She had been restless to return ever since.

"You can't keep me here. I'm almost nineteen!"

Lena turned away to avoid saying something she would regret. And so that Ans wouldn't see her tears. She walked through the door to the barn, then outside to where Pieter was repairing a bicycle tire. "I could hear you fighting with Ans again," he said.

"She insults me and our way of life, Pieter. I don't know how to get through to her."

Pieter removed his cap and wiped his forehead on his sleeve. "You can't, Lena. She's been strong-willed and determined to get her own way since the day she was born, remember?"

Oh yes. Lena remembered. Ans had never been a quiet, contented child like Wim or Maaike. "She's so stubborn!" Lena said. "Why won't she listen to reason?"

"Her stubbornness might be her greatest asset one day."

"Or it might bring her to ruin."

Pieter pulled his cap over his sweaty hair again. "Ans spent the past year watching her grandmother slowly die. Let her go, Lena. Trying to hold on to her is like holding on to sand. The tighter you grip, the faster it slips through your fingers."

Impossible. Lena was the glue that held the farm and the family together. Everything would fall apart if she let go. She moved forward into Pieter's arms, loving his strength and solidity, a tree with deep roots and strong limbs. Lena had married him when she was eighteen—Ans's age—and had never regretted it for a single moment. "What about her soul, Pieter? She's rejecting the church and everything we've taught her."

"I don't know what to tell you," he said with a sigh. "Talk to your father. See what he has to say."

She kissed him and left him to his work, walking slowly back toward the house. She had work to do as well, but she was too worried to concentrate on any of it. She looked for Maaike and Wim and found them crouched in the tall grass by the edge of the canal, their blond heads bent together as they examined a frog or a bug or some such treasure. "I'm going into the village," she called to them. "Want to come?"

They wanted to stay home and play, so Lena rode her bicycle into town by herself. She found her father sitting at his kitchen table in the manse, writing a letter. He laid down his pen and sat back in his chair as she greeted him. "Well, this is a pleasant surprise, Engelena Everdina. What brings you here?"

He always smiled when he used her full name. He seemed softer since Mama died, as if grief and pain had filed away some of his sharpness and certainty. He was more patient with his parishioners, more understanding of their faults.

He gestured to an empty chair at the table and listened as Lena told him about her escalating arguments with Ans and her daughter's comments about the church. Ans had lived here in the manse during her last months in secondary school, taking care of her grandmother until she'd died. Grief still etched a deep cavern in Lena's soul that she hadn't climbed out of yet. She would be sucked back into the darkness when she least expected it by the sight of an empty place at the table or a basket of abandoned knitting. Lena couldn't lose her daughter, too.

Her father paused a moment before replying, removing his wire-rimmed glasses and polishing them with a corner of his sweater. "Ans's faith has to become her own, Lena. She can't inherit yours or mine, no matter how much we may wish it. She has to find God through what she sees and experiences with Him."

His advice surprised Lena. "But . . . what if she doesn't come back to the church? What if she keeps turning away from it—and from us?"

"Ans belongs to God, not to us. He will be faithful to pursue her. The Bible says no one can snatch her from the Father's hand." He seemed certain of it.

"What about her reputation—and yours? People are already asking why she doesn't come to church with us anymore."

"You don't owe anyone an explanation."

His words should have reassured Lena, but they didn't. She couldn't help feeling that her daughter's rebellion was her fault. "Ans wants to leave home all by herself and move to Leiden. I must have done something wrong as a mother to make her feel that way."

Her father gave a gentle laugh, shaking his head. "No, Engelena. Don't blame yourself. Adam and Eve had a perfect parent, yet they rebelled."

"What should I do?"

"If you love her—and I know you do—you have to let her go."

Tears filled Lena's eyes. "Just let her go? All alone? She has no plans at all for the future except to leave home and live in Leiden."

"God created Ans the way He did for a reason. He can use her strong will and independent spirit. Maybe this isn't rebellion as much as it is the need to become herself."

"She's just a child, Papa." Lena's throat tightened as she swallowed a lump of sorrow—or maybe fear. "She's naive about the ways of the world beyond our farm and village."

He stood and walked around the table to rest his hand on her shoulder. "Listen, I'll talk with one of my colleagues at the Pieterskerk in Leiden. I'll see if he knows of a position for Ans with a family from his congregation. Maybe living away from home for a while will help her figure out her next step."

It wasn't the answer Lena wanted to hear. She had to stop her bicycle and sink down beneath a tree on the way home, her vision blinded by tears. Lena had imagined a different future for her beautiful firstborn child. Yes, she knew her children would eventually grow up and leave home, but she had always pictured them living nearby, with armfuls of her grandchildren. They would sit in church together every week and eat Sunday dinner at her farmhouse table. Ans might even marry a preacher like her grandfather and live in the manse beside the church. Never had Lena imagined setting her daughter loose in a university city like Leiden. In letting Ans go, Lena would have to let go of all her dreams for her.

A tractor coughed as it rumbled across a distant field scribing tidy rows. A colony of ants busied themselves in their hill beneath her feet. Lena found order and safety and purpose in the rhythms of nature. She could see no purpose in Ans's flight from home.

"If you love her . . ." Oh, how she loved her daughter! Ans, her firstborn, special to her in so many ways. She possessed an outward beauty that frightened Lena because Ans didn't know the power of it yet. Lena clasped her hands into fists as if longing to hold tightly to her.

"If you love her, let her go." She had to entrust her daughter to God. Lena knew her faith wasn't strong enough to do that. She lowered her head as her tears fell and asked God to teach her how to let go.

CHAPTER 2

COLOGNE, GERMANY

Miriam Jacobs put her hands over her ears to block out the bickering. Her family was quarreling again. Abba argued with Uncle David. Uncle David argued with Uncle Nathan. And Uncle Nathan argued with Abba. Aunt Shoshanna and Aunt Louisa squabbled with Mother and with each other. Mother disagreed with Abba.

Miriam didn't want to hear any more. She pushed her chair away from the table and stood, gathering up the delicate bone china plates. She carried them into the kitchen to escape the noise and yanked the door closed between the butler's pantry and the dining room. She could still hear them quarreling.

Miriam longed for the meals around her family's dinner table to be as they used to be, when there was laughter instead of fighting and generous platters of food spread across the white tablecloth. A time when the silver candlesticks were lit in celebration, not to save on the cost of electricity. Mother would sit down at the grand piano after dinner, and Miriam and Uncle David would take out their violins, and they would make lovely music together. Her cousin Saul would join them on his cello when he was home from the music conservatory. Sometimes Aunt Louisa would sing a Mozart aria in her beautiful soprano voice, making chills run down Miriam's arms.

"Our lives will never be the way they used to be," Abba shouted. "It's foolish to expect them to."

"This madness will pass," Uncle Nathan replied. "We just need to be patient and wait it out. People will come to their senses, you'll see."

"We should apply for visas and go to Palestine," Cousin Saul insisted.

"Don't be absurd! Palestine is a backwards, desolate place!"

"We should go to America," another cousin said. "They don't hate Jews there."

"No? Well, if that's true, why don't they issue more visas so we can immigrate? They turned away all those desperate people on that ship, didn't they?" No one could forget the SS *St. Louis*, sailing from Germany last month with more than nine hundred Jews on board seeking asylum in Cuba. The visas the Cuban consulate had issued its passengers were declared invalid by the time the ship reached Havana, and the passengers were forbidden to disembark. Urgent appeals to the American and Canadian governments for refuge were rejected. The desperate passengers had no choice but to return to hate-filled Europe.

"We're staying right here," Uncle Nathan said. He was the older of Mother's two brothers and once the wealthiest.

"But they are boxing us in," Abba said, removing his glasses. "Our lives have grown intolerable. We aren't wanted. We must leave."

"It will get better."

"It will get worse."

Dishes and pots teetered in the kitchen sink. Miriam would help wash them tomorrow. There was little else for her to do all day besides practice her violin, and besides, it was too dark in the kitchen to see what she was doing. She waited for a lull in the arguing, then returned to the dining room to bid everyone good night.

"I wish Saul hadn't gone out," she heard Aunt Louisa say. "It's past curfew."

"I warned him not to," Uncle David said. "It's too dangerous."

"He'll be all right," Uncle Nathan replied. "He knows how to take care of himself."

"Where would we go if we were to leave?" Mother asked. She was still beautiful and delicate, as lovely as the music she'd once performed. It was the first time she'd shown any hint of listening to Abba's arguments.

"I told you, to the Netherlands. They are allowing Jewish refugees to flee across their border. Some people I knew from the university have already gone there."

"How would we move all of our belongings to the Netherlands?" Mother asked. "It's impossible."

"When we go, we must leave everything behind," Abba replied. "Our lives are more valuable than any of our possessions."

"How would you get there?" Uncle Nathan asked.

"I'm told there are guides who will take us across the border in places that aren't guarded," Abba said. "I'll walk if I have to."

"And you think the Dutch people are going to accept Jews any better than our fellow Germans do here in Cologne?"

"There has been a synagogue in Amsterdam since the seventeenth century," Abba replied. "The Dutch don't hate us. They don't have propaganda posters plastered on every wall, demonizing us, or signs in their shops saying no Jews allowed."

"How would you make a living?" Mother asked.

"They have some very fine universities. Jews aren't forbidden to teach there. I've already been making inquiries—"

"I'm getting worried! I wish Saul would come home." Aunt Louisa had risen from the table and was pacing between the foyer and the dining room, lifting the curtain from time to time to gaze into the darkened street.

"Now that it's after curfew," Uncle David said, "Saul might have decided to stay where he is rather than get caught outside in the streets."

Miriam's concern for her cousin grew by the minute. They had all heard horror stories about Jews being assaulted and beaten for no reason. Jewish men who'd had their beards set on fire, women molested. But she also understood her cousin's restlessness, his longing for freedom in spite of the danger. She wouldn't say it out loud, but the prospect of living the rest of her life in this joyless house was unimaginable. Abba's arguments had begun to sway her.

"I'm going to bed," Miriam said. She kissed Mother's cheek and gave Abba a hug, then lit a candle from the one in the center of the table and carried it upstairs. She could still hear them arguing, even with her bedroom door closed. A dark curtain of anxiety began to settle over Miriam, wrapping itself around her, snatching her breath, making her queasy. Her battles with this sudden, nameless dread had begun on Kristallnacht as she'd sat with her parents in their darkened apartment near the university, listening to angry shouts and shattering glass in the streets below, the sky lit by the glow of flames. Now she struggled to control this panic attack, knowing it would grow to uncontrollable proportions until she would be gasping for air as if she'd run up a steep hill. The best way to control it, she'd learned, was to lose herself in her music.

Miriam's hands trembled as she lifted her violin from the case. Her lungs squeezed tighter, but she began to play a Tchaikovsky violin piece by memory, unable to read the music by candlelight. She offered her music as a plea for Saul's safety and as a prayer that God would end the bickering and show her family what to do. Slowly, slowly, her nausea eased and she could breathe again.

◦◦◦

"That's it," Abba said. "We are leaving." He spoke calmly and with great certainty. Two Jewish neighbors on their way to morning prayers had found Miriam's cousin a few blocks from home. Saul had been beaten and left for dead by a gang of Hitler Youth. The neighbors carried him home. He would live, the doctor said, but his injuries would take a long time to heal. Miriam wondered if his soul would ever heal. And if his crushed fingers would ever play the cello again.

The entire family had gathered in Saul's bedroom, trying to comprehend what had happened and why. The room grew very still when Abba announced they were leaving. "If any of you wants to join me, you are welcome to come. But I am taking my wife and daughter and we are leaving Germany for good."

Miriam's heart stuttered at his words, like a leaf tumbling down the street in the wind. The shroud of anxiety floated around her, threatening to settle over her. She couldn't imagine leaving Cologne. Yet she couldn't imagine staying. Who could live in a place where such things happened? "When, Abba?" she asked.

"By the end of the week, if not sooner. I will need a few days to finish making arrangements, then we will go. We must get out."

He told Miriam and her mother to pack one suitcase each. They would have to carry it themselves, and they might have to walk part of the way. Miriam would take her violin, too, of course. She packed and repacked her suitcase countless times in the next hurried days, unable to decide what to bring and what to leave behind. At the very last minute, she tossed out some clothes and added her photograph album and her grandmother's silver candlesticks. Her former life might be ending, but that didn't mean it had never happened. Miriam wanted to remember the laughter and the holidays by Lake Constance so the hope for happier days in the future wouldn't fade.

The night before they were to leave, Abba loaded their bags, Miriam's violin, and an extra suitcase with some of his books and research papers into his car, gathering dust in the carriage house all these months. One of his former physics students, Rolf, came to fetch it and drove it to his apartment in a different part of town.

Saying goodbye to her family and her home the next morning was one of the hardest things Miriam had ever done. Knowing her parents would be right beside her was the only thing that made it bearable. But when the final moment came and they stood in the foyer with their coats on, Mother sank down on one of Grandmother's antique chairs and said, "I can't leave. I'm sorry, but I can't." It was as if her home and her way of life exerted a pull as strong as gravity, and she couldn't free herself from its grip. "You go first and get settled. Miriam and I will join you later.

That way you can let us know what furniture and other household goods we should bring with us."

"My dear, don't you understand? The Nazis won't let us bring anything with us." He spoke gently as if explaining it to a child. "The moment they see us moving our things, they will arrest us. Remember how they took everything in Nathan's store? The Nazis are already moving into Jewish homes and taking whatever they wish. It won't be long until they take this house, too."

Mother looked away as if unable to face him or the incomprehensible truth. It was the same way Miriam had looked away when she first saw her cousin's beaten body. "I can't leave my home," she said softly. "I can't."

"And what about you, dear one?" Abba reached for Miriam's hand. "Will you come with me?"

"I . . . I . . ." She looked from one parent to the other, her stomach as tight as a fist.

She heard a soft sound, like a groan. Her cousin Saul was trying to speak. He looked at Miriam through swollen eyes. "Go . . . ," he rasped. "Miriam, go!"

She looked at her mother.

"Yes," Mother said, closing her eyes. "Yes, you should go." Miriam knelt beside Mother's chair and hugged her fiercely. She embraced her in return, then gently pushed her away. Miriam stood and went to join Abba.

"Dry your eyes, Miriam," Abba said, "so the neighbors won't know that we're leaving." Miriam wiped her eyes on her coat sleeve and walked through the front door with him. She heard weeping behind her and couldn't look back as the door closed. "You remember what we must do?" he asked when they reached the sidewalk.

"Yes, Abba." They walked through the streets together to the crowded market district, carrying empty shopping bags. With the crush and press of shoppers all around them, Miriam and Abba quickly tore off the loosened yellow stars that identified them as Jews and stuffed them into their pockets. They faced imprisonment if caught without them. No one seemed to notice. They continued walking, stopping at a produce vendor to buy fruit, adding it to their bags as if they were ordinary people on an ordinary shopping day. Surely the fruit vendor saw Miriam's shaking hands as she paid for her purchases, or noticed her ragged breaths. And the soldiers idling on the street corner—could they tell that she and Abba were Jewish? What if they stopped them and asked to see their identity cards? Miriam's insides churned as she struggled to breathe, battling her rising fear. And sorrow. She mustn't cry.

Abba filled their bags. He and Miriam continued walking through the marketplace, then out of the Jewish district for the first time in months. Grotesque posters in shopwindows and on billboards depicted Jews with exaggerated facial features and denounced them as an inferior race. What if Rolf had tricked Abba, and the Nazis were waiting inside his apartment to arrest them? "Everything will be fine, Miriam," Abba said as her breathing became labored. "We're almost there."

Abba rang the bell to Rolf's apartment. He answered a moment later and invited them inside. Miriam needed to sit down as fear threatened to overwhelm her. Rolf brought her a glass of water. "Where's your wife, Professor Jacobs?" he asked.

"She isn't coming." Miriam saw pain in Abba's eyes as he removed his glasses and rubbed them. He'd been forced to choose between staying with his wife of twenty-five years and leaving with his daughter. Miriam wondered if Abba would have stayed behind if she had.

"Shall we go, Professor?" Rolf asked after they'd rested and regained their composure. Abba nodded. They left through the back door and went down a rear staircase to where the car was parked behind the building. Miriam gripped the railing on the way down, her knees trembling. They were three ordinary people, traveling west out of Cologne, going on a holiday in the countryside the way they had when Miriam was a child.

Rolf drove for a very long time. It was growing dark when they stopped at a house in a small German village near the Dutch border. It belonged to the guide who would help them cross the border. The guide's wife offered coffee and sandwiches at her kitchen table. They barely spoke as they waited until midnight. It all seemed like a dream to

Miriam, and she longed to wake up in her bed in their apartment near the university. But it wasn't a dream. She thought of Saul and wished they had all left together weeks ago as Abba had begged them to do.

"It's time to go," the guide finally said. They went out into a cold wind and walked across a meadow and into the woods behind the village, carrying their suitcases and the violin. The ground was wet, soaking Miriam's shoes, the night dark and frigid. After living inside for months, it seemed strange to feel the wind blowing her hair across her face.

They emerged from the woods several minutes later, and after crossing another pasture, they came to a river where a man waited with a rowboat. The boat rocked as the man helped her and Abba board and then tossed in their suitcases. Miriam shivered as if she might never be warm again as they crossed the river, the wind blowing straight from the Noordzee. When the boat reached the other side, the man helped Abba lift out their suitcases and haul them up the embankment.

"Head straight west across that field and you'll come to a road," the man told them. "Turn right and follow the road north until you come to a small village. The Dutch people will help you from there. They're good people."

The trip across the damp field and up the dirt road into the village took more than three hours. Abba had to stop several times to set down his heavy suitcase and rest. Miriam was grateful each time. Her feet felt frozen, her hands blistered from gripping her bag and her violin. Her lungs ached. All around them, the countryside rustled with strange sounds.

Dawn shimmered along the horizon beneath the clouds, like a window shade slowly rolling open by the time they reached a farm on the edge of town. The farmer had just stepped from the barn with his dog, and the animal hurtled toward them, barking a warning. The farmer silenced it with a shout and walked out to the road to meet Miriam and Abba. "From Germany?" he asked. Abba nodded. "Many, many are coming," he said in clumsy German. "I will show you the train. It takes you to Westerbork, the camp for refugees."

CHAPTER 3

Ans de Vries arrived at the Leiden train station toting all of her belongings in two canvas bags and a pasteboard suitcase. She couldn't help grinning as she walked down busy Rapenburg Street, thrilled to be moving to such a bustling place. The air smelled of coffee and of the fishy canals and rivers, not of manure. The streets hummed with traffic. Bicycles whooshed past and leaned in tangled piles outside shops and houses. Church steeples and the domes of an observatory poked above the trees in the distance.

Ans followed the directions Opa had given her to meet with her potential employer, Professor Herman Huizenga. She would have skipped like a schoolgirl all the way there in her eagerness to begin her new life, but the cumbersome baggage slowed her steps. A fifteen-minute walk brought her to his office at the university, a venerable old building of aged brick and polished wood, rich with centuries of history. She climbed the stairs to the second floor. His door stood open. Ans set down her luggage, straightened her blouse, and smoothed back her fair hair before knocking on the doorframe. She hoped she didn't smell of cows.

"Come in, please."

She stepped through the doorway with what she hoped was a confident smile and extended her hand to the gentleman seated behind a desk. "Hello, Professor Huizenga. I'm Ans de Vries. I'm here about the job as a lady's companion?"

He stood, unfolding his lanky body, grasshopper-like, and shook her hand. "Very nice to meet you. Please, have a seat." She had never seen an office like his, lined with shelves of leather-bound books that spilled over onto the floor and every available surface. Scientific gadgets and contraptions she couldn't begin to recognize adorned every pile and table and shelf and chair. What an interesting person he must be to have such an office.

"Thank you for coming, Miss De Vries," he said when they both were seated. "You have been told what this job entails?"

"You would like a companion for your wife." Ans had been surprised and pleased that no cooking or cleaning was required. It seemed too good to be true.

"Yes, an assistant of sorts, keeping Eloise company when I'm at work or when I need to travel to conferences. You'll escort her when she goes out and help her pass her days agreeably and be a friend by her side. Sometimes she will ask for help dressing for the day and preparing for bed at night."

"May I ask why she needs my help, Professor Huizenga? Has she been unwell?" The professor wasn't old, probably in his early fifties. Surely his wife had friends and family members who could accompany her.

He took a moment to reply as if searching for a place to begin, running his hand over his reddish-blond hair, stroking his trim goatee. "You wouldn't know it from meeting Eloise, but she is a very fragile woman who struggles, from time to time, with melancholia." He spoke as if it pained him to disparage her. "You were recommended to me as a bright, cheerful young lady, who I hope will be good medicine for her. Have you ever known someone with melancholia?"

"No, I'm sorry." Ans wondered if the truth would cost her the job.

"Eloise goes for days, weeks, even months at a time when all is well, and no one would ever guess that anything was wrong. But then something triggers her sadness, and she falls into a pit that she can't easily climb out of. It isn't your task to keep her happy but to walk beside her in the darkness and make sure that she doesn't . . ." He looked down at his desk for a long moment before looking up again. "That she doesn't harm herself." His words fell as soft as snowflakes. "Does that possibility frighten you, Miss De Vries?"

"To be perfectly honest, yes. But I took care of my grandmother during the final months of her life, and that was often difficult too." Ans paused, then decided to take a chance. "May I ask why your wife might choose to harm herself?"

"Yes, of course. Her background is important to know." He took a deep breath, then continued. "Eloise grew up in Belgium. She was a young woman like you when the surrounding nations decided to wage a war in the middle of her country. She lost her home and her parents to the violence and then her only brother, who was very dear to her. He was gassed and suffered horribly before he died. I'm not sure one ever recovers from such tragic losses, but Eloise has spent her lifetime trying. Valiantly."

Ans had read accounts in school of the Great War in neighboring Belgium—the hellish trench warfare, the poison gas attacks, the endless devastation. "I'm so sorry, Professor. I can't imagine suffering through such a terrible war. What can I do to help her?"

"There are certain events . . . sounds . . . even smells that distract her mind from the present and hurl her into the past. Into the pit. In time, you will learn what some of those trip wires are. You must become her lifeline, her tether, linking her to the present. You serve as a reminder of what is real and what isn't. I need you to be a companion and a friend without giving the impression that you are her jailer."

"I see." A niggle of fear burrowed into her stomach. The job would be challenging, but hadn't she wanted something different?

"In recent months, the darkness has been calling to her more and more often," the professor continued, "triggered by the looming threat of another war. It's impossible to shield her from all of the news. She has read about the German invasion of Czechoslovakia and heard about it on the radio, and she is well aware of what will likely happen there because she knows what happened in her own country. I can't always be with her, Miss De Vries."

"I hope you will both call me Ans."

"Yes, of course. Much of your time will be your own when I'm able to be with her, Ans. We will pay you a weekly salary in addition to room and board. You would still like the job after everything I've told you?"

She drew a deep breath. "I would. Your wife sounds like a remarkable woman. It would be a privilege to walk alongside her."

"Thank you . . . thank you." The relief on his face was touching. Tears glistened in his eyes. He must love his wife a great deal. The professor cleared his throat and pushed papers around on his desk for a moment as if gathering himself. "Now, if you will give me a minute to finish up here, I will take you to meet her. Our home isn't far."

The Huizengas lived in a tall four-story town house on a tree-lined street overlooking the Witte Singel canal. Eloise Huizenga greeted Ans as if she were a relative who had come to visit. "Welcome to our home. Come in, come in! What a pretty young woman you are! I hope you'll feel very much at home with us." Eloise Huizenga was a beautiful, elegant woman in her forties with fair skin and dark hair cut in a stylish bob. A striking streak of white blazed through her sideswept bangs. She gave the impression of boundless energy, yet at the same time, she seemed as fragile and delicate as the fine Meissen china pieces that decorated her home.

"I'm very glad to be here, Mrs. Huizenga. Please, call me Ans."

"And you must call me Eloise. Come in and we'll have tea."

"I'll leave you ladies to get acquainted," Professor Huizenga said, kissing his wife's cheek. "Tell the cook I'll be home around six."

The town house was so beautifully decorated with antiques and artwork and luscious carpets that Ans was almost afraid to walk into the sitting room. She knew she was gaping like a country peasant, but she'd never been in a home like this one before. Eloise poured tea from a sterling silver teapot as they sat at a tiny table overlooking the street and the nearby canal. "What do you think of Leiden so far?" Eloise asked.

"It's wonderful. I'm very excited to be here. To be honest, I was eager to leave the small village and the farm where I grew up."

"Oh? Why is that?"

"I love my parents very much, and they're wonderful people, but I want to see new things and do new things. After I finished secondary school last spring, I wasn't sure what I wanted to do in the future. I'm hoping that coming here will help me figure it out."

Eloise gave a clap of delight. "What a marvelous place to be in, Ans! You're a lovely young woman with your whole future ahead of you and endless possibilities to explore. I hope we'll become friends and that you'll let me show you all the things I love about this city. It will be exciting for both of us."

"That's very kind and generous—"

"We'll explore Leiden, then take the train to Amsterdam and Den Haag. We'll attend concerts and see artwork—the greatest artists in the world are from the Netherlands, you know. I believe you'll see the exquisite beauty of your farm life in a new way when you view it through their eyes. Are you familiar with the Impressionists?" Her pale skin grew flushed as she spoke, her voice breathless. She didn't wait for Ans to reply as she gushed on. "You must see the Impressionists' artwork. I could lose myself in their vision of the world. And there are a host of lectures on a fabulous variety of new ideas. Like phrenology! Are you familiar with phrenology?"

"No, I—"

"I find it endlessly fascinating! Oh, there are so many astonishing new ideas to explore. I will make you my apprentice and fellow sojourner in their discovery!"

"I would like that."

"You aren't eating, Ans. Here, you must try one of these pastries.

They're from my favorite coffee shop near the university, and although they aren't quite as good as the ones back home, we must make do when we're in exile, mustn't we? No one makes a croissant like the French do—even the Belgians, sad to say. Please, try one."

Ans was overwhelmed by everything—Eloise's home, her zest for life, and her generosity in sharing them. Yet something about her glittering enthusiasm seemed out of proportion to their brand-new friendship. After learning of Eloise's fragile mental state, Ans felt as if she were trying to sip from a teacup filled dangerously close to the brim.

They toured the house when they finished their tea, and Ans wondered how long it would take to feel at home here. She carried her own bags and suitcase to her bedroom on the second floor, a room every bit as lush and elegant as the rest of the home, the suite of a guest, not a servant. She would have the luxury of a bed all to herself, not shared with her little sister. Ans would miss Maaike's warmth on cold winter nights but not her sprawling, poking elbows and knees. Her room was on the same floor as the Huizengas' bedroom suite, even though there were two more vacant bedrooms and another bath on the third floor. It seemed surprising until Ans recalled that the professor wanted her near Eloise when he couldn't be.

"Please, take your time unpacking and getting settled," Eloise said before leaving. "There's no hurry at all. I need to attend to some correspondence downstairs." She closed the door behind her. Ans was unsure what to do. Should she follow Mrs. Huizenga around like a lapdog, checking on her, making sure she was all right? Was it okay to leave her alone for a few minutes? The professor said to be her friend, not her jailer, but did that mean it was okay to leave her alone sometimes? And if so, for how long?

Ans opened her suitcase and began filling the wardrobe and dresser with her things. The shining enthusiasm she'd felt when she'd stepped off the train this morning had been dimmed by the realization of what a huge responsibility she'd agreed to. Ans wondered if she was in over her head.

CHAPTER 4

The Westerbork refugee camp was still under construction when Miriam and Abba arrived. It squatted on a bleak stretch of heathland, seven miles south of Assen, the nearest town. They were assigned to a small space in a long wooden barracks with two beds and two blankets, separated from the rest of the noisy, restless refugee families by a curtain. The space was open to the rafters above them, which were crisscrossed with strings of drying laundry. The dank odor of wet wool filled the air and stuck in Miriam's throat. Sharing toilet facilities with the other women in her barracks robbed her of the last remnants of her dignity. With bare wooden walls, floors, and ceilings, the barracks were how Miriam imagined prison might be. But she wouldn't cry. Or perhaps she couldn't cry. She told herself it was no more a prison than her home in Cologne had been.

With so few belongings, it didn't take long to settle in. Abba fashioned a makeshift shelf for his books from a discarded vegetable crate and used his suitcase as a desk, where he sat for most of the day writing endless letters. Rain added to the damp mugginess in the barracks.

"Are you writing to Mother?" Miriam asked as he sat scribbling.

"Yes. She'll be very glad to know that we arrived and that we're safe."

"She would have hated it here, you know. It's very primitive, and the lack of privacy would have distressed her." Especially the toilets. Mother would have been appalled by them. The unfamiliar sounds of wildlife in the barren heathland would have kept her from sleeping, as they did Miriam. The construction racket would have gotten on her nerves. Miriam hadn't expected luxury, but she found everything about the camp dreary and grim, including the tasteless food. Nevertheless, she knew she should be grateful to be here. To be free.

Abba stopped writing and looked up at her. "Your mother will join us once we're settled in our own place. After I find work and an apartment. The others will come, too. You'll see."

Miriam remembered her debilitating fear as they'd crossed the German border, slogging across the wet fields until her feet were soaked and chilled, picking their way through the dark, dispiriting woods. If Mother knew what lay ahead, she would never agree to come.

"Do you think it will be all right if I practice my violin?" she asked on their third day in camp. Isolated in her tiny living space, Miriam had been battling panic attacks ever since they'd arrived and hoped to find relief if allowed to play.

"I think it would be lovely. This place could use a little music to brighten things, don't you think?"

The rain had paused, so Miriam found a secluded place outside behind the barracks, away from the play area, where the children squealed and splashed in puddles. The pressure in her chest eased as she lifted her violin from its case. She played the melody from Tchaikovsky's Violin Concerto in D Major from memory and allowed the violin to weep in her place. Miriam closed her eyes and poured all of her fear and sorrow into her music. The sounds of hammering and sawing faded into the background. She felt lighter when she reached the end of the piece several minutes later, then a rustling sound behind her made her turn around.

A young man in his twenties stood near the barracks as if trying not to be noticed.

"Is my playing disturbing you?" she asked. "I'll stop if it is."

"Not at all! Please, don't stop. It's beautiful." His smile lit up his eyes and his face. Had she seen anyone smile in this place?

"It's just that . . . with such tight quarters here . . . I would hate to disturb anyone."

"No, please continue."

Miriam tucked the violin beneath her chin but couldn't recall where she'd left off. She was self-conscious now.

"Would you like me to go away?" the young man asked.

She glanced at him again. "No, you don't have to . . . but I need to keep practicing if I hope to stay in shape. Abba thinks I can apply to a music conservatory once we're settled."

He approached and offered his hand for her to shake. "I'm Avraham Leopold—Avi." He had wiry black hair and a thick beard and eyes the color of strong coffee. His high forehead and thin, wire-rimmed glasses gave him a scholarly look. He was perhaps two or three years older than Miriam, with the slim build of a long-distance runner. His smile warmed her and she smiled in return.

"I'm Miriam Jacobs. My father and I just arrived from Cologne a few days ago. Where are you from?"

"I've lived in Berlin all my life—until now."

"Have you been here very long?"

He exhaled so wearily that Miriam was sorry she'd asked. "Nearly four months already. My barracks wasn't even finished yet. And I didn't have this beard!" He grinned and stroked his face. "I've been trying to get a visa to move to Palestine. They were right when they told me it would take a long time. The British have enough headaches trying to appease Hitler. They don't want to stir up trouble in Palestine by letting Jews come back to their homeland. Where are you planning to go?"

"I think my father wants to stay here, in the Netherlands."

He shook his head. "They won't let us stay. This camp was built for Jewish refugees, but only until we can find a permanent place somewhere else. That's why it's way out in the middle of nowhere. We aren't supposed to mingle with the Dutch people. It's a small country, and there are hundreds of us. They would like us to move on."

"My father has been writing letters to his fellow professors in several countries, trying to find a position in one of their universities."

"I wish him well. I was an engineering student until they forbade Jews to study at the university."

"Is your family here with you?"

He sighed again. "No, my parents couldn't read the handwriting on the wall."

"What do you mean?"

"Don't you know that story? It's from the book of Daniel the prophet."

"We're not religious."

"Neither is my family," he said, laughing. "Believe me! But I've had a lot of time on my hands here, so I've been studying the Bible. I've read through the Torah three times, in fact. Now I'm reading the Prophets."

"Papa thinks it's absurd that we're being persecuted for being Jewish when we aren't even religious. We rarely celebrated Passover or the other holidays. We sometimes had dinner with Mother's family on Friday night, but we don't keep kosher or anything like that."

"I understand. My family is the same." He sat down on the barracks steps and motioned for Miriam to join him. She hesitated, then sat beside him, her violin on her lap. He seemed nice. And she needed a friend.

"Anyway, in the story in the book of Daniel, all the warnings of a coming disaster were there, plain as day, written on the wall by a ghostly hand. But the people couldn't interpret them. And my family couldn't accept the fact that we weren't wanted in Germany. That we were hated, even. We had no future there. The persecution will only get worse and worse, until . . . well, who knows what will happen to us. So I escaped by myself. Once I'm settled in Jerusalem, maybe I can convince the rest of my family to join me."

"My cousin Saul plans to leave for Palestine as soon as he's well again. He was beaten by a gang of Hitler Youth and left for dead. He says nothing he might face in Jerusalem could be any worse than what the Nazis did to him. He isn't going to wait for his immigration papers but plans to sneak into Palestine somehow."

"Maybe I should do that." Avi scooped up a handful of pebbles and absently tossed them as they talked.

"So how do people stay occupied all day while they wait for a visa or someplace to go—besides reading the Torah?"

"They've given us some garden space to grow our own food. And we can volunteer to plant trees for the government. As you can see, there aren't very many around here."

Miriam looked down at her hands, holding her violin. "I don't think either of those choices are for me."

"I've also offered to teach mathematics in the school they're setting up. I think they'd be grateful if you taught music classes."

"I would be happy to. Anything to keep busy so I can stop thinking about . . ." She faltered, desperate to erase the picture of her family and a way of life that had vanished. "To stop thinking of other things," she finished.

"I know. It's hard not to dwell on the past, isn't it? And all that we've lost?" Miriam nodded as tears stung her eyes. Avi gave an apologetic smile as he stood. "I'll go away now so you can practice. It was nice talking with you, Miriam."

She realized after he left that the fist in her chest had relaxed while she'd spoken with him. She could breathe again.

By the end of Miriam's first week in the refugee camp, Avi had become a regular fixture at her daily practice sessions, sitting quietly off to the side, sometimes closing his eyes as she played. Even when she lost herself in the music, Miriam was aware of him sitting nearby, listening. His quiet serenity made her feel calm. He and many of the other refugees told her how much they enjoyed her music and thanked her for making Westerbork a little less bleak. She had just finished practicing one day and was putting her violin away when Avi rose from his customary place on the steps of the barracks and approached her.

"Miriam—I've been searching all week for a way to thank you for your music and the hours of enjoyment it has brought me, and I've come up with something." He waved a book in the air. "If you'll allow me, I would like to read a psalm to you." He motioned to the place where he usually sat, inviting her to sit down. He smiled his familiar warm grin, then began to read:

"Listen to my words, Lord,
    consider my lament.
Hear my cry for help,
    my King and my God,
    for to you I pray.

In the morning, Lord, you hear my voice;
    in the morning I lay my requests before you
    and wait expectantly. . . .

But let all who take refuge in you be glad;
    let them ever sing for joy.
Spread your protection over them,
    that those who love your name may rejoice in you.

"That psalm is about us, Miriam," he said when he finished. "We're refugees in this place, but our true refuge is in Him."

"Will you read it again, please?"

He did. The words summed up Miriam's unvoiced prayers and made her feel that her unshed tears were noticed.

Every afternoon after that, Avi read a psalm to her. Miriam looked forward to it as much as she did to losing herself in her music. Slowly, in spite of her losses, in spite of her stark surroundings, Miriam's panic attacks became less frequent and she began to feel hopeful again. The psalmists knew suffering and what it was to wait in confident hope. To wait with countless questions and no answers. She wasn't alone in her loneliness. Avi became a trusted friend.

CHAPTER 5

Ans chose an outdoor table at the little café along the canal even though the sky sagged with heavy clouds. She was grateful for a few minutes alone, away from the pristine town house and the breathless intensity of her employer's personality. Eloise hadn't fallen into the pit of melancholy the professor had warned about, but she set such a hectic, frantic pace that Ans feared it was only a matter of time before she collapsed. She and Ans had been coming to this café regularly, and the friendly young waitress, Jansje, smiled as she walked over to greet Ans.

"Your mother isn't with you today?"

"Pardon? . . . Oh . . . no, Eloise isn't my mother. I'm her companion. She went out for coffee with her husband today."

"I'm so sorry for assuming . . ."

"That's okay."

"You seemed so close, like mother and daughter or at least good friends, always running off to do things together."

"Well . . . yes, I suppose we are friends. I sometimes forget that I work for her. She's been good to me, taking me to so many interesting places that it hardly seems like work."

"Do you want your usual?" Jansje asked.

"Yes. Thank you." Ans watched her disappear into the café and realized how much she longed for a friend her own age, someone she could daydream with and talk with about silly, unimportant things. Someone uncomplicated, who didn't keep Ans always on edge. "Do you have time to visit a bit?" Ans asked when Jansje returned with her coffee and pastry. "I'd like to ask you a question."

Jansje glanced around at the other outdoor tables. "Sure. We're never very busy in the afternoon." She pulled out one of the metal chairs and sat down but couldn't seem to resist straightening the sugar bowl and the ashtray and other items on the table while they talked. "What's your question?"

"I'll have some free time this Saturday night while my employers attend a dinner, so I was wondering what there is to do around here."

"Do you want to meet some boys?"

"Not especially." Ans smiled at Jansje's look of surprise. "I mean, I'm not looking for anything serious—I just want to meet some people my age and have some fun. I grew up in a dreary farm village where nothing much happened. It's so small that if I looked twice at a boy, everyone in town would start discussing our wedding."

Jansje laughed. "And you didn't like any of those boys?"

"They were as interesting as wooden clogs. All they knew about were cows and crops. This is a university town. There must be someplace fun where the students go."

"Do you like to dance? My boyfriend, Bram, and I sometimes go dancing."

"You have a boyfriend? Tell me all about him!"

Jansje glanced at her other customers as though checking to see if she was needed. She was a plain girl, but her smile made her seem pretty as she talked about her boyfriend. "Bram and I are planning to get married when he finishes at the police academy. I'm working here to earn money so we can get a head start."

"That's exciting!"

"I can't wait to be his wife! Have you ever been in love?" Ans shook her head. "Oh, it's wonderful! We go dancing nearly every weekend or else to this other club to listen to the music. You're welcome to come with us sometime."

"I wouldn't want to limp along like a third wheel."

She tilted her head in thought. "Bram's roommate is awfully cute. I don't think he's dating anyone special. How about a blind date? We could all go together."

"What's his roommate like?"

"Erik already finished at the academy and he's a policeman here in Leiden. He's kind of quiet and serious, you know? But you're so lively and friendly I think you'd be good for him. And Erik is good-looking, too—although not as handsome as Bram," she added with a laugh.

The offer intrigued Ans. She felt a shiver of excitement, or perhaps it was guilt. Should she ask which church Erik belonged to? Her parents would forbid her to date a man from another religion—or worse, someone with no church background at all. She took a sip of coffee and decided she didn't care. "I'm willing to try it if Erik is."

"Great! What do you want me to tell him about you? Besides that you're gorgeous."

The compliment caught Ans off guard, and she felt her cheeks burning. She'd been taught that it was vain and prideful to acknowledge her own physical beauty. "Just tell him I'm new in Leiden and that I'm working for a university professor and his wife as her companion. Please don't mention that I'm from a farm town."

A customer beckoned to Jansje from another table, and she stood. "I'll talk to Bram and Erik tonight. Stop by tomorrow and I'll let you know what they say."

It was quickly arranged. Ans would meet Jansje at the café on Saturday evening and they would walk to the dance hall where the men would be waiting.

Erik Brouwer's first words when Jansje introduced Ans were "You weren't lying when you said she was gorgeous! I'm very glad to meet you, Ans—before some other lucky fellow did!"

"You're not bad yourself," she replied, laughing. "Are you sure you don't have a girlfriend already?" Erik was strong and well-built with wide shoulders and a square, handsome face. His thick, wavy hair was the color of sand and had an intriguing, tousled look that made Ans want to run her fingers through it.

"No, I've never had a girlfriend."

"Erik is married to his job," Jansje said. "Come on, let's dance." She pulled her boyfriend onto the dance floor. The walls pulsed with music—a swing style that Ans had enjoyed listening to on the radio but had never heard from a live band.

"Would you like to dance?" Erik asked her.

"Can we just watch for a minute? To tell you the truth, I don't really know how, and I want to see how it's done first."

"Sure. I'll be glad to teach you when you're ready." Erik led her to a table and ordered two glasses of Amstel. There was something exotic about him that made the farm boys back home seem dull and lumbering in comparison. She thought she detected a slight accent in his speech but couldn't place it.

"Have you always lived in Leiden?" she asked.

"Only for the past five years. I was born in Bandung, Java, in the Dutch East Indies."

"That's amazing! What's it like?"

"Well, very hot for one thing." He had a shy, sweet smile. "But lush and beautiful. My father was a civil servant for the Dutch government, but he died five years ago. He wanted me to return to the Netherlands, where he and my mother were born."

"Do you miss Java?"

"In some ways, yes. Especially the food. But Leiden is my home now."

"What made you decide to become a policeman?"

"I don't know . . . I think it must be in my blood to want to make sure everything runs smoothly and in order. My father was the same way. There are parts of the East Indies that are still untamed compared to here."

"Would you ever want to go back and help tame them?"

"Maybe . . . someday. But I like it here very much at the moment."

Ans relaxed as they chatted, relishing the freedom from the pressure of her job, savoring her life in a new city away from home, enjoying the company of an interesting, attractive man. Erik was polite and engaging, but after a while she noticed that he never fully relaxed. He always seemed alert and aware of his surroundings, scanning the room as if watching for danger, watching the other people. "Are you on duty as a policeman tonight?" she finally asked. "Or are you looking for someone in particular?"

"Me? . . . No, I'm off duty tonight. Why?"

"Well, you seem to be always looking around, as if expecting something to happen."

He gave an embarrassed grin. "Sorry. It's my job to be vigilant and notice things. Sometimes it's hard for me to turn it off. Does it bother you?"

"Not really. I was just curious. My job with the Huizengas also requires a certain amount of watchfulness, but I'm grateful for the chance to be free from the responsibility for a few hours. I'll bet you're a very good policeman."

The music changed to a slower tempo, and Erik reached for her hand. "Are you ready to try dancing? It'll be easier now that the band is playing a slow song."

"Sure! I'll give it a try." Erik was a patient teacher, and Ans liked dancing once she got the hang of it. Being in his arms was the best part of all. He smelled wonderful, like mysterious spices from distant places. She hoped he would ask her out again and wondered if it would be too bold of her to suggest they go to the cinema some night. She was working up the nerve to try when two men at a nearby table got into a heated argument. Erik immediately became alert as their voices grew louder, and when one of them shoved the other, Erik stepped over to intervene.

"Hey. This isn't the place for roughhousing. There are women here. Why don't you go outside and cool down?" For a moment, it looked like one of the men might take a swing at Erik. Ans held her breath. But the man seemed to change his mind after assessing Erik's strong build and ready stance. He turned away and stormed out.

"You did that very well," Ans said, breathing again. "Do you know him?"

"I've seen him here a few times. He always drinks too much."

"I told you Erik was married to his job," Jansje said with a laugh as she joined them.

"Well, I think what he did was wonderful," Ans replied. "I bet he'll be chief of police someday."

When the evening ended, Ans accepted Erik's offer to walk her home. "I had fun tonight," he told her. "Would you go out with me again sometime?"

"I was hoping you would ask."

"How about a noon picnic in the park by the Burcht tomorrow?"

"The Burcht? I don't think I've been there yet."

"It's in the oldest part of Leiden, right where the two branches of the Rijn meet. It was a fortress in ancient times. It has a great view of the city."

"I would like that, but . . . um . . . I have to go to church with the Huizengas in the morning. It's part of my job. Can I meet you afterwards?"

"Sure."

They shared a lunch of bread and cheese the next day, spread on a blanket near the canal. Swans and ducks floated in the water, undisturbed by the pleasure boats drifting past on the peaceful Sunday afternoon.

In the weeks that followed, it wasn't easy for Ans and Erik to arrange time off together, but when they did, they spent it with each other. Along with dances and leisurely picnics in the park, they watched the boat traffic on the canals, ate in little cafés along the Rijn, and rode bicycles together over Leiden's lumpy brick streets. Ans took Erik through the conservatory at the Hortus Botanicus and browsed through Leiden's bookshops, where they found a book with photographs of Erik's native Java. Ans introduced Erik to Eloise Huizenga when he came to fetch her one evening, and Eloise declared him "a decent and charming young man." On one beautiful Sunday morning, Ans asked to be excused from church, and she and Erik rode their bicycles to the beach at Katwijk. Erik took her hand as they walked through the sand near the shore and admired the old lighthouse. She loved the feel of his hand in her own.

"Are you and Erik getting serious?" Jansje asked one day when Ans stopped at the café alone for coffee. "You're together all the time now."

"We're just good friends. That's the way we both want it, for now. We have fun together." But Ans couldn't deny the prickle of excitement she felt every time she waited for Erik to arrive. Or the deep contentment she felt when she walked beside him, holding his hand. She began wishing he would kiss her, and when he finally did, holding her face in his strong, square hands, his fingers tangled in her hair, it was the most wonderful feeling Ans had ever experienced.

"I've been wanting to do that for quite a while," he murmured, his breath tickling her face.

"Me too . . ." They stood in the shadows along the Witte Singel, the water rippling gently against the shore, the twinkling city lights reflected on the water. Erik pulled her close and kissed her again, and Ans never wanted to leave his arms. Was this what love felt like? Was she falling in love? Whatever it was, Ans had never felt freer or happier.

CHAPTER 6

"I've come up with an idea," Avi said one afternoon. "I'd like to know what you think." Miriam couldn't imagine what he might say, but she was touched that he valued her opinion. "The Sabbath begins tomorrow at sundown, and I'd like you and your father to celebrate it with me. We can invite other families too, if you'd like, but I would especially like to celebrate it with you. Will you help me with the arrangements?"

The idea delighted Miriam. "You'll have to teach me what to do. I've never made Sabbath preparations before."

"The most important things are the bread, the wine, and the candles. I have a book with all the prayers and readings." His enthusiasm was contagious.

"I brought my grandmother's silver candlesticks from home. We can use those."

"Perfect! Will you light the candles for us? The woman of the household has the honor of welcoming the Sabbath."

"Yes, of course. Where will you get candles? And wine?"

"I'm going to ask permission to walk to Assen tomorrow."

"Isn't that a long way?"

"It is, but it'll be worth it. And I might be able to hitch a ride with one of the supply vans."

Abba's enthusiasm for the idea surprised Miriam. He pushed money into Avi's hand, offering to pay for the wine and candles. Two other families wanted to join them, along with three single men who lived in Avi's dormitory. They got permission to pull a table aside in the dining hall for their Shabbat table, and Miriam decorated it with wildflowers and the silver candlesticks. She and Avi were adding the finishing touches when Abba rushed in, waving a letter and his dark-rimmed spectacles in the air. "Miriam! We got a letter from your mother!"

"How is she? What did she say?" Abba's joy made her certain that Mother must be coming to join them. There was life in his gray face again and a sparkle in his hazel eyes.

"Here, you can read it. It's to both of us."

Miriam held her breath as she read, pushing against the anxiety she always felt when she thought of home. According to Mother, everything was the same. Saul was hobbling around on crutches now, but Mother said nothing about him playing his cello. She said nothing about joining them, either. Miriam wondered if the arguments around the dinner table were the same too, now that Abba was gone. Abba watched as she read, and when she finished and looked up at him, she still saw glee on his face. She hadn't read anything in the letter that accounted for it.

"You're pleased about something, Abba. What is it?"

"I received another letter today, as well. My labors to find a university position may finally be bearing fruit. The letter is from a colleague at Leiden University, right here in the Netherlands. We met at a conference in Berlin, and he remembers my work. He's trying to arrange a position for me as a lecturer in physics. I may even be able to continue my research there."

Miriam hugged him. "That's wonderful, Abba!"

"Congratulations, Professor Jacobs," Avi said. "I'm glad you and Miriam may be getting out of this place." Avi was happy for them, Miriam could tell. But she heard regret in his voice and saw it in his eyes.

"It isn't definite yet," Abba said. "But my colleague will continue to lobby on my behalf. He thinks it looks very hopeful."

Avi turned to her. "You can pursue your musical studies there."

"Is Leiden far from here?" Leaving her new friend would be a great loss for Miriam, even if it meant Mother would be able to join them.

"Leiden is in the western part of the Netherlands," Abba replied. "Twenty-five miles or so from Amsterdam. Not far from Den Haag."

"They allow Jews to be professors there, Abba?"

"Yes, of course. Leiden is a very old university, founded in the sixteenth century."

"Maybe you could come too," Miriam told Avi. "You could finish your engineering degree."

He nodded, but his smile was an indulgent one, as if he really didn't believe it could happen. "Now we have even more reason to thank the Almighty as we celebrate the Sabbath," he said. He gestured to the tall white candles he'd fitted into the holders and pushed a box of matches into her hands. "It's time to light the candles, Miriam."

"Wait!" Abba said. He pulled a small skullcap from his pocket and fitted it over his dark, slicked-back hair. "There is a blessing you are supposed to recite, Miriam. Shall I say it for you this time until you have a chance to learn it?"

She looked at him in surprise. "How do you know it, Abba? Mother never lit candles that I can remember."

His eyes glistened. "I heard my mother and grandmother recite the blessing every week when I was a boy. I will tell you about it after you light them." She lit the candles, then listened in amazement as he recited words in Hebrew, his voice choked with emotion.

"Abba . . . I didn't know . . ."

"Everyone sit down and we can begin," he said.

Miriam looked around at the other guests as they took their places and saw their hushed excitement. Miriam didn't know the traditional Sabbath rituals, but the flickering candlelight and expectant joy in Avi's eyes made the rustic dining hall seem like a holy place.

"First, it is a father's privilege to say a blessing for his children on Shabbat." Abba laid his hand on Miriam's head as he recited in Hebrew again, then kissed the place where his hand had rested.

"Professor, would you do us the honor of saying the blessings on the bread and wine, too?" Avi asked.

Abba poured wine into the silver goblet that one of the guests had contributed and recited the blessing. They passed the goblet around, each taking a sip. He blessed the bread, then broke it into pieces and passed them around.

The food was the same dining hall fare as usual, but it seemed different tonight as they laughed and talked and listened to Avi explain what the Torah said about celebrating the Sabbath day. Later, when the food and wine were gone and a happy glow had settled over the table, Miriam asked Abba how he'd learned the Sabbath rituals.

"My parents were Orthodox. My grandfather was a rabbi."

"I never knew that!"

"No one in my family was happy with me when I left home and went to the university to study physics instead of to the yeshiva to study Torah. But Torah and physics are perfectly compatible in my mind. The Almighty is a God of order and laws, and I wanted to study how He had created and ordered the universe." He looked down at the table. "My family and I became even more estranged when I married your mother—a woman from a nonreligious family."

Miriam knew the story. "You heard her performing at a piano recital and fell in love with her."

"With her and with the exquisite music she created." His eyes glistened in the candlelight. "How could I explain that her music drew me closer to God? My family didn't understand."

"I understand, Professor. Miriam's music does the same for me."

"I didn't tell your mother, Miriam, but since losing my position at the university, I have returned to Torah study. I am asking God why we are being persecuted. What have we done? And what He wants to teach us in this dark trial."

"That's why I began reading it too," Avi said. "Have you found any answers, Professor?"

"No. But I think God likes it when we ask questions. My best university students were the ones who asked questions. I think God is pleased when we engage in a dialogue with Him. I regret that I've ignored Him for much of my life, but at least we are talking again. I was raised to study the Torah with a *chavrutah*—a study partner. Would you do me the honor of being my *chavrutah*, Avraham?"

"I'm the one who would be honored, Professor Jacobs."

Later, after the evening ended and Miriam and Abba had returned to their stark barracks, Abba turned to her and said, "I like your young man very much, Miriam."

"Why do you call him my young man? We're just friends—"

"Yes, I can see that you're friends. And I see much more. I saw your faces when I mentioned the possibility of moving to Leiden. I heard how quick you were to invite him to join us if God sees fit to move us there. It's probably too soon to call it love, but I already see great affection between the two of you. I wouldn't mind if you and young Avraham grew closer, dear one." He laid his hand on her head as he had when he'd blessed her. "No, I wouldn't mind in the least."

If Miriam were asked to name the time or the day when she fell in love with Avraham Leopold, she couldn't have done it. Her love for him grew the way a plant does—so slowly you can't see it but becoming steadily stronger every day until a dazzling flower unfolds. He held her hand as they walked to meals. He sat on the steps during her daily practice sessions. And she sat on the bed in her tiny, curtained home, listening to the lively discussions as he and Abba studied Torah. Their friendship grew until they became inseparable.

By the time Abba was officially appointed to lecture in physics at Leiden University, Miriam and Avi knew they wanted to spend the rest of their lives together. She would follow him anywhere, even to Palestine.

She could forget the sorrow of the past, forget her dismal surroundings with Avi beside her. Joyful music now poured from her violin to match the joy that filled her heart. She was in love! There was no other feeling in the world quite like it.

Abba had smuggled money out of Germany, glued between the cover and flyleaf of several of his books. Enough to rent a small, furnished apartment in Leiden. Avi would join them after his records from the university in Berlin arrived. Hopefully he would be granted a visa to enroll in Leiden as an engineering student.

"See?" Abba said as he and Miriam packed their suitcases again. "We'll flourish once more, my dear one. Your mother will join us in Leiden, and we'll start all over again—the four of us. Love grows in the most unlikely places, doesn't it?"

"Yes, Abba! It surely does!" For the first time in over a year, the tantalizing possibility of joy seemed within Miriam's grasp. She leaned toward it like a flower to the sun.

CHAPTER 7

"How would you feel about welcoming two overnight guests, my dear?" Professor Huizenga asked his wife during dinner one evening. His reddish hair and beard glinted like gold in the candlelight. Ans dined with the Huizengas in their elegant dining room nearly every evening as if she were a family member instead of a mere caretaker. The delicate china, polished silverware, and rich, savory food were welcome reminders of her happy escape from her country upbringing—although she still felt like a farm girl much of the time, in spite of Eloise's efforts to introduce her to high culture.

"Guests?" Eloise replied. She speared a small piece of potato with her fork. "Who are they, Herman? Do I know them?"

"A brilliant German colleague I once met at a conference in Berlin—"

Eloise's fork clattered onto the dish. "You want to invite *Germans* here? To our home?" There was a note of panic in her voice as the color drained from her fair cheeks, and Ans grew alert. This was the first hint she'd seen of Eloise's altering moods. Ans watched Professor Huizenga to see how he would react.

"Eloise. Look at me." He reached for her hand, waiting until she did. "Our guests have also suffered from their tyranny. Professor Jacobs and his daughter came to the Netherlands for refuge, just as you did after the war. The foolish Nazis will no longer allow him to teach at the University of Cologne because he's Jewish."

"So they know what it's like?"

"Yes, my love. They know. But I can make other arrangements—"

"No. No, don't do that. Of course they may stay here." Her smile seemed forced. Ans saw the heroic effort Eloise was making to regain her balance.

"I've arranged for him to lecture at the university. His daughter, Miriam, is about your age, Ans. They've been living in a refugee camp, but I've offered to let them stay with us until they find an apartment. Perhaps you could help them?"

"I would be happy to," Ans said. He had directed attention away from his wife, smoothly and deliberately, to give her a chance to recover. "I know my way around Leiden pretty well now. Will they want to live near the university?"

"I assume so. Or perhaps near the synagogue off Korevaarstraat. Do you know where that is? Across the canal from the science buildings?"

"I don't think I've ever noticed a synagogue."

"You wouldn't, necessarily. It's a plain brick building. Jews don't build steeples like we do or draw attention to their synagogues in any special way."

The only Jewish person Ans knew was the wizened tinker who made his rounds in a horse-drawn cart, sharpening knives and selling pots and pans in her village and the surrounding farms. But like everyone else in the Netherlands, Ans had heard about the persecution of Jews in Germany. Jewish families had been streaming across the border into her tiny country in the tens of thousands. She'd seen pictures in the newspaper of the overcrowded Westerbork refugee camp.

Eloise was no longer eating. She had pushed her plate away, unfinished. Her hands fluttered like trapped birds as she straightened her silverware and moved her water glass. "Those poor people . . . ," she murmured. "What they must have endured. When will our guests arrive, Herman?"

"Later this week, by train. You need to finish eating, my dear."

Eloise didn't seem to hear him. "We'll make them feel welcome, won't we, Ans?"

"I'll be happy to—"

"First thing tomorrow, we'll get a listing of available apartments from an agent. It will have to be a furnished apartment, naturally, because they won't have brought much with them, will they? I'll insist on one with lots of windows. Good light is very important when so many of our winter days are gray and dreary. Of course, they may stay with us for as long as it takes, but I understand the importance of having a place of one's own after an upheaval like the one they've suffered."

The professor reached for his wife's fluttering hand, stilling it. "Eloise, my love. You haven't eaten. You'll need your strength if you're planning a busy day."

"No, what I need is sleep. Plenty of sleep. I think I'll go to bed now so we can get an early start." She rose from the table, and Ans knew her well enough by now to be certain she wouldn't be convinced to return.

⁙

Eloise poured herself into the task of finding a furnished apartment with a feverish intensity that worried her husband. He cautioned Ans not to leave her side. By the end of the week, they'd found three possibilities, and Eloise turned her attention to readying her town house for their guests. She asked Ans to help put fresh linens on the beds in the spare bedrooms, ignoring the housekeeper's protests that it was her job to do it. They shopped for flowers and French pastries. While the professor drove to the station to meet the train, Eloise set out coffee and tea in her best china cups and arranged the pastries on a platter. Queen Wilhelmina herself might have been coming to visit. By the time their guests arrived, Eloise's agitated state made Ans feel more dread than anticipation.

Ans greeted the Jewish father and daughter at the door, struck by how haunted and ghostly they looked, as if the essence of them had been left behind in Germany. They arrived with only three suitcases and a violin case, which the daughter held closely. Mr. Jacobs looked as though he'd once been heavier and could use some of Mama's hearty farm dinners with potatoes and butter and fresh cream to regain his vigor. Miriam Jacobs was slender and pale, like a plant in need of sunlight and fertile soil. She was strikingly pretty, with dark hair and eyes, and she moved with the graceful elegance of a ballerina. But Ans noticed how her hands trembled as she reached for her teacup or selected one of the pastries from the plate.

"You speak German?" Miriam asked in surprise as Ans began chatting with her.

"Yes, a little—I could use practice."

"I learned some Dutch in the camp," Miriam said. "Maybe you can teach me more."

"I'd be happy to. We can practice both languages together." Ans liked Miriam immediately and looked forward to having another friend her age. But she also kept an eye on Eloise, who seemed to withdraw inside herself, not saying a word, as everyone around her spoke in German.

"You seem tired, Eloise, my dear," Professor Huizenga said when they finished their tea. "Why don't you go upstairs and rest?" He turned to their guests. "You must be weary too. If you'll please excuse my wife and me, Ans will show you to your rooms and help you get settled."

Ans carried one of the suitcases as she led Miriam and her father to their rooms on the third floor. Miriam's room was small and stuffy from lack of use, even though Ans had opened the windows to the warm September air. She was about to apologize for its condition, but before she could get the words out, Miriam twirled in a circle like a child, taking everything in.

"This room is so pretty!" She ran her hand over the flowered bedspread as if caressing it. "We were grateful for the refugee camp, but there was nothing lovely there. I've missed color and beauty." She lifted the vase of flowers from the dresser and inhaled their scent. Ans was glad she and Eloise had walked to the flower market to purchase them.

"I know the Huizengas are very happy to have you here, Miriam. I'll leave you for now so you can rest and get settled. Let me know if you need anything else."

"Well . . . to be honest, I would love to go for a walk outside, if it's safe."

"It's very safe to walk around Leiden. We can go for a walk right now, if you'd like."

Miriam smiled for the first time. She crossed the hall and knocked on her father's door to ask if he wanted to join them.

"Next time, perhaps. I'm going to write a letter to your mother and tell her where we are."

The walk seemed to energize Miriam and put life and color back into her cheeks. "Cologne, where I grew up, was also a beautiful city," she said. "But by the time we left, it was no longer safe for us to go for a walk. And there were very few places to go, since we weren't allowed in the public parks or theaters or other ordinary places."

"Because you're Jewish?"

She nodded. "I was a prisoner in our house. It was the same at Westerbork except the camp is in the country. There was still no place to go."

"You'll like Leiden. People walk everywhere, and they especially enjoy an evening stroll after dinner. There are a lot of nice cafés, or you can go to a concert or the movies. Sometimes I go to dances with my friends."

"The city looked very pretty as we rode from the train station. It seemed like there were so many bridges and rivers."

"The Rijn river flows through the city and branches into two forks in the middle—the Oude Rijn and the Nieuwe Rijn. There are several canals, too." She looked at Miriam. "Your father mentioned writing to your mother—is she still in Germany?"

"Yes. It was very hard to leave her and the rest of our family behind. Abba hopes Mother will join us once we're settled. She would have hated the refugee camp. She grew up in a home very much like yours."

"Oh, it isn't my home. I work as Eloise Huizenga's companion." Ans led Miriam in a wide circle through a portion of the old city, showing her the parks and canals along the way.

"I wish Avi was here to see all this!" Miriam said. "I wish he could know freedom like this!" She glanced shyly at Ans and said, "Avi is my boyfriend. Abba and I are hoping that he'll be able to join us here soon."

"Then I'll hope so, too."

⟨≈≈≈≈⟩

Dinner that evening felt oddly subdued. Miriam and her father seemed overwhelmed by all the food and formality. Ans could well imagine what a shock it must be to go from a bleak refugee camp to so much luxury. Professor Huizenga seemed worried and preoccupied. "Tomorrow we'll tour the university," he told Mr. Jacobs, "and I'll show you the classrooms and your office. Eloise and Ans will show your daughter some apartments to consider."

Eloise spoke very little throughout the meal, and when she did, her usual cheerfulness had a brittle quality to it. Ans acted as an interpreter between Miriam, who knew only a little Dutch, and Eloise, who couldn't or wouldn't speak German.

"You play the violin, Miriam?" Eloise asked. "How wonderful!"

"Music was a huge part of my life in Cologne. I had hoped to study at the conservatory like my mother and uncle and cousins did, but Jews were no longer allowed."

"Well, we'll see what we can arrange for you here. If not in Leiden, we can certainly find a place for you to study in Amsterdam. It's easy to travel there by train."

"Thank you. I'm so grateful."

Ans knew that Eloise would pour herself into the task with the same frenzied energy she'd used when finding an apartment, and Ans felt weary at the thought of keeping up with her. Eloise seemed incapable of relaxing and ran on two speeds—frenetic activity or exhausted sleep.

When the meal ended, they moved into the front room for coffee. Eloise sat down for only a moment before springing up and crossing to the boxy radio in the corner. "Let's turn on the BBC and see if there's a concert tonight."

Her husband leaped up right behind her. "Let's not, my dear. I'm afraid the radio will disrupt our conversation." He reached for her hand to lead her back to her chair, but she shook him off.

"A little background music, Herman. Miriam is a musician. She might enjoy it."

"Eloise, my love. It isn't a good idea right now." He reached for her again, but she shoved his hand aside, roughly this time, and gave him an angry glare. He looked helpless, as if he needed to stop her and didn't know how. Ans couldn't see how listening to music would do her any harm. The professor closed his eyes as if in pain as Eloise gave the knob a triumphant turn and the radio hummed to life. The announcer spoke English, so Ans didn't know what he was saying, but his somber tone and rushed words told her that something terrible had happened.

The professor tried again. "See, Eloise? I don't believe there's going to be any music tonight—"

She swatted his hand away, listening intently. It seemed to take a moment for her to get the gist of it, but when she did, she stumbled backwards to the nearest chair as if stunned. "He's talking about a war with Germany!" she said in astonishment.

"I had hoped to spare you and our guests the news. Please—"

"I want to know what's happening, Herman!"

"Let me turn it off, my dear, and I will tell you." He twisted the knob, silencing the spitting static and the announcer's urgent jabber. Eloise didn't stop him this time. "The Nazis invaded Poland the day before yesterday," he told her in Dutch. "They're bombing Warsaw. Hitler has broken the agreement he made in Munich with England and France, so both countries have declared war on Germany."

"That's how the last war began," Eloise said. "Just as quickly, after that awful assassination." She looked like a frightened child. Ans hurried over to kneel beside her chair, taking her hand to comfort her as she would her little sister, Maaike.

"Excuse me, please," Miriam's father said, "but could you tell us what has happened?"

Professor Huizenga removed his glasses and ran his hand over his face before sitting down. He repeated the news in German. Mr. Jacobs appeared shocked. Miriam covered her mouth as if to hold back a cry. They had seemed at peace only a moment ago. "What a terrible way to begin your first day in your new home," Professor Huizenga said.

Miriam's father cleared his throat. "And the Netherlands? What will this country do? Will they take sides with Hitler or with the others?"

"Our government has vowed to remain neutral in any armed conflict," the professor said, fixing his glasses in place again, "just as we did in the Great War. Only last month, Hitler assured our leaders that he'll respect our neutrality. It's in his best interest for us to remain neutral." The professor's words didn't seem to soothe Mr. Jacobs. The news had aged him even more, his body capsizing as he sank deeper into his chair.

"My wife and family are still in Germany."

"I'm so sorry," Professor Huizenga said. "I'll do everything I can to bring them here as quickly as possible." He leaned forward, his gaze holding Mr. Jacobs's. "What happened to you in Germany can't happen here. Our government will keep us out of Europe's mess."

Ans glanced at Miriam and saw panic on her face. The room fell silent.

Eloise stood, rising from her seat as if sleepwalking. "I apologize to everyone, but I'm feeling very tired." Her voice was strangely flat. "I know you've had a long day too. Perhaps we should all say good night."

Ans rose and took Eloise's arm.

Miriam and her father also stood. "Thank you for the meal and for all you're doing for us," Mr. Jacobs said.

"Would it bother you if I played my violin in my room?" Miriam asked.

"Not at all," Eloise said. "I think it would be lovely."

"I'll join you in a moment, dear," Professor Huizenga said.

Ans helped Eloise climb the stairs and get ready for bed. Neither of them mentioned the upsetting news. The faint sound of a violin drifted down from Miriam's bedroom upstairs, the tune haunting and plaintive.

"Those poor people . . . ," Eloise murmured. "What they must have endured."

Ans nodded, remembering Miriam's timid smile as they'd walked Leiden's peaceful streets and the way she'd glowed when she talked of the man she loved. She had seemed as happy to be in beautiful Leiden as Ans was. "Can I get you anything else?" Ans asked when Eloise was in bed.

"No. You may go. And leave the light on, please. I need to sleep with it on."

"Good night, then."

It was too early for bed. Ans went downstairs again to the front room, where Professor Huizenga was listening to a Dutch news program. He switched it off and looked up. "Does Eloise seem all right?"

"She's a bit shaky. She wants to sleep."

"Did she take her medicine?"

Ans nodded. "I can only imagine how upsetting the news must be for her."

"Yes, and for the Jacobses as well. I'll need to help Professor Jacobs get settled at the university tomorrow, so I'm glad you'll be here for Eloise. We'll need to watch her closely."

The doorbell rang, and Ans offered to answer it. Her heart did a little dance when she saw Erik on the doorstep. She hadn't seen him in more than a week, occupied with the preparations for the Jacobses' visit. "Erik! What a nice surprise. Would you like to come in?"

He shook his head. "Can you come for a walk with me, Ans?"

"Sure. Let me get a jacket and tell the professor I'm going."

"Have you heard the news?" he asked when Ans returned. He reached for her hand and they started walking.

"About the war? Yes. It's awful, isn't it? I hope it isn't as long or as horrible as the last one. The news upset Mrs. Huizenga terribly. We have guests staying with us—Jewish refugees from Germany—and they were also upset."

"I came to tell you that I'm being called up for military training with the Dutch army."

"Military training? Why?"

"All men between age eighteen and forty are required to go. They say as many as three hundred thousand of us will be mobilized."

Ans halted in place. She squeezed his hand tighter. "But . . . the Netherlands is neutral. Professor Huizenga said Hitler promised not to attack us. He thinks the other nations will respect our neutrality too, as they did during the first war."

"Yes, the Netherlands will remain neutral." He tugged her hand to start her walking again.

"Then why are we mobilizing our men?"

"It's just a precaution. We need to let the other countries know that we won't take sides in this war, but we'll defend our borders." Erik encircled her waist and pulled her close as they continued down the street and across the bridge to the park.

Ans wrapped her arm around him too, wondering how much longer she would have him beside her. "When do you have to leave? Do you know where you'll be sent?"

"I'm not sure about any of that. I haven't received orders yet. But very soon, I expect." In his understated way, he seemed excited by the prospect.

"How do you feel about going?" she asked.

"I think army life might suit me. And it's not like anyone will be shooting at me."

"I should hope not!"

He halted by the water's edge and took both her hands in his as he gazed down at her. He seemed shy suddenly. "I came to ask a favor. I know we've only known each other a few weeks, but . . . will you be my girlfriend?"

Ans hoped it was too dark for him to see that she was blushing. Her fair skin always betrayed her. "I would like that very much," she replied. "I'm going to miss you, Erik." She leaned close and hugged him tightly. The thought of Erik going away or fighting a war made her realize how much she cared for him.

He lifted her chin and gave her a quick kiss. She wanted more, but he gave her a teasing smile. "Wait. I have another favor to ask. May I come back tomorrow and take some pictures of you? And of us together? A friend of mine has a camera he said I could borrow."

His request made her laugh.

"I can't wait to show off my beautiful girlfriend to the other men. They'll be so jealous!" He took her into his arms, and they kissed until they were both breathless.

Ans had never seen Erik this happy. She thought of Miriam again, how happy she'd looked when she'd described the man she loved. A shiver of joy spread through Ans as they walked back to the house together. She was thrilled to call this handsome man her boyfriend. Her parents would like him, except for the fact that he wasn't interested in going to church. But then, neither was she.

For the first week of the new war, Ans stayed beside Eloise every moment of the day whenever her husband was away. They showed Miriam the three apartments they'd found and helped her choose one. But Eloise had none of her usual energy and barely spoke a word. It had been hard for Ans to adjust to Eloise's nonstop chatter when she'd first started working for her, but now her long silences seemed ominous. Ans realized how fragile her employer's facade had been all these weeks as she saw it begin to fracture. The task of preventing her from falling into despair might prove nearly as exhausting as keeping up with her frenetic activity.

Erik's mobilization orders came the following week. Ans managed to get away for a short time to see him off at the Leiden train station. A deep foreboding stole over her as she kissed him goodbye, as if a storm cloud had stolen the sun's warmth. Her tears started falling, and she was helpless to stop them.

"Don't cry," Erik soothed. "I'm only going away for training, not to fight."

"I know. But everything's changing, and I don't want it to. I was so happy . . . We were having so much fun together, and now . . ." She wiped her cheeks, searching for a way to explain how she felt. "I remember riding my bicycle out in the country one time, and I suddenly heard thunder booming in the distance. A storm was racing up behind me, moving closer and closer, and I felt so vulnerable out there on the empty road. There was no place to hide or take cover from the lightning. I feel that way now, with all the rumbles of war thundering around our little country."

Erik pulled her close. "That's why I'm going into the army, Ans. I want to be that shelter for you. I want to always keep you safe."

Her tears continued to fall as she watched Erik's train leave the station. He and dozens of other young men waved and blew kisses from the open windows, buoyed with the idea of a great adventure. Ans watched the train until it was out of sight, then gathered her strength to hurry home to Eloise.

CHAPTER 8

Lena attacked the tub of laundry with the plunger as if it were her enemy. She wished she had gone into town with Pieter. He should have been home by now, but he wasn't. It didn't take three hours to sell their milk and eggs and pick up the items Lena had asked for. That meant he was probably talking about enlisting with some of the other farmers again.

Steam from the boiling tubs fogged the porch windows where she worked. Lena removed her sweater, then pulled the kerchief off her head and mopped her brow before running the finished load through the wringer. She and Pieter had done all of the usual autumn chores together—harvesting the fall crops, butchering pigs, smoking the meat, and making sausage—but now that the work was finished and winter approached, Pieter was growing restless. Deep creases had furrowed his brow like a plowed field as they'd sat in the kitchen last evening listening to news of the war on the radio.

"Why does it bother you so much?" she'd finally asked. "We don't have to worry. We aren't at war with anyone."

"You expect me to be content just sitting around all winter," he'd replied, "while other men are doing their duty?"

"You're too old for the draft. Besides, you're exempt because you're a farmer."

"I'm thinking of joining the reserves."

"Pieter, no! This war is none of our country's business. If our government wants to muster troops as a show of strength, let them do it without you."

"That show of strength kept the Netherlands neutral the last time, remember? I need to do my part." He had grabbed his jacket and stormed off to the barn, slamming the door. Lena had let him go. They rarely argued, and she didn't want this disagreement to come between them. But she feared it would.

She was pegging clothes on the line a half hour later when she heard their truck coming up the road. She left the basket where it was and walked across the yard to meet him outside the barn. She could tell by the way he squared his shoulders and lifted his chin that he had something important to say.

"I know you won't be happy, Lena, but it's all arranged. Six of us have enlisted in the reserves together. We'll be reporting to army headquarters in Den Haag for training."

"When?"

"Monday."

Lena grabbed his jacket sleeves, wishing she could shake sense into him. "Pieter, please don't do this. I'm begging you."

"It's already done. You know I have to go. You know it's the right thing to do."

"But it isn't! You have a wife and children to think about. A farm to look after. No one will fault you for not going. Tell them you changed your mind. Please!"

"I'm not changing my mind." He twisted free. Lena knew she was supposed to submit to her husband's decisions, but she couldn't face the thought of him going away. Or of being left alone.

"Pieter, I'm afraid for you."

He sighed and pulled her into his arms. She thought he was going to give in and listen to reason, but he released her after only a moment and walked toward the open barn door. She followed him inside. "You're getting all worked up for nothing, Lena. You didn't carry on this way when I trained during the first war."

"We weren't married yet," she said, keeping pace with him. "You didn't have three children to think about."

"And now I do!" he said, raising his voice. "They're the reason I have to go!"

"If you're truly thinking about us, you'll stay home."

Pieter halted and closed his eyes for a long moment. Then he opened them again and looked intently at her. "The first war was more than twenty years ago. I need to take a retraining course with the latest weapons. There's no reason for you to worry because we aren't at war and we aren't going to be. But our military needs to demonstrate that we're prepared to defend our borders. And I need to be ready too."

"What about our farm?"

"I'll get everything in order before I go. Wim will help with the milking. He knows what to do. The training only lasts eight weeks."

She turned away without answering and walked back to her clothesline. Her anger grew as she shook the wrinkles from each piece of clothing and hung it up to dry. She was angry at the war, angry at Pieter's stubbornness, angry at her own helplessness. Pieter and Ans would both be gone, and with the two younger children in school all day, Lena would be alone. She had felt helpless as she'd watched Ans board the train to Leiden. She'd felt helpless to stop the march of time when she'd watched her youngest child walk down the road to start school. And now she was helpless to stop Pieter from leaving. This wasn't how she'd imagined her life would be. How had it spun out of control?

Before dawn on Monday morning, Pieter fed and milked the cows for the last time, then returned to their bedroom to pack. Lena's anger transformed into panic as she watched her husband place his neatly folded clothes in an empty feed sack and gather his shaving gear.

"It isn't fair," she fumed. "Why does there have to be another war? Why does it have to upset everything we've worked for?"

"We endured a European war once before."

Lena moved to block his path, stopping him as he turned to the open dresser drawer. "You know how much I worry about Ans, far away in Leiden. Now I'll be worried about you, too."

Pieter rarely lost his temper, but his voice grew louder, his tone sharp. "You have to stop this useless fretting, Lena! The Bible says, 'Do not be anxious about anything'!"

She gaped at him in surprise. Pieter was a man of faith, but he rarely spoke of it. And he never quoted Scripture.

"You can't just say 'stop' and expect me to—"

"Lena, listen to me!" His hands squeezed her arms. "You're wound so tightly, worrying about every little thing, trying so hard to hang on to control, but you never were in control to begin with. It's an illusion. The sooner you realize that, the sooner you'll put everything into God's hands and find some peace and maybe even get some sleep at night." He released her and lifted the sack. "Now will you drive me into town, or should I ride my bicycle?"

She stared at him. She wasn't going to win. Europe was at war, and Pieter was going away for training. "I'll drive you," she said, then threw herself into his arms, hugging him tightly one last time.

She woke Wim and Maaike and told them to get dressed for school while she was gone. A cloud of dust billowed behind the truck as Lena drove Pieter into the village—like the billowing clouds of war that were quickly overshadowing the Continent. The other five farmers who'd enlisted along with Pieter were already at the station, waiting for the train. Lena knew all of these men and the families they were leaving behind. Did their wives hate this decision as much as she did?

Lena couldn't wait for the train. She had to get home to her children and her chores. "I'll write," Pieter said as they kissed goodbye. "I love you."

Lena nodded, her heart too sorrowful for words.

CHAPTER 9

Miriam lowered her head against the wind as she hurried to her apartment. She usually enjoyed the freedom of walking everywhere in this pretty city, watching the boats on the glittering canals or winding through the maze of centuries-old cobblestone streets and imagining how she would share all these things with Avi. But November had brought weather that was cold and damp, along with shorter days. The sun set by late afternoon, and Abba had to walk home from the university in the dark. She knew Leiden wasn't like Cologne, with gangs that randomly attacked Jews, but the memory of what her cousin Saul had endured made her stomach churn whenever Abba was late.

A cold rain began to drizzle, and Miriam walked faster, hugging her bag to her chest. Inside were two warm sweaters and a pair of wool trousers, gifts from Mrs. Huizenga's own wardrobe after she'd learned how few clothes Miriam and Abba had brought from Germany. "Winter is coming, Miriam. Take these," she'd insisted. "Leiden can be frigid." The professor's wife had been helping her and Abba get settled, inviting Miriam to lunch every week so she could practice her Dutch.

Ans had become a good friend as well, ready to help Miriam with anything she needed. "I'll take you shopping, if you'd like," she'd offered. "It'll be fun! I know where all the best shops are. And you can get some bargains on market day." Mrs. Huizenga was friendly, but in a more distant way than Ans—perhaps because she didn't speak German.

Miriam checked her mailbox before unlocking the door to her apartment building, hoping for a letter from Avi. The box was empty. Maybe the mailman hadn't come yet. She climbed the steep, narrow stairs to her second-floor apartment, brushing icy raindrops from her coat, shaking them off her hat. This apartment was a place to live, but it wasn't quite home yet. She and Abba lived here like two incomplete souls, missing the other halves of themselves, missing the people they loved.

Ans and Mrs. Huizenga had helped her and Abba rent this apartment, then had taken her shopping for the other essentials necessary to start a household. The front room had two comfortable chairs and a sofa, lacy curtains at the windows, and a radio they could listen to at night. The kitchen had a sink, two small gas burners and an oven, and a table that Abba used as a desk, writing endless letters, desperate to rescue their family in Cologne. Now that Germany was at war, their loved ones' futures were more uncertain than they'd ever been. Abba had given Miriam the larger bedroom so she would have room to practice her violin. And they had a modern bathroom for Mother. If she ever made it out of Germany, she would find it comfortable here.

"We'll be fine," Abba had assured Miriam on the first night they'd lived here. "The Netherlands is at peace. Once our family is together again, everything will be fine, you'll see." But as they'd listened to the German news channel each night and heard the Führer's manic rants, Miriam didn't see how anything could ever be fine again.

The unpleasant smell of her wet wool coat filled the room as it dried. Miriam didn't know quite what to do with herself while she waited for the mailman. It hadn't taken long to put away the new clothes Mrs. Huizenga had given her. She'd practiced her violin all morning and was bored with that. Abba would be teaching at the university all day. With nothing else to do, she decided to write another letter to Avi rather than wait for one from him. She was worried he would need warm winter clothing in the refugee camp, and asked if he wanted her to send some.

At last Miriam saw the mailman coming up the street and hurried downstairs to the mailbox to give him her letter. "Sorry, nothing for you today," he said when he saw her waiting. Abba would be disappointed too. There had been no mail at all from Germany since the war began two months ago. But there was a letter for her widowed landlady, Mrs. Spielman, who lived in the apartment below theirs and wasn't able to get out much because of her rheumatism. Miriam knocked on her door.

"Mrs. Spielman? It's Miriam, from upstairs. You got a letter. I thought I'd save you the trouble of going outside in the cold." A moment later, the door opened.

"Come in, come in! Quickly!" She beckoned for Miriam to hurry inside while she held on to her squirming cat, Oliver. The fat gray- and black-striped tiger seemed to take great delight in trying to escape every time the door opened. "Would you like a cup of tea? I saw you walking home in the rain a while ago."

"That would be lovely, if it isn't too much trouble."

"Not at all. I could use the company." She limped into her kitchen— a larger version of the one upstairs—and put the kettle on the burner. Mrs. Spielman, also Jewish, was a pleasant, gray-haired woman in her seventies who was as round and plump as the potato dumplings Mother's cook used to make. She set out a teapot and cups, her crippled fingers knotted and bent.

"I hope my Dutch is not too bad. I am still learning."

"I can understand you just fine."

"Something smells good," Miriam said, inhaling the aroma of cooking food.

"*Ach* . . . it's just some soup I'm throwing together. It's not so much fun to cook for only myself. Do you enjoy cooking, dear?"

"I . . . um . . . I do not know how. In Germany, our family hired a cook. Abba and I have been eating what is already made."

"I can teach you if you'd like."

"Yes? You would not mind?"

"Not at all. Although you probably eat different things in Germany than we do here."

"It does not matter. We must eat something."

"Tell me what you have in the house and I'll help you make something with it for supper."

Miriam hung her head, embarrassed. "I have nothing. I must go to the market later."

"No wonder you're so thin! I'll write a grocery list for you. Show it to the Jewish butcher on the corner and tell him I sent you. He'll help you. Then bring everything home and I'll teach you how to cook it."

Miriam ran upstairs for her coat, purse, and shopping basket after finishing her tea and the gingery cookie Mrs. Spielman offered with it. "We Dutch love our tea biscuits," she'd said, laughing.

Thirty minutes later, Miriam was hurrying through her door again with the groceries while Mrs. Spielman wrestled with the cat to keep it from escaping. Miriam's eyes watered as she peeled and sliced the onion. She added it to the roasting pan and learned how to sear and season the meat before putting it into Mrs. Spielman's oven to roast.

"Tomorrow I'll teach you how to make soup for the cold winter months."

"How will I thank you, Mrs. Spielman?"

"There's no need. It isn't only your father you must think about, little Miriam," she said as they peeled potatoes and chopped carrots to go with the meat. "A pretty young girl like you will surely have a husband to feed one of these days."

Miriam decided to confide in Mrs. Spielman. She struggled with the language as she groped for words. "I am in love with a man from the refugee camp. His name is Avraham Leopold. He must have a visa to be a student, but the needed papers are in Berlin."

Mrs. Spielman saw Miriam's tears. She dried her hands on her apron and pulled her into her arms. They were soft and warm and wonderfully comforting. "You poor dear."

"I am sorry. I didn't mean to cry."

"That's okay. You can go ahead and cry anytime you want. That's what my arms are for."

"I miss Avi so much," she said, wiping her cheeks. "We write letters but it is not the same. Avi thinks of running from the camp, but if he is caught, they will send him back to Germany."

"What a tragedy that would be." She smoothed Miriam's hair from her face with her knotted fingers.

"In Germany, they made Jews suffer—what is the word?—persecution. I didn't think anything worse could happen. But now there is a war, and we have no letters from our family. We are so worried."

"That's the worst thing about war—all the separations."

"To me, the worst thing is not dreaming of a future. When there is peace, anything seems possible. Now, nothing does. The future is taken from us and we cannot get it back."

"At least we're at peace here in the Netherlands."

"Yes. And Abba is happy at the university." Miriam pulled out her handkerchief to wipe her eyes and blow her nose. "When Avi and Mama come, everything will be perfect." She stuffed her handkerchief back into her pocket and returned to peeling. It seemed like half of the potato was coming off with the peels. "I am not good at this," she said with a sigh.

"Cooking takes practice. Like learning the violin, I suppose."

"What about your family, Mrs. Spielman? Have you always lived in Leiden?"

"My husband and I both grew up here. He was a pharmacist and owned a shop on Rapenburg for years. We raised two sons who both live in Amsterdam now, with their families. And I have eight grandchildren."

"How wonderful!"

"They surely are. You'll meet them when they come for a visit. I've had a happy life, Miriam. The Netherlands has been a good place for Jews to live."

"You give me hope, Mrs. Spielman—and cooking lessons."

"Here, let me finish peeling," she said, taking the knife and potato from Miriam. "By the time your young Avraham arrives, you'll be able to cook him a feast."

"That will be wonderful. But will this food be cooked when Abba comes home?"

"Oh yes, my dear. And won't he be surprised?"

"He will think he's in paradise."

CHAPTER 10

Lena's days fell into a lonely rhythm without Pieter. She did the farm chores—her own as well as his—bundled the children off to school each morning, listened to the news and did mending every evening, tossed and turned in the cold, empty bed at night until the sheets were rumpled and loose, then rose before dawn to do it all over again. There was less laundry to wash, fewer people to cook for, no one to talk to during the day. Winter brought short days and endlessly long nights. She wasn't sleeping well. Pieter was a quiet man, but she missed his warm, solid presence during the day, his gentle snoring at night.

December could be a dreary month, but today, December 5, the wind blew the clouds toward the sea and a wintry sun made an appearance for the first time in days. Lena put on her warmest coat and tied a kerchief over her hair to bicycle into the village, hoping for a letter from Pieter. He wrote once a week. Lena could tell that he struggled to find something different and interesting to say each time. Tonight was Sinterklaas Eve, and she would love to have a letter to read aloud to the children since Pieter himself couldn't be home.

She climbed off her bike when she reached town, stopping first at the post office, where her cousin Truus's husband worked as postmaster. He was five years older than Pieter and hadn't enlisted in the reserves. "No mail for you today, Lena. Sorry."

She disguised her disappointment as she thanked him and climbed the stairs to her cousin's apartment above.

Truus poured them each a cup of coffee. "What do you hear from your soldier boy?"

"His training was supposed to last eight weeks. He should be home any day now."

"Maybe in time for Sinterklaas Eve?"

"That would be the best present I could imagine. But I doubt if the army thinks about sentimental things like Sinterklaas and hopeful children. I already bought presents for Wim and Maaike. I'm stopping at the bakery next for treats."

"Well, if he doesn't come tonight, there's always Christmas. And what do you hear from Ans? Do you think she'll be home for Christmas?"

"I don't know. Maybe. The woman she works for isn't well."

"What's wrong with her?"

"I don't know, exactly." Lena knew from Ans's letters that Mrs. Huizenga suffered from spells of melancholia, but she decided not to tell her cousin. Truus loved a juicy morsel of gossip. Her husband also seemed to know everyone's business and was jokingly accused by some villagers of reading all the mail.

Lena finished her coffee and hugged Truus goodbye, then went to the bakery for *pepernoten* and the traditional holiday *banket* shaped in a *W* for Wim and an *M* for Maaike.

"No *A* for Ans this year?" the baker asked.

Lena shook her head, willing away tears. "Her job in Leiden is very demanding."

Her last stop was the manse to visit her father. She went in through the kitchen door and wandered through the dining room and front room on the way to his office. The rooms had seemed barren and lifeless since Mama's death, and Lena always passed through them quickly. Papa had hired a housekeeper to clean and cook for him, but the manse lacked the warmth and cheer that her mother had always given it. A basket of knitting still sat beside her mother's chair near the window, the needles holding a half-finished pair of socks. Neither Lena nor Papa had the heart to stow the knitting away.

"Engelena! You look hearty and rosy-cheeked!" Papa rose and walked around his desk to kiss her.

"I bicycled into town to buy Sinterklaas treats. I let the sun fool me into thinking it was warm."

"Any news of when Pieter is coming home?"

"Soon, I hope. Papa, I wanted to ask—do you think you could come out to the farm tonight for Sinterklaas Eve? I know the children will really be missing their father. I will be, too, naturally. Pieter always made the holiday such fun for them."

"I'll try. But I'm sure you've heard that Mrs. Hoekstra is in her last days. I'm leaving in a few minutes to be with the family."

"I understand." Lena had grown up with the demands her father's role as pastor required. He loved his family, but his work often had to come first. She'd lost track of the number of times he'd been called away from the dinner table or from a special occasion like tonight.

She took her time cycling home to the farm, searching for beauty in the barren tree limbs and drying grasses, finding none. She removed her kerchief to feel what little warmth the sun provided, but it failed to cheer her. Once home, she hid the presents and treats she'd bought for the children and started supper.

Wim and Maaike burst through the kitchen door that afternoon, chattering about Sinterklaas Eve and the school holiday tomorrow. Wim no longer believed that Sinterklaas would arrive on his white horse tonight, bringing presents to all the children, but he gallantly played along for Maaike's sake.

"Have you been good, Maaike?" he teased as they removed their shoes and hung up their coats. "Or will Zwarte Piet be paying you a visit?" Piet was Sinterklaas's servant who punished naughty children.

Maaike looked worried as she tugged Lena's sleeve. "I've been good, right, Mama?"

"Yes, little one." Lena combed her fingers through Maaike's wind-tangled hair, as thick and golden as Pieter's.

"I wish Ans was here," Maaike said.

"And Papa," Wim added.

"I know. I miss them, too." She bit her lip, remembering how Pieter would sneak outside when the children weren't watching and run around to knock on the front door after leaving presents from Sinterklaas on the front step. Then he would race back inside and reappear when the children opened the door to see their treats. Lena couldn't do the trick by herself.

She and Wim milked the cows together and fed the animals, then the three of them sat down at the kitchen table to eat supper. The children didn't want much, their tummies full from parties at school. "Is it time to put our shoes outside, Mama?" Maaike asked afterwards.

"Yes, let's do that." They went into the barn for a fistful of hay and then down to the root cellar for carrots. These were placed outside in one of their wooden shoes to feed Sinterklaas's horse. Sinterklaas would fill the other shoe with treats and presents.

"Let's sing," Lena said, attempting to lift everyone's spirits, including her own. She sat at the piano in the front room and played the traditional holiday songs while the children sang along. They were in the middle of a song when a loud knock on the door startled them. Maaike's face lit up, her mouth open wide in anticipation.

"It's Sinterklaas!" she giggled. Or maybe Opa. Maybe he'd been able to stop by tonight after all, although Lena hadn't heard his car.

They all hurried to the door. And there was Pieter!

"Papa!" Maaike cried. Lena thought she might burst with joy as Pieter dropped his sack of belongings and pulled her into his arms, kissing her on the lips, right in front of the children. He hugged Wim and tousled his hair, then scooped Maaike into his arms for a hug.

"Well, I'm sorry I'm not Sinterklaas," he said, "but it looks like he's been here already." He pointed to the children's shoes, overflowing with treats. The carrots and hay were gone.

"See, Wim? I told you I've been good," Maaike said, elbowing him.

The children hauled their loot inside, and Lena nestled on the sofa beside her husband as they watched the children tear into their gifts.

"Why didn't you write and tell me you were coming?" Lena asked.

"I wanted to surprise you." He lifted her hand and kissed it.

"Well, you certainly did. I thought for sure you were Sinterklaas."

The children were so excited that Lena didn't know how she would ever get them to sleep. Pieter sat on the sofa with Wim beside him and Maaike on his lap and told tales of his life as a soldier. At last Lena grew impatient to have Pieter all to herself and sent the children to bed.

"It's so wonderful to have you beside me in bed again," she said later. "I've been so lonely."

"Me too. And I'll tell you one thing, I like being a farmer more than a soldier."

"Promise you won't leave me again? It's terrible here without you."

Pieter propped himself on one elbow and looked down at her in the darkened room, his expression serious. The half-moon shone through the curtain and lit up his fair hair like spun gold. "I can't promise that, Lena. They said if there's a crisis, I'll have to report back to Den Haag for deployment."

"Do you think there will be one?"

"Well, not much is happening in the war right now. No major battles between the Nazis and the Allies. They're calling it a 'phony' war."

Lena pulled him down beside her again. "Let's pray for peace."

CHAPTER 11

In the months since England and France declared war against Germany, Ans had stayed alert for signs that Eloise might be sliding into depression. It was like watching her navigate a rushing streambed, stepping over slippery rocks, trying not to lose her footing and be swept away. She admired Eloise's courage. When Ans first arrived in Leiden, Eloise had thrown herself into every task with frantic cheerfulness, talking fast, her graceful hands nervous and fluttery. Now she often had to be coaxed from bed in the morning. She ate very little and was obsessed with listening to news of the war. Not much had been happening so far, but the anxiety of waiting made Eloise's melancholy worse, as if she feared the approach of a violent storm.

"The battles will surely start any day, now that winter is over," she repeated each morning.

"Yes, but the Netherlands is neutral. The war won't come here," Ans tried to assure her. She made sure Eloise continued with their usual routines, getting out of the town house for a walk, planning trips to Amsterdam or outings in Leiden, eating lunch with Miriam.

The three women were having lunch on a rainy afternoon in one of Eloise's favorite cafés when a man rushed in, shouting to the owner, "Have you heard the news? The Nazis just invaded Norway!" Waiters froze with trays of food in their hands. Everyone in the restaurant stopped eating to listen. "Nazi warships have landed in Oslo with thousands of troops!" the man continued. Ans wanted to shout at him to be quiet. Norway was neutral, like the Netherlands.

Eloise set down her fork and removed her napkin from her lap, laying it across her half-finished plate. "Tell the waiter we need our check. We're going home."

"Let's finish our lunch first," she said, resting her hand on Eloise's arm. But Eloise grew increasingly agitated as the man continued to describe the invasion of Norway and a simultaneous attack on neutral Denmark.

"Tell me what has happened," Miriam said. "Is it something with the war?"

Ans nodded. "The Nazis invaded Norway and Denmark." She spoke softly, hoping no one would overhear her speaking German, aware of strong anti-Nazi sentiment in the Netherlands.

Eloise pushed her chair away from the table and asked for the check. "Come, Ans. We need to hurry home." Eloise's slender body trembled so badly on the way home that Ans and Miriam had to support her, juggling umbrellas and dodging puddles. Vendors shouted out the headlines from every newsstand they passed, and Eloise made Ans stop and buy them.

They arrived at the town house soaking wet, their feet drenched. "Let me fetch some towels for everyone," Ans said, combing her fingers through her rain-matted hair. Eloise didn't reply as she went into the front room and switched on the radio.

"Eloise, maybe we should wait for Professor—"

"Oh, do be quiet, Ans. I'm trying to hear this." She sank onto the sofa, white-faced and trembling.

Ans asked Miriam to get the towels. "Can you stay and help me?" Ans whispered when she returned.

"Yes, of course."

What the man in the restaurant had said was true. Nazi warships had sailed past British mines to land in major Norwegian ports from Narvik to Oslo. Thousands of troops poured ashore. A Norwegian military commander who was a Nazi sympathizer had ordered Norwegian troops not to stop them. The Nazis also had invaded Copenhagen and other Danish cities, demanding that the overwhelmed Danish government surrender.

"Norway and Denmark were neutral," Eloise said. "Neutral! Just like Belgium was in the Great War. Just like we are here in the Netherlands. See, Ans? Neutrality means nothing to those people. Nothing!" Her voice sounded shaky at first but seemed to grow stronger along with her anger.

"Eloise, please," Ans said, handing her a towel. "We need to turn off the radio until your husband comes home. It's only going to stir up memories that you need to forget."

"Forget! I won't ever forget! You weren't even born when the Kaiser decided to use neutral Belgium as a shortcut to Paris. They killed my parents and took over our house in Antwerp."

Ans had never seen Eloise this upset. Should she telephone the professor? She had a number where he could be reached at the university in an emergency.

"My older brother escaped to France and fought with the Allies," Eloise continued. "He was gassed in the war. I saw him one last time, and he begged me to kill him and end his suffering." Eloise turned to Miriam, commanding her attention as if both of their lives were now at risk. "We nearly starved to death, Miriam!"

Miriam seemed to have trouble breathing whenever she became upset, and she was clearly in distress now.

"Eloise, stop. You're upsetting yourself and Miriam, too. Please—"

"You both need to know that wars always bring famine and disease and starvation. Thousands of innocent people died of hunger in Belgium before the world stepped in to help us."

"But you survived and you moved here—"

"There were too many horrible memories for me in Belgium."

"And you married the professor," Ans said, desperate to steer her memories in a different direction. "He loves you very much, I can tell. You have a beautiful life together. I hope I find a husband someday who loves me half as much as he loves you." Eloise managed a smile. "When your thoughts go to the past, why not think of the present, instead? And the future?"

Eloise's eyes filled with tears. "There won't be a future—that's what I'm trying to tell you, Ans. It's going to happen all over again. Enemy occupation. Starvation and death—"

"Stop!" Ans grabbed Eloise's flailing hands, squeezing them tightly. "You don't know that, Eloise. Our country has already mobilized hundreds of thousands of troops who are positioned to defend us if—"

"We Belgians did the same thing." She shook her hands free. "The troops won't do any good. Ask the Danes and the Norwegians."

"Our country was spared in the last war—"

"It won't be spared this time." Eloise stared into space as tears washed down her cheeks. Ans wondered if she dared to leave her side long enough to call Professor Huizenga.

"Maybe you're right. Maybe it will happen again. But until it does, let's be happy, Eloise. Let's take the train to Amsterdam tomorrow and see the artwork. Miriam can come with us and—"

"It's too dreary to travel in the rain."

"Then let's enjoy the rain! We'll walk Miriam home with our umbrellas up and our boots on, and we'll slosh through all the puddles like children. We can stop at the flower market and buy flowers for every room in the house. And when we get home, we'll drink pots and pots of tea and listen to beautiful music on the gramophone."

Eloise looked up at Ans with a weak smile. Her tears continued to fall. "You're right, dear, dear Ans. We do have today, don't we? But our lives could change in an instant, just as they have for those poor Norwegians. And then nothing will ever be the same."

Ans was scrambling to think of what to say next when she heard a key turn in the front door. Professor Huizenga hurried in. *Thank God.* He sat down beside Eloise, still wearing his wet overcoat, and gently pulled her into his arms. "I was afraid you might have heard the news, my love, so I came home right away."

"You won't leave me, Herman?"

"Never." He looked up at Ans over his wife's head and nodded. She could go.

"I'll walk you home," Ans whispered to Miriam. They put their wet coats back on and headed out in the rain again with their dripping umbrellas. It wasn't far to Miriam's apartment, but neither of them said a word, as if exhausted by the afternoon's events.

Miriam turned to Ans when they reached her door. "I fear Eloise is right," she said softly. "What happened to her in Belgium and what happened to us in Germany—it could happen all over again."

"But maybe—"

She held up her hand to stop Ans. "But you are right, too, Ans. We still have today. We must live in hope today and not in despair." She hugged Ans and said goodbye.

By the time Ans returned to the town house, the radio was off and the professor had coaxed Eloise upstairs to her bedroom. Ans made a pot of tea and was sitting in the kitchen, drying off and warming up by the range, when Professor Huizenga found her there. He looked cold and pale and even thinner than the day Ans first met him. "I fear this war will be the end of her," he said with a sigh.

"Is she okay?"

"For now. Eloise has taken her medicine. It will make her sleepy."

"Would you like a cup of tea?" she asked, lifting the pot. "There's plenty."

He shook his head. "I'm taking Eloise away for a few days. The sea air always refreshes her. I thought you might like to go home to see your family while we're away."

"Thank you. I think I'll do that."

"Ans, I don't know how to thank you for being such good medicine for Eloise—no, you're much more than that. You're her friend."

"I like her very much, Professor. I hope this trip will be good for her."

"Yes. So do I."

Ans decided not to take the train home, needing time and space between her life in Leiden and the farm. It was a long bicycle ride, but she left early Sunday morning and arrived just as her family was returning from church. Her mother held her tightly and seemed reluctant to let go. Ans thought of Miriam and Eloise, who had both lost their mothers, as she embraced her own. Both women had also lost their homes, and Ans felt guilty for having wanted so badly to leave hers.

"My turn! My turn!" Maaike danced around Ans, pulling on her hands and begging to be picked up and carried, even though at six years old she was no longer a baby. Ans gave her and Wim the chocolates she had brought.

"But you have to wait until after dinner to eat them," she warned. Maaike gave an impish grin and slipped a piece into her mouth when she thought no one was looking. "Spoiled girl!" Ans said with a laugh. She gave her sister a playful swat before following their mother into the kitchen. "Need help, Mama?"

"No, I think everything's ready."

Mama always set the table the night before and peeled the potatoes and carrots. They had gone into the oven with the smoked pork before church and smelled heavenly now. When Opa arrived, they all sat down for Sunday dinner.

Ans looked at her beloved family gathered around the table, and it was as if she'd never left home. Nothing had changed here on the farm, which was comforting in a way. But Ans knew she had changed. She'd done so many new things, had made new friends, had even learned to dance. And she had a boyfriend whose kisses awakened all sorts of new possibilities.

"Is the job working out well?" Opa asked as platters of meat and mashed potatoes and carrots made their way around the table.

"I like Professor Huizenga and his wife a lot," she replied. "I'm supposed to be Eloise's companion, but it's almost the other way around. She takes me to so many interesting places like concert halls and art museums. I'm getting a wonderful education from her." She didn't mention Eloise's frailty. It seemed wrong to expose her weakness. She wondered how much Opa knew about the situation.

"I'm glad," he said. "And that you like it there."

"I've also met an interesting family from Cologne, Germany. Miriam Jacobs and her father are Jewish refugees. Professor Huizenga helped Mr. Jacobs find work as a lecturer at the university, and Mrs. Huizenga and I helped them get settled in an apartment."

"From the looks of things," Papa said, "they got out of Germany just in time."

"Miriam's mother and the rest of her family didn't make it out. They're still there. And Miriam's boyfriend is stuck in Westerbork."

"War brings so many horrible disruptions," Mama said. "All of the boys you went to school with, Ans, have gone off for military training."

"I wish I was old enough to be a soldier," Ans's brother said.

"Oh, Wim!" She punched his shoulder. "You're just a boy." She could tell by the stubborn jut of his chin that he disagreed.

"We have work to do now that spring has arrived," Papa said, "and we're shorthanded."

"Your father went away for military training too—" Mama began.

"And I'm still in the reserves," he finished. "I'll be called up if I'm needed. This invasion of Norway and Denmark worries me. In the meantime, I'm needed on the farm. The government has been stockpiling food so our country will survive if the war disrupts trade."

"Like Joseph and Pharaoh in the Bible," Opa said. "Storing food in times of plenty is a very wise thing to do."

"Wars always bring famine and disease and starvation," Eloise had

told Ans. She looked at the bountiful meal in front of her and couldn't imagine it.

Papa read from the Bible and prayed after dinner, as he'd done for as long as Ans could remember. Mama asked polite questions about the city and Ans's job as they did the dishes but seemed hesitant to pry into her personal life. Ans longed to tell her about Erik and how much she missed him now that he was away. But mentioning Erik would bring unwelcome questions about his background and his faith, questions that Ans wasn't ready to answer.

When the dishes were done, Ans slipped into the barn to talk with Papa. He was diligent about not working on the Lord's Day, but he still made sure his animals were cared for. He'd changed from his Sunday suit and looked more like the papa she loved in his well-worn work clothes.

"Do you think we'll be caught up in the war?" Ans asked.

"We managed to stay neutral the first time. We should be able to do it again."

"Then why do you seem so worried?"

"Do I?" He raked his hand through his thick hair, and Ans thought she saw a few silver strands among the blond ones.

"Yes. Mama seems worried too. Mrs. Huizenga grew up in Belgium, and she told me horrible stories about what happened to her country when the Kaiser's armies invaded. She thinks it will happen here."

He didn't reply right away.

"Your mother and I both remember how the first war disrupted our lives, even though our country wasn't involved. I was a young man—in love with your mother," he added with a shy smile. "And I think this war is already disrupting our lives. All of the farmers are shorthanded, for one thing."

"We feel the tension in the city, too. Professor Huizenga says so many students have gone off for military training that the university is half-empty."

"Your mother worries about you, Ans. Maybe you could write to her a little more often so she knows you're all right?"

"Yes, I'm sorry. I'll try harder from now on. There isn't a lot to say sometimes."

He pulled her close in a one-armed hug. "I worry about you, too, my girl. It's a father's job to protect his daughter, no matter how old she is."

Ans thought of the lengths Miriam's father had gone to protect her and knew Papa would have done the same. "I know, Papa, and I love you for it."

"You aren't going to forget how to milk a cow while you're away, are you?"

She laughed. "Not likely!"

"Well, if you need some practice while you're home, let me know."

⌇⌇⌇

When it was time for Ans to return to Leiden, Wim rode alongside her for a mile or two, chattering about the war and his best friend's brother, who had gone away for training. "The Nazis have tanks that can roll over anything in their path and smash it flat," he said. The wind ruffled his pale hair like wheat. "Nothing stops them! And they have so many planes that they fill the sky from one end to the other!"

"How do you know so much about it?"

"The radio," he said, shrugging as if it were obvious. "But their tanks won't get very far in our country. If they try to invade us, we're going to open the dikes and flood the land and drown them all."

"Did you learn that from the radio, too?"

"Papa makes me turn it off when they start talking about gruesome things, like what the Nazis did in Poland."

"I should think so! You're only twelve!"

"But my friend Hans listens to all of it, every night, and he tells me what I missed."

Ans wanted to plead with Wim not to listen, to remain an innocent child for just a while longer. She understood what Papa meant when he'd said the war was disrupting their lives.

"Hey, you won't tell Papa about all the stuff Hans tells me, will you?" Wim asked suddenly.

Ans shook her head. If Wim didn't hear the war news from Hans, he would hear it from somebody else. "Your secret is safe with me," she replied. They pedaled together for another mile before Wim had to turn back. "Thanks for riding with me, Wim. You're still my favorite brother, you know."

He grinned at the joke they always shared, then turned serious. "Are you ever coming back home to live with us again, Ans?"

She hesitated—then decided her brother needed to hear the truth. "I don't think so, Wim. Leiden is my home now. I'm sorry."

"*Ja* . . . so am I."

CHAPTER 12

Three weeks after Ans's visit to her family, she awoke to the sound of distant thunder. She listened for rain, thinking she might need to get up and close her bedroom window. The distant booms continued—sometimes one or two, sometimes a cluster of them. Yet the thunder didn't rumble any closer or fade into the distance like a regular storm.

Maybe it wasn't thunder.

Now there was another odd sound from far away—a low, droning roar like a rushing waterfall. It grew steadily louder. Closer.

Airplanes. Not one, but many.

Ans scrambled out of bed and parted the curtains to peer out. She couldn't see anything. The rumbling was on the other side of the town house. She left her room and felt her way downstairs toward the dining room windows. A shadowy figure in the foyer startled her. Ans gasped and backed up a step. Eloise turned to face her.

"Did you hear them, too?" she asked. Her face was as pale as the streak of white that swept through her dark hair, as pale as her delicate silk nightgown. Ans's heart raced faster. Professor Huizenga had gone to Den Haag on an overnight trip. They were alone.

"What is that sound?" Ans asked.

"Airplanes. And they're dropping bombs."

"That can't be true. We aren't at war. Why would anyone bomb us?"

"Because Hitler intends to conquer all of Europe, and we're next. Remember Norway and Denmark?"

Ans couldn't reply. She didn't want to believe it. "Lightning warfare" they were calling it—*Blitzkrieg*. Hitler's armies invaded with lightning speed and overwhelming power, forcing a quick surrender. Had the lightning struck the Netherlands? Ans wanted to go back to bed and wake up all over again.

"Come on," Eloise said. "We need a better view." She turned and raced up the stairs, climbing all the way to the third floor before Ans could catch up with her. Eloise opened the child-size door that led up narrow wooden steps to the attic. Ans followed her, barely able to see in the dusty gloom at first. But as her eyes adjusted, she could make out an old dresser, a battered steamer trunk, a chair with a broken leg. Cobwebs draped from the rafters above her head. The attic didn't have a floor, but Eloise was already navigating across some loose planks between the joists, making her way to a dormer window in the rear of the attic as if she knew every inch of the space. She dragged a wooden crate closer to the window and climbed up on it.

"Eloise, wait! What are you doing? Maybe we should—"

"We have to go out on the roof. We'll be able to see above the trees from there."

"The roof? I-I don't think that's a very good idea. We don't have shoes on, and—"

"Help me open this window. It's heavy, and I think it's stuck." Eloise grunted as she strained to open the grimy window. Dust and filth soiled her hands and beautiful nightgown. She beckoned to Ans. "Come on! Hurry!"

Ans picked her way across the splintery boards, arms outstretched for balance. This made no sense at all. She needed to stop Eloise, but how? "Maybe we should wait until morning."

"Why wait? They're bombing us right now." The drone of airplanes sounded louder up here. There must be hundreds of them. "I told you this would happen, didn't I, Ans? It's just like the last war when they didn't care if Belgium was neutral or not, and they marched in and took whatever they wanted, but this time they'll not only take Belgium, but the Netherlands, too—you can be sure of it." Her voice had the manic intensity that Ans recognized as a sign of danger. The higher Eloise's mood soared, the further she might eventually fall.

"I still don't think we should go out on the roof in the dead of night and—"

"Fine!" Eloise gave an exasperated sigh. "Stay inside if you're afraid of heights. But help me open the window." Eloise seemed determined, and Ans didn't dare let her venture out onto the roof by herself.

She climbed up on the crate beside her. "I'm not afraid of heights," Ans said. "I used to play up in our hayloft and climb to the top of our windmill. It's just . . . it's dark outside. And cold. And we're in our nightgowns. Shouldn't we get dressed first? Or at least put on shoes and coats?"

Eloise ignored her.

"One . . . two . . . *three*!" They shoved together and the window slid open, bringing a blast of damp air. Ans was slightly relieved to see a flat, narrow ledge about two feet below the dormer where they could stand. But they were four stories above the street and the wind was blowing. And there was nothing to hang on to. Eloise braced her arms on the windowsill and hoisted herself through the opening. Her silk nightgown snagged and tore. Ans's instinct was to stay inside on the crate, but she had no other choice but to follow Eloise outside into the cold, clear night. She linked arms with her, gripping the window frame with her other hand.

"You're shaking," Eloise said.

"It's cold out here. And it's an awfully long way down."

But Eloise was looking up, not down. "There! Look!" she said, pointing. "Den Haag is in that direction."

Ans saw faint flashes of light on the horizon, followed by a rumbling sound several seconds later. "Are they bombing the city?"

"My guess is they're bombing the airport. There's an army airfield over there."

"Maybe it's a training exercise."

"Why would our army use Nazi airplanes for training? Look, over there." She pivoted in the narrow space and pointed to an entire formation of planes that filled the sky like migrating birds. Ans felt the deep throb of their engines in the pit of her stomach. Dread filled every inch of her.

"See? Nazi planes," Eloise said. "It looks like they're heading toward Scheveningen on the Noordzee coast. And look! They're dropping paratroopers!" Ans watched in disbelief as the planes spewed out tiny specks like soot that drifted slowly to the ground. "See? They're invading us."

"Heaven help us . . . ," Ans murmured.

"You can save your breath, Ans. Heaven didn't help us the last time."

Ans studied Eloise's face in the dim light, searching for signs of an emotional collapse. The professor said that sights and sounds or even smells might act as trip wires, triggering dark thoughts of harming herself. If the news from Norway had nearly created a crisis, what would the sight of a Nazi invasion do?

"Oh, my poor, dear Herman," she said. "He's caught in the middle of that mess."

"I'm sure he'll be fine, Eloise. They'll have shelters and a safe place for him to go."

"Yes, but how will he ever get home?"

Ans scrambled for a reply. "I'm sure our soldiers are fighting back. We have troops stationed in Den Haag to protect the queen and the royal family."

Eloise gave a harsh laugh. "Our tiny Dutch army doesn't stand a chance! Name one other country that has been able to stand up to the Nazis."

Paratroopers fell from the armada of airplanes, filling the distant horizon. Ans's stomach churned as she thought of Erik fighting against such an overwhelming enemy. And Papa would be deployed in this crisis too. "I heard that there's a plan to open the dikes and flood the land so enemy tanks can't get through," Ans said, desperate to offer hope.

"A flood won't stop paratroopers from dropping out of the sky. Look at them all!" Eloise made a sweeping gesture with her arm, and for a moment, Ans feared she would lose her balance. She had to get Eloise off this roof.

"Can we go inside now? I'm cold."

"Our brave Belgian army tried to fight back in the Great War, but they were outnumbered." She seemed immune to the cold.

"Please, Eloise. My teeth are chattering."

"Oh, I suppose. If you must." She led the way inside and they closed the heavy window together. Then Eloise trotted across the rickety floorboards and down the stairs to the front room while Ans struggled to follow her through the darkened house.

"Shall I turn on the lights?" Ans asked.

"What for? We'll need to get used to the darkness."

"What do you mean?"

Eloise didn't reply. She switched on the radio and turned the dial through the haze of static until she found a station. Any news was certain to be devastating, and Ans knew she had to keep Eloise calm until the professor came home, but how?

Oh, Lord, please help me, she silently prayed. *Please show me what to do.*

CHAPTER 13

Lena startled awake. Pieter had suddenly thrown back the covers and leaped out of bed. She sat up in alarm. "Pieter? What's wrong?" Their bedroom was dark. Not even a crack of light appeared on the eastern horizon.

"Shh! Listen!" He held a finger to his lips. A low thrumming sounded in the distance, like a tractor running. No, like dozens of tractors.

"What is it? What's that noise?"

"It sounds like airplanes. A good many of them, I would think, to create such a roar."

The telephone downstairs began to ring, never a good sign in the middle of the night. Pieter hurried down the narrow stairs to answer it with Lena close behind. She glanced at the tall clock in the front room. Four thirty in the morning.

"Hello? . . . *Ja*, this is he . . . *ja* . . . *ja* . . . I'll be there as soon as I can."

Lena's first thought—her greatest fear—was that something terrible had happened to Ans. "Pieter, who was that? What's wrong?"

"The Nazis are invading us."

"*What?*" It wasn't what she expected to hear. She gaped at him in astonishment.

"That sound is their planes. They're bombing our airfields, dropping paratroopers." He raced back up the stairs, calling behind to her. "I've been deployed, Lena. I have to go."

She watched him put on his uniform and gather his things as if he knew exactly what he was doing. She couldn't comprehend what had happened. "I-I don't understand . . ."

"Remember how Hitler invaded Norway and Denmark last month? Now it's our turn."

"Oh, Pieter! What are we going to do?"

"Fight back. We're not giving up without a fight."

Lena closed her eyes. It had been bad enough when he'd gone off for training and she'd worried endlessly about him. But this wasn't training. This was the real thing. She longed to cling to Pieter and never let go, but their homeland, their very existence was being threatened. She couldn't beg him to stay. Lena yanked him into her arms, holding him tightly. "I love you."

"I love you too, Lena. Pray for our soldiers and for our country." He pried her arms away and hurried downstairs again. Lena followed and wrapped bread and cheese and an apple for him to take. "I'll ride my bike into town," he said. "They're sending a vehicle to pick us up."

"No, take the truck. It will be faster. I'll ride my bike there when the children wake up and drive it back home. I don't think they'll have school today, do you?" She wouldn't send them even if they did, unwilling to let her children out of her sight with the Nazis invading. Yet she knew it was a delusion to think she could protect them or that they would be safer with her. "What should I tell them, Pieter?"

"The truth."

"What's going to happen to us? Do you think we'll be able to stop the invasion? Will England and France help us, do you think?"

"They weren't much help to the other countries the Nazis invaded." He seemed distracted. She knew he was eager to leave. She started to cry, unable to stop her tears as fear engulfed her. "Lena . . . don't," he said. "You have to be strong. We both do."

"I'm sorry . . . I'm sorry . . ." She wiped her eyes but couldn't stop crying.

He held her again, kissing her one last time. Then he was gone. She heard the truck's sputtering engine start up. The headlamps shone briefly into the front windows as Pieter turned and drove away. The house was quiet again except for the ticking clock. The hum of distant airplanes seemed louder, closer. Lena went upstairs to get dressed, feeling chilled. She saw the rumpled sheets where Pieter had slept only a few minutes earlier, and dropped to her knees beside the bed to muffle the sound of her weeping as she prayed.

By the time the children awoke, Lena had regained control. She fed them breakfast and calmly explained what was happening. "Your papa left to join the other soldiers. He took our truck early this morning, and we'll have to go pick it up after our chores are finished."

"Are Nazi tanks and soldiers coming here?" Wim asked.

Lena hesitated. Pieter had advised her to tell them the truth. "They will probably try, Wim. But our army is going to fight back."

"Do we have tanks like they do?"

"I don't know. You can ask Opa when we see him today."

Later, Lena, Maaike, and Wim climbed onto their bicycles and pedaled into town to fetch Pieter's truck. She felt exposed and vulnerable riding through the open flatland with Nazi planes overhead, and she breathed a prayer of thanks when she finally saw houses and the village church steeple on the horizon. Pieter had parked the truck in the square beside the church. "Load the bicycles, Wim, while I talk to Opa." Lena took Maaike's hand and went inside.

The manse was empty. Lena came outside again and crossed the market square, finally finding her father in the bakery, talking with a group of villagers who had gathered there. He kissed the top of Maaike's head and steered them in the direction of the church. "Pieter has been deployed," she said.

"I know. I prayed with him and the other men before they left this morning."

"I'm so scared, Papa." She spoke softly as they walked toward the truck, hoping Maaike wouldn't overhear. She saw Wim waiting beside the truck and told Maaike to run across the street to join him. "I've been praying all morning that our country will be safe and that Pieter and the others will be safe, but—"

"Do you want your way or God's way?"

She stopped walking. The question made her angry. "Of course I want my way. Isn't that why we pray and bring our requests to Him? But I've never understood why He doesn't answer our prayers if He loves us. He didn't keep Mama from getting sick and dying, even though everyone in the village prayed for her. Now we're at war, and if anything happens to Pieter or one of our children, I . . . I don't think I could handle it."

"God has His reasons for allowing this great upheaval. Maybe He's asking us to join the fight against evil and help redeem this fallen world."

"I don't have enough faith for this, Papa."

"None of us do. All we can do is ask Him each day what He wants us to do."

She nodded, keeping her tears at bay. She saw Maaike gazing up at the distant airplanes and Wim pointing to them. Two of his friends had stopped to talk with him. "Mama! There's no school today!" he shouted when he saw her. The seriousness of the war would impact him soon enough, but for now he seemed to think of it as a holiday.

"I need to go home, Papa."

He stopped her as she started to cross the street. "Lena, never forget that God is in control."

CHAPTER 14

"Please, Abba," Miriam begged. "We need to find out exactly what's going on." They had awakened to the sound of airplanes, some flying so low she wondered if they would crash. Sirens had wailed, adding to their panic. She and Abba had been sitting beside the radio since the early morning hours, trying to interpret what the Dutch newscasters were saying. "I hope we're wrong and that this country isn't at war. But please, let's go downstairs and ask Mrs. Spielman what's going on."

"Go without me," he said. His voice was soft, and Miriam could see that he was struggling to control his tears. He didn't know Mrs. Spielman as well as she did, and he probably didn't want to lose control in front of her. Miriam understood Abba's distress. She shared it and had been battling for the last several hours to draw a deep breath.

"Please, Abba. If we're right about what the broadcast is saying, and Hitler's armies have truly invaded our new home, then I need you beside me when we hear the news so we can decide what to do."

"Give me a moment, then." He went into the bathroom, and Miriam heard water running in the sink. Then he went into his bedroom, and when he came out, his dark hair was slicked back. He was wearing his suit coat, as if the news would be easier to bear if he was in a suit. He followed Miriam downstairs as she knocked on the landlady's door.

"Mrs. Spielman, it's me, Miriam." Every breath she drew felt labored.

"Come in, come in," she said, opening the door a crack. "But be careful . . . don't let Oliver out!"

Miriam bent to hold back the squirming cat while Abba hurried inside and shut the door. "We're very sorry to bother you, Mrs. Spielman, but we have been listening to the radio and we want to make certain we have not misunderstood."

"*Ja,*" she replied with a sigh. "I'm afraid the news is bad, no matter which language you hear it in." She beckoned them into her sitting room, where her radio was on, and invited them to sit down.

"We cannot stay," Abba said, refusing to sit. "But we need to know for certain." Miriam hoped Mrs. Spielman would understand his need to digest the news in private.

"We're at war," she said. "Hitler's armies invaded the Netherlands early this morning, dropping bombs and soldiers from the sky with parachutes. Our army is fighting back, and we've opened the dikes to stop them with a flood. But we don't have news from all the battlefronts yet, and no one really knows for certain how the battles are going."

A sharp pain twisted through Miriam's stomach at the news. Abba groaned and ran his hand over his face. "Where can we go now?" he said, speaking in German. "Where is there a place where we'll be safe? That monster and his goons have found us again." Miriam hugged him tightly and felt his body trembling. "Your mother should have come with us. She should have gotten out while she had a chance," he said. "At least we would die together. Now I don't think we will ever see her again."

"Don't say that, Abba. We have to hang on to hope—"

"How? We will be trapped again with no way out. Once the Nazis take over, how long do you think it will be before they do the same things to us here that they did in Germany?"

Switching to Dutch, Miriam said, "Mrs. Spielman, my father is afraid the Nazis are going to take over like they did in Germany. Is he right?"

"According to the news, our soldiers are putting up a very brave fight." But Miriam saw the fear in the older woman's eyes and was concerned for her.

"What about your sons in Amsterdam? Will you try to go to be with them?"

"I don't think I can. It's not safe for any of us to go outdoors until the fighting stops."

Abba crouched in front of Mrs. Spielman's chair, facing her, speaking in broken Dutch. "Do you know how Nazis do to Jews? Do you hear what happens to us in Germany? Why we leave our home?"

"*Ja*. Everyone knows how they persecute Jews."

"If the Nazis win this country, they will do the same. You and me and Miriam, we must get out."

"Where would we go?" She was clearly frightened as she looked from Abba to Miriam, twisting her knotted hands.

Abba stood again. "Maybe to Belgium. Maybe they will let us cross to France or Spain—"

"They invaded Belgium, too," Mrs. Spielman said.

Abba stared at her, swaying as if dumbstruck by the news. "Then . . . then there is no way out," he mumbled in German. "We are surrounded. Germany on one side, Belgium on the other . . ."

"We could cross the channel to England," Miriam said. "Surely the British will change their immigration laws and give us refuge there. Maybe the Americans or Canadians will finally let us come to their countries."

Abba shook his head. "Remember that ship full of Jewish refugees? The Americans and Canadians both turned those people away. More than nine hundred passengers—desperate men, women, and children— forced to return to Nazi hands."

"So there's no place to go?" Miriam asked. "There must be someone who'll take pity on us. Why doesn't the world see what the Nazis are doing and how desperate we are?"

"We escaped from them once, Miriam. We can do it again."

Miriam saw his determination and believed he would find a way. "But I don't want to go without Avi. Can't we wait until we get a letter from him and find out what's happening to him at Westerbork?"

"Who knows how long a letter will take to get here with a war on? By then, it may be too late. We will be trapped again. Like your mother is." He sounded close to tears. "We must go upstairs, Mrs. Spielman, and decide what to do," he said, speaking in Dutch again.

"I'll keep listening to the news and let you know if anything else happens." She sounded dispirited. Abba had upset her. She remained in her chair as they made their way to the door. "Watch out for the cat when you leave . . . ," she called after them.

Abba was right. They should run before the Nazis caught up with them again. But how could Miriam leave without Avi? And where could they go? She helped her father upstairs as if leading a blind man, his words echoing in her heart and stealing her breath: *How long do you think it will be before they do the same things to us here . . . ?*

CHAPTER 15

The fact that Eloise had barely spoken since they'd come down from the roof worried Ans more than her manic chatter had. They listened to the radio in the front room, sitting side by side on the sofa as news of what was happening slowly trickled in. The Nazis had invaded at three o'clock that morning, targeting airfields and destroying nearly all of the Dutch army's aircraft before they had a chance to take off. Thousands of Nazi paratroopers had landed near Amsterdam. More had landed outside Den Haag, intending to capture the queen and government officials. The Dutch army was fighting back, but they were badly out-armed and had already sustained many casualties. *Please, not Papa or Erik.*

At times, Eloise would rise and pace the length of the room as she listened, muttering to herself. Sometimes she would stop and part the draperies to look out the front window before returning to her seat beside Ans, gripping her hand until Ans's fingers ached.

As the sun rose and the terrible news repeated endlessly, Ans had switched off the radio. "Let's get dressed. Professor Huizenga will know more when he gets home."

She helped Eloise change out of her ruined nightgown, then quickly got dressed herself, afraid to leave her alone for more than a minute, afraid she would run upstairs to the roof again. "Come into the kitchen with me while I make breakfast."

"Who can eat at a time like this?"

Ans couldn't stop thinking about Papa and Erik, wondering if they were all right and if she would ever see them again.

Sirens wailed as morning turned into afternoon, and planes continued to roar overhead, sometimes flying so low that the windows rattled. Eloise refused to do something to take her mind off the news, such as reading a book or listening to the gramophone.

"I can't concentrate, Ans. I'm so worried about Herman. If anything happens to him, I don't think I can go on. Why doesn't he call?"

"I'm sure he will as soon as he can. Maybe the telephone lines are down."

"He's in Den Haag, Ans, where the fighting is!"

"I think you should take some of your medicine. I'm worried about you."

Eloise lowered the volume on the radio and turned to look at Ans, her eyes oddly bright and alert. "I'm going to do everything differently this time. I was so fearful the last time, and I let the war overwhelm me. Mother and Father worked with the Resistance, and my brother fought in the trenches. They were strong and brave, and they lost their lives, but I was a coward. I was afraid to die."

"I'm sure there were a lot of people who were afraid—"

"This time I know better. I know that dying isn't the worst thing that could happen to me. Doing nothing and losing everyone I love is the worst thing. That's why I'm going to fight back this time. Are you with me, Ans?"

She didn't know what to say. If she agreed to fight, she feared Eloise might do something crazy like rush out into the street and chase down the Nazis with a carving knife. Yet Eloise needed to know that Ans was her friend. "How can we fight back?" she finally said. "We don't have any weapons. Shouldn't we let the Dutch army do the fighting?"

"I don't want to alarm you, Ans, but they aren't going to win. The Nazis are going to conquer the Netherlands just like they've conquered everyone else."

"Please, God . . . no . . ."

She didn't realize she'd spoken aloud until Eloise said, "Praying won't help. I already told you that. But once the Nazis take over, there are lots of things that civilians like us can do. So are you with me?"

It occurred to Ans that Eloise might be able to battle her depression better if she had another enemy to fight. "Yes, of course I'm with you. But you'll have to teach me what to do."

"We won't be the only ones. Others will fight back too. We—"

The telephone rang, interrupting her. Eloise raced to answer it. "Hello? . . . Herman! I'm so relieved! Are you all right, darling? Where are you? . . . When are you coming home? . . . I see . . . No, don't put yourself in danger. We're fine here . . . No, don't worry about us . . . I love you, too, my darling . . . Yes, just a minute . . ." She put her hand over the receiver and turned to Ans. "Herman is still in Den Haag and can't get out because of the fighting. He wants to talk to you."

Ans took the receiver. "Hello, Professor Huizenga."

"How is Eloise? Is she okay?"

"Yes, so far." She decided not to worry him by mentioning their trip to the rooftop. Besides, Eloise was standing right beside her.

"Listen, Ans, I don't know when I'll be able to get home. Please keep Eloise in the house where it's safe. And promise me you won't let her out of your sight for a moment! Especially if she starts to spiral down."

"Yes, I promise."

"Promise what?" Eloise asked after Ans hung up.

"That we would both stay inside where it's safe. I think that means no more trips to the roof." They returned to the radio in the front room, but Ans was no longer listening to it.

She knew she had turned away from the church for the past few years, but she still believed in God. Would He even listen to her prayers now that she and the people she loved were in danger, or would He ignore her the way she'd been ignoring Him? Ans wanted to believe that Eloise was wrong and that God would hear her prayers.

Papa had read the Bible aloud after dinner for as long as Ans could recall, and the story that came to mind now was the Prodigal Son. The father who ran down the road to welcome his son home was God. He would forgive Ans and welcome her home if she told Him she was sorry. And she was sorry! She needed His help.

As the radio blathered on, Ans silently prayed for her country. For Papa and Erik. For her family. And she prayed that God would help her fulfill her promise to Professor Huizenga to keep Eloise safe.

CHAPTER 16

By Sunday, the third day after the invasion, the Dutch army was still fighting valiantly, in spite of the Nazis' superior weapons. Lena had kept the radio on constantly as she did her chores, trying to remain calm so the children wouldn't be frightened. Wim acted brave but he was only twelve years old. And Maaike had been having nightmares and wanted to sleep with Lena. But so far, Lena's hope had remained alive as she'd prayed for Pieter.

An announcement came over the radio that the queen and her ministry officials were fleeing across the channel to England to form a government in exile. Lena was clearing the breakfast table, and the news stole her breath. "She abandoned us!" she said aloud. "The queen abandoned us to our enemies!" She sat down heavily, her strength gone. Was this the end of their country? How could the queen give up hope and leave when Pieter and the other brave soldiers were still fighting? The queen's desertion struck Lena like news of a death.

She stood again when her strength returned and called to Wim and Maaike. "Put on your Sunday clothes. We're going to church."

Since the invasion on Friday morning, Lena had been afraid to leave the house with Nazi bombers and fighter planes crisscrossing the skies, but now she put her concerns aside, desperate for friends to talk to. The truck bounced as she sped down the unpaved road, and she breathed a sigh of relief when she finally reached town. But she was surprised to see a motley array of vehicles blocking the narrow main street. Most were farm vehicles loaded with bundles and crates and household goods. Hundreds of refugees filled the market square, mostly elderly people, women, and children.

Lena parked the truck in the only spot she could find and hurried toward the square, holding Maaike's hand. Wim sprinted ahead to where Papa stood on the church steps in his black liturgical robe and white collar, shouting as he invited everyone to come inside the church.

"Lena! I was going to call you," he said when she and Maaike reached him.

"What's going on?"

"They opened the dikes to stop the Nazis, and all of these families were flooded out of their homes. I got a call from a pastor in Amersfoort, asking if our church would take some of them."

"I'll take a family," she said.

"I was hoping you would."

Lena steered Wim and Maaike ahead of her into the sanctuary, and by the time the villagers and refugees also made their way inside, the building was packed. The elders were bustling around the chancel, preparing to serve Communion, and it seemed like an odd time for the sacrament amid all the chaos of war. The worship service began, and the words of the hymns and the sound of voices surrounding her lifted Lena's spirits, reminding her that she wasn't alone. *"O God, our help in ages past . . ."*

"It's natural to wonder where God is in times like these," Papa said as he broke the bread for the sacrament of Communion. "He is here, in Christ's broken body and spilled blood. He understands our suffering and confusion. He is here, with us." Lena ate the Communion bread, desperate to feel God's presence, to know He was with her, beside her.

After the service, she helped her father and the deacons assign refugee families to the various parishioners who'd volunteered to house them. Lena took in the Zylstra family. Tina, who was in her midthirties, was with her three boys ages four, six, and ten, and her mother-in-law. Tina's husband, like Lena's, was fighting in the army. Lena would have taken a second family, but so many people came forward to volunteer that it wasn't necessary.

Tina had pulled a loaded farm wagon behind her truck with crates of squawking chickens tied on top of the swaying load. "We emptied our root cellar and smokehouse," she explained, "and brought everything with us. No one knows how long we'll be away."

"What about your dairy cows?"

"We set them free in our highest pasture, farthest from the dike. There wasn't time to take them anywhere else, and besides, where could they go? Now we must hope for the best."

Lena became anxious on the ride home from the village, feeling exposed and vulnerable in the flat, open countryside. It was taking too long, their progress slowed by the heavy farm wagon and muddy road. She longed to be home, to be safe. But was any place truly safe? A deadly war was raging across her nation, and these refugee families had made it real to Lena, bringing the war to her village, her farm. Pieter wasn't the only one who was battling the enemy. Everyone was being swept up in the fight.

Suddenly she heard the murderous roar of enemy aircraft approaching, coming in low and fast overhead. Her instinct was to press the accelerator to the floor and race home. But no, she needed to slam on the brakes and yell to the children to jump from the truck into the ditch. Before she could do either, the planes thundered by overhead and were gone, leaving Lena shaking and furious and struggling not to weep. Wim and Maaike were looking at her, their eyes wide. Maaike had her hands over her ears.

Lena exhaled, her heart still pounding. She squeezed Maaike's knee. "It's all right. We're all right." For their sakes, she couldn't surrender to fear.

Her knees were still trembling as she parked in her barnyard. The Zylstras' truck halted behind hers. "Your farm is very beautiful," Tina said as she looked around. "I don't know what will be left of ours."

Lena's fear slowly settled into place along with the settling dust. They unloaded the farm wagon, and Wim set the Zylstras' chickens loose in the fenced yard with Lena's hens. But as Lena worked, a deep, bottomless rage began building inside her, a hatred greater than any she'd ever known. No one was safe from the Nazis. They threatened everyone and everything she loved. She could disguise her fear, but her hatred seemed uncontrollable, growing stronger with each passing hour. And there seemed no end to it.

At last, everything was unloaded. Lena was surprised by how few household goods the Zylstras had brought with them. "There wasn't time," Oma Zylstra said when Lena mentioned it. "We decided food was more important than possessions." Oma wasn't able to do much heavy lifting, so Lena encouraged her to sit in the rocking chair and comfort Tina's smallest son, upset by the upheaval. He sat on his grandmother's lap, clutching a stuffed bear and sucking his thumb.

"The boys and I carried everything we could up to the attic," Tina said. "They told us the floodwaters might reach as high as the second floor . . ." Lena pulled Tina into her arms as she dissolved into tears. So much responsibility on this young woman's shoulders.

"We'll get through this together," Lena said.

Oma Zylstra helped Lena fix lunch while Tina unpacked their clothing and bedding. Maaike would sleep in Lena's bed with her, Wim would share his bedroom loft with the three boys, and Tina and her mother would sleep in Maaike's room. They talked about the days ahead as they ate, and how they were all praying for victory over these invaders.

"I don't know how long we'll have to live here," Tina said. "Even if the war ends quickly, we won't be able to return home until the floodwaters go down. Who knows how long it will be before we can plant crops again."

"We may not be able to plant this spring, either," Lena said, "with all of the men away." They sent the children outside to play afterwards, cautioning them to stay close to the house, then Lena turned on the radio. There was news of the battles that were still raging and of the Dutch fortifications that had been forced to surrender. When she heard that Den Haag was now under attack, Lena drew a shuddering breath. "I think my husband is in Den Haag," she said.

Tina reached for her hand. "My husband is on the eastern front."

Lena heard the rumble of approaching planes, flying low. She sprang from her seat to call the children inside, but then she heard Wim's voice and the sound of laughter outside as the planes flew on. *"You're trying so hard to hang on to control,"* Pieter had told her, *"but you never were in control to begin with. It's an illusion. The sooner you realize that, the sooner you'll put everything into God's hands and find some peace."*

Lena exhaled and sat down again.

CHAPTER 17

Ans parted the curtain to stare out the front window, wondering how the May afternoon could be so beautiful with flowers blooming and new green leaves on the trees, when war was raging all across her country. She would soon turn twenty, and this should be the springtime of her life, but her youth had been suddenly snatched away. The safe, carefree world she'd grown up in was gone, and she wondered if she'd ever feel safe and carefree again.

She let the curtain drop and turned to Eloise, perched on the sofa in the same place she'd been for days. As uncertain and traumatic as these past days had been for Ans, she couldn't imagine living through them for a second time as Eloise was doing. No wonder she was so fragile. A dish that had been shattered was never as strong, even when the pieces were patiently glued back together. Ans was weary of being the glue.

"Can we turn off the radio for a little while?" she pleaded. "They're saying the same things over and over."

Eloise shook her head. "We have to know what's happening. It's important!"

Ever since Ans awoke to the sound of bombs five days ago, each day had passed as slowly as a year. Professor Huizenga still had not returned home. The Huizengas' cook and housekeeper had stayed home with their families, and Ans had been doing all the cooking, making do with whatever she could find in the cupboards. Neither she nor Eloise had an appetite. Nazi planes flew over constantly. Sirens blared. Leiden, located between Amsterdam and Den Haag, felt like the crossroads of the war. At night, Ans and Eloise dozed beneath piles of blankets in the front room beside the radio in case they needed to flee to the basement. Ans was exhausted, afraid to sleep for fear Eloise would do something rash, like go up on the roof again.

Eloise had been inconsolable after learning that the Nazis invaded Belgium on the same day as the Netherlands. She refused to take her medicine, knowing it would make her sleep. "I have to know what's going on!" she'd insisted. Ans feared they would both lose their sanity, cooped up in the house beside the radio. Two days ago, she had decided to take a chance and coaxed Eloise to leave the town house.

"It's Sunday. I think we should go to church." She'd promised Professor Huizenga she'd keep Eloise inside, but the Pieterskerk was only a five-minute walk away.

Eloise had looked at her with a mocking grin. "Why do you want to go to church? God isn't answering any of your prayers."

"But . . . you and the professor have always gone to church. Every Sunday since I moved here."

"Only because Herman finds comfort in it."

"Well, I would like to go, but I won't leave you here alone. Please come with me. I need comfort too." She'd managed to convince Eloise. The church had been packed.

Today, Tuesday, was the fifth day of the war, and Eloise seemed to be pulling out of her slump once again by planning how she would fight back. "We'll take to the streets, if necessary, and fight the enemy hand to hand," she said. Ans didn't know whether to discourage her or play along. She wished the professor would come home.

Late in the afternoon, an urgent news bulletin interrupted the broadcast. Ans heard the trembling emotion in the newscaster's voice and immediately went to sit beside Eloise, gripping her hands. She tried to brace herself for more bad news, but the announcement was even worse than she imagined. The Nazis had bombed the city of Rotterdam. The center of the city had been demolished. Estimated civilian deaths approached one thousand. Tens of thousands were homeless. "No . . . This can't be happening . . . ," Ans moaned.

But there was more.

If the Netherlands didn't surrender immediately, the Nazis threatened to destroy Amsterdam and Utrecht the same way. The Dutch government had surrendered. The five-day war was over. Hundreds of thousands of Dutch soldiers were prisoners of war and could be sent east to labor camps.

"Papa! They have my papa!" Ans sobbed. "And Erik!" The losses overwhelmed her—her security, her future, her hope. She now lived under enemy occupation.

Eloise no longer talked of fighting back. She sat on the sofa as if in a trance, staring speechlessly at the radio until night fell, listening to the horrifying descriptions of the devastation in Rotterdam. Grappling with fear and despair herself, Ans couldn't hope to cheer her. *God, help us! Please, please, help us.*

Her prayers were answered before dawn on the morning after the surrender when Professor Huizenga arrived home. Ans and Eloise had been asleep in the front room, where they'd been ever since the invasion, and Eloise sprang up to run to him. Ans was so relieved she wanted to hug him too. He gently enfolded Eloise in his arms as if wrapping a priceless object in cotton batting.

"I've been desperate to get home ever since the invasion," he said. "I finally decided to start walking. I've been on the road all night. Den Haag is only a dozen miles from here, but the Nazis have tanks and troops and roadblocks everywhere. Bridges are gone, and there are craters in the middle of the roads. I made detour after detour. It's madness!"

"What happened in Den Haag, Herman? Was it terrible?" Eloise asked. "We heard about Rotterdam."

He hesitated before saying, "It was just what you'd expect in a war, Eloise; that's all I will say. I won't stir your memories by giving details."

She started to protest, but he stopped her. "Look, my darling. I'm here with you now. And we're both unharmed. The Nazis are promising a benevolent rule if we cooperate."

"Cooperate! I have no intention of cooperating, and I hope you don't either!"

"We'll talk about it after we've rested, yes? Right now, I could sleep for a hundred years." He wrapped his arm around her shoulders the way Mama's hens would use their wings to protect their chicks and led her up the stairs.

Later that day, the church bells at the Pieterskerk summoned everyone to a special service. Ans went alone to mourn with the entire country for the soldiers and civilians who had died. A year ago, she had wanted so badly to leave the farm and move to Leiden, but now she longed more than anything else to go home. Yet she couldn't desert Eloise, who needed Ans more than ever. After what they'd experienced together these past five days, the loss would be too much for her.

Ans was leaving church afterwards when she heard a distant rumbling sound. The people milling around outside the church stopped to listen. "What is that?" someone asked. The roar of powerful engines swelled and grew, along with a rhythmic cadence that Ans recognized as marching footsteps. The Nazis had arrived in Leiden.

Ans left the church square, following the sound toward the city's center. The ground shook as Nazi tanks rolled down Breestraat, their treads rumbling on the cobblestones. They were followed by hundreds of Nazi soldiers, marching in step.

Tears streamed down Ans's face. She couldn't move, frozen in shock at the sight of the enemy who had invaded her peaceful nation, bombing innocent men, women, and children, forcing a surrender. It was one thing to hear about it on the radio, another to see the horrifying reality in front of her as soldiers fastened bloodred banners with black swastikas to Leiden's buildings. A deep rage filled her at the injustice.

She couldn't let Eloise see this. Ans turned and sprinted toward the town house, thanking God that they lived on the opposite side of the ancient city moat from the Nazis.

CHAPTER 18

Miriam hadn't slept well since the Netherlands surrendered. On the surface, Leiden seemed to be returning to normal, yet enemy troops now occupied the city, and the menacing Nazi presence hovered over it. She avoided the city center whenever she shopped, unable to bear the sight of swastikas or hear soldiers speaking her native tongue in Leiden's beautiful streets. This was supposed to be her place of refuge. She and Abba had endured so much, given up so much to reach this place of safety, and overnight that safety had vanished.

Abba had returned to work at the university but went regularly to the synagogue to pray and talk with the other men. Miriam would hear his quiet rustlings in the apartment after she went to bed and knew he was awake for much of the night. "Please, Abba, you need to get some sleep," she had pleaded one night.

"I must find a way to save us," he had replied. It seemed impossible. There was no place to go. Along with Norway, Denmark, the Netherlands, and Belgium, the Nazis had also invaded France. No one had been able to stop them as they continued to push the Allied forces back.

Now, as Miriam lay tossing in bed, she knew tonight was going to be another sleepless night. She glanced at her little alarm clock—twenty minutes past midnight—and sighed. The crack of light beneath her bedroom door told her that Abba was also awake. She punched her pillow and closed her eyes, then sat up again when she heard a sound outside. Was someone knocking on the downstairs door? It was right below her bedroom window. She rose, and when she opened her bedroom door, she saw that Abba had heard it too. Miriam followed him downstairs, thinking it might be one of Mrs. Spielman's sons from Amsterdam, and the elderly woman might not have heard the knock. It was after curfew, so whoever it was needed to get inside quickly.

Abba unlocked the door and opened it a crack. A moment later, he flung it wide. "Avraham!"

Miriam gave a cry of joy and rushed into Avi's arms. He crushed her to himself, and she rocked in his arms, both of them weeping. His body was so cold. And wet. Yet Avraham Leopold was wonderfully alive—and here! Miriam prayed she wasn't dreaming.

"I thought I would never see you again!" she said.

"I had to find you, Miriam. I had to be with you."

"Shh, shh!" Abba said. "Come inside, quickly!" He pulled them into the tiny vestibule and led the way upstairs. Miriam and Avi stumbled up the steps behind him, clinging to each other, unwilling to let go.

"How did you get here?" Abba asked when they were safely inside. "There are Nazi soldiers everywhere."

"I walked a good part of the way," he said with a little laugh.

"All the way across the country?"

Avi nodded. He looked exhausted, his clothes and shoes in tatters. Miriam led him to the sofa and he sank down with her still clinging to him. She wouldn't let go of him, couldn't stop looking at his beloved face, afraid he would disappear.

"When we learned that the Nazis had invaded," Avi said, "everyone in Westerbork was terrified. We knew we would be trapped there and probably shipped east if the Nazis won."

"There is a great deal of despair among our people," Abba said. "My rabbi said hundreds of Jews in Amsterdam have committed suicide rather than fall into Nazi hands."

The news made Miriam shiver. Abba had kept it from her until now. But it made Avi's safe arrival all the more miraculous. He was here! In their apartment!

"At dawn on the second day of the invasion," Avi continued, "a group of us left camp and walked to Assen. Nobody stopped us because the country had much bigger things to worry about than a bunch of Jewish refugees. The Nazis weren't in Assen yet, so we boarded a train, planning to travel to the coast in Zeeland. We hoped to hire a fishing boat or some other ship to cross the channel to England. I planned to come here and get both of you so we could escape to England together."

"I also looked into booking passage to England immediately after the invasion," Abba said. "A few ships were able to make it across in the early days before the surrender, but the Nazis quickly took control of the Dutch coastline. Crews and passengers of any vessels they caught trying to cross the channel were sent to the labor camp in Mauthausen or shot on sight."

Avi closed his eyes for a moment, shaking his head. "We never made it that far. On the very first day, our train was forced to stop near Zwolle because the railroad bridge across the IJssel River had been blown up. We boarded a different train, planning to head toward the northern coast instead. We made it only as far as Leeuwarden when the war halted us again. The people in Friesland were very kind when they heard our story and offered us food and shelter in their homes. But we were a large group and difficult to hide, and the Nazis soon found out about us. We fled once again rather than endanger our hosts, but the Nazis chased us down and took us back to Westerbork."

"You were trapped again?"

Avi nodded. "But before the Nazis had time to count and register everyone, I decided to escape across the heath alone. I've been traveling ever since."

"All the way across the Netherlands?"

"Yes. Mostly at night, avoiding the main roads and Nazi road-blocks. So many bridges have been destroyed that I had to swim across canals and rivers in places. The main roads are well guarded. But many wonderful people helped me along the way, feeding me and ferrying me across rivers . . . And now I'm here."

Miriam gripped his icy hand, trying to warm it between her own. Avi had nothing with him—no bag, no extra clothing.

"You must be starving!" Miriam said. She was reluctant to leave his side, but she rose and quickly filled a plate with leftovers and bread from their supper. She sat beside him at the table, watching him wolf it down.

"That bread is from our Shabbat dinner," Abba said. "Miriam has learned how to make challah." Abba's smile, so rare these days, was warm and tender. He loved Avi too.

"You're still keeping Shabbat?" Avi asked.

Miriam nodded. "Yes. Our landlady has been teaching me how to cook and bake. She eats Shabbat dinner with us sometimes. Families from Abba's synagogue have also invited us."

"We continued celebrating Shabbat at Westerbork, too," Avi said. "Our simple dinners grew until we filled the entire dining hall on Friday nights."

"And now you need to go to bed and rest," Abba said when Avi finished eating. "You look exhausted." Miriam stroked his bearded cheek. How she loved his broad grin, his beautiful, shining eyes.

"Yes, thank you. I will." He stood, pulling Miriam to her feet. "But before I sleep, Professor Jacobs, there's something I must ask you. None of us has any idea what will happen now that the Nazis have occupied this country, and—"

"I know exactly what will happen, Avraham. The same things that happened to us in Germany will happen here. The Nazis will forbid me to teach. We'll be required to register and to wear yellow stars. They will take our property and our money and our freedom. They will demonize us and persecute us and turn us into their slaves."

"I know . . . I know," Avi said sadly. "I fear it as well. Right now, there's no way out of the Netherlands, no sympathetic border we can cross, no neighbor to offer asylum. The Nazis surround us on every side. That's why, with your permission, I would like to ask Miriam to marry me. I'm in love with her."

His words stole Miriam's breath, but from joy this time. She had yearned to hear him say those words during the long weeks they'd written to each other. She'd dreamed of this moment on the endless nights when she couldn't sleep. She had never dared to hope it would happen.

"I know we're young," Avi continued, "but these are uncertain times, and I would like to bind my life to Miriam's for as long as our lives may last."

"Is this what you also want, Miriam?"

"Yes, Abba. With all my heart."

Tears filled Abba's eyes. "Of course you have my blessing, my children. Of course you do!"

"I'll find work to support us, Professor. From now on, the three of us will live every day to the fullest for as long as we're able. May we make our home here with you?"

His tears brimmed and rolled down his cheeks. "Yes! Our new little family will stay together always."

Miriam hugged him tightly. "Thank you, Abba!"

"How soon would you like to marry?"

"I would marry her tonight if it was possible!" Avi replied. "No one knows what tomorrow will bring."

Miriam released her father and took Avi's hand. "I'll ask my friend Ans what we're required to do in this country."

"And I will talk to the rabbi," Abba said. "You will be married beneath a chuppah at the synagogue."

Miriam filled the bathtub for Avi. Abba convinced him to sleep in his bed afterwards. Miriam returned to her own room but found it impossible to sleep, her mind racing with joy and hope. Avraham was here! They would start a new life together. For the first time since leaving Westerbork, Miriam fell asleep happy.

After Abba left for the university the next morning, Miriam and Avi walked hand in hand to the Huizengas' town house. "This is Avraham," she told Ans when she answered the door. "He's here! He made it!"

Ans gave a cry of delight and pulled them inside. "What an answer to prayer!"

"Yes. We're together again, and we want to get married—"

"That's marvelous news!" Eloise interrupted. She had followed Ans into the foyer. "You must come in and have some coffee and tell us everything so we can help you plan your wedding!"

Ans served the coffee as Avi retold the story of his escape. He perched on the edge of the brocade settee, looking out of place in his raggedy clothes. His discomfort in these luxurious surroundings was obvious. Miriam had seen him only in the rustic barracks at Westerbork and briefly in her tiny apartment. Her grandmother's home had once been this opulent, but Avi came from an ordinary middle-class family in Berlin, his father an accountant, his mother a homemaker.

"We're hoping to get married as soon as possible," he said. "We don't know what the future will bring, but we want to face it together."

"What do we need to do in your country to be married?" Miriam asked.

Eloise quickly took over in her breathless, chatty way. "I will take you to the registry office myself. You'll need to apply for a marriage license, which isn't difficult to do, and then there will be a civil ceremony. Do you have identification? Birth certificates?"

"We brought everything with us from Germany," Miriam replied.

"Avraham isn't a Dutch resident, but you are, Miriam. You and your father have been legally registered as residents, and he has a good job at the university, so that should be enough to make it official. I'll go with you to be one of your witnesses. Ans will, too, won't you? I can be ready to leave for city hall as soon as you are. What do you say? Shall we get things started?" She stood, ready to leave immediately, but Ans held her back.

"Eloise, wait . . . Miriam will want her father to be there. And perhaps their other friends—"

"Of course, of course. We can finish our coffee first. But anyone can see that they're eager to be together, and I'm ready to help any way I can. Perhaps we can go to city hall—"

"Wait," Ans said again. "Eloise . . . you haven't been to city hall since the surrender. You need to prepare yourself . . . There are enemy soldiers and swastikas everywhere."

"Do you think the Nazis will forbid them to get married?" Eloise asked.

Miriam drew a quick breath. Abba believed the persecution would begin all over again, here in the Netherlands. Avi reached for her hand, squeezing it to reassure her.

"I'm not saying that," Ans replied. "As far as I know, the Dutch clerks working in all the public offices are still doing what they've always done."

"Then what's the problem?"

"I . . . I'm worried that it will upset you to see the enemy occupying Leiden."

"Don't coddle me, Ans. You're as bad as Herman." Eloise glared at Ans.

Miriam wasn't used to seeing tension between the two women. Yet she'd noticed how fragile Eloise was and knew Ans was wise to discourage her from witnessing the Nazi takeover.

"Eloise, there is something else you can help us with," Miriam said. "Avi escaped with only the clothes on his back. He's going to need clothes and shoes."

"It would attract too much attention if I had carried a suitcase," he added.

Eloise seemed to size him up. "You're not as tall as Herman, but my seamstress can do wonders with sewing needles and scissors." Eloise became animated again, and Miriam knew she would pour her breathless energy into helping Avi. "Naturally, you must be married in a suit. And I'll look after the rest of your wardrobe, too, so don't worry about a thing."

"How can we ever thank you?" Miriam asked. "You've done so much already, and—"

"And you, my lovely Miriam, deserve to be wed in silks and lace. Let me see what I have that might suit you. Ans, call my seamstress straightaway. Her number is in my address book."

The paperwork required more than a week to process, then Miriam and Avi were married in a civil ceremony in the registry office with Abba and Ans as their witnesses. That afternoon, Miriam stood beneath a chuppah in the synagogue with the man she loved, reciting their marriage vows in a quiet ceremony. They invited Ans and Eloise and Professor Huizenga, along with Mrs. Spielman and some of Abba's colleagues and friends from the synagogue. Eloise's dressmaker had altered a beautiful peach-colored silk dress and matching jacket for Miriam to wear, and a dark suit for Avi.

"You look beautiful," Abba said with tears in his eyes. "As beautiful as your mother. If only she could be here with us." Before leaving for the ceremony, Miriam had paged through her photograph album with Abba, remembering their loved ones. Their absence tempered Miriam's joy. She and Avi should be surrounded by family and friends, dancing with them in a joyous circle as they celebrated.

Eloise poured her high-spirited energy into hosting a reception at the town house afterwards. "With herring, of course. It's a Dutch tradition!" She turned the top floor into a bridal suite, insisting that Miriam and Avi spend their first married days there. "You will have the third floor all to yourselves," she had whispered to them. "My cook will bring room service just like a fancy hotel."

"This is the happiest day of my life," Avi said as he closed the bedroom door and pulled Miriam into his arms.

He smelled wonderful, the scent of Professor Huizenga's expensive cologne lingering on his newly tailored clothes. Miriam breathed deeply, the pressure in her chest gone. She could have soared to the treetops if she'd had wings. "It's my happiest day as well. When I fled from Cologne, I thought I'd never feel joy again."

He took her face in his hands, their foreheads touching. "I want to fill your life with love until it overflows, Miriam." He kissed her, tenderly at first, then with slowly growing passion. She tasted the wine they'd used to toast their marriage on his lips. "I wish I could take you on a proper wedding trip and give you the home you deserve. Living under enemy occupation isn't the way I'd hoped to begin our new life."

Miriam stroked his freshly trimmed beard. "I'm not afraid of anything now that you're here, my love. We'll face whatever the future holds, together."

CHAPTER 19

"Let me help you get dressed, Eloise," Ans begged. "We should go for a walk today."

Eloise shook her head as if the effort to speak was too much for her. For the past week, she'd remained in her nightgown and robe all day, floating listlessly around the town house like a ghost of herself. The only reason she would agree to rise at all was to go downstairs and listen to the radio.

Planning Miriam and Avi's wedding reception had buoyed Eloise's spirits. But Ans knew from experience that the higher Eloise's moods soared, the steeper her fall might be when the euphoria burst. Her despair had deepened throughout the last week of May as the news became increasingly grim, with reports of Nazi victories and crushing Allied defeats. She seemed to shrivel inside herself as they listened and no longer talked of fighting back.

Professor Huizenga gave up trying to plead with his wife to turn off the news. There was no way to shield her from it. Europe's fate—their future—hung in the balance.

The Nazis had stranded the British and French armies on the beaches at Dunkirk, and for a few dread-filled days, it appeared that France and

Britain would be forced to surrender too. Then a miracle had lifted their spirits when the Royal Navy and hundreds of civilian vessels had evacuated the British army to safety across the channel.

But the Netherlands' last hope for liberation had disappeared with the British forces. The Nazis and their allies now occupied Belgium, leaving the Netherlands cut off from the world and surrounded by Nazi-controlled nations. The French army was in tatters. The Nazis marched relentlessly toward Paris.

Ans finally coaxed Eloise out of bed, but she cringed when Eloise went to the front room first and switched on the radio. "Let's wait until after breakfast—"

"No, wait! Listen!" The excitement in the announcer's voice was unmistakable. Ans held her breath, hoping it was good news for once. It was. All Dutch soldiers being held as prisoners of war would be set free to return to their jobs and homes.

"Papa!" Ans shouted. "My papa is coming home! And Erik! Oh, Eloise, thank God!"

"You must go home and celebrate with your family this weekend."

"Thank you! I think I will!" Erik would be coming home too. They'd exchanged letters while he'd been away, and the bond between them had grown stronger as they'd shared their hopes and fears with each other. She could hardly wait to see him.

❦

Ans packed an overnight bag and set out for the farm on her bicycle early Saturday morning, knowing that the trains would be crammed with Nazis and returning Dutch soldiers. "If Erik comes while I'm at the farm," she'd told Eloise before leaving, "please let him know when I'll be back. And that I can't wait to welcome him home."

The air was warm with the promise of summer, the fields green and scented with freshly mown hay. Even the manure smelled good to Ans as she pedaled home, thanking God for sparing Papa and Erik when so many others had died. And thanking Him that the good news had helped Eloise find her footing again in the delicate balancing act she performed every day. The journey was tiring, but Ans sped up as she cycled the last mile home.

How wonderful it was to hug her family and be with them again. The simple farmhouse with its red-tiled roof, and the attached barn full of cows, and the squawking chickens, and the stately old windmill—none of these familiar sights had ever looked so beautiful to Ans.

Her down-to-earth papa seemed uncomfortable with the fuss everyone paid him. Mama wouldn't take her eyes off him. Maaike clung to him like a third leg. Wim followed him around like an unweaned calf.

"You rode an awfully long way just for me," he said as Ans hugged him.

"I needed to make sure you were all right." Ans thought she saw more wrinkles on his tanned brow. And he looked weary.

"We did our best," he said quietly. "It wasn't enough."

When Opa learned that Ans was home, he joined them at the farm for dinner. Mama had cooked Papa's favorite treat, smoked eel.

"The village looked unchanged as I cycled through it," Ans said as they sat around the table. "I didn't see any red banners or swastikas like the ones all over Leiden."

"I suppose that's one advantage of living in an unimportant, out-of-the-way village," Mama said. The village Ans had been so eager to leave.

"They'll find us eventually," Papa said.

"Have there been a lot of changes in Leiden?" Mama asked.

"Everywhere you look it's obvious that we're under enemy occupation. Yet some people think everything will be fine, and life will be just as it was before, so let's all go back to work or to school. They think nothing has changed except for the handful of people at the top who are in power."

"We've heard their propaganda too," Opa said. "They say, 'Come under the protection of the Reich. Don't be afraid. The Dutch are fellow members of the Aryan race.'"

"They're tempting a lot of people to trust them," Mama said. "The war unnerved them, and people want to believe the lies. They want to go back to how it was before. After all, there aren't any signs out here in the country that we've lost our freedom." She passed the bowl of potatoes to Opa, but he held up his hand and shook his head.

"There's a story in the Old Testament," he said, "about a time when the Assyrian army laid siege to Jerusalem. They surrounded the city with their superior forces and demanded that the king surrender. The enemy leader shouted to King Hezekiah and the people who were watching from the top of the wall, saying, 'Make peace with us and come out to us. Then you'll be able to eat from your own vines and fig trees.' But King Hezekiah placed his trust in God and stood firm. His tiny nation was outnumbered, just like ours, but he refused to surrender."

Papa frowned and pointed upward. "I don't think Hezekiah's enemies had airplanes dropping bombs."

Opa tilted his head, acknowledging Papa's point. "But God performed a miracle," he continued, "sending the angel of the Lord and killing 185,000 enemy soldiers with a plague in a single night."

Papa's frown deepened. "The time to perform a miracle would have been before the Nazis bombed Rotterdam or while we were still fighting for our freedom." His face flushed a deeper bronze, a signal of his growing anger.

Ans had rarely seen Papa lose his temper. He usually would simply walk away. She knew he wasn't angry with Opa, but with the Nazis. Or perhaps with God.

"I watched men die," he said.

"Pieter . . . the children . . . ," Mama whispered.

"No, Pieter made a good point," Opa said. "A timely miracle would have been welcomed by all of us. But the point of my sermon isn't going to be the miracle."

"Is this your Sunday sermon?" Ans asked.

"It will be." He pushed his chair back from the table as if to give himself room to gesture when he spoke. "Right now, we're all standing where King Hezekiah and his people stood. The enemy says, 'Trust us. Join us. All will be well.' But we each face three choices." He ticked them off on his fingers, one by one. "We can lie low, mind our own business, and simply adjust to Nazi rule. Or if we like the way they're doing things and we want to get ahead, we can collaborate with them, join the Dutch Nazi Party, and help them usher in their new Reich. Or, like Hezekiah, we can resist, refusing to surrender and assimilate."

Ans thought of Eloise and her determination, at first, to fight back against her enemy. News of Allied defeats had destroyed her will to resist. Depression had pulled her down into a pit like quicksand.

"And will you be telling our congregation to resist?" Mama asked. Ans saw new lines in her face too.

"I will be telling our people that we need to make a conscious choice. To do nothing is to choose the enemy's side. So there are really only two choices in the end—give in or fight back."

"Do you think that's wise, Papa? Please don't put yourself in danger."

"Engelena, it would be much more dangerous for me to face God at the end of my days and explain why I did nothing."

"Your father is right," Papa said. "I may have been sent home from the battlefield, but I'm going to continue to fight. Any nation that would bomb an unwary city and kill a thousand innocent civilians must be stopped." His words and the urgency in his voice made Ans's heart speed up. Was this her calm, quiet papa?

Mama was biting her lip, struggling against tears. "But, Pieter . . . our family . . ."

"I know. But what will their lives be like if they grow up under Nazi rule, learning their values and imitating their hatred?"

Ans understood Mama's fear. She also knew that what Papa and Opa said was true. She thought about their words as she bicycled back to Leiden the following day, and about the question Eloise had asked when she'd first made up her mind to fight back: *Are you with me, Ans?* If so, Ans knew she would need to learn what it meant to fully trust God.

Erik came to the town house the day after Ans returned home, looking as handsome as ever, yet in some ways older and more hardened. His wheat-colored hair had been shorn when he first joined the army, but it had grown back while he'd been a prisoner and was as thick and tousled-looking as before. She had almost forgotten how wonderful it was to feel his arms around her and to enjoy his soft kisses when they were alone. She reveled in the knowledge that she belonged to him, that he was watching out for her as they walked hand in hand, passing the ever-present Nazi soldiers.

Ans knew her parents belonged together; Professor Huizenga and Eloise seemed made for each other; Miriam seemed more whole and fully herself now that Avraham was beside her. And with every moment that Ans spent with Erik, she grew more and more convinced that he was the perfect partner for her, and she for him. They balanced each other—she the impulsive and adventurous one, he steady and cautious. His letters had revealed so much more about him as he'd talked about his childhood in Java and what he thought about the war and what his hopes and dreams were for the future. Ans was thrilled to read that he included her in those dreams.

They sat side by side on a bench, their hands entwined, watching a pair of swans in the canal. "What's next for you, Erik?"

"They said my job on the police force is waiting if I want it back."

"I could never work for the Nazis. They disgust me."

"Ans . . . shh . . . ," he whispered, looking all around. "You can get into a lot of trouble for talking like that."

There were other people in the park, couples reunited, strolling the paths, watching the swans and ducks on the Steenschuur. Ans lowered her voice for Erik's sake. "Don't you feel the same about them after the way they brutally attacked our country? How can you work for them?"

"I'm not working for them. I'm working for the people of Leiden. Protecting them. And you." He glanced around again as if to see whether anyone was listening, then continued in a soft voice. "Isn't it better for us to keep order and police our own streets instead of letting the Nazis do it? Because if we don't, they will—and their policing will be brutal."

"I believe you. But aren't you afraid they'll demand you take an oath to Hitler or the Reich?"

He looked away for a moment as if he couldn't face her.

"What? Tell me, Erik."

"There are rumors that we may need to become members of the NSB if we want to stay on the police force."

"The Dutch Nazi Party? Oh, Erik!"

"It would be in name only. I don't agree with anything they stand for. But the police chief is being pressured to give preference to party members when deciding who gets hired. And if I lose my job—if any man loses his job—we'll be sent east to work in German factories. We'll be slave laborers."

"Do you think my Jewish friends will be persecuted here the way they were in Germany?"

Erik shrugged. "Who knows? So far, they're saying the Jews won't be bothered here. The Nazis have promised that if our people cooperate, things will return to normal."

"Do you believe them?"

"What choice do we have?"

Ans stood again and walked toward the water. She was weary of hearing that everything would be all right when the mere sight of the two Nazi soldiers strutting down the street across the canal made everything all wrong.

She recalled her family's conversation at the dinner table and wondered if she should share her grandfather's assessment with Erik. Surely he would agree that the only two options were to cooperate or resist. Yet it seemed that, at least on the surface, Erik had chosen to adjust to Nazi rule and float with the tide. And if he joined the NSB, wouldn't that be considered collaboration? But how could she blame him if the alternative was to be sent to a labor camp?

Ans's stomach turned at the thought of Erik becoming a Nazi puppet. He'd been forced to choose the lesser of two evils, but she didn't like either choice. "If only we hadn't lost the war," she murmured.

Erik had come alongside her, and he wrapped his arm around her waist. "We fought hard, Ans. Remember my roommate Bram, Jansje's fiancé? He was killed on the first day of the invasion."

Ans closed her eyes, thanking God that it hadn't been Erik. Or Papa. They walked home together, clinging to each other.

❦

In mid-June, Hitler marched triumphantly into Paris. Eloise's mood spiraled even lower. As the days passed, she slept too much, ate too little, and stared into space as if her body and mind were vacant. Ans tried to get her to talk, wondering if she was reliving the past, which seemed to be merging with the present in a terrifying way.

One warm afternoon, Ans managed to convince Eloise to walk with her to nearby Van der Werff Park. As they strolled down one of the paths, a young woman strode toward them as if in a hurry. Her hand suddenly reached out as she marched past, and she thrust a piece of paper into Eloise's hand. She halted to read it.

The flyer urged people all across the country to take part in patriotic demonstrations on June 29 by celebrating the birthday of Queen Wilhelmina's son-in-law, Prince Bernhard. "Here's our chance to fight back," Eloise said. "We're going to do this!"

Ans heard life in her voice for the first time in weeks. She read the details of the peaceful demonstration again and couldn't see any harm in going, especially if it lifted Eloise's spirits. "But let's see what Professor Huizenga thinks first," she said.

Eloise showed him the flyer at the dinner table that evening. "Ans and I are planning to go," she told him.

"Absolutely not!"

"But, Herman, why not?"

"Because this is certain to provoke the Nazis. How can I keep you safe if you go about provoking our enemy?"

"But it's a peaceful demonstration. All we're going to do is wear something orange in support of the queen and the House of Orange and carry one of those white carnations that the prince so famously wears."

"That's *all*?" His voice rose in alarm.

Eloise smiled and ran her hand down his arm, then clasped his fingers. "Maybe we'll wave a few pictures of Prince Bernhard and the royal family too. There's nothing wrong with that, is there?"

"My dear, I know you aren't that naive."

"It's just a birthday celebration. And the prince himself is German."

"It's a political protest against Nazi rule. The prince has publicly denounced the Nazis." His gaze was stern.

Eloise's smile faded. "I have to do *something*," she said softly.

"Remember how worried you were for my safety when I was trapped in Den Haag after the invasion? Do you understand how much I would worry about you if you went to this demonstration?"

"But I will go *mad* if I don't do something to fight back! I can't stay hidden away at home all day. Do you want me to end up in the asylum again? Let me stand up and protest. It's the very least I can do."

The professor looked at Ans, pleading for help. Ans had seen the positive change in Eloise today and believed that fighting back would be good for her. She decided to take a chance and defend her. "We have so little hope at the moment, Professor. To be honest, I would like to fight back, as well."

"See, Herman? Think of the proud history of your ancestors here in Leiden. They defended the city against Spanish rule and refused to surrender. Leiden was besieged for more than six months, and even though people were starving, they didn't give up. After the siege lifted, the House of Orange rewarded the citizens of Leiden by founding the very university where you're a professor." She punctuated each of her last dozen words with a poke in the center of her husband's chest.

He gave her a gentle smile. "I know my city's history, darling. But listen—"

"What's the worst that can happen to me—prison? Any prison the Nazis put me in would be no worse than the prison of fear that held me captive during the last war."

He didn't reply. His love for her was so tender, so touching. He must be relieved to see his wife happy and animated again. Yet Ans sensed his internal struggle.

"When is the demonstration? Perhaps I'll come with you."

"On June 29. It's a Saturday. Will you come, too, Ans? You don't have to, you know."

"I want to come."

"Then it's settled."

A huge crowd gathered in the park by the fortress on Saturday, most wearing articles of orange clothing and sporting white carnations. Dutch flags had been forbidden, but people held up pictures of Prince Bernhard and the royal family, a sign of patriotism that the Nazis couldn't miss. The Dutch people weren't giving up or switching loyalties as the Nazis had hoped. Ans felt proud and unafraid as she stood chanting with the others, *"So there!"* and *"Orange will triumph!"*

Professor Huizenga seemed nervous and kept his wife close to his side. But Eloise was positively beaming.

Then the police arrived, flanked by Nazi troops. Ans's happiness vanished when she saw Erik among them, alert and vigilant as if anticipating trouble. The demonstrators were ordered to break up and go home or face arrest.

Ans tensed as she heard angry shouts from the middle of the crowd. She watched Erik, wondering if he'd seen her among the demonstrators.

After a few anxious minutes, people slowly began to leave the park, still chanting as they laid their carnations and their pictures of the royal family against the fortress wall like a memorial. Ans tossed her white carnation onto the pile along with everyone else. She and the professor and Eloise turned toward home.

Eloise seemed happier than she'd been in months that evening as they listened to the radio, even though the news was as hopeless as usual. Ans said good night and went upstairs to her bedroom early. She tried to read a book but couldn't concentrate. She turned out the light and stared at the ceiling for a long time, unable to sleep, unable to forget that she and Erik had stood on opposing sides.

CHAPTER 20

Sweat ran down Lena's face and into her eyes as she attacked the weeds in her kitchen garden with a hoe. Prayer had taken on a new urgency these past few months, and she'd developed the habit of pleading silently with the Almighty while she worked. Today she prayed that she would remain strong for her children. She prayed for courage to fight against the enemy and that God would show her when and how to do that. At times, she found it difficult to continue with her regular farm chores as if nothing had changed, while the Nazis proclaimed victory after victory. Her nation had depended on the British and French armies for help, but they'd suffered devastating defeats. The Fascist dictator of Italy had now joined forces with Hitler.

Lena paused when she reached the end of the row and removed the kerchief to wipe sweat from her eyes. "How are you doing, Maaike?" she called to her daughter. "Are you getting many blackberries?"

"Some . . . ," she said, holding up the bowl she carried. "They're so prickly, Mama!"

Lena smiled, suspecting that more berries were going into Maaike's mouth than into her bowl. Lena had always loved her life in the countryside, far from the hectic pace of Amsterdam and Leiden. But ever since the Nazis took control of the radio broadcasts and newspapers, she'd felt cut off from the world with no way of knowing what was truly happening. Then word had whispered around the village to tune into the British BBC station in the evenings, which had begun a special broadcast of *Radio Orange* in Dutch. Last night, Queen Wilhelmina herself had spoken to her fellow citizens, offering words of encouragement, urging them not to give up. Her speech had brought tears to Lena's eyes and renewed her courage.

She was about to attack the next row of weeds when she heard engines rumbling in the distance. She cocked her head to listen. They weren't airplanes. The droning was much closer and traveling on the ground, not in the air. The sound grew louder, approaching. "Maaike, come here," she called. "Right now."

Maaike plucked one last blackberry and popped it into her mouth before making her way toward Lena. "What's that sound, Mama?"

Lena didn't reply. She put down her hoe and grabbed Maaike's hand, hurrying inside through the back door, then continuing through the door into the barn to look for Pieter. He and Wim had been spraying trees in the orchard, but he must have heard the approaching engines too. He was striding toward the barn with Wim beside him. A dust cloud plumed in the distance, accompanying the sound. A car was coming up the road, followed by two motorcycles. Nazi flags fluttered from the car's antennae. Lena stood close to her husband, gripping Maaike's hand.

"What do they want, Papa?" Wim asked. "Do you think they've come to make sure we've turned in all of our copper?" There had been rumors about such searches.

"It's possible," Pieter replied.

Good thing we buried it. Lena didn't say the words aloud, not wanting the children to hear. The Nazis had ordered that all metal be turned in to the authorities—especially copper, which was needed for bullets. They kept careful records, making sure everyone in the village and surrounding farms had complied. Pieter had turned in some of their things so they wouldn't attract suspicion, then Lena had helped him bury the rest in her kitchen garden after dark so the children wouldn't know.

The motorcade came to a rumbling halt. Lena's knees trembled, not with fear so much as anger. "They have no right!" she said through clenched teeth.

"Hush, Lena. We need to remain calm. Wim, take your sister into the house. Stay there until I say so." Wim obeyed, but he walked backwards all the way as if unable to take his eyes off the motorcycles. He hadn't seen a Nazi soldier before. The children disappeared inside, and a moment later, Lena saw the lace curtains part in the front room and Wim and Maaike peeking out. She turned her attention to the vehicles again as the motors switched off. Her heart pounded faster than the ticking car engine as it cooled.

Pieter leaned down to whisper in her ear. "Don't let them know you understand German."

She nodded in agreement.

The soldiers dismounted their motorcycles and removed their goggles. They wore pistols in holsters at their sides. The car door opened and a Nazi officer stepped out, smoothing the front of his uniform. Lena heard him issuing orders to the others, telling the soldiers to begin the inventory of her farm. A second man in uniform stepped from the car, older than the others and stoop-shouldered, lacking the bearing and authority of a soldier. "Tell them we've come to take inventory," the officer told the man in German.

The little man stepped forward. "We must make lists of your farm," he said in clumsy Dutch. He mimicked writing on his hand as if it were a tablet. "A record of all animals. The crops. Everything." He swept his arm wide to encompass the barn and fields and pastures. Lena stared at him as if she didn't understand, but she did. And it made her furious. They were going to inventory the farm so they could steal everything from them. Conquering armies always did. It was summer, and the pigs and cows had growing offspring. The hay had been mowed and stored away. Sugar beets, cabbages, and potatoes grew in neat rows in the fields. Fruit ripened on the trees. Everything they'd worked so hard for would go to feed the Nazis.

"They have no right," she whispered again.

"They believe that 'might makes right,' Lena."

The interpreter gestured to Pieter. "You must come and show us." Lena had no intention of leaving Pieter's side. Together, they followed the officer around the farm, answering the questions he asked through the translator. Lena heard them first in German, then in Dutch. The soldiers made notes in their ledgers. They even tromped around to Lena's kitchen garden, writing everything down. They counted piglets and cows and chickens, demanding to know how many gallons of milk the farm produced each day, how many eggs the chickens laid. They inspected the tractor and the farm truck and made note of Lena's bicycle, the children's bicycles. They pointed to the windmill and asked how many bags of grain it could grind. Pieter tried to explain that it was used to pump water for irrigation, but Lena wasn't sure from the interpreter's translation that he'd understood.

The inspection ended with what the officer probably thought was a stirring speech. "We hope for your cooperation," he said. "Other nations are populated with inferior races, but we consider the Dutch to be our brothers, members of the Aryan race. Our victories are your victories. When we prosper, you will also prosper. Working together, we will build the great Third Reich."

Lena longed to shout, *Never!* How could he expect her people to forget what the Nazis had done to Rotterdam?

Pieter remained silent after the translator finished. He seemed to sense that she was about to explode and he took her hand, signaling her to be quiet. "Tell your captain," he said at last, "that I think you will find it impossible to befriend a country and a people who were subdued by brute force. You're like a bully who marches onto the playground in the middle of a friendly children's game and grabs the ball, threatens all the other children, and then demands that they play with him. Do you understand what I'm saying?"

The interpreter turned to the captain and mumbled a few words, but he didn't repeat Pieter's reply, which was probably for the better.

Two hours after they arrived, the Nazis returned to their vehicles. "Good thing our farm is on a dead-end road," Pieter said as the roar of motorcycles faded and the dust cloud settled. "We'll always hear them coming."

"What's going to happen to us, Pieter? To our family and our village? I'm glad Wim and Maaike are on summer break, but oh, how I wish Ans was home!" Having the Nazis nearby was like knowing a dangerous beast was on the prowl, and she longed to hold her children close where she could see them and protect them. But as Pieter had once told her, the illusion that she was in control was just that—an illusion. A foreign army occupied her country. The Netherlands was no longer free.

Lena went into the barn to fetch her bicycle. "I'm going into town," she told Pieter.

"Now? What for?"

"I need to find out what's going on, where the Nazis are staying."

"There's nothing you can do, Lena."

"And I want to talk with my father. I won't be long." She hopped onto her bicycle and hurried off. Lena found her father in his office in the manse, standing by the window that looked out on the market square. His Bible lay open on his desk. Several crumpled sheets of paper littered his desk and the floor. "Are you writing your sermon, Papa?"

"I'm trying to." He kissed both her cheeks, then sat down on the edge of his desk. "I've been writing sermons all my life, but the task has taken on a new urgency in these precarious days. I see what our country and our community are going through, and it brings me to my knees, asking God what He would have me tell them." He gestured to the open Bible. "I'm still waiting for His reply."

"Nazi soldiers came to our farm today. Two on motorcycles and two in a car. They took an inventory of everything we have so they can steal it from us."

"I saw them in town. They've spent the past few days here, looking everything over. I think they went to a couple of other farms besides yours."

"I feel so violated!"

"I understand. When I saw the motorcycles, my first thought was to thank the Lord that He took your mother home before all of this happened. She was such a gentle, sensitive soul. This would have hurt her deeply."

"I miss her so much. But she was stronger than everyone thought she was, Papa. I think her response to the invasion would have surprised us."

"And you're also much stronger than you think. I know you're struggling with a great deal of worry and fear right now, and naturally so. Offer it to the Lord, Lena. Let Him be the source of your courage."

She nodded, her throat tight with emotion. She waited until she could speak. "So what will you be telling us this week, Papa? I've never seen our church as packed as it's been every Sunday."

"I'm not sure yet." He paused for a moment. "The Nazis preach a doctrine of hatred, and I've always believed it's wrong to hate. But Proverbs says that to fear the Lord is to *hate* evil. And Romans says we are to *hate* what is evil and cling to what is good."

"Aren't you afraid people will misunderstand what you're saying? Pieter thinks there may be Nazi sympathizers among us."

"I'm sure both things are entirely possible. Time will tell. But I think we can all agree that what the Nazis have done—invading a nation at peace, killing our young men, bombing and slaughtering innocent civilians—that these actions are wicked and evil. God asks in the words of the psalmist, 'Who will rise up for me against the wicked? Who will take a stand for me against evildoers?' Each of us must decide how we will respond."

"Please be careful, Papa."

He straightened and reached out to embrace her. "Don't worry about me, Engelena. I must learn to fear God more than I fear men. He is the One I must answer to."

CHAPTER 21

Miriam found Ans and Eloise waiting at the café for her when she arrived. Ever since the Nazi invasion six months ago, Eloise's emotional struggles meant she and Ans were unable to leave the town house to meet with Miriam as often. This lovely fall day seemed to be one of her better ones. Miriam savored the rich aroma of coffee as the waitress set the cup in front of her. "That smells wonderful," she said, glad to be free of the nausea that had plagued her these past months.

Eloise poured tea from a little pot into her cup. "I wonder how much longer we'll be able to enjoy such luxuries as coffee and tea. In the last war—"

"Let's not spoil the day by talking about the war," Ans interrupted. "We haven't seen Miriam in weeks."

"Yes, and I have exciting news to share," Miriam hurried to say. "Avi and I are expecting a baby."

Ans leaned close to hug her. "I'm so thrilled for you! When?"

"Sometime next year. In early March, I think."

"You and Avi must be overjoyed," Eloise said. "Naturally, you'll need a bigger apartment. And we'll need to go shopping with you for baby clothes and diapers and—"

"We'll have plenty of time for all of that," Miriam said, laughing. "Our current apartment fits us just fine for now. Our landlady, Mrs. Spielman, has become a second mother to me, teaching me how to cook and bake, and she would be heartbroken if we moved."

"Have you heard from your mother or the rest of your family in Germany?" Eloise asked.

Miriam shook her head, looking down at her coffee as she blinked away tears. How quickly her moods bounced from joy to sorrow these days. She thought she understood how Eloise's painful past could bring so many ups and downs.

"I understand that Avi has found work?" Ans asked.

"He's doing odd jobs for Abba's friend from the synagogue. It's not ideal, but he's glad to be working. And Abba is happy to be back in the classroom, lecturing to his students. He loves to teach."

"I'm so happy for all of you," Ans said. "Let us know what we can do to help you prepare for the baby."

"Thank you. I will." Miriam gazed at these friends who'd become so dear, wishing she could express her thoughts better. "At times this past year I thought I would never be happy again, but—"

"It's nearly impossible to be happy with this terrible war ruining our lives," Eloise interrupted.

Miriam drew a deep breath and exhaled. "Avi and I decided that we would live one day at a time. We both know better than anyone what could happen. But until it does, we will be happy every single day."

Eloise rested her hand on Miriam's. "Dear little Miriam. I wouldn't dim your happiness for all the world . . . but I've experienced the terrible things that modern warfare brings. Life in Leiden seems untouched at the moment, but the war will catch up with us one of these days. We're already beginning to feel the effects now that the Nazis' *Reichskommissar* for the Netherlands has been passing these new laws."

"Eloise . . . don't . . . ," Ans murmured.

Miriam's chest squeezed with dread. "What laws?" She needed to know.

Eloise started to reply, but something in Miriam's expression seemed to stop her. She looked away, fussing with her teapot. "I didn't mean to frighten you, Miriam. You're like a daughter to me. You and darling Ans. Herman and I were never able to have children, you know, and so I'd like to think of you as the daughters I never had." Ans leaned forward to comfort Eloise as her eyes filled with tears, but she shooed her away. "Never mind my silly blubbering. Let's talk about happier things."

She pulled a handkerchief from her purse while Ans smoothly changed the subject, talking about the baby again and asking if they preferred a boy or a girl.

Miriam couldn't stop worrying about Eloise's ominous words as she walked home. The Nazis had appointed a *Reichskommissar*. He was passing new laws. The laws the Nazis had passed in Germany had gradually restricted the daily lives of Jewish citizens until nearly everything was taken from them and they'd become prisoners in their own homes.

She tried to calm her fears by practicing her violin after returning home, but Tchaikovsky's moving melody didn't soothe her the way it usually did. Her fingers wouldn't move right and she kept making mistakes until she finally returned the instrument to its case. She would ask Avi about the new laws as soon as he arrived home.

"I had coffee with Eloise and Ans today," she began before he'd even removed his jacket. "I told them about the baby."

"I'm sure they were very happy for you." He took her into his arms and kissed her as he did every day when he got home.

Miriam didn't release him. "But then Eloise told us something sad. She said she and her husband were never able to have children. I felt so sorry for her, Avi. She started crying in the restaurant."

"Mrs. Huizenga has always seemed very fragile." He smoothed a strand of Miriam's dark hair from her face, a tender gesture that should have comforted her but sent a ripple of dread through her instead. Would she and Avi always be together?

"What's wrong?" he asked.

"Eloise told me that the new *Reichskommissar* for the Netherlands is passing laws. Do you know about this?"

"A little bit . . ."

"Why haven't you told me?"

"Because so far the laws haven't affected us. I didn't want you to worry."

"You aren't protecting me by shielding me from the truth, Avi. We promised to share everything with each other, the good things and the hard things."

"I'm sorry."

He tried to hold her close again, but she pulled away and looked at him. "Tell me about the laws."

He exhaled with a weary sigh. "A few months ago, they passed a law saying that Jews can't be hired for civil service positions. Jews who are already civil servants can't be promoted. That includes staff positions at the university. University professors all over the country signed a letter of protest, but it didn't do any good."

"They passed the same law in Germany in the beginning, remember?"

He nodded, closing his eyes.

"Is there more?"

"A second law requires all civil servants to submit a letter in writing, stating whether they are Aryan or Jewish."

"Abba has to do that?"

Avi looked down for a moment as if reluctant to reply. "Yes. But the Dutch Protestant churches issued a public protest, calling the law an outrage."

"Did the protest do any good?"

"No."

Miriam felt a boulder drop into the pit of her stomach. "Avi, this is how it started in Germany, remember? The persecution began gradually, a small step at a time until we ended up—"

"Miriam, don't."

He held her tightly, trying to soothe her as she struggled to breathe.

She hadn't suffered a panic attack in months—until today. "But we can see what's coming. We've been through this before."

"And yet we're alive, Miriam. And we're together. We escaped from them once before and we can do it again."

Tears slipped down her face. "What kind of a world will our baby be born into?"

"Only God knows."

Miriam was curled on the sofa in Avi's arms, still tearful, when Abba arrived home.

"You've heard the news?" he asked when he saw them there. He had a newspaper in his hand. He looked grief-stricken.

"No, Abba. What's wrong?"

"I told Miriam what's been happening these past few weeks," Avi said. "Is there more?"

Abba sank onto a chair as if his legs could no longer hold him. "Oh, my dear ones . . . Today there was another new law from the *Reichskommissar*." He cleared his throat and loosened his collar as if struggling to speak the words. "All Jewish teachers and university professors are no longer allowed to work."

"Abba, no!" *Just like in Cologne.*

"I've been dismissed. The university community is outraged. The professors and students are all fighting against this, and there's talk of a strike. They're holding a public protest at the university tomorrow."

"I want to go with you, Abba."

"And do what? What is it you think you can do, Miriam? No, my dear, you and your child must stay here where it's safe."

"If enough people at the university protest," Avi said, "the Nazis will have to listen."

Abba shook his head. "The law will be backed by Nazi troops and the Gestapo. The Dutch people will have no choice but to carry them out." He drew a deep breath as if gathering strength. "We need to find a way out of this country, Avraham. We must apply for visas—"

"I agree, but where can we go? How will we get there?" He released

Miriam and struggled to his feet as if he wanted to run. "The consulates have all closed. I was promised a visa for Palestine, but then the British declared war and the Nazis invaded us and there's no longer a British embassy here."

Abba stood too, taking control, halting Avi's frantic pacing. "Enough of this, now. We will eat our dinner and walk to the synagogue for evening prayers. The other men are also searching for a way out. We'll find one together."

After Abba and Avi left for work the next day, Miriam walked to the town house to ask Eloise if she knew more about the firings at the university. She found her in the breakfast room with Ans, having their morning tea. "I'm sorry to barge in—"

"Nonsense. Ans, fetch another cup for Miriam."

She sat down at the table, determined to remain calm, breathing slowly. "Yesterday you mentioned the new laws that the Nazis have passed. But have you heard about the latest one?" Eloise shook her head, frowning. "All Jewish teachers and professors have been fired. Including Abba."

Ans froze, her cup halfway to her mouth. Eloise slumped back against her chair. "I knew Herman was upset when he came home last night, but he just mumbled about problems at work."

"Abba said that the other professors and students are holding a protest at the university today. They're calling for a strike. Maybe if there's enough public outrage . . . maybe they'll change their minds."

Eloise sprang to her feet as if a jolt of electricity had shot through her. "We're going! I'm not going to sit by without adding my voice to the protests. Give me a moment to change my clothes and we'll be on our way." She headed toward the stairs before Ans could stop her.

"I'm sorry, Ans," Miriam said. "I was sure she must know about it already. I just wanted to ask if she had more information."

"I don't think I can stop her from going. But will you come with me in case I need help?"

"Yes, certainly. I feel like this is all my fault."

"It's not. I understand why her husband tries to shelter her, but I don't think he realizes that she actually copes better when she's doing something."

"I'm ready," Eloise said when she returned. "Do you know where the protest is being held?"

"No. Abba didn't want me to go."

"We'll find it. Let's go."

Miriam and Ans could barely keep up with Eloise as she strode from the house, crossed the bridge, and headed toward the cluster of university buildings off Rapenburg Street. It was easy to follow the shouts and chanting voices of protesting students as they drew close. Students handed out flyers with details about the new anti-Jewish laws.

"We can't let them do here what they did in Nazi Germany!" one student shouted. "We must stand up for our freedom and our rights!"

His words gave Miriam hope. She linked arms with Ans and Eloise so they wouldn't get separated and followed the flow to where the public speeches had begun.

"Who is that man?" Eloise asked a student as a distinguished-looking gentleman mounted the platform.

"That's Professor Cleveringa, dean of the law faculty."

The crowd stilled as the professor told how his distinguished mentor and colleague, Professor Meijers, had been dismissed from Leiden University because he was Jewish. Cleveringa read the letter of dismissal, and Miriam cringed at the ugliness of the hatred it spewed. It was happening again. Her lungs squeezed until she could barely draw a breath.

The police and Gestapo arrived moments after he finished his speech.

"Let's go! We need to go home!" Ans said. She linked arms with them, dragging them away from the campus and rushing toward the town house.

Miriam felt dizzy. She had to keep stopping to catch her breath.

They were almost to the bridge when a student brushed past them, shoving a flimsy newspaper into Eloise's hand. She halted to read it. "It's an underground newspaper! From the Resistance!" She hurried after the student before Ans could stop her, calling, "Wait! Please listen. I want to help."

The student halted. He looked wary, ready to run. "The truth of what's happening should be spread all across the country," Eloise said. "Can you put me in contact with your editor? I can help. I was a journalist in Belgium."

He looked all around before saying, "Go to the Leiden Observatory tomorrow morning at nine. If he agrees to meet with you, he'll be there."

"Eloise, are you sure about this?" Ans asked.

"How can any decent person stand by and allow this to happen?" she asked.

"Let's go home," Ans said. They started walking again.

"When this started happening in Germany, there weren't many people who were brave enough to stand up for us," Miriam said. "The Nazis had already created such a climate of terror and hatred that everyone was afraid of them. Thank you for helping us."

"I can't promise it will do any good," Eloise said, "but I'm going to try."

Miriam was able to breathe again by the time she reached her apartment. It helped to know that her friends and others at the university were standing up for Abba. She told him so as soon as he arrived home. "Don't be angry with me, Abba, but I went to the university this morning with Mrs. Huizenga and Ans. We heard the law professor's speech. People are going to support you. They won't let you be fired. I heard them calling for a strike." He started shaking his head before Miriam even finished.

"The strike won't do any good. The Gestapo arrested Professor Cleveringa right after he finished his speech. They've closed the university."

"So Professor Huizenga is out of a job too?"

"It would seem so."

Avi took the news very hard when he returned home. He had taken off his coat and hat, but he put them back on again right away. "Come, Abba," he said. "Let's go to the synagogue for evening prayers."

CHAPTER 22

Ans grew more and more concerned for Eloise's state of mind after returning from the protest. Trying to calm her seemed hopeless. Eloise paced through the town house, ranting nonstop about the Nazis and their unfair treatment of the Jews. She was waiting to speak with her husband the moment he came home from work, which was earlier than usual.

"I know all about what happened at the university this morning," she told him without a word of greeting. "Come and sit down, Herman. There's something I need to tell you." Ans tried to excuse herself so they could have privacy, but Eloise insisted she stay. "We're all in this together, Ans."

The professor sank down on the sofa, his long legs outstretched, his body limp. He ran his hand over his face. "Go ahead and tell me, Eloise. This day couldn't possibly get any worse."

"I was there," she said. "I heard Professor Cleveringa's speech. It was brilliant."

He sat up in alarm. "What were you doing there? Ans, did you let her go—?"

"Don't get mad at Ans—she couldn't have stopped me if she had bound and gagged me and locked me in the closet."

"But why? How did you even hear about the protest?"

"Miriam came over to tell us that her father and all the other Jewish professors had been fired. She said there was going to be a public protest. I simply had to do something."

"Do you also know that the Nazis closed the university, for now, after the speech?" he asked. "And arrested Professor Cleveringa?"

"I'm not surprised. But it won't do them any good. It won't stop the students and the people of Leiden from protesting this outrage. We simply can't stand by and allow them to persecute our Jewish people the way they did in Germany."

"The Nazis don't tolerate protests, Eloise. You're putting yourself in their crosshairs."

"I don't plan on standing in the street with a placard. I have something else in mind."

"Eloise, please . . ." Ans had never seen him look so weary and worried.

"I plan to do *this*." Eloise handed him the underground newspaper, then waited, watching while he skimmed it. "Now don't be angry with me, Herman. It won't do any good because I won't change my mind. I'm going to work for this newspaper."

"Doing what?"

"I can monitor the radio broadcasts in both English and French. Ans knows German. We can report the real news so the Dutch people will know the truth, not the lies and propaganda that the Nazis want us to believe. It's what I studied to do."

"But it always upsets you when you learn what's really going on. I couldn't bear to see you have another breakdown—"

"Herman, listen to me." She moved closer to him on the sofa and took his face in her hands. "I feel stronger when I'm fighting back. I can push the terrible memories away because this time I'm going to write a different ending to my story. I won't be a coward. I'm not going to hide from them. We can do this work together. It seems you're out of a job at the moment, aren't you?"

He gave a weak smile, and Ans saw the love in his eyes. "Yes, but let's think about this for just a minute . . ."

"The Resistance is rising up, Herman, and I need to be part of it. We can't give in to the Nazis' demands without a fight. This persecution of the Jewish people isn't just a cause to me. It's personal. This is about standing up for my friend Miriam and for her husband and her father and for the child she's carrying."

The professor captured Eloise's wildly gesturing hands and stilled them in his. "I know you're well aware of what happened to your parents—"

"They died while helping the Resistance. I survived. And I've been dying every day since then. The doctors said when the bad memories come, I should replace them with different thoughts. Positive thoughts. And positive actions. Working for the newspaper will save my life—I'm certain of it."

"And if you're arrested? Imprisoned? Eloise, I couldn't bear it."

"It would be no worse than the prison that my own mind has kept me in."

The professor turned to Ans, his expression pleading. "Ans, what do you think? Should Eloise do this? Is this wise? The Nazis will see this newspaper as treasonous. Anyone caught working for it will be imprisoned—or worse."

Ans chose her words carefully. "I'm not sure I'm qualified to give an opinion. But I'm also disgusted by what the Nazis are doing. I would like to work for the Resistance too. If Eloise decides to work for them, I will help her."

"This isn't what you signed on for, Ans," he said. "You need to talk with your family first. They may object to you putting yourself in danger."

"I don't need to talk to them. I already know they'll agree. They plan to fight back too. My grandfather said that everyone needs to make a conscious choice, whether they're going to be for or against the enemy.

He said if we choose to do nothing, then we're choosing to be on the enemy's side."

"I've arranged to meet with the editor of this newspaper," Eloise said, waving it. "Tomorrow, in fact. Ans will come with me, won't you? We'll fight the Nazis on every possible front." The professor looked up at Ans, pleading silently.

"Yes. We'll go together."

⁓⁓⁓

"I hate it that we've had so little time together lately," Ans said as she went into Erik's arms the following afternoon. "Can we go for a walk?" Evenings out together were no longer possible with the new curfew laws, so they snatched whatever moments they could.

"There won't be time. I'm going on duty soon. Maybe we can just sit out here on the steps for a few minutes."

Ans sank down on the cold stone step beside him, her head on his shoulder. "This terrible war is interrupting everyone's life," she said. "Will we still be able to see each other this weekend?"

"That's what I came to tell you. There's a meeting I have to attend."

"Is it about the protests at the university?" Erik had never mentioned seeing her at the demonstration for Prince Bernhard's birthday, so Ans assumed that he hadn't. Should she tell him that she'd gone to the protest at the university yesterday?

"I can't talk about it. I'm sorry."

"Erik, please tell me you don't agree with this persecution of Jews. Firing an eminently qualified physics professor or law professor because he's Jewish is just wrong!"

"Don't get involved, Ans. Please!"

She pulled away to look at him, her heart racing. She already was involved. Should she tell him? She and Eloise had met with the editor of the underground newspaper this morning and had volunteered to work with him. Eloise would do her reporting and writing under a pseudonym; Ans would help her gather the news and then distribute the newspapers.

"Please," Erik pleaded. "I know that one of the Jewish professors is a friend of the Huizengas, but—"

"He's my friend too. And so is his daughter and her husband. I can't stand by and let them be persecuted. What the Nazis are doing to them is monstrous. Surely you can see that." She felt the muscles in his body tense.

"What you and I believe doesn't matter. We can't fight them, Ans. They're too powerful. And they're ruthless. They'll arrest you and anyone else who speaks up without thinking twice about it. The Dutch Nazi Party is everywhere, watching and listening."

"I hope you're not thinking about joining them and becoming a party member."

"I had no choice."

She heard his words, spoken in the past tense, and froze. "You already joined them?"

"I had to. I didn't want to be sent to a labor camp." His beloved face looked strained, the muscles in his jaws tight.

"Wasn't there any other choice?"

"Not at the moment. No."

"Then we're on opposing sides?"

"Ans, no! I don't want that! I love you!" He held her tightly again, and she leaned against him, wanting to melt into him, change him, merge their hearts and their minds into one. It was the first time he'd said that he loved her, and her heart leaped with joy in spite of her inner turmoil.

"I love you too." It was true. She loved this sweet, shy man who only wanted to keep order and protect people. They kissed, and nothing mattered in that moment except their love for each other, their future together. If it weren't for the war, their future could begin today.

Ans thought she understood Eloise's anger and grief after the Great War had altered her life forever. And she grieved for Miriam, who wanted the same thing that Ans did—a future with the man she loved.

Ans was still thinking of Miriam when Erik said, "Promise me you won't get involved, Ans. I want you to be safe. I want a future with you.

I can't give you the life you deserve right now, but when things get better, when the country stabilizes, will you marry me?"

In a way, it seemed too soon. They'd met only a year ago. And ever since Erik went into military training, they'd been apart more than they'd been together. But Ans loved him. She wanted to spend her life with him. She knew they could make a happy life together. In that moment, she hated the Nazis for coming between them. She and Erik were on opposing sides because of the Nazis.

"Yes, Erik, yes! I would love to be your wife! But I don't want to start our life together under these horrible conditions. I think we should wait until the war ends and life returns to normal and we're free again." She expected to see joy on his face, but he winced. "Did I say something wrong?"

"When I see the power the Nazis wield . . . how much they control us and every nation around us, and how no one has been able to stop them . . . I don't think we'll ever be able to break free from them."

"Don't say that! We can't lose hope, Erik. We can't!"

Ans felt like singing when she went to her room that night. She wanted to announce to the world that she was in love and Erik had asked her to marry him. She had said yes! Yet she couldn't tell anyone. Herman and Eloise wouldn't understand. They would see Erik as a policeman who worked for the Nazis, their enemy. And Miriam would never understand how she could fall in love with a member of the Nazi Party. Ans couldn't explain it to herself, much less to her friends. Or her family. Mama and Papa didn't even know about Erik. But Ans loved him. When this war ended, they would be together forever.

In the months that followed, Ans was able to snatch only short moments of time with Erik. Her days were spent working with Eloise on the underground newspaper, spreading the news about the Nazi persecution of Jews in the Netherlands. Her work was important. She was rising up against the enemy, resisting their evil.

In January, the outrage at the treatment of Jews reached a boiling point when the Nazis passed a law requiring all Jews to register their names and addresses and carry identification cards marked with a *J*. Strikes were called and riots broke out in Amsterdam as people protested, demanding that the Nazis rescind the law.

Erik arrived at the town house early one morning while Ans was still eating her breakfast. She hurried outside to talk with him on the front step, afraid to invite him inside. After working late into the night, she and Eloise had been too tired to clear everything away before going to bed. Eloise's typewriter sat in plain view on the dining room table, strewn with drafts of reports and editorials. The latest issues of the newspaper, detailing the unrest in Amsterdam and the Nazis' brutal backlash, were stacked on a chair for Ans to deliver.

"I came to tell you that I've been ordered to assist the police in Amsterdam," he told her after they'd kissed. "I'm leaving now to help put an end to the rioting."

"Will you be in danger?"

"We're armed. The rioters aren't."

The thought occurred to her that Erik could provide an eyewitness report. People all over the Netherlands would learn the truth about what the Nazis were ordering the Dutch police to do. "When will you be back?"

"I have no idea."

"I love you, Erik."

"I love you too." He kissed her and was preparing to leave when she stopped him again. There was something else she needed to know.

"But you agree that what they're doing to the Jews is wrong?"

He sighed and ran his hand through his hair. It was the color of damp sand and reminded Ans of their walks on the beach in Katwijk in happier times. "Everything that's happening in the Netherlands is wrong," he said. "But if I show any sympathy at all, I'm finished. I'm hoping I can urge the other officers to exercise restraint. Right now, the situation in Amsterdam is out of hand." He kissed her again and said,

"I'm concerned for you, Ans. I know you have Jewish friends, but please be careful. Riots don't help anyone."

"I'll be praying for you. And for us."

He looked surprised. "You believe in prayer?"

"Yes, don't you?"

"I don't know anything about it. I wasn't brought up with religion. Life is very different in Java than it is here."

"Maybe we can talk about it when you get back. You can come to church with me sometime."

He nodded, but Ans thought she detected more skepticism than enthusiasm. Had she really never talked about her faith before? It had taken on renewed importance since the invasion. Erik waved, then turned and walked away without looking back.

CHAPTER 23

MARCH 1941

Miriam and Avi's baby girl was born on a sunny morning in early March, after Miriam had labored for eighteen hours. A Jewish doctor delivered the baby in their apartment, avoiding the hospital and official records. The moment the doctor placed baby Elisheva in Miriam's arms, she felt more joy than she ever thought possible—and with it, more fear than she'd ever known. Elisheva was as delicate and perfect as a flower blossom, from her halo of fine, dark hair to her tiny, precious toes. Miriam stroked her soft cheek and kissed her perfect fingers, unable to take her eyes off her. Avi laughed and wept when he held her for the first time. But in his unguarded moments, Miriam caught him looking at their child with a mixture of love and dread and fear. "There is so much more at stake," he whispered.

Abba had never stopped searching for a way to escape, and when the baby was three months old, a man from the Dutch Resistance came to their apartment after curfew one evening. Miriam had expected an underground freedom fighter to be fierce-looking, but he arrived wearing a business suit and tie and carrying a briefcase. Miriam had been saving every guilder she could spare to pay for their escape and had no coffee or tea to offer him.

"I don't need anything, thank you," he said, waving away her apologies. He sat down at their kitchen table and took a book from his bag, carefully removing a delicate map that had been rolled inside the spine. He spread it out on the table. "I can put you in contact with a network that has been very successful in smuggling people into Switzerland, Professor Jacobs, but it's costly. The money is needed to purchase Dutch and Belgian identity cards that won't identify you as Jewish. The next step will be to cross the Belgian border—"

"Belgium?" Abba said. "The Nazis occupy Belgium."

"They do," he replied. He placed his book on one side of the map to keep it from curling while he traced his finger along the route. "Once across the border, you will be given your Belgian identities and taken to a safe house in Brussels. There you will meet a *passeur* who knows the route from Belgium, through France, and into Switzerland, avoiding checkpoints and border controls. The *passeur's* fees can be very expensive but are well worth the cost if you want to escape. So far they've proven very reliable. None of their passengers have been caught."

"And are Jews accepted in Switzerland?" Avi asked. "I've heard that some have been turned away at the border."

"And I've heard that some of the Swiss officials cooperate with the Nazis," Abba said, "hiding Nazi money and other assets in Swiss banks."

"I've heard all of these things, too," the man said. "But the *passeur* will avoid Swiss border controls. Once you're there, your documents will disguise who you are."

"How soon can we leave?" Abba asked.

"Producing the false documents will take time. Two or three months, at least. And that's if we start the process right away."

"I will pay any price," Abba said.

"Can we assume that the terrain will be rugged?" Avi asked. "We have a small child." He gestured to Miriam, who had been pacing the tiny living room while the men talked, rocking Elisheva to sleep in her arms.

"The child is going?" he asked in alarm.

"Yes, of course. All four of us are going," Abba replied. "I can pay for all of us."

"A child will be a problem, especially one that small. The route is physically demanding and dangerous. A crying baby can give you away. I don't know of anyone who has tried to do it with a small child. I'm not certain the *passeur* will even agree to try."

Miriam's hope evaporated, and despair rushed in to take its place. She held Elisheva tightly as if someone might snatch her from her arms.

"You said it will take a few months for all our papers to arrive?" Abba asked. "The baby will be stronger by then."

"I can strap her to my chest and carry her," Avi said.

"Smuggling two men will be no problem. Even you," he said, gesturing to Miriam, "if you have sturdy shoes." He lifted the book, and the map curled up on its own. He rolled it tightly and pushed it back into place in the spine. "But traveling with a baby will be close to impossible."

Disappointment nearly crushed all three of them. Abba gave the man a down payment to begin the process and asked him to please inquire about taking Elisheva. "It's unthinkable for any of us to leave without her," he said.

◠◡◠

In July, the synagogue was vandalized with painted swastikas and slogans reading, "Jews die!" Miriam remembered Kristallnacht and everything that had happened to her family after that terrible night. It was happening all over again in the Netherlands.

New rules for Jews appeared in the newspapers, including a summary of all the places they were forbidden to go. They could no longer ride on trams or buses or trains. They couldn't visit parks or do business with non-Jewish shops. They could no longer visit non-Jewish households.

Miriam's world shrank to include only the synagogue, the Jewish grocery store, and the streets around her apartment.

As her life grew more confined, her fear grew more expansive, enlarging with each new proclamation until it nearly overwhelmed her. She had to protect her daughter, but how? She and Avi searched for a way as they lay in each other's arms at night, whispering their love and their fear. They found no answer.

"Just remember," Avi murmured, "the Nazis may take everything else away, but they can never destroy our love."

CHAPTER 24

Eloise found reserves of strength that Ans had never seen as she poured her seemingly boundless energy into her work with the underground newspaper. Ans enjoyed working with her. The only problem was getting Eloise to stop to sleep or eat. "I'm not stopping until we're free again," she would say whenever Ans tried to coax her. The higher Eloise flew, the lower Ans feared she eventually might fall. Together, they monitored foreign radio broadcasts in German, English, and French, then reported what they'd heard.

Besides monitoring the news, Ans also delivered copies of the newspaper as soon as they came off the press, riding her bicycle or traveling by train to Amsterdam or Den Haag. She was standing on the platform at the Leiden station with a bundle of newspapers hidden in the lining of her bag, waiting for the train to Den Haag to arrive, when she saw Erik approaching. He wore his police uniform, and he was with two Nazi soldiers. He looked surprised when he saw her, but he continued walking toward her as if not in a hurry and didn't smile or greet her with a kiss. "What are you doing here, Ans?"

"I'm . . . um . . . running an errand for Eloise. Are you going someplace too?"

"We're checking ID cards." He wouldn't meet her gaze. He seemed embarrassed. The latest Nazi regulation now required everyone over the age of fifteen to carry an identification card at all times.

"Oh. I should let you get on with your job, then. Will I see you this weekend?"

He lowered his voice. "I have to check your ID card, Ans. They're training us to do it correctly." Her heart beat faster.

This stranger was the man she had laughed with and kissed last night, the man she'd snuggled beside at the cinema. Before the movie started, a Nazi propaganda film had aired. It had disgusted her. She'd tried to talk about it afterwards, telling Erik how outraged she was, but he'd warned her to be quiet. "There are listening ears everywhere," he'd whispered. She knew he was right. If they identified her as a Jewish sympathizer, it would endanger her work with the newspaper and put all of their coworkers at risk.

"My ID card is in here somewhere." She laughed, trying to make light of it as she fumbled through her purse. She was afraid of Erik in his role as a policeman, afraid of the power he wielded for the enemy. By carrying forbidden newspapers, she was breaking the law that he was sworn to uphold. Erik glanced at the two soldiers watching him from a short distance away. He must see that she was nervous. What would he do if he found the newspapers?

"Here it is," she said, handing the card to him. Her heart raced faster as Erik studied it, wondering if he'd been trained to spot a fake. Miriam and Avi were making plans to escape with false identity cards.

Erik stared at the flower on her lapel as he handed it back. She'd pinned it there so her contact could identify her. Erik knew she didn't wear flowers. "Open your bag for me, please." She did, watching his face as he poked around inside. A trickle of sweat ran down his temple. He was in as much danger as she was. Her bag contained physics textbooks borrowed from Professor Huizenga so she could pose as a student. Erik would know they weren't hers. The newspapers that were sewn inside the lining called for active resistance and exposed the Nazis' propaganda.

They also reported the latest news from the battlefront, news that the Nazi-controlled papers wouldn't report.

Erik suddenly looked up at her in alarm. Their gazes locked, then Ans looked down at what he'd seen. The weight of the textbooks had torn some of the stitching loose. The masthead on one of the newspapers was clearly visible behind the tear.

Time stood still.

Then Erik cleared his throat and said, "You may go." With those three words, he broke the law for her. He'd placed himself in danger. For her.

Her train to Den Haag rumbled into the Leiden station, shaking the platform. The doors opened, and she boarded on legs barely able to carry her. She stood in the aisle for the entire ride, unable to find a seat in the crowded car, gripping the strap as the train sped up and slowed down, stopping in towns along the way. She was so nauseated she feared she might be sick. Ans had been delivering the underground newspaper for months, but this was her first close call. She would have to warn everyone to be more careful.

At last, the train reached Den Haag. Ans stepped onto the platform, waiting for her contact to spot the flower on her jacket. Within minutes, a young man carrying an identical bag approached and greeted her like an old friend, kissing her cheeks. He chatted as he led her to a café near the train station, talking about the weather and how crowded the trains were these days. Ans knew the routine and had done this before with other contacts in other places. But he must have noticed that she was upset.

"Did you have a close call?" he asked after they were seated at a small table near the window.

Ans nodded. "They check ID cards and bags now. But I'm okay . . . I mean . . . I will be okay in a minute."

He leaned across the table. "Go ahead and cry if you need to. We'll pretend you're giving me bad news."

Tears filled her eyes, but not because she was afraid. Ans knew how much Erik's work meant to him, how committed he was to upholding the law. The Nazis would execute him if they suspected he was collaborating with the underground. Her tears were for what he had just risked for her. And because she feared he would ask her to choose between her love for him and her work for the Resistance.

"I'm okay," she said again. She had a twenty-five-minute wait until the return train to Leiden. Maybe her knees would stop trembling by then.

When it was time to leave, she and her contact said farewell and picked up each other's bag. The new one had a botany textbook in it and a bird guidebook. Ans had no idea what messages, if any, were sewn into the lining.

She boarded the train, hoping the Leiden station would be crowded when she got off, hoping Erik would be gone. What could she say to him? No explanation or apology seemed sufficient, no expression of gratitude enough to thank him for saving her.

She hurried home without looking up at anyone, then picked at her supper and went to bed early, telling Eloise she felt unwell.

Ans wept and worried all night long. She loved Erik. She feared this would be the end of their relationship, and she didn't want it to be. She raged at the war that had made their love impossible. Erik had been trained to obey authority. How could Ans explain that she had to obey a higher authority?

The first thing she said when Erik arrived at her door early the next morning was "I'm so sorry. I know you must be angry with me and—"

But he pulled her into his arms, cutting off her words. He held her tightly, his face pressed against her hair. "Do you want to come in out of the rain?" she asked when he released her again.

"I'm already wet. Let's walk."

Ans tied a kerchief over her head and went outside with him. They walked with their arms around each other. Rain dampened her face along with her tears as they followed the street beside the canal until it joined the Rijn, the trees sheltering them from the worst of the rain.

"May I explain why I—?"

"Do you have any idea what would have happened to you if one of those Nazi soldiers had been the one who'd looked in your bag instead of me?" He halted, letting go of her. His voice trembled with emotion.

She couldn't tell if it was sorrow or relief or anger. Perhaps all three. "They would have arrested you. And when you got to the police station, they would have tortured you until you gave up the names of all your contacts. All of the people who were responsible for that newspaper."

Her stomach rolled with nausea. "You've seen this happen, Erik? You've witnessed them torturing people?"

"I couldn't stop thinking about you all night! I kept playing the scene over and over, horrified by how close . . ." His breath caught. "Why would you do such a stupid thing? Doesn't our love or our future mean anything to you?"

"It means everything to me! That's why I'm doing this. What kind of future will we have under Nazi rule? Under a regime that tortures people? The Netherlands is my home, Erik. If there's any chance at all that I can help free my country, then I need to take that chance."

"I can't . . . I can't . . ." He shook his head as if waging an internal battle. "I can't sleep or eat or live knowing how much danger you're in! I love you, Ans, and I need to protect you from them! Don't you understand that? I know what they're like! I know the things they'll do!"

"How can you keep working for them?" she asked.

He looked away. A bicycle swished past, splashing water from the wet street. "You know the answer. We've had this conversation before." And they'd also heard stories about life in a Nazi labor camp. He reached for her hand. "I need you to promise me you won't deliver those newspapers again. Otherwise . . . I don't think I can do this, Ans. I can't love you as much as I do and know how much danger you're in. You're naive and idealistic, and you imagine that it'll do some good to fight them, but it won't. You can't win. They'll break you. And I couldn't bear that."

"I love you too—"

"Then *promise* me! Promise me right now or I'll have to walk away!"

"I promise," she whispered. She could do that much for the man she loved. She would tell Eloise and the others that she had to stop delivering newspapers.

But she hadn't promised anything else.

CHAPTER 25

DECEMBER 1941

The warm farmhouse kitchen was the same as it had always been for the more than twenty years that Lena had lived here, the fire burning brightly in the stove, her family listening to the boxy wooden radio on the stand in the corner, her knitting needles flying as she worked to finish a pair of socks for Wim. Maaike had her new set of paints and brushes spread out on the table, a gift on Sinterklaas Eve. Wim sat on a chair by the stove beside his father, learning how to carve with the pocketknife that had been his present. The fragrant aroma of hotchpotch from their evening meal still lingered in the air. Everything seemed the same as always.

And yet nothing was the same. Every day, the Nazis issued new regulations that curbed their freedom and made the enemy occupation more difficult to endure. Lena and Pieter loved farming their land, but now that most of their efforts went to feed the enemy, they felt enslaved. The only radio newscasts not under Nazi control were the few minutes of nightly *Radio Orange* broadcasts from England. As Lena waited for tonight's news, she worried that even those broadcasts would be taken from them soon. One of the Nazis' new laws had required all radios to be registered. Lena guessed that the next step would be to confiscate them, and she hadn't wanted to register. "Who's going to know whether or not we have a radio?" she'd asked Pieter.

"Every person who has visited our home will know. Everyone who comes in and out of our kitchen can't miss seeing it."

"But our friends—"

"We must forget the idea that anyone is our friend. We have no idea who we can trust. Besides, what if Maaike or Wim says something at school about listening to the radio at night?"

"You're right; you're right." They had registered their radio.

Lena paused in her knitting and leaned forward to see the picture Maaike was painting—a green field with black-and-white cows, a blue sky. Marring the expanse of blue was a formation of airplanes. Had they become such a common sight that her daughter included them in her tranquil farm scenes instead of a flock of migrating birds? Lena wanted to grab the brush and paint over the airplanes, erasing them. But no one had been able to stop the Nazis, let alone with a simple brushstroke. She turned her attention to her son. "What are you carving, Wim?"

He held up a lump of wood the size of his fist. "It's going to be a duck."

She exhaled with relief, fearing he would fashion a tank or a gun. Their St. Nicholas Day celebration had been leaner this year. Rationing made many goods more expensive and harder to find, but she'd managed to buy a few treats for Wim and Maaike. Lena remembered the night two years ago when Pieter had returned home from his military training to surprise them for St. Nicholas Day. They'd had no idea it would be their last holiday as free people.

Lena resumed knitting as the *Radio Orange* broadcast began. A moment later, she stilled with news of a special bulletin. *"Early yesterday morning, at 7:48 a.m. on the Pacific islands of Hawaii, the Japanese launched a surprise attack on the United States' naval base in Pearl Harbor. The US fleet suffered the loss of its eight battleships anchored there. One hundred and eighty-eight US aircraft were also destroyed in the raid. The loss of life is expected to reach nearly 2,500. In response to this unprovoked attack, the United States has now declared war on Japan.*"

"This is overwhelming," Lena breathed.

Pieter stared at the radio as if waiting to hear it was a joke or a mistake. As the announcer repeated the news bulletin, he looked up at Lena, raking his hand through his thick blond hair. "America is in the fight. They have the resources and manpower to help us win. Remember the first war? Finally there's hope."

"Will the Americans help us beat the Nazis?" Wim asked. He had stopped carving, his brow furrowed like his father's.

Pieter rested his hand on Wim's shoulder. "*Ja*, they'll help us."

Lena didn't know whether to feel relieved or horrified by the news. She barely heard the rest of the broadcast, her knitting forgotten as she tried to comprehend this triumph of evil on the other side of the world. The escalation and scope of the war made it seem like something from the biblical book of Revelation. How could God stand by and remain silent?

Pieter switched off the radio when the program ended, returning Lena's thoughts to her kitchen and her family. "Off to bed with you two," she said. "School tomorrow."

Wim shaved a few more slivers from his creation before laying it aside with a sigh and thumping up the wooden steps to his bedroom.

"But my painting isn't finished," Maaike complained.

"You can finish it tomorrow after school. Close up the paints so they don't dry out." Lena swept up the shavings from Wim's carving project and fed them into the fire.

"I'll be up at the windmill," Pieter said. Lena nodded. She would join him when the children were asleep. She followed Maaike upstairs and helped her get ready for bed. Her room beneath the eaves was warm from the kitchen stove, but by morning, Maaike would be burrowed beneath her comforter. She and Ans had shared this bed, and both Maaike and Lena felt her absence nearly every night.

"Is Ans coming home for Christmas?" Maaike asked as Lena loosened her braid and brushed her golden hair.

"I'm not sure. Let's hope so." Lena listened as Maaike knelt by her bed to say her prayers, then tucked her into bed. It wouldn't take her long to fall asleep. Lena peeked into Wim's loft afterwards. "Did you say your prayers?" she asked.

"*Ja.*" At thirteen, he'd outgrown their nightly bedtime rituals, but Lena couldn't resist crossing to his bed and kissing his forehead.

"Good night, then."

Downstairs, Lena stoked the kitchen fire, adding fuel before putting on her coat and hat. She turned out all the lights and slipped outside into the freezing night. The wind swirled dried leaves across her path as she plodded up the rise to the windmill in the dark. She found the door and stepped inside, waiting for her eyes to grow accustomed to the even-darker interior. A faint light from Pieter's candle flickered high above her. The old mill creaked and groaned in the wind as she climbed the narrow steps and then the steep wooden ladder to the very top, where Pieter crouched beneath the massive wooden beams. It was cold in the unheated mill. It smelled of old wood and dust and the oil Pieter used to grease the pump.

"It's nearly finished," he said. "Just a couple more nights." It would be one of several hiding places she and Pieter were building around their farm to prevent the Nazis from stealing everything they labored for all summer.

More than a year and a half had passed since the Nazi invasion, a year and a half since their freedom was stolen. After the first summer, when the enemy had inventoried their farm and then carried off their harvest, Pieter had begun building these caches to keep more of their crops out of Nazi hands. Working at night, after the children were asleep, he and Lena also had created a false floor beneath the hayloft in the barn. They'd dug another chamber beneath the abandoned chicken coop. A false wall in the root cellar hid a secret room behind a row of shelves. They would be arrested or shot if the Nazis discovered what they were doing. Lena lived with the fear of what might happen to her and Pieter and to their children every moment of every day. Yet giving in to the Nazis was unthinkable.

A breeze blew through the open rafters, nearly snuffing out their only candle. They were forced to work in this dim light, afraid that a lantern would shine for miles in the clear December sky. Airplanes droned above them from time to time, a constant reminder of the war, a constant source of fuel for Lena's hatred. The Nazis had stolen her life and her children's secure future.

Lena yawned as the hours passed, struggling to keep her eyes open as she held the boards in place for Pieter to hammer. It must be well past midnight by now. They would have only a few hours of sleep before they'd have to get up and begin their chores again.

"That's it. We're done for now," Pieter said at last. He gave a satisfied sigh and blew out the candle, plunging them into darkness. They needed both hands to descend the steep wooden ladders. He closed the door to the outside behind them and took Lena's hand in his. He had worked without gloves, and his fingers were icy.

She shivered, wanting to hurry along the path to the warm farmhouse, but he pulled her to a stop. "Look up at that sky, Lena. Isn't it beautiful?" He stood behind her, his arms wrapped around her.

She took comfort from his warmth and strength as she gazed up at the midnight sky. At the moment, there were no airplanes, and she could almost imagine that the war had never happened and everything was as it used to be.

"So many stars!" she murmured. "And they say the universe goes on and on forever, without end. I can't imagine that, can you?"

"Only an amazing God could create such a wonder."

She remembered this evening's news bulletin and felt a tug of fear in her stomach. "How He must grieve when He sees what we're doing to His beautiful earth. The entire world is at war." They stood in place for a few minutes, the great swath of the Milky Way shining like a river of starlight. "How can God remain silent and do nothing in the face of all this evil?" she asked.

"He isn't silent as long as we're His voice and His hands."

"It doesn't seem like we're doing enough."

"Each little thing we do to hinder the enemy is enough for now. When the Almighty needs us to do more, He'll tell us."

But to do more would mean putting themselves in more danger. Lena's fear wrestled with her deep hatred for the Nazis. She longed to fight back, to get even, to free her family from their power. Yet she would be a fool not to fear them. She wished her faith was stronger, that she could trust God completely and give her fear and anger to Him. But why had He allowed the Nazis to win in the first place? She exhaled in frustration and felt Pieter's arms tighten around her.

"What, Lena?"

"I want our life back. I want everything to be the way it used to be. I'm tired of living each day in suspense, not knowing what will happen to us tomorrow, not knowing how long we'll be forced to live this way. Will it be forever? Will we have to live this way for the rest of our lives?"

"God knows," he said softly.

They started walking again, following the path by the irrigation ditch, the barn and farmhouse looming shapes against the starlit sky. Lena washed up and put on her nightgown in the dark. But before climbing into bed, she slipped into her children's rooms, tucking the covers around them. Each day that she managed to keep her family warm and safe and fed felt like a victory.

CHAPTER 26

JULY 1942

The July sun pressed down on Ans like a hot iron as she walked to Leiden University's observatory. The water in the canal, motionless in the still air, reflected the sun's fire like a mirror. She slowed her steps as she neared the building with the rounded domes, glancing around for her contact from the newspaper.

Today's messenger was a new woman, recognizable by the flower she wore and the bag she carried. They greeted each other like friends who'd met by chance and chatted about the warm weather while Ans surveyed their surroundings. She felt safer meeting her contacts in a crowd where they could blend in, but few people were out and about at this time of day, probably due to the heat. The two women quickly exchanged bags.

Ans's bag hid the news reports that she and Eloise had written, while her contact's hid the latest edition of the newspaper. Ans didn't dare read it until she was safely home, but she pulled it out and began scanning it as soon as she was inside. She made her way upstairs to the workroom they'd created in one of the bedrooms on the third floor, her feet moving faster and faster as she climbed, horrified by what she was reading.

"They're doing it, Eloise!" she said as she arrived upstairs, perspiring and breathless. "The Nazis are actually doing it!"

Eloise stopped typing. "Doing what?"

Ans saw the weariness in Eloise's eyes and was sorry for springing the news on her. Eloise hadn't been sleeping well, pacing the town house at night and worrying everyone. Ans should have waited until Professor Huizenga was home, but it was too late.

Eloise huffed with impatience. "Tell me what they're doing, Ans."

"The Gestapo in Amsterdam is rounding up Jews during the night, registering them at a theater they're using as an assembly point, then transporting them out of the country. They're forcing the Dutch police to help."

She had an unwelcome image of Erik doing the same thing to innocent people here in Leiden, and her heart squeezed. She'd hoped he would change his mind about helping their enemies after the Dutch East Indies fell to the Japanese in March, but nothing had changed. "I'm not in Java," he'd said. "Anything I try to do here isn't going to help my homeland."

Ans had wanted to shake him. "Don't you see?" she'd asked. "The world is slowly being swallowed up by evil!"

"Of course I see! But right now, right here in Leiden, there's nothing we can do to stop it without losing our lives."

She'd known he was right, but it grieved her every time their arguments ended in this stalemate.

Meanwhile, the Nazis devoured more of their freedom every day. Earlier this spring, all Jews had been ordered to sew yellow stars on their clothing. It seemed like a little thing, but Ans knew that it wasn't.

"They passed the same law in Germany," Miriam had told Ans, "and it was no longer safe to go out. Anyone who saw us on the street could persecute us." Another new law forbade Jews to visit non-Jews, but it hadn't stopped Ans and Eloise from visiting Miriam. "The Nazis told Mrs. Spielman she no longer owns this apartment building," Miriam said on one of Ans's visits. "Dutch Nazis now control all Jewish assets. Every day we wake up wondering what they'll do to us next."

Ans had watched in speechless outrage as Miriam had sewn a yellow star onto the sweater Mrs. Spielman had knit for Elisheva's first birthday.

Then, two months ago, another shocking proclamation announced that all Jews in Nazi-occupied Europe would be transported east to resettlement camps. Churches across the Netherlands protested, and Ans had dared to hope that the Nazis would relent. But according to the newspaper Ans had just received, midnight razzias had begun in Amsterdam, with the Gestapo pounding on doors and rounding up entire families. Ans wished she hadn't shared the news with Eloise so abruptly.

"So all of our protests were for nothing?" Eloise asked. "They're going through with the deportations?"

Ans nodded and dropped into a chair, still holding the newspaper. She didn't tell Eloise that the former refugee camp at Westerbork was now being used by the Nazis as a prison and deportation camp.

"The editor is calling for more active resistance," Ans said.

"Meaning what? Are we supposed to fight them in the street? What will we use for weapons? They say that the pen is mightier than the sword, but so far my pen hasn't done much good." Eloise ripped the half-finished page from her typewriter and crushed it into a ball. Ans knew from experience that taking action might keep Eloise from despair, but what more could they do?

Ans rose to her feet again. "We have to help the Jews here in Leiden find safe places to hide. We can't stand by while the Nazis round them up and take them who knows where. I'm going to warn Miriam and her family. Are you coming with me?"

"Of course."

They stepped outside into the stifling afternoon and were both perspiring by the time they reached Miriam's apartment. The haunting violin music that floated down from an open window on the second floor stopped when they rang the doorbell. Miriam was alone with the sleeping baby, her father and husband out working odd jobs to put food on their table.

Ans sat down in Miriam's living room to tell her about the newspaper report. "The Gestapo in Amsterdam are going from house to house every night, rounding up Jews. They know exactly where everyone lives because of the address registrations last year." The color seemed to drain from Miriam's face. Ans hurried to finish. "You can't stay here and let them take you and your family. We need to find a way to help you escape before it's too late."

"Where? . . . How? There's no place to go!" Miriam stood as if preparing to run, and Ans could tell that one of her panic attacks was starting to take hold. Eloise made her sit down again.

"Let's think this through," she said. "What about your father's plans to escape to Switzerland? Elisheva is older now, and—"

"It's too late. They told Abba that the *passeur* has been arrested. Escaping by that route is no longer possible."

The news brought a dread-filled silence that seemed to swallow all the air. The baby whimpered as she awoke from her nap, and Miriam hurried into the bedroom to get her. Elisheva wore only a diaper and had been sweating in the hot apartment. Her little round face was red, her damp hair plastered to her head, but she recognized Ans and gave her a sleepy grin. Ans reached for her. "Come here, sweetheart."

Miriam set her down, and she toddled over on wobbly legs. Ans held her close, remembering when her sister, Maaike, was that age, waddling around the farmhouse and pointing to everything with delight. Ans ached to see her family, but it was impossible. She couldn't leave Eloise. Working with Ans on the newspaper was the only thing that kept her afloat most days.

"You can't stay here and wait for the Nazis to take you," Eloise said. "Move into our town house. We'll hide all of you there."

"How will we get there with these on our clothes?" Miriam plucked at the hated yellow star on her dress. "It's illegal to be caught in public without them."

"We'll figure out a way," Ans said.

"If they stop us and ask for our identity cards, they'll see the *J*. And if we're carrying suitcases . . ."

Miriam was right. The Nazis had thought of everything as they'd patiently laid their trap.

"Show this newspaper to your father and Avi when they get home," Ans said, pulling it from her bag. "Then burn it. I'll come back tomorrow with a plan."

Eloise trudged up the stairs after they returned home and went into her bedroom instead of her workroom. "I would like to sleep now," she told Ans. "Please leave me alone." She tried to stop Ans at the door, but Ans followed her inside.

"I need your help, Eloise. We have to come up with a plan to move Miriam's family here without being noticed. Do we know if we can trust your neighbors?"

Eloise turned away to stare out the window. "We can't fight the Nazis. They're too strong. This war is different from the last one. This time we're going to lose."

"So you're just going to give up, Eloise? You're going to let those monsters take Miriam and Avi and that beautiful little baby away?"

"I can't watch everyone I love die again. I can't! I won't!"

Ans crossed the room and grabbed Eloise's shoulders, turning her around and shaking her. "Eloise, stop it! I just heard you promise Miriam that her family could hide here. Are you going to break that promise?"

Eloise grasped Ans's wrists, pulling her arms down and pushing her away with surprising force. "I told you I need to sleep! I'll think about everything later!" She had never argued this way before, and it terrified Ans.

"Let me get your medicine—"

"I can take it myself! I'm not a *baby*!" The word seemed to trigger something inside her, and Eloise collapsed to the floor, sobbing. "That baby . . . that beautiful little baby . . . I watched everyone die in the last war, and I can't do it again . . . I can't!"

Ans sank down beside her, holding her tightly and letting her cry.

When Professor Huizenga arrived home an hour later, he found them there. It had been one of the longest hours of Ans's life. "Come, darling, take your medicine now," the professor soothed. He waited in their bedroom until she finally fell asleep.

"What happened?" he asked Ans afterwards. She saw his concern. He wasn't accusing her.

"We read in the underground newspaper that they're starting to round up all the Jews in Amsterdam, and it was too much for her. I know she handles things better when she has something to do, so we went to Miriam's apartment to warn her and her family. Eloise offered to hide them here. But seeing the baby triggered Eloise's grief, and . . ." She couldn't finish as sorrow clogged her throat.

"Did the newspaper say when the roundups might start here in Leiden?" Ans shook her head. "Might your friend on the police force know?"

"I-I could ask him. I'll run over to his apartment right now and see if he's home."

"Ans—thank you for helping Eloise today," he said, stopping her. "She told me she pushed you, and I'm sorry—"

"Neither of you needs to apologize. I never should have let Eloise see the newspaper. I'll be more careful from now on."

"I agree that we need to hide Miriam's family here, but we'll all be in danger when we do. I can't ask you to stay here and risk your life, Ans."

She drew a deep breath, aware of the danger she would be in but also aware of her love for her friends. "I want to stay." She didn't lie and say she wasn't afraid, because she was. "I'll be back after I talk to Erik."

It was too hot to run all the way across Leiden, but Ans walked as quickly as she could, hoping to catch Erik between shifts. Thankfully, he was home, just changing out of his uniform after a long day at work, and he answered the door without his shirt. "Ans! What brings you here?" His skin felt hot as she hugged him. She wanted to kiss him and linger in his arms, but her errand was much too important.

"I need to ask you something," she said. "I just read the news that—" She halted, realizing her mistake. She had read the news in the illegal underground newspaper. The newspaper that she'd promised to stop distributing. She felt the blood rush to her face and cleared her throat to start again. "I learned that the Gestapo is taking Jews from their homes in Amsterdam and transporting them out of the country. The Dutch police are being forced to help them do this, and—"

Erik put his finger to his lips to shush her and pulled her inside, closing the door. He gestured for her to sit, then turned away for a moment to put on his shirt. "Ans, you must be more careful about what you say," he said, fastening his buttons. "Someone might overhear you."

Ans wanted to shout the news of this injustice from the rooftops. She struggled for control. "I came to ask if you knew when—?" She thought of baby Elisheva and swallowed a sob. "If you knew when the Jews will be rounded up in Leiden? The Gestapo does their dirty work after curfew so people won't see what's happening to these innocent men, women, and children, but I need to know when it's going to happen here!"

He sighed and sat down on a chair across from her as if sensing that she didn't want to be close to him right now. He bent forward, arms on his thighs, hands dangling between his knees. "We haven't been told anything specific. But something must be about to happen because they're reworking our schedules, assigning more of us to the night shift."

Ans closed her eyes, unable to stop her tears. "And you'll have to help them?"

Erik started to speak, but she stopped him. "Don't say you have no choice. If every man on the police force refused to—"

"If we refused, we would be sent to the labor camps along with the Jews we're defending. Listen, Ans, I'm as trapped as your friends are. They have no place to run or hide, and neither do I. How can I get out? Where would I go? Home to Java? The Japanese are all over the Pacific, and they're even more bloodthirsty than the Nazis. There's nothing we can do."

"Don't tell me that! There must be *something*!"

Erik slowly shook his head. She thought she saw tears in his eyes. Then the muscles in his face tensed as he clenched his jaw to keep his tears from falling. He stood. "I was just about to fix something to eat. A dish with spices from home. Stay and have dinner with me, Ans, and then I'll walk you home before curfew." He reached for her hand, but she hesitated. "Please? I'll show you how we cook in Java. You'll need to know for after we're married."

Ans wiped her eyes and accepted his hand.

Erik had told her what she needed to know. Miriam and her family had to go into hiding right away. But Ans couldn't bear to think that Erik might be the one who pounded on their door in the middle of the night.

CHAPTER 27

Miriam had the Sabbath table set and dinner prepared by the time Abba and Avi came home. She'd had only enough flour to bake two tiny loaves of bread, and the *cholent* had more beans and potatoes than meat, but they would light candles and share the special meal together. She dreaded showing them the underground newspaper. Each time her husband and father left the apartment to look for work with yellow stars conspicuous on their clothing, Miriam's fear for their safety made the hours apart seem endless. Today, after reading about the persecution in Amsterdam, she listened with even deeper anxiety for their return.

Their footsteps sounded slow and weary as they trudged up the stairs, but she breathed a prayer of thanks and opened the door to greet them, holding Elisheva in her arms. Avi smiled and kissed both of them. "No hugs until I wash," he said. His clothes were damp with perspiration.

"Where's Abba?"

"Right behind me. There was a letter in our mailbox."

Miriam took one look at her father's pale face when he entered with an open envelope in his hand and felt a panic attack grip her. "What does it say?" Miriam thought she already knew the answer.

"We must be ready to be transported to Amsterdam next week." His voice trembled with emotion. "They will come after curfew to fetch us. We are each allowed one suitcase, which we must carry ourselves."

"No!" Miriam buried her face in Avi's chest and wept, not caring that he was dirty and sweaty. His arms came around her, enveloping her and the baby. "Ans and Eloise warned me this would happen, but not so soon! Everything's happening too fast!"

"It seems we have no choice," Abba said. "I see no way out this time."

"Yes, there is." Miriam dried her eyes, determined to be strong. "Ans and Eloise said we shouldn't wait for them to take us away. They offered to hide us in their town house."

"How will we get there without being seen?" Avi asked. "If we wait until after dark, we'll be breaking curfew."

"Ans is coming back tomorrow with a plan."

"God bless them," Abba said as tears ran down his face. "They are saving our lives for a second time. May the Almighty One bless them for this." He and Avi bathed and changed their clothes, then walked to the synagogue to pray. The other men would have received the same notice by now. The sun wouldn't set until after curfew on these long, hot summer days, but as soon as the men returned, Miriam lit the candles and they sat down to eat the Shabbat meal.

"The Sabbath is our island of peace and rest," Avi said as he broke the bread. "Tonight, let's not talk of tomorrow." But Miriam knew the future was on everyone's mind and a prayer for deliverance in each of their hearts while they ate.

It was still the Sabbath the following afternoon when Ans arrived at the apartment with an old-fashioned hatbox. They sat around the table, still spread with the white tablecloth, to hear her plan.

"Professor Huizenga and I came up with the idea last night," she said, opening the box. "The safest time for all of you to be out in the open will be on Sunday, when everyone in Leiden will be walking to church. I brought each of you a Sunday hat, and a dress and white gloves for you,

Miriam." She pulled the items from the hatbox and handed them out. "We also added ties like the Dutchmen wear on Sunday."

Abba looked uncertain as he fingered the necktie. He used to seem so strong and robust to Miriam with his broad face and sturdy body, but he'd been whittled down in the years since leaving Cologne, and silver threads now peppered his dark, thinning hair. "And you believe these disguises will work?" he asked Ans.

"We are praying that they do. Get dressed on Sunday morning and hide all the belongings you want to take in the bottom of Elisheva's baby carriage. Then stroll out the door and walk to the Pieterskerk for the morning service like all of the Christians will be doing. We'll be waiting to meet you at the front entrance. Professor Huizenga said he hoped you wouldn't be offended, but he thinks it's best if you sit through the church service with us. He'll be telling people that you are refugees from Scheveningen, on the coast, and that the Nazis forced you to evacuate to build their fortifications. We'll all walk back to the town house together after the service."

"But won't there be people there who know me from the university?" Abba asked. "You will all be in danger if someone reports this deception."

"That's why Professor Huizenga thinks it would be best if you and Avi shave off your beards. And, Miriam, you'll blend in better if you cut your long hair and wear it in a modern bob. I can help you cut it if you want me to."

Miriam reached up to touch her hair. Avi loved it long, but she would shave it all off to save her family. "Yes, of course I will."

"What about our identification cards?" Avi asked. "The police can ask to see them at any time."

"That's another reason why we chose a Sunday morning. So far, the Nazis still show respect for that day. And there will be so many people coming and going to church, they can't possibly check everyone's ID."

Abba rose from the table and took both of Ans's hands in his. "I will never be able to thank you and the Huizengas for your kindness and generosity. But I wonder if I may impose upon you for one last favor. I'll show you what it is." He disappeared into his bedroom and came out with the suitcase he'd used to carry his books and papers from Cologne, opening it to show Ans what was inside. "This is the scientific research I've been doing. Please give it to Professor Huizenga for me. If you are stopped, you might well be carrying it for him. He knows what I've been working on. He'll understand what all of it means. Someday, when Leiden is free again, perhaps an enterprising graduate student can finish where I left off."

The words sent a jolt of alarm through Miriam. "You'll finish it yourself when that day comes, Abba."

He smiled. "Then he will keep it safe for me until then."

"I'll take it to him," Ans said. "And I agree with Miriam—you'll finish your research yourself one day. The tide of this war is certain to change soon."

"I pray that you're right."

"What about your violin, Miriam?" Ans asked. "Shall I take that for you too?" Miriam froze for a moment, unable to imagine being without it.

"I think it's a good idea," Avi said.

"Y-yes. Thank you." She went into the bedroom to get it, pausing to run her hand over the violin's smooth wooden case. She opened it and peeked inside as if checking to see that a baby was safely asleep, then closed the lid and fastened the latches. She held it to her chest for a moment, feeling foolish. After all, it would be waiting for her at the town house tomorrow. Yet it was much more than that. This move brought another change in her life, wrenching her from a place of relative comfort and security to a new and more dangerous stage. She pulled air into her lungs, determined to be strong for Elisheva's sake.

They didn't talk about Ans's plan after she left. Avi lit the havdalah candle that evening, reciting the words that marked the end of the Sabbath day, then blew out the candle, plunging their apartment into darkness.

When church bells tolled across Leiden on Sunday morning, Miriam left her little home for the last time, wearing white gloves and a summer dress without a yellow star. A flowered straw hat covered her head, which felt lighter without her long hair. Ans had cut it for her, declaring her new style a fashion success. Avi said he liked it too.

Elisheva had stared in confusion at her father and grandfather, as if not recognizing them without their beards, but then Avi had laughed and tickled her and all was well. Miriam would have laughed at how different Avi looked too, with his bare face and strange tie and even stranger hat, but she was much too nervous as they prepared to leave for church to think anything was humorous.

She walked down the apartment stairs and propped Elisheva in her baby carriage. They had already said a tearful goodbye to Mrs. Spielman last night. She would go with the authorities to Amsterdam, she'd said. She would live with her sons and grandchildren in the resettlement camp.

Abba had acted oddly all morning, staring at Miriam and Avi and the baby as if memorizing their faces. When he halted in the downstairs doorway instead of continuing forward, dread suddenly filled her. "Come on, Abba. The church bells are ringing. We need to go."

"I'm not going with you, Miriam. You and Avi and Elisheva will be safe with the Huizengas."

"Abba, no!"

"When the authorities come, I will tell them you already moved to Amsterdam so Avi could find work. I'll give them an address there."

"Abba! No! You can't do this! I won't let you! You have to come with us!"

"Shh . . . shh . . . you mustn't make a fuss. Someone will hear."

"Why won't you come? Please! They'll hide you, too."

"Because I know we won't be able to hide there forever. There are too many of us. The three of you will stand a better chance without me. The baby is the most important one of all of us. She is the future."

"But you're a renowned physicist! Your research—!"

"It's safe." Miriam remembered how he'd given it to Ans yesterday and realized he had never intended to come at all.

"Don't do this, Abba! Remember how Mama refused to come? Remember how much it hurt us?"

He cupped Miriam's face in his hands and looked into her eyes. "I'm tired of running, dear one. If I know that the three of you are safe, it will be enough for me. Who knows? Maybe I'll find your mother in the resettlement camp."

"Abba, please listen—"

"This is what I want. Mrs. Spielman won't have to go to Amsterdam on the transports alone. I promised I would go with her." He held Miriam close and kissed her forehead. "I love you, Miriam. Dry your tears now." He looked at Avi. "Take good care of them, Avraham."

Miriam whirled to face her husband. He hadn't said a word to try to dissuade her father. "You knew about this?" she asked. "You knew he was staying behind and you didn't talk him out of it?"

"I tried! I begged him to come!" Avi's tears were overflowing as well.

"Nothing Avi said would have changed my mind."

The church bells were so loud. Nagging, clamoring, as if to say, *Hurry, hurry!* One of them was a deep bass note that pounded in the pit of Miriam's stomach.

Avi encircled her shoulders and tried to move her and the baby carriage forward. "We have to leave, Miriam. Come."

"No, I can't! I won't leave you, Abba!" She stretched out her hand to her father, but he wouldn't take it.

"You must go," he said. "And God go with you." He turned his back and went inside, closing the door behind him.

CHAPTER 28

The trauma they'd endured in the past few days made everyone in the town house sick at heart. Ans didn't know how to comfort any of them. Miriam and Avi mourned for her father, enduring yet another loss after suffering so many others. "Why wouldn't he come with us?" Miriam asked again and again. "He should have come with us." Professor Huizenga mourned the loss of his friend and colleague, saying he didn't understand it either. Eloise continued to insist that she didn't want to live in a world with so much evil and hatred, and Ans could hardly blame her. Eloise had to be coaxed to leave her room, and when she did, she stared through vacant eyes as if afraid to look at anyone, fearing she would lose all the people she loved. Ans hadn't seen or spoken to Erik in more than a week, and she thought she knew why. In spite of the many protests, the Gestapo and local police were systematically rounding up Leiden's Jews and transporting them to Amsterdam. Everyone wondered if Professor Jacobs was among them.

"I'm going over to your old apartment to see what's happening," Ans told Miriam and Avi when she could no longer stand waiting. She didn't know if facing the truth would change anything, but at least she would be doing something.

"Please be careful," Professor Huizenga said.

"I will." She thought about concocting an excuse for why she was in the Jewish neighborhood in case anyone stopped her but decided it didn't matter. She had her identity card. She didn't need a reason to walk Leiden's streets in daylight.

The area around the synagogue and Jewish shops seemed silent and deserted. Ans pressed the apartment's doorbell and heard it ring inside. No one answered. She remembered finding this apartment for Miriam and her father nearly three years ago. They'd lived happily here, working hard, putting down roots, building a family and a new life together. How could they and an entire community of innocent people be targeted this way? What was the root of such hatred? And what could she do to fix it and make it right? There were no answers. She stood in the street, looking up at the vacant building through her tears, and understood Eloise's sadness and despair.

Ans was about to leave when something rustled in the bushes beside the door. She backed up a step, then saw that it was a cat—Mrs. Spielman's cat. It mewed when Ans crouched to pet it. "You poor thing. You were left here all alone."

She heard heavy footsteps on the cobblestones behind her and turned to see a man striding toward her. The cat disappeared into the bushes again. The figure drew closer.

Erik.

She stood, ready to run into his arms and let him comfort her, then stopped. He was in his uniform. He wasn't smiling. Nor did he reach to embrace her.

"What are you doing here?" he asked in a tight voice. "You're not supposed to associate with Jews. You'll be in a lot of trouble."

"What Jews?" she asked angrily. "They're all gone! And what are you doing here—arresting them?"

"We've been ordered to watch this apartment and several others. Two of the Jews who lived here are missing."

"Those two *Jews* are my friends, Miriam and Avi Leopold. They moved to Amsterdam to find work. I suppose you and your Nazi friends have already taken Miriam's father, Professor Jacobs, and their landlady, Mrs. Spielman." She wanted Erik to hear their names, to know that they were real people. "Do you know where they took them?"

"Amsterdam, I think."

"And then what? From Amsterdam they'll go to Westerbork—and then where? What happens to them after that?"

Erik looked away. "They'll go to resettlement camps."

"How can you do this, Erik? How can you help the Nazis destroy innocent people's lives?"

"I don't have a choice!"

"You keep saying that, using it as an excuse—"

Erik moved closer, lowering his voice. "You promised me you wouldn't get involved."

"I'm involved because they're my friends. I heard there were round-ups in Leiden, and I came to see if Professor Jacobs was still here. He isn't. This is his landlady's cat." It had reappeared from beneath the bush and was rubbing its head against her leg.

"You're not hiding your friends, are you?" She didn't reply. "Please, Ans. You'll be in terrible danger if you are. I don't want anything to happen to you."

"I told you. They already moved to Amsterdam. Now, unless it's against the law, I'm going to take Mrs. Spielman's cat home so it doesn't starve to death." She bent to pick it up and it clung to her, its claws sharp, its motor purring. She walked away from Erik without another word. She loved him. But she hated what he was doing.

"The police are looking for you and Miriam," she told Avi when she returned. The rage she felt was beyond any anger she'd ever known. "They know you're missing and they're watching your apartment. We need to create a hiding place here, in case the Nazis come to search."

"Would they do that?"

"Yes. They would."

They decided that the Leopolds would sleep on the third floor at night but keep their meager belongings in the attic, stowed in an old dresser and in a decrepit trunk that was falling apart. It was much too hot in the attic to stay up there for any length of time. The baby's diapers were the hardest things to hide. Several of them always needed to be hung on a rope in the attic to dry. Miriam and Avi kept their bedroom neat, sitting on the floor and keeping the bed made so it appeared unused. The curtains on all three floors remained closed so no one could see inside from the street, making the house as dark and gloomy as they all felt.

Ans held drills so they could practice hiding in the attic quickly, without making noise. She timed how long it took them, practicing until they could do it in under two minutes. They also practiced climbing through the dormer window and crouching on the flat, narrow ledge beneath it, where Eloise and Ans had stood watching the bombs fall during the Nazi invasion. The baby didn't like the drills and would cry as if sensing everyone's anxiety. The Huizengas shared a wall with neighbors on both sides, and everyone worried that they would report the baby crying. The cook and housekeeper had been dismissed.

A week after the Leopolds arrived, Ans was sitting in the parlor one evening with the cat curled on her lap, listening to the radio with the Huizengas, when someone pounded furiously on the front door as if intending to break it down. They pressed the doorbell relentlessly. The cat bolted when Ans sprang to her feet. The color drained from Eloise's face.

"Go warn them," Professor Huizenga whispered. "Quickly!"

Ans sprinted up the stairs, two at a time. By the time she reached the third floor, the Leopolds were already crawling through the little door to the attic. "Is it the Nazis?" Avi asked.

"I didn't wait to see. Hurry!"

They crossed the attic, balancing on the joists as they had practiced, yanking the diapers off the clothesline as they went. Avi climbed onto the crate and opened the window, letting Miriam climb out onto the ledge first. He handed her the baby, then climbed out behind her. Ans closed the window again, praying that Elisheva would be accustomed to the drills by now and wouldn't cry. Ans moved the crate away from the window without making any noise, then hurried back to the attic door. With every careful, hurried step, her fear and anger mounted. Had Erik sent the Nazis here? Had he betrayed her? Her anger and suspicion soared by the minute. What part had he played?

She was out of breath by the time she reached the doorway leading out to the third floor. She closed it behind her quietly and paused to listen, trying to catch her breath, her heart somersaulting. The Gestapo moved swiftly through the house, tromping in their heavy boots, shouting to each other in German. They were already on the second floor, searching the Huizengas' bedroom. Ans hurried to the third-floor bedroom that the Leopolds had used and made sure it looked untouched. Then she ducked into Eloise's office and switched on the lamp. The soldiers were right below her now, searching her bedroom. The workroom was strewn with Eloise's papers. Would the soldiers read them and see what she'd been typing? Ans spotted a copy of the underground newspaper beside the typewriter and her heart leaped into her throat. She snatched it up and thrust it under her blouse, then tucked her blouse into her slacks. They would need to be more careful next time. Would there be a next time? She stood in the doorway as if she'd been working and had been startled by the commotion downstairs.

Moments later, two soldiers thundered up to the third floor, demanding to know who she was and what she was doing here. She shrugged and spread her shaking hands, pretending she didn't understand. They searched both third-floor bedrooms, flinging open the closet doors, pounding on the walls as if looking for secret compartments. Ans watched to see how thoroughly they searched so she could write a newspaper report about it. When they finished, the soldiers opened the attic door and climbed the steep steps. Ans and her friends had practiced moving around on the narrow joists, but she didn't think the soldiers could balance their way to the attic window in their heavy boots.

She waited, barely breathing, until they came out again. She got a good look at the two men and saw how young they were, no older than Erik. She longed to ask them how they could do this terrible work and if they missed their families and their homes in Germany. Were they so committed to Adolf Hitler and the Third Reich that they were willing to sacrifice their humanity? She didn't want to hate them, knowing it was wrong to hate, but she couldn't help it.

After the Gestapo left, Ans hurried downstairs to console Eloise. She sat frozen on the sofa as if she wanted to disappear into the cushions, while her husband knelt on the floor in front of her, holding her hands. She was trembling from head to toe, staring into the past.

"Eloise! Look at me," her husband said. He waited until she did. "You're all right, darling. They're gone. The soldiers are gone."

"But those dear people . . . Did the soldiers find them?" she whispered.

"No. They're safe. All three of them."

"They can't live this way, Herman. Sooner or later the baby will cry at the wrong time and—"

"But she didn't cry. They're safe."

Ans sat down on the sofa beside her. She needed to penetrate Eloise's fear and get her to do something so she would feel in control again, fighting back against this obscene invasion of her home. "I watched how they searched the house, Eloise, and listened to what they were saying. We need to write an article about it for the newspaper. We can warn others what to expect."

Eloise turned to face her. "We could hide more people here. There may be others we can help." She was back with them again.

"Yes. And we will help others," her husband said.

None of them wanted to go to bed, still feeling vulnerable. They waited an hour, then Ans went up to the attic to let Miriam and Avi back inside through the window. Like Eloise, Miriam was pale and trembling from head to toe. The baby was asleep, but Miriam refused to let go of her. "We're going to sleep up here in the attic tonight," Avi said.

Ans didn't sleep at all. As soon as curfew ended the next morning, she ran to Erik's apartment to confront him. She pounded on his door the same way the Nazis had. Erik had been shaving and he answered with half his chin covered with lather. "Ans—?"

you believe in God?" she asked.

hat does that have to do with anything?"

We both answer to a higher authority. For now, you answer to the
s, but my higher authority is God. He's the One I must obey. If God
me to disobey the Nazis, I have to obey Him. Just like you have to
y the authorities over you."

"That makes no sense. What kind of a God would ask you to risk
ur life for someone else?"

A Bible verse suddenly sprang to Ans's mind: *"Greater love has no one
than this: to lay down one's life for one's friends."*

Ans understood those words now. She understood what Jesus did
for her. During all the years she'd spent sitting in church and hearing
Papa read Scripture every night, the Bible had merely been nice words
and inspiring stories that didn't apply to her life. Now they were real.
God's love for her was real. And the love she felt for her friends was just
a small taste of God's love. Yes, Ans would risk her life for them. She
remembered another verse she'd memorized in Sunday school: *"What
does the Lord require of you? To act justly and to love mercy and to walk
humbly with your God."*

"Erik, the God who would ask me to risk my life is the same God
who gave His own life for us. Because He loves us."

Ans could tell from his expression that he had no idea what she was
talking about. They had laughed and kissed and talked and dreamed of
the future together, yet Ans had never shared her faith with him. *Lord,
forgive me.*

"I have to finish getting ready or I'll be late," Erik said. "Ans, please—"

"Stop! Don't ask me to promise anything until you give me a chance
to explain what my faith means to me. Let me tell you why I can't make
any promises."

She turned and left without saying goodbye. Without kissing him.

She pushed her way inside and closed the d
last night and searched our town house. Did you
Did you send them there to look for my friends M
Tell me the truth!"

"No! I don't know anything about it. Are you accu

"Why did they search our house then?"

"I don't know. Maybe because your boss was the one w
your friends. Didn't they live with you in the beginning?"
slowly faded. He picked up a towel and wiped off his face.

"I'm sorry, Erik. I shouldn't have assumed . . . But it was t
to have them pound on our door, then barge in and search our
that way."

"Do you believe me now when I say you're in danger? If you had be
hiding them and you were caught, you'd go to prison!"

She looked away, closing her eyes. When she opened them again,
she saw the small table by the door where he always tossed his keys
and police badge when he came home. She also saw a brochure from
the Dutch Nazi Party with a swastika on the front and an exaggerated
caricature of a Jewish man with a hooked nose. To see it here, in Erik's
apartment, turned her stomach. She swallowed bile and looked up at
him again.

"I don't want to be on opposites sides of this war. Don't you have any
compassion at all for the Jewish people?"

"Yes, of course I do, but—"

"You're supposed to catch criminals, Erik. These are innocent people!"

"The Jews will all be together in the resettlement camps. It can't be
as bad there as everyone imagines."

"What if it's worse?"

Erik was silent for a moment. Then his gaze met hers. "I love
you, Ans. I want both of us to survive. I want a future with you. The
Americans are in this war now, and that gives us hope. In the meantime,
promise me you won't defy the Nazis or hide any Jews. It's either our
lives or theirs."

CHAPTER 29

The Gestapo returned to the town house two nights later, pounding on the door and ringing the doorbell at two o'clock in the morning. Ans leaped from her bed and ran up to the third floor, ducking through the little door to the attic. Avi and Miriam now slept there at night and were already climbing out the dormer window. Ans teetered across the joists to close it behind them and move the crate. She heard the baby whimpering from being awakened and Miriam soothing her. Ans glanced around to make sure the attic looked untouched, then raced downstairs again, praying they wouldn't see her emerging from the tiny attic door. The men were older than the first two and had no regard for the mess they left in their wake. They took longer, searching more thoroughly. They didn't find the Leopolds.

Ans huddled in the parlor with Eloise and Herman after the Gestapo left, sipping tea as they tried to calm down again. No one would be able to get back to sleep. Eloise stared at nothing the way she had on the night the Nazis invaded the Netherlands, only this was much worse. The Nazis had invaded her home, her bedroom.

The Gestapo returned a third night, in the pouring rain this time. Miriam and Avi were drenched and shivering by the time the men left, the baby wailing in distress.

The intrusion roused Eloise from her lethargy. "The Leopolds need a better hiding place," she said. "I'm not afraid for my own safety, but if the Gestapo keeps coming back, sooner or later we might make a mistake. Besides, that poor baby can't hide on the window ledge in the wintertime." If the Leopolds were discovered, Eloise would never recover from their loss.

"How do we go about finding a safer place to hide them?" Ans asked.

"Someone from the underground newspaper will know. We should start there. Every issue has called for greater action, more resistance. Surely they'll have contacts with a network of people. That's how the Resistance operated during the first war."

"It's worth a try," Ans said. "We already know we can trust them. But who can we ask?" Ans had been delivering Eloise's news reports and editorials to an unknown contact in a variety of meeting places, making a simple exchange. This month, it had been on the observatory grounds. Neither Ans nor Eloise knew who else was involved with the newspaper or where the underground press was located.

"Start with your regular contact person when you meet with them tomorrow."

Ans was waiting at the observatory the next day at the appointed time. "Listen," she said, after the exchange had been made. "I need help. My friends need to go into hiding."

"Are they Jewish?" she whispered.

Ans nodded. "The newspaper is calling for active resistance, so I know there are people who feel the same way I do, people who want to fight back. I assume you have contacts in the Resistance. Can you put me in touch with them?"

The woman glanced around as if afraid they'd already talked for too long. "I'm just a link in the chain. I don't know the answer. But I'll convey your message."

As the days passed, Ans longed to see Erik and explain her faith. They'd spoken on the telephone a few times, but he still worked at night and slept during the day, and she wanted to be with him in person when she shared her faith with him. "I love you, Ans," he said each time. She loved him, too, and needed him to understand why she made the choices she did.

After Ans's next meeting with her contact from the newspaper, she found this message inside the bag: "Go to the Hortus Botanicus on Sunday at one o'clock. Look at the plants. Someone will find you."

The enormous glass greenhouse at the botanical gardens was almost unbearably hot on the July afternoon when Ans arrived. She wandered around, gazing at the tropical plants, until a middle-aged man with wire-rimmed glasses approached her. He had fair hair and a bushy blond mustache and appeared unremarkable—an ordinary schoolteacher or bank clerk—and not at all how she pictured a Resistance fighter.

"Hello, my dear cousin!" he said, spreading his arms. "So wonderful to see you again!" He kissed both of her cheeks. "Now walk beside me," he said in a low voice. "We're admiring the plants. Call me Havik."

Ans's heart thudded in her chest as if trying to escape. She could see how his hawklike nose and alert eyes had earned him the code name Hawk. He strolled by her side for a few moments, giving her time to calm down. "I understand you're dating a policeman," he said at last. "A member of the NSB."

She halted, frightened by his knowledge of her private life. "How . . . how do you know that?"

"It's our business to know. That's why you deliver your articles to a contact and not to the newspaper. It's why you don't know where the printing press is."

"You don't trust me?"

"Spare me your outrage. Lives are at stake. They can't torture you into revealing our whereabouts if you don't know where we are. Or who we are. Keep walking." He tucked her hand into the crook of his elbow.

Few people had come to the greenhouse in the summer heat, but as Ans and Havik passed another couple, he murmured softly, pointing to plants and trees as if enjoying a leisurely afternoon. "Does your policeman friend know you're meeting me?" he asked when they were by themselves again. "And that your Jewish friends need to go into hiding?"

"He knows they're my friends and that I'm outraged by what the Nazis are doing to them—and what they're forcing him to do. But I told him my friends moved to Amsterdam. I didn't tell him I was contacting you."

"Good."

"But Erik isn't like them. He's just playing along with the Nazis. He joined the Nazi Party to keep his job."

"Then why didn't you ask him for help? Why didn't you tell him you needed to hide your friends?"

The question startled her. She didn't know why. And yet she did know.

"You aren't sure if you can trust him, are you?" Havik asked.

"I don't want to get Erik into trouble. He saved me after he caught me delivering your newspapers. He didn't turn me in."

"You've learned the first lesson of working with the Resistance—don't trust anyone."

"I'm trusting you."

Havik waited until another couple walked past. "Never forget, if we were able to follow you and learn all about you, then your boyfriend and his Nazi friends could too."

It frightened and enraged Ans to think that she was vulnerable. Then she thought of Miriam and Avi being hunted and pursued by the Nazis, and she put her own feelings aside.

"I would do anything to save my friends. Please tell me how I can do that."

"How many are there?"

"Three. Mir—"

"Stop. Don't tell me their names."

She let out her breath and started again. "They came to the Netherlands as refugees from Germany. My friend is a little older than me, married to a man from Berlin. They have a baby—"

"A baby!" Havik stopped walking. "How old?"

"She was one year old in March."

He shook his head. "It's very difficult to hide small children with their parents. Families are too conspicuous. Babies cry and give away hiding places. Alone, a child can pose as an orphan."

"I know. That's why we need to move them to a safer place. The Gestapo has searched our house three times. They haven't discovered my friends, but we're worried that the baby will cry at the wrong time or that our neighbors will hear her."

"You're wise not to trust your neighbors. Some of them notice too much. That's why we hide small children by themselves, ideally with families in small towns or out-of-the-way farms."

Ans immediately thought of her parents' farm. Elisheva would be safe there.

"Could either the mother or father pass for Dutch?" Havik asked before she could mention it.

Ans pictured their dark hair, the dark stubble on Avi's chin. "No. Neither of them could. They speak Dutch with a German accent."

"That's a problem." Havik appeared to be deep in thought. His expression didn't look hopeful.

"Can you help my friends? Will you help them?"

"Yes, yes, of course. The baby will be the hardest to place. I can find places for the parents, but not together." Ans's heart ached for them, forced to endure even more separation. And giving up Elisheva was unimaginable. "Many of our hiding places are fluid," he continued. "There are raids, informants; people get moved around and seldom stay in the same place for very long unless they're native Dutchmen and can pose as a maid or a distant cousin who has come to stay. By necessity, families get separated in the shuffle—a place for one here, for two there. Often, they're hidden for a while, then something puts them in danger and the cards are shuffled all over again. You understand?"

"I think so . . . and I may know a place for the baby. My parents own a farm in the country outside of Leiden. But we would need to invent a story to explain where the baby came from because everyone in their village knows each other's business."

"Would your family understand the risk and be willing to take it? They'll be arrested if they're caught hiding Jews."

Ans hesitated. Mama and Papa would gladly do it. She knew their unshakable faith. The question was, did she want to put her family at risk? Not just Mama and Papa, but Wim and Maaike too.

"I can go there and ask."

"No. Don't be seen traveling back and forth without a reason. Don't do anything to make their neighbors or your boyfriend suspicious."

"Erik cares about me. He's a good man—"

"Is he friends with this Jewish family as well?"

Ans looked away, shaking her head, remembering all the excuses Erik had given for why he couldn't meet them or eat at their apartment. "Erik never met them."

"Trust no one!" he said vehemently. They had circled the paths inside the greenhouse a second time and had come to the door leading out. Ans felt relieved as they stepped from the steamy mugginess. "When was the baby born?" he asked.

"March 7 of last year."

"Her name?"

"Elisheva. Her Dutch name is Elisabeth."

"You know the bridge over the Oude Vest near the Beestenmarkt?"

"Yes."

"Stand on the bridge one week from today at four o'clock, tossing bread to the swans."

"With my friends?"

"Just you. But bring their identification cards with you. Tell your friends to be ready to leave at a moment's notice. Do you have any cousins?" It seemed like an odd question.

"Yes. Several."

He kissed her cheek again. "I am one of them."

She watched Havik go, then walked back to the town house to tell her friends the hopeful, heartbreaking news.

CHAPTER 30

Miriam stood on a wobbling board in the center of the airless attic, as far as she could get from the walls of the adjoining town houses, and drew her bow across the strings of her violin. Avi had fashioned a mute that fit over the bridge of her instrument to help dampen the sound, but she still worried every time she played. But she had to play. The sound soothed Elisheva to sleep, and it helped Miriam feel alive and whole.

Elisheva was asleep on a blanket beside Avi, wearing only her diaper as he fanned her to cool the air. He loved hearing Miriam play too. Her music had drawn them together in the refugee camp and had comforted them along with the psalms Avi read aloud. He read sorrow-filled ones now, laments that asked the Almighty One *Why?* and *How long?* This afternoon, as they waited for Ans to return from her meeting with a Resistance contact, they had used a psalm as a prayer: *"Have mercy on me, my God, have mercy on me, for in you I take refuge. I will take refuge in the shadow of your wings until the disaster has passed."*

Miriam played Tchaikovsky's haunting theme, still grieving for Abba. "Why wouldn't he come with us?" she asked again and again.

"He couldn't have endured this," Avi explained after the Gestapo returned for yet another surprise raid. "He didn't want to ruin our chances for survival. I think your mother knew the same thing. I think that's why she didn't leave Cologne with you."

The air in the stifling attic made it difficult to breathe. She and Avi lived up here all the time now. The Gestapo came at random times, each unannounced visit heart-stopping. Professor Huizenga had installed a buzzer near the front door that rang in the attic to warn them when they needed to hide. So far, the heavy pounding on the door alerted them, but what if the Nazis decided to knock softly and catch them by surprise? Or if a nosy neighbor came?

Miriam couldn't remember the last time she'd slept soundly or had gone outside in the daylight and fresh air. How lovely it would be to walk along the canals again and sit beneath the trees. And how lovely it would be to feel warm sunlight on her face again. But Miriam and Avi were too frightened to even sit outside in the tiny backyard after dark, fearing the neighbors would see them, fearing the Gestapo would return. If they kept the attic window open, they could sometimes glimpse stars through the canopy of trees at night.

"We're not trying to get rid of you," Professor Huizenga had said when they'd made the decision to contact the Resistance. "But you need a better place to hide, a safer place. The Americans are still a long way from freeing Europe, and you can't live this way much longer." He didn't say it, but the Gestapo raids and the possibility of being discovered were taking a toll on everyone, especially Eloise.

Miriam had just begun playing the theme from Mendelssohn's violin concerto when she heard the attic door open and footsteps ascending the stairs. "I'm back," Ans said. "Come downstairs and I'll tell you and the Huizengas what I've learned."

"Is it good news?" Avi asked as he lifted the sleeping baby.

Ans exhaled. "It's hard news."

They gathered in the Huizengas' bedroom, a frilly, ethereal space that seemed to Miriam like something from a fairy tale. She had slept in a pretty bedroom like this in her grandmother's house in Cologne. She wondered if Elisheva would ever be able to sleep peacefully in a room of her own. Avi laid the baby on the bed and sat beside her, patting her gently so she wouldn't wake up. Miriam was too nervous to sit, ready to run at any moment to their attic hideaway.

Eloise sat in a chair by the window, the closed curtains ruffling gently in the warm breeze. She appeared calm today as she waited for Ans to tell them what she'd learned. Her moods seemed to swing wildly up and down, seldom settling in the middle, and she either raced around expending nervous energy and typing reports and editorials, or sat staring at nothing. Her husband and Ans knew how to keep her stable, but Miriam sometimes wondered if the war might drive all of them crazy.

"Tell us what you learned, Ans," Professor Huizenga said. "We're all hoping you have good news." He'd just returned from work and stood beside his wife, his hand caressing her shoulder. He no longer worked at the university. Even after the Nazis reopened it, the faculty and students had chosen to let its doors be closed for good rather than sign the loyalty oaths the Nazis demanded. "It's the first time Leiden University has closed since its founding in 1575," he'd told them. The professor's older brother, a banker, had offered Herman a job rather than allow the Nazis to send him to a work camp.

Ans seemed nervous as she prepared to explain what she'd learned. "The good news is that they're willing to find a safer hiding place for you. The Resistance will provide false ID cards for you without the *J*. But I'm sorry to say that the three of you can't stay together."

Miriam's lungs squeezed as if gripped by a giant fist.

"But surely Miriam and the baby can remain together, can't they?" Avi asked.

Ans shook her head. "I'm so sorry . . ."

Miriam sank down on the bed beside Avi, her thoughts whirling. "But . . . Elisheva is still nursing! She needs me!"

"I know; I know. But you and Avi will need to hide in out-of-the-way places, and you may be moved around a lot. The biggest obstacle to finding a permanent place is that you're not Dutch. Your accents give you away. Dutch Jews can hide as servants or evacuees, and they're familiar enough with this country to pass interrogation. But as soon as you speak, they'll know who you are."

"And the baby?" Miriam wheezed. "Where will she go?"

"I'm going to take her to my parents' farm, where she'll be safe. We all know how hard it's been to confine her and keep her quiet. She can't grow up properly if she's hidden away. The safest place for her is in the country-side. The Resistance can provide papers saying that she's an orphan."

Miriam moaned.

"I know it's going to be hard," Ans said, kneeling in front of her. "But my parents will raise her and love her like their own daughter until the war is over. They're wonderful people, and Elisheva will be safe there. She'll have plenty of food and milk to drink, and she can run and play outside with my sister, Maaike, in the sunshine and fresh air."

Miriam lowered her face into her hands and wept. Everything Ans said was true. But how could she leave her baby? And her husband? Avi wrapped his arms around her, rocking her. His body shook with his sobs. The room was silent for a few minutes, then Eloise spoke.

"Tell your Resistance contact that while Herman and I may not be able to hide Miriam and Avi, we could hide Dutch Jews posing as maids or a nurse."

"Yes, I'll tell him," Ans said.

The baby stirred and woke up, gazing around with a worried look as if wondering where she was. Miriam snatched her up and held her close. Avi thanked Ans, and they went back up to the sweltering attic with its dusty rafters and dangling cobwebs to be alone. Elisheva squirmed, wanting to free herself from Miriam's arms and crawl around. This was no place for her to grow up. "You and Elisheva are the only two people I have left," Miriam sobbed. "How can I leave my baby? How can I leave you?"

"I know; I know." Avi held her as she wept. "But they're right, Miriam. If we're apart, there's a better chance that one of us will survive. We can't let Elisheva grow up in constant fear this way. She isn't able to cry or run or play. She'll have a better life, a safer life, with Ans's family. And we'll know where to find her when this war is finally over."

"I don't think this war will ever be over. The Nazis are going to hunt us down until the day we die."

"But at least our daughter may live."

If she didn't let Elisheva go, she might lose her forever. If there was any chance at all that her daughter would survive, Miriam had to take it. She asked Eloise for paper and a pen and sat down in the office to write two letters. She could hear Avi's soft voice as he played with Elisheva in the hallway outside the room and her daughter's delighted laughter as she took toddling steps, clinging to her papa's hand.

Tears spotted the paper as Miriam wrote first to Ans's mother. When she finished, Miriam wrote a second letter to her daughter:

Darling Elisheva,

From the moment you were born, you've been our joy, our life. Saying goodbye and letting you go is the hardest thing I've ever had to do. But there is no other way for your father and me to save you. The only chance you'll have to be safe, to live, and to grow and become a woman someday is to release you into another mother's loving arms. You're much too young to understand these dark times and the painful choices we are forced to make. Many good, loving people are giving their lives to free the world from the evil that is causing our separation. People have risked their lives to save our family, and I pray that we can find a way to thank them.

If we meet each other again, dear Elisheva, the day will be as joyous as the day you were born. If we don't see each other again until the World to Come, please remember your father and me from the photographs in this album and know that we love you with our very life and with our every breath.

May God be with you, my beloved child.

Your loving mama

Miriam tucked the two letters inside her photograph album, planning to send it and her grandmother's silver candlesticks with Elisheva.

"Do you think God has abandoned us, Avi?"

"No, don't ever think that. See how He has provided for us through the Huizengas and Ans and her parents? Never doubt His goodness. And don't ever give up hope."

"I know I must be strong. And I will be." But the pain in her heart at the thought of leaving Avi and Elisheva was so great that she feared she would die from it. She took out her violin again and played the Tchaikovsky theme for them, hoping they would remember her whenever they heard violin music.

CHAPTER 31

Ans walked to the bridge near the Beestenmarkt at the appointed time, trying to stroll casually along the canal without glancing around or acting nervous. If she ran into Erik, she would have to lie and tell him Havik was her cousin. It seemed odd to her now that after dating for nearly three years, Erik had never asked about her family. There was no one waiting on the bridge, so she took the crusts of stale bread from her bag and tossed pieces into the canal below. A rush of squawks and feathers greeted her as the ducks fought over each morsel.

A few minutes passed before she saw Havik strolling from the direction of the train station with a bag over his shoulder as if out for a late-afternoon walk. Ans wished she could act as nonchalantly as he did and not let her nervousness show.

He smiled and kissed her cheeks. "Greetings, cousin!" Then they stood side by side, tossing stale bread over the railing.

"The child is now Elisabeth Jager from Noordwijk. Her mother died of consumption, and her father can't take care of her on his own after the coastal evacuations. He works for the railroad and travels often. I'll leave it to you to invent a connection to your family. Practice the story until it feels natural to tell it."

"I brought her parents' ID cards in my bag." They would exchange bags before they parted.

"I suggest you travel to your family's farm by train, as late in the day as possible so you'll arrive near curfew, when it's dark. Leave as soon as the curfew ends the next morning, from a different station, if possible. If you encounter anyone you know and they ask about the baby, can you lie convincingly?"

"Yes." She would do anything for Elisheva.

"I wish you and the child well."

"Thank you."

"We'll need a week to forge new ID cards for your friends. We already have a few possible hiding places for them in mind. A physician, Dr. Elzinga, will come to your town house with instructions."

"You know where we live?"

"Of course." The knowledge sent a shiver through her. It would take only one mistake, one slip from someone in the Resistance to expose her, the Huizengas, and the Leopolds to great danger. And soon she would put her parents at risk too. Ans wanted to believe that this was the source of Erik's concern for her, the reason why he'd begged her not to get involved. She refused to believe that the man she loved shared the Nazis' beliefs.

"The family I work for are willing to help others, as well. Two or three women could live there as servants or a live-in nurse. If the refugees are Dutch Jews, they could pose as relatives. Mrs. Huizenga is Belgian."

"Good. And are you willing to help as a courier?"

"What would I need to do?"

"People in hiding like your friends need to be fed, which means they need ration books. We acquire them by robbing post offices, but we need couriers to distribute them to the safe houses along with forged IDs. Are you willing?"

She had promised Erik not to deliver underground newspapers, but ration cards and fake IDs were different. And even more dangerous. Still, Ans didn't hesitate. "Yes, of course I'll help."

"Do you have a bicycle?"

"Yes."

"And courage?"

"I think so." Her heart hammered faster with each question.

"You may also need to travel by train to Den Haag or Utrecht or Amsterdam or one of the many small villages where people are hidden. If you're caught with a supply of false ID cards or ration books, you'll be arrested and sent to prison."

Ans remembered the injustice that had led to this work. *"What does the Lord require of you? To act justly and to love mercy and to walk humbly with your God."* "I understand," Ans said. "I still want to help."

"Good. We're grateful. The underground's work is growing, and we need to expand our network. When the Nazis recalled all of the Dutch military officers a few months ago, many of them went into hiding as *onderduikers*. We need trustworthy people who can offer hiding places."

"My grandfather has been telling his congregation to resist the Nazis. He knows which of his parishioners you can trust. I can speak with him."

"It would be better if we do it. How can we contact him?"

"I'll write it down for you."

"No. Just tell me. Never put names and addresses in writing where they might fall into the wrong hands. Can you lie? Or, more importantly, will you lie?"

"Yes."

"Take the child to your farm as soon as you can think of a plausible excuse to travel there. Her papers are in this bag."

"Should I call and let them know?"

"Never assume that a telephone is safe. I'll be in touch again."

Ans took Havik's bag and went home to tell Miriam and Avi the news.

CHAPTER 32

Elisheva was finally asleep in Miriam's arms. They'd given her a small dose of Eloise's sedative before wrapping her in a blanket for the trip to the farm. "It's time for me to go," Ans said. She thought her heart would break as Miriam gave a little sob and pulled Elisheva close to her heart one last time.

"I love you, my darling girl," she said before kissing her goodbye. Avi took his daughter from Miriam's arms and did the same, murmuring a prayer over her before laying the sleeping baby in her carriage for the walk to the train station. Tears streamed down his face.

Ans needed to leave the house quickly to avoid causing the Leopolds further pain. Professor Huizenga helped Ans maneuver the carriage through the front door. He and Eloise would go with Ans to the train station and bring the carriage home again. If the Gestapo raided the town house while the three of them were away, Avi and Miriam would hide on the ledge outside the attic window. Avi had added a handle to the outside of the window frame so he could close it behind them without Ans's help.

The walk to the station took fifteen minutes. Eloise pushed the carriage, and the professor carried the suitcase with Elisheva's clothes and a few of Ans's things for her overnight stay on the farm. The suitcase also contained the photograph album Miriam had brought from Cologne.

She had begged Ans to take it with her, saying, "Please keep this for Elisheva so she'll remember us. Tell her these silver candlesticks once belonged to my grandmother." If the Nazis saw the photographs, they would know in an instant that the owner was Jewish. Carrying it would be extremely dangerous. Yet Ans couldn't refuse Miriam's request.

They arrived on the platform only minutes before the train was scheduled to leave in order to decrease the chances of running into Erik. Eloise lifted the baby from the carriage and handed her to Ans. She felt heavy in her arms, the weight of her responsibility heavier still.

"Be careful," Eloise whispered. "Be safe. Don't take any unnecessary chances." She kissed Ans goodbye as if they were mother and daughter, and the professor handed her the suitcase.

Ans boarded quickly and took a seat. She felt enormous relief as the train steamed from the station without encountering any Nazi soldiers or Leiden police officers. It wasn't a long trip, but she would have to change to a different rail line along the way.

She made it safely to her first stop and waited on a bench in the station to transfer trains. Again, there were no Nazi soldiers in sight, and she boarded the second train without incident. She was almost home. But as the train pulled into an out-of-the-way station, Ans saw Nazi soldiers on the platform waiting to board. They entered one of the middle cars and moved in opposite directions, one going toward the front of the train, the other toward the rear, asking everyone for their identification card. Ans prayed that the train would depart quickly and that the soldiers would get off again. But when the whistle blew and the train lurched forward, the Nazis were still on board.

Ans couldn't act nervous. She needed to sound convincing. Her turn came and the soldier halted beside her seat. "ID card, *bitte*." She took it from her purse, hoping he wouldn't notice her trembling hand. He took an eternity to look it over, studying her face and comparing it to her photograph. Her heart froze when he pointed to the card, then to the baby.

"You are not married," he said in accented Dutch. "Who is child?"

Ans swallowed a knot of fear. "Her mother died of consumption, and her father can't take care of her. They were from Noordwijk, on the coast, and had to evacuate. I'm taking her to live with relatives."

He stared at her for so long she wondered if he'd understood her. Then he held out his hand again. "You show proof of this?"

Ans dug into her bag for Elisheva's birth certificate. Would he be able to tell that it was a forgery? Ans looked down at the baby's beautiful face as the soldier studied the papers for another eternity, praying as she never had before. At last he gave back the papers and moved on to the next passenger. Ans battled tears of relief as she thanked God.

The sun was low on the horizon when the train pulled into Ans's village. Havik had said it wasn't safe to telephone ahead, so she'd planned to walk to the manse and ask her grandfather to drive her to the farm. She climbed down from the train without waiting for a porter and hurried away from the station, struggling with the sleeping child and the awkward suitcase. Elisheva didn't wake up. Ans crossed the street, walking quickly, her head lowered, hoping she wouldn't meet anyone she knew. Her hope collapsed when she heard someone call her name.

"Ans? Ans de Vries, is that you?"

She wanted to keep going, pretending she hadn't heard. But she recognized the voice. The Van Dams lived in the house she'd just passed. Corrie van Dam had been her best friend in school. It would seem suspicious if she didn't say hello. She turned to Mrs. Van Dam, who was sweeping her front stoop in the fading twilight.

"Oh, hello, Mrs. Van Dam."

"I thought that was you! We haven't seen you in ages! How are you, Ans? Corrie was just saying the other day how much she missed her best friend."

The bag and the baby were growing heavy. Ans set down the suitcase and shifted Elisheva to her other arm. "It's been a while since I've been home. I work in Leiden now."

"Is this your baby? Your mother never told us you'd married."

"No, she isn't mine," Ans replied, trying her best to laugh. "Her mother died, and her father can't take care of her. We're hoping the fresh air on the farm will do her good."

"She's a relative of yours?"

Her heart thumped faster. She mustn't get trapped in a web of lies. Everyone in the village knew Mama and Papa and their relatives. "The baby's parents were friends of mine. I'm sorry, but I really can't talk right now, Mrs. Van Dam. I need to get out to the farm before curfew."

"I'll tell Corrie you're home. I know she'd love to see you."

"Yes. It's been ages."

Ans picked up the suitcase and hurried across the market square to the manse. As she neared the front door, she saw lights on behind the curtains and what looked like several people moving around inside. She set the suitcase down and shifted the baby to her shoulder. Opa had guests, and she needed to avoid meeting them. She was about to walk around to the back when the front door opened and one of the church elders stepped outside. He saw her before she had a chance to turn away.

"Hello, Ans. I didn't know you were back in town."

Her composure nearly shattered. He was one of the most unbending men in the church and had let his disapproval of Ans and her wayward behavior be known in the past. "I just arrived on the evening train." Her cheeks burned as if on fire. "I'm hoping Opa will drive me out to the farm before curfew."

"Is that your baby?"

"No, her mother died, and her father isn't able to care for her. He thought our farm would be a good place for her until he can."

The man had the grace to hold the door open for her and help with her suitcase. But three other elders stood just inside the door, preparing to leave. One of them, the village postmaster, was married to Mama's cousin, Truus. They'd all overheard what Ans said and were certain to tell their wives the big news. The prodigal daughter had returned home and was sneaking around in the dark of night—with a baby. She should have given more thought to how her arrival would look.

Ans moved into the parlor, where chairs had been gathered into a circle for the meeting. Opa looked surprised when he saw Ans, but he recovered quickly and came to her rescue, pretending not to be surprised at all.

"You made it. Come in, my child. Can I hold the baby for you? How was your trip?"

"Tiring," she said, laying Elisheva in his arms. "But at least she slept." He parted the blanket, smiling as he looked at the baby's face.

"I'll say good night to you gentlemen," Opa said, shooing them out the door. He was still cradling the baby. "It was a good meeting. We'll talk again." The moment he closed the door and turned to Ans, she burst into tears. He embraced her with his free arm and kissed the top of her head. "Come, let's sit down for a moment." He led her to the sofa and sat down beside her.

"I'm sorry. I'll need to be stronger if I'm going to do this work," Ans said between sobs. "And I'm sorry for surprising you this way. I didn't plan ahead for what I would do if you had company . . . and I ran into Mrs. Van Dam outside the train station and . . . and I wasn't prepared."

"Is the child Jewish?" he asked.

"How did you know?" She wiped her eyes on her sleeve.

"Because I know you, my dear girl. What's her name?"

"It's Elisabeth now. Her parents are my friends. The Nazis are rounding up all of the Jews in Amsterdam and Leiden and everywhere else and transporting them to resettlement camps."

"Yes, we've heard about it through the underground newspapers."

"My employers and I are helping to hide as many people as we can, but it's difficult to hide babies as young as Elisabeth. I'm hoping Mama and Papa will take care of her for us."

"She's beautiful," he said, gazing down at her.

"The thing is . . . I hated to put Mama and Papa in danger, yet I couldn't stand by and do nothing to help."

"Don't worry about your parents. The compassion you feel for this child—and your desire to do what's right—are things you learned from them. They won't hesitate to take her, in spite of the risks."

"But I'm putting Maaike and Wim in danger too."

"Every one of us is in danger as long as the Nazis remain in power. The only truly safe place to be is in God's hands."

Ans began to feel calm again as she listened to Opa's soothing voice.

For the first time since leaving Leiden, her heart wasn't flailing wildly as if trying to escape from her chest.

"I've had to tell so many lies, Opa, and I know what the Bible says about lying. Ever since I was Maaike's age, you've drilled into me how much God hates liars. But I'm working with the Resistance now, trying to save lives, and that means I have to lie all the time."

"Here, take her for a moment," he said, shifting the baby into Ans's arms. "I want to read you the verses from Proverbs that I used in last week's sermon." He stood and retrieved his Bible from the table, then sat beside her again, paging through it. The familiar rustling of the thin pages was somehow comforting. "Here's what it says, Ans—and it's a command: 'Rescue those being led away to death; hold back those staggering toward slaughter. If you say, "But we knew nothing about this," does not he who weighs the heart perceive it? Does not he who guards your life know it? Will he not repay everyone according to what they have done?' I believe God is on our side in this work we're doing. And you're certainly not alone in doing it."

"So it's okay to lie?"

"It's not. But the Jewish midwives lied to Pharaoh in order to save Jewish babies. Moses was one of those rescued children, and he led millions to freedom. There's a difference between lying to save yourself and for your selfish ends—to get yourself out of trouble or make yourself look good—and lying to save another person's life. A huge difference."

"The people I work with in the Resistance may be coming to see you. They need safe hiding places, and I told them you might be able to help. You know which people in the village to trust."

"Yes, of course I'll help. But now look at the time," he said as the mantel clock struck the hour. "I need to drive you out to the farm before curfew."

"It's already past curfew. Won't you get into trouble?"

"I'm allowed a little leeway as a pastor. Deaths and illnesses and other crises have no respect for curfews. But perhaps you'd better sleep at the farm tonight rather than risk coming back with me. Let me turn out these lights, and we'll go."

CHAPTER 33

Lena was reading Maaike a bedtime story when she heard a car coming up the road. She stopped reading, suddenly alert. It was after curfew. The car halted outside. The engine turned off. Two car doors slammed. "Who's here, Mama?" Maaike asked.

Not the Nazis. Please, not them. "I don't know. Your papa will see to them." She continued to read, hoping to finish the chapter quickly as voices drifted up from the kitchen. She recognized her father's voice and felt only slightly relieved. It would take something important to bring him out here this late. And then she heard another familiar voice.

Ans!

She closed the book and hurried downstairs, knowing that Maaike would surely follow her. Lena reached the bottom of the stairs, and there was her beautiful daughter, standing in the kitchen, holding a bundled baby in her arms.

"Ans! My goodness! What are you doing here?" Lena rushed to embrace her. Ans handed the baby to her grandfather and hurled herself into Lena's arms as if she might never let go. "Let me look at you!"

Lena said when they finally parted. Footsteps thundered down the steps as Maaike and Wim joined them.

"You're home!" Maaike cried. "You're finally home!"

"Hi, Ans," Wim said shyly.

"Wim! My favorite brother!" Ans replied. They all laughed and cried and embraced each other, then Lena remembered the baby. She was just waking up, stretching and yawning and rubbing her eyes as if she'd been asleep for a hundred years.

Lena reached out for her. "And who is this little one?"

"Her name is Elisabeth. Her mother died and she needs someone to take care of her."

"Well, hello, Elisabeth. Welcome to our farm." She had lovely dark eyes the color of chocolate and ebony hair that fell in soft curls around her face. She blinked as if wondering where she was, then smiled at Lena, revealing teeth like tiny pearls. Lena smiled in return. She had a thousand questions she wanted to ask, but they could wait until after the children were in bed.

"Let me see; let me see!" Maaike begged. Lena sat down on a kitchen chair, loosening the blanket and allowing Elisabeth to sit up and look around. "Hi, Elisabeth!" Maaike said. "We'll call you Bep, shall we? My friend is named Elisabeth and that's what she likes to be called." Maaike and the baby seemed intrigued with each other, holding hands and grinning.

"Are you hungry, Ans?" Lena asked.

"*Ja*. I didn't eat much before leaving. I was too worried about how the baby would manage the trip." Lena handed the baby back to Ans and let them visit with Maaike and Wim while she fixed something to eat. She made tea for Pieter and her father and warmed a pan of milk to put into one of the bottles Ans had brought.

"Now," Lena said when Wim and Maaike had been sent off to bed again. "Tell us about Elisabeth." She lay in Ans's arms, guzzling the bottle of milk.

"She's Jewish," Ans said softly. "She and her parents needed to go into hiding. The Nazis are rounding up all of the Jews in Leiden and deporting them. I hoped you'd be willing to take Elisheva."

"Yes, of course we will," Pieter said. "We'll help any way we can."

"The Dutch underground supplied a false birth certificate that says she's Elisabeth Jager from Noordwijk and that her mother died. Her father supposedly travels with the railroad. The certificate should be sufficient if the Nazis inspect her papers. I hesitated to put you in danger, and especially Wim and Maaike—"

"We're trusting God to keep them safe," Pieter said. "They don't know anything at all about our underground activities."

"We've prayed about it," Lena said, glancing at her father. "And we believe God is asking us to do whatever we can to fight against this evil. The baby's parents are welcome to hide here, too. Surely they'll want to be together." Lena could well imagine the grief Elisabeth's mother must have felt when she released her child into a stranger's arms. Only desperation could have torn one of Lena's children from her.

"It isn't safe for them to hide together. Elisabeth's parents are refugees from Germany and speak Dutch with an accent. The Resistance will find hiding places for them."

"Is it dangerous living in Leiden?" Lena asked. "Because you know you can always move back here with us." It was what Lena wanted with all her heart, just as Elisabeth's mother had wanted her child to be safe.

"I need to go back and help all the others, Mama. The Resistance is also hiding *onderduikers*—men who'd otherwise be sent to Nazi labor camps."

"Tell your contacts they can send people to us," Pieter said. "Your mother and I have built hiding places to store food, but we could easily hide people there too."

"And I know several trustworthy people in my congregation who'd be willing to help," Papa added.

"Thank you. I know they'll be grateful."

"We've formed a local group of resisters," Pieter said. "We've been stockpiling food and doing things to disrupt the Nazis any way we can. We're willing to do more if you tell us what needs to be done."

"Well, besides hiding places," Ans said, "they need a supply of ration cards to feed the people in hiding. The Resistance steals them when they're delivered to post offices each month. I know they're breaking one of the Ten Commandments, but—"

"We'll ask the Almighty for forgiveness," Papa said. "Jesus commanded us to love our neighbor, first and foremost. I think we can put underground work into that category."

The baby finished eating, and Ans passed her to Lena so they could grow used to each other. How Lena loved the feeling of her warm, wiggling weight in her arms, the scent of her soft hair and skin, the sweet babbling sounds she made. Lena loved being a mother and missed having children this age now that Maaike was in school. Yes, she and Bep would get along splendidly.

"Elisabeth's mother sent this photograph album," Ans said, pulling it from the suitcase. "They wanted Elisabeth to remember who they are if anything happens to them. She wrote you this letter, Mama. And one for Elisabeth to read in the future. But you'll need to keep the album hidden in case the Nazis search your house. The photographs will give away her Jewish identity."

"Do you think they might search here?"

"The Gestapo has come to the town house several times. That's why we had to find another place for the family to hide." The baby squirmed in Lena's arms, so she set her on the floor. She leaned against Lena's legs as she gazed around the kitchen. Ans handed the letter from Elisabeth's mother to Lena, and she unfolded the page to read it.

Dear Mrs. De Vries,

In giving you my daughter, I'm giving you part of my heart. For however long this war lasts, you'll be the one who will watch her grow and teach her to skip and run and sing. You'll brush her hair in the morning and hug her good night and dry her tears.

I pray that you will love her as if she is your own daughter and that she'll know comfort and security in your arms.

If God wills it, we will meet one day, and I will be able to thank you for protecting my little girl. If He wills otherwise, I ask that you tell her about her father and me, Avraham and Miriam Leopold, through these photographs. Tell her that her Hebrew name is Elisheva, and that it means "God's promise." Tell her how much we love her. And how very hard it was to let her go.

Gratefully,
Miriam Leopold

"What difficult decisions this war forces us to make," Lena said. She wiped her eyes and slipped the letter between the pages of the album. She knew this mother's pain and fear. Tomorrow she would have to release her own daughter. Ans would return to Leiden and put herself in danger by helping the Resistance. Until Lena held Ans in her arms again, her soul-deep fear for her wouldn't go away. How she hated the Nazis for what they were doing to her family.

"Pieter, you'll need to fetch Maaike's old crib from the attic," she told him. "Put it in our bedroom for now."

She padded the bed with feather pillows after scrubbing off the dust and cobwebs, using the work to keep her emotions under control. If she ever stopped working, she would surely fall apart.

The house quieted after Papa returned to the village and Pieter and Ans went to bed. But Bep couldn't seem to fall asleep in her strange surroundings and in a stranger's arms. She cried and cried for her mama as Lena walked through the downstairs rooms with her, and nothing Lena did could console her. "Poor little thing," she murmured as Bep pushed away the bottle of milk Lena offered her. "I'll bet your mama is weeping for you too."

Lena's tears fell along with Bep's as she paced through the darkened house, praying and pleading with God, desperate to feel His peace. How long would they have to endure this war, these painful separations, this agonizing uncertainty day after day? Would their lives ever be the same? *Have mercy, God. Have mercy on this child and on us all.*

When Lena ran out of tears, she began to sing, humming the melodies of her favorite hymns, finding consolation as the words flowed through her mind. She rocked little Bep in her arms as she sang, and at last, at last, the music soothed the exhausted baby to sleep.

Lena and Pieter were up before dawn to milk the cows and do their chores. Papa came back to drive Ans to the train station. Lena couldn't hide her tears as she hugged Ans goodbye. There was no way to know when they would see each other again.

Papa prayed for all of them before leaving. "Just remember," he added as he kissed Lena goodbye, "nothing any of us will ever face, now or in the future, is out of God's control."

It didn't take Lena long to get used to doing her chores with a baby riding on her hip again. Bep was curious about everything on the farm, and she stared in wonder at the squawking chickens and the huge black-and-white cows. Maaike loved having a living doll to dress and feed and play with. But Bep cried for her mama when she was tired or hungry, and it took Lena a long time to comfort her.

The baby went to church with them on Sunday, although Lena spent most of the service walking with her outside. Lena's friends swarmed around her afterwards, asking questions and saying what a beautiful child she was. Lena told them the story she'd rehearsed with Ans—Bep's mother had died, and her father traveled for the railroad and couldn't take care of her. They'd lost their home after the Nazis evacuated their neighborhood in Noordwijk.

At last the other parishioners left to eat their Sunday dinners. Lena was about to leave too, when she noticed her cousin lingering behind to talk with her. Truus pulled Lena aside, whispering as if what she had to say was top secret.

"I think you should know there are rumors all over town about your baby."

Lena's stomach did a slow turn. If people in town guessed that Bep was Jewish, Ans would have to find another hiding place. Lena watched Bep toddling near their truck, holding Maaike's hands. She already loved Bep's smile and her dark eyes and the soft black ringlets at the nape of her neck.

"I don't listen to rumors, Truus, and you shouldn't either."

"Well, in this case, maybe you should. It reflects badly on you and your family, so you'd better defend yourself for their sakes."

Lena's stomach rolled again. If someone informed the Nazis, they would take Bep away and send Lena and Pieter to prison for hiding her. Sad to say, Lena didn't know who to trust—or if her own cousin would keep her secret safe. "I don't understand, Truus. How can it reflect badly on my family to adopt a motherless child from Noordwijk?"

Truus leaned closer. "People are saying she's Ans's baby."

"What?" The accusation took Lena by surprise. Her heart pounded with outrage.

"Nettie van Dam saw Ans bringing her here late Friday night," Truus continued. "She said Ans acted very suspiciously. Nettie's husband is a church elder, and he saw Ans, too, as he was leaving the consistory meeting. So did my husband."

Lena didn't know how to reply to such a scandalous accusation. She was blushing, and she knew that her flushed cheeks made her appear guilty. It took her a moment to find her voice. "Yes, Ans brought her here . . . but . . . you mean . . . Nettie van Dam just assumed . . . ?"

"Everyone knows Ans is a willful girl. Nettie's daughter, Corrie, was Ans's best friend before she suddenly and mysteriously disappeared."

"It isn't a mystery! Ans works for a college professor and his wife in Leiden!"

"Don't get mad at me, Lena. I'm just telling you what Nettie said. We all remember how Ans refused to come to church before she moved away. And she hasn't been home for how long, now? A year or more? If you don't want this gossip to spread, you need to speak up right away and quell the rumors."

"I've already told everyone about Bep's parents," she said in a tight voice. "Ans brought her here because she was friends with them. If that explanation isn't enough . . . !" She was too furious to finish. She turned away from Truus and watched her children playing as she struggled to control her temper. Maaike was enraptured with Bep and was like a fussy little mother. Wim proudly stood guard, ignoring his friend who called to him to play. Should Lena defend her honor and pride with the truth and endanger this baby? Or was she willing to sacrifice her reputation to save a Jewish baby's life? "People will believe whatever they choose to believe," she finally said. "If they want to accuse my daughter, they should have the decency to do it to my face."

Truus glanced all around as if someone might be listening, then lowered her voice again. "Lena, we've known each other all our lives. We're family. You know I would never betray your secrets. You can trust me with the truth."

Lena turned back to her. "Are you asking me if it's true? You think Bep is Ans's daughter?"

Truus shrugged as if to say, *Yes, why not?*

Lena hesitated. Bep would be safer if Truus and everyone else in town believed the rumor. The orphan story sounded too convenient and a bit suspicious. Yet Lena's instinct was to protect Ans's reputation. Yes, she'd been rebellious in earlier years, but Ans was strong and beautiful and kind and good. She'd risked her life to bring Bep here and to help her Jewish parents. She was risking her life every day by working with the Resistance. Ans would gladly sacrifice her reputation for this beautiful child. And as difficult as it would be, Lena knew she would have to sacrifice her own reputation as well. She would become the mother whose scandalous daughter had brought home an illegitimate baby for her to raise.

"You can't tell anyone, Truus," Lena said quietly.

Truus's eyes grew wide. "So she *is* Ans's baby?"

"Bep is our daughter now. Pieter and I will raise her as our own."

꧁❦꧂

Lena and Pieter were about to go upstairs to bed a week after Bep's arrival when there was a soft knock on the kitchen door. They looked at each other. "Are you expecting anyone?" she whispered. Pieter shook his head. Lena scrambled to her feet and raced upstairs to make sure all the children were asleep. She heard the door squeal open, but she didn't hear any voices. When she was certain that none of the children were awake, she crept downstairs again to the kitchen. Pieter was talking with a man, their voices so low she couldn't hear what they were saying. One of the stairs creaked, and when Pieter saw her, he motioned for her to come closer.

"This is Wolf," he told her. "He works with Ans's network." Wolf was in his midtwenties, dark-haired and thin. He looked more suited to sitting in a student café and discussing philosophy than to being a soldier with the Dutch Resistance.

"We need hiding places for Jews and *onderduikers*," he said simply. "I understand you're willing to help."

"We're willing," Pieter said.

"Do you know the risks?" He looked at Lena when he asked the question. "To you and your family?"

Lena's heart sped up. She wanted to protect her family and keep them safe, not put them in danger. Once again, fear and faith waged war in her heart. Fear warned her not to defy the Nazis and risk imprisonment or death, while faith encouraged her to stand against evil and hide these people. It had been faith that gave her the courage to shelter Bep, and if Lena's faith was real, then it must win this struggle. Yet she couldn't deny the sickening dread that lay coiled in her heart at the thought of her loved ones in Nazi hands.

Then she thought of Bep's mother. Miriam Leopold had placed her daughter in Lena's hands, releasing her and trusting Lena to care for her child. Lena must do the same with her children. She must place them in God's hands, trusting Him to protect them.

"Yes, we understand the risks," Lena said. "We believe this is what God is asking us to do."

"I'll start sending them to you in a few days. And if anyone sees me coming and going to your farm, tell them I'm Elisabeth's father. I work for the railroad."

"My father is willing to help too," Lena said. "Did you talk to him? He's the village dominie."

"I will. But it's safer not to reveal any details about the workings of the underground. The Gestapo is ruthless in their use of torture to learn our secrets. That's why we never use real names or reveal the scope of our network. Your father will know nothing about what you're doing. And we'll advise him not to tell you about his involvement."

After Wolf left, Lena needed the reassurance of Pieter's arms around her. She leaned her head against his chest, comforted by the steady thumping of his heart.

"I won't say that I'm not afraid," she told him, "because I am."

"Remember why we're doing this, Lena, why we're taking risks and putting ourselves and our family in danger. Know in your heart that this is what God is asking us to do."

"I've been a Christian all my life, and I've wanted to serve Christ. But I never imagined it would mean this. I love my life here on the farm with you. I love being a mother and raising our children. But the war has turned our lives upside down."

"They're not upside down, Lena. They're growing outward. God gave us this farm and the work that we both love to do, and now He wants us to offer it back to Him."

"You're right; you're right. But you may need to remind me from time to time. I've never had to lean on God so hard before."

Lena covered Bep with a blanket before climbing into bed beside Pieter. As much as she longed for the world to be different, she had to believe that God knew the bigger picture of what He wanted to accomplish. And she had to believe that she and Pieter and the people she loved all had a part to play in what He was doing.

CHAPTER 34

The Gestapo returned to search Eloise's town house just before dawn. "They're never going to leave us alone and stop looking for us, are they?" Miriam whispered to Avi as they huddled outside on the ledge. He held her tighter in reply. Insects buzzed in the warm August night, and a smoky half-moon shone through the rustling treetops. It should have been lovely, but Miriam no longer saw beauty in a world gone mad.

Elisheva was safe on the farm, for now. Miriam was relieved when Ans returned, reporting that all had gone well. "She'll be safe with my parents. She can be a happy child there." Miriam tried to picture her daughter playing outside in the fresh air, feeling the breeze ruffle her hair and laughing as clouds, like fluffy sheep, drifted across the sky above her head. But Miriam's arms ached with longing for her daughter. How long would it be until she could hold her again? Would Elisheva even remember her?

Miriam was practicing her muted violin the following afternoon when Ans came up the attic stairs to speak with her and Avi. Her face was red with exertion, her hair sweaty.

"I just returned from meeting with my contact, and I have news to share. Come down to the office where it's a little cooler." Her somber expression warned Miriam that the news would be difficult to hear. She held tightly to Avi's hand as they went downstairs.

"They've found hiding places for both of you," Ans said. "Here are your new ID cards with your new names." Avi was now Andries Bakker. Miriam was Christina Bos. "Someone is coming for Avi this afternoon, and—"

"This afternoon!" Miriam cried. "That's too soon! I'm not ready! I can't say goodbye again after just losing Elisheva! I can't!"

Avi drew her into his arms. There was still so much she wanted to say to him. A few short hours weren't long enough to tell him how much she loved him and how much his love meant to her.

"I know, Miriam. I know," he murmured. "But the Almighty One brought us together in the refugee camp, and He brought me here to you after the invasion. If it's His will, He'll bring us together again when this war finally ends."

But what if it isn't His will? She was afraid to ask that question.

Avi released her, and she saw him struggling to compose himself. "What do I need to do?" he asked.

"Someone from the underground will come to our back door, posing as a repairman," Ans said. "You need to pack a bag, a winter coat if you have one, and be ready to leave with him. Someone will come for Miriam tomorrow at ten o'clock."

After all of the endless hours in the attic, time was passing too quickly now. Miriam lay beside Avi on the bed they'd shared after their wedding, trying to say all the things they wanted each other to remember. Her heart felt as if she were keeping watch beside a deathbed. This was really happening. Avi was really leaving today. Who knew how long it would be until they could sleep beside each other again?

Much too soon, Ans knocked on their door. "He's here, Avi. I'm sorry."

Avi took Miriam's hands in his to pray one last time, fighting his tears. "We place our lives in Your hands, Almighty God. We entrust our future to You. You brought us together in the beginning, and now You are separating us. We pray that it be Your will to unite us with each other and with our daughter, Elisheva, once again."

The man waiting in the kitchen wore coveralls. He had unstrapped a large toolbox from his bicycle and carried it inside as if making repairs. A second bicycle had mysteriously appeared on the back stoop. The man gave Avi coveralls like his to wear and a hat to cover his hair. He put Avi's clothes and belongings inside the toolbox and an extra rucksack. Miriam felt as if she stood at a great distance, watching everything happen to someone else, not to the man she loved.

"Ready?" the repairman asked.

Avi nodded. Tears filled his eyes as he pulled Miriam into his arms one last time. "I want you to live, Miriam! Live! Do whatever you need to do to stay alive, and I will too. We must believe that we'll be together again when this is all over."

"I love you, Avi."

"I love you too." He kissed her. The door closed behind him. Miriam couldn't bear to go to the kitchen window to watch him ride away. They'd wrenched her heart away when they'd taken Elisheva. Now her soul was gone as well.

She walked upstairs to the attic as if in a dream. She was alone. Alone. All of the people she loved most in the world were gone. She took her muted violin from the case and began to play, weeping tears of grief through the music, tears she could no longer shed.

A long time later, Miriam heard footsteps on the wooden stairs. Eloise and Ans both joined her, carrying a tray of food. "You missed supper," Eloise said. "We brought you something to eat."

"Thank you. That was nice of you." Miriam didn't tell them she was too heartsick to eat. She hoped they would leave again. But Eloise sat down on the dilapidated trunk with a sigh. She was an elegant, delicate woman and looked out of place in the dreary attic, like a priceless jewel in an ugly wooden box.

"Miriam," she said softly. "I know how you feel. I know. And I won't lie and tell you that it will get better, and that you'll find a way to go on, because right now you probably don't want to go on."

Miriam looked away, staring at the dormer window that had been her family's only door of escape these past few weeks. She knew Eloise's story. She knew how much her friend had lost in the first war and the toll it had taken on her mind and her health. If anyone understood Miriam's losses, it was Eloise.

"I hate them!" Miriam said. "They've taken everything from me. My home in Cologne, the life I had there, my mother and aunts and uncles and cousins. Then they took my home and my family away for a second time when they took Abba. Now they've separated me from my daughter and my husband. They're even taking my name. I have nothing left. Nothing."

"I understand," Eloise said. Miriam looked into her eyes as if into her soul and knew that she truly did. "Don't escape into the darkness like I did, Miriam. Don't let them do that to you. The darkness isn't an escape; it's the pit of hell. Don't believe the voice that whispers that ending your life is the only way out."

Alone in the attic that night, Miriam longed to fall asleep and never wake up. But her mind refused to shut down, replaying every wonderful moment she'd spent with Avi and Elisheva. She stayed awake, afraid to allow those memories to fade. Tomorrow she would begin a new life all over again. She would stay alive as Avi had begged her to do. She would live one day at a time.

At ten o'clock the next morning, a man arrived at the front door carrying a medical bag. Ans showed him into the front room, where Miriam waited with Eloise. "Good morning, I'm Dr. Elzinga. And you must be Christina Bos."

It took her a moment to react to her new name. "Yes. Yes, I am."

"I'm here to take you to a safe house, Christina. I've been allowed to keep my car, you see, so I can care for my patients. I can travel relatively freely." Miriam heard his words but barely comprehended them. He pulled a folded white dress and cap from his bag and handed them to her. "This nurse's uniform is for you. Go ahead and put it on. I'll stay for a while as if I'm attending a patient, then we'll leave together."

The mumble of voices faded behind Miriam as she carried the uniform upstairs to change. It was too baggy, but she supposed it didn't matter. The cap felt strange on her short hair. She fetched the suitcase she'd packed and ran her hand across the smooth wood of her violin case for a final time, as if caressing a loved one's face. It would be ridiculous to bring the instrument into hiding.

She started to leave, then turned back, unable to leave her violin behind. It was the last piece of her life that still remained, and she would cling to it, whether she'd be able to play it or not. She dumped some of her clothing out of the suitcase and put in the bow and violin, wrapping a sweater around it to protect it.

"If people need to be moved, I'm often the one who transports them," Dr. Elzinga was saying when Miriam returned to the parlor.

"We're very willing to house new guests," Eloise replied.

Miriam felt the slow thudding of her heart when it was time to say goodbye. Eloise hugged her fiercely. "I know I'll see you again," she said. "You're a strong woman, dear Miriam."

Ans was trying to be brave but couldn't stop weeping. "You'll be in my prayers every single day," she said as she hugged her.

Miriam didn't cry. Or perhaps she couldn't cry. She felt strangely dead inside as she closed the door and walked away from the friends she loved. It seemed strange to be outside on a hot summer day, hearing sounds that had been muted in her attic shelter and feeling the sun on her skin. She resisted the urge to run to the doctor's car for safety and looked back only once as they drove away, memorizing the house and the friends who lived there.

Leiden's canals and buildings and bridges moved past her window as if she were watching a film. The Molen de Valk towered in the distance. She remembered how pretty and picturesque the city seemed when she'd first arrived here with Papa—before the Nazis defiled it with their swastikas and their hatred.

"Are you all right, Christina?" the doctor asked. He kept glancing at her as he drove as if worried that she would break down.

"I'm fine." Her eyes remained dry. Every part of her felt numb. Her heart had begun to die the day Ans took Elisheva away. And when she and Avi crouched on the ledge outside the window that night, hiding from the Gestapo, a deadening paralysis had spread slowly through her. It reached her heart the moment she'd kissed Avi goodbye. Miriam had stopped feeling. Now it was pure survival. She must stay alert, stay alive, so they would all be together again.

"I don't know how long you'll be able to stay with the Ver Beeks," Dr. Elzinga said. "They're eager to help, feeling that it's their Christian duty, but you're the first person they've hidden and they're nervous about making a mistake. We have no idea how nosy their neighbors are. Be warned that you may need to be moved several times."

"It doesn't matter," she said. The fewer attachments she made, the less pain she would feel at their loss.

"We hope to get you out of Leiden altogether and away from the larger cities, where the Nazis are more active." They crossed the bridge over the canal, the tires humming, and left the old city, passing the train station, where Nazi soldiers strolled the platform. Miriam turned away so she wouldn't have to see them.

Twenty minutes later, the car pulled up to a tidy brick home, nestled close to its neighbors in a row of similar houses lining the narrow street. It seemed cheerful and welcoming with colorful flowers beneath a large bay window and pretty lace curtains. Miriam gazed up at the blue sky as they waited for Mrs. Ver Beek to answer the door, wondering if it would be her last glimpse of it for a while.

The Ver Beeks were a quiet, plainspoken couple in their fifties who lived a simple, hardworking life without frills or frivolity. They welcomed Miriam into their home as if she were a guest, not a fugitive, giving her a bedroom on the second floor across from theirs and inviting her to eat with them at their round kitchen table. They bowed their heads to thank the Lord for their food before eating and read from the

Bible each evening when they finished. Miriam would only need to hide when someone came to the door.

"As long as you don't go outside, Christina, and you stay away from the windows, no one will know you're here," Mr. Ver Beek said. Miriam wasn't sure if he meant the Nazis or nosy neighbors. She helped cook and clean and wash their clothes, but Mrs. Ver Beek was a reserved woman who seemed content to work in silence and not ask questions, which was fine with Miriam. Evenings were spent reading or listening to the radio.

"I'm mindful each moment of the day that you're risking your lives for me," she told the Ver Beeks after supper one evening. "I will always be grateful to you." She hoped her words conveyed her sincerity, spoken in her accented Dutch.

Mrs. Ver Beek's reply was matter-of-fact. "I'm sure you would do the same for us."

Miriam had nothing to do during the day when Mr. Ver Beek was away at his job as a school janitor and Mrs. Ver Beek was busy at her church. Miriam longed to play her violin but knew it was impossible. Instead, she would take the instrument from its wrappings and close her eyes, fingering the silent strings and practicing the bowings without making a sound. She silently rehearsed the Tchaikovsky concerto and the Mendelssohn piece, melodies that Elisheva and Avi had loved, then composed imaginary letters to them, telling them about her days and asking if they were safe and happy. Each night before falling asleep, Miriam cradled a pillow in her arms, pretending it was Elisheva and that she was singing her to sleep. She imagined Ans's mother holding her at this very moment and singing the same song to her before tucking her into bed. Those thoughts were the only things that kept the darkness, which Eloise had warned about, from closing in.

CHAPTER 35

Ans held Erik's hand as they crossed the bridge over the Witte Singel and made their way to Van der Werff Park. Swift-moving clouds blew across the afternoon sky, erasing patches of blue the color of Erik's eyes. A damp breeze from the Noordzee promised rain, but Ans didn't care if she got soaking wet, as long as Erik was beside her again. "It seems like our times together are becoming very scarce," she said as she sat down beside him on a bench.

"It's not by my choice. I would be with you every day if circumstances allowed." His arm tightened around her shoulder, anchoring her to him as if he feared she would float away. The last time she'd seen Erik, she'd left without kissing him goodbye, and she had regretted it. Loving someone was so wonderful and yet so difficult.

Ans had asked Erik for a chance to explain what her faith meant to her and why she needed to fight the Nazis and help her Jewish friends. And now here they were.

Ans had become even more involved with the underground, meeting regularly with Havik, delivering false ID cards and stolen ration books. She'd helped Miriam and Avi hide in the town house attic and had carried Elisheva to the farm past terrifying Nazi soldiers. Any one of those actions could have gotten her arrested, imprisoned, or shot. But she wouldn't stop doing this work, even if it meant losing the man she loved. Miriam said Avi had assured her that the Nazis couldn't destroy their love, but maybe he was wrong. Weren't they coming between Ans and Erik, sabotaging their love for each other?

"Life under the Nazis is becoming unbearable," Ans said after searching for a place to begin. "I hate that they're pulling us apart. You're working for them, and I . . . I'm working against them."

She paused, fearing his reaction. Havik had warned her not to trust anyone, and now that she'd told Erik the blunt truth, she wondered if he would feel it was his duty to report her.

When he didn't respond, she dismissed the thought, trusting his love. "I don't think either of us is going to change our mind, are we? You aren't going to stop . . . and neither am I." She looked at him, waiting for his reply.

He gazed forward at the canal, shaking his head. "I'm in too deep," he said. "They'll never let me leave." And he would never be allowed to quit the NSB. She remembered the disgusting Nazi propaganda she'd seen in his apartment. The Dutch Nazi Party held rallies around the country, and the thought of Erik participating in one of them made her sick to her stomach.

She swallowed hard, struggling to speak the next words. "Then we have to decide what we're going to do. Should we keep seeing each other even though we're on opposite sides, or say goodbye?"

"No," he groaned. "I don't want to say goodbye. You're the only person who makes my life bearable. I need you, Ans. I need your goodness and your love to make up for all the things I'm forced to see and do every day."

"Would it help if you talked to me about it?" She knew how much she longed to unload the burden she was carrying.

"I can't talk about my work."

"Because you aren't allowed to or because it's too hard?"

"Both." They sat in silence watching a duck waddle out of the canal, shaking its feathers. Erik gently caressed her shoulder, giving her comfort.

She lifted his other hand to her lips and kissed it. "I don't want to lose you, Erik. But I can't stop doing my work."

"Ans, please . . . how can I make you understand how dangerous—?"

"I know how dangerous it is. But I'm a Christian, and my faith compels me to fight against evil."

Erik wouldn't know what she meant because he didn't know Jesus. But maybe that was why she needed to stay with him, so she could share her faith with him. She swiveled on the bench to face him. "Erik, you know that what the Nazis are doing is wrong. You know it."

"Yes, but please don't talk about it in public," he said in a low voice. "You might be overheard."

"And then what? What would happen if someone overheard me?"

"I can't speak of the things they would do."

"That's exactly what I'm talking about! They're evil! The whole point of my faith, the whole point of why God sent His Son, is to destroy evil and rescue mankind. I have to do the same. Any goodness you see in me is only because of Christ."

Erik tilted his head back and gazed up as if searching for words written in the sky. "It's very hard for me to understand your . . . zeal," he said when he looked at her again. "I've seen Christianity only as an outsider, and I have to say that what you are *compelled* to do seems . . . extreme. And foolhardy." He searched her face, perhaps afraid he'd been too blunt.

"It didn't make much sense to me, either, even though my parents and grandparents are Christians. I grew up going to church and hearing my papa read from the Bible after our meals, but it didn't seem to have any connection with my life. Attending services twice every Sunday didn't make any difference in people's lives, as far as I could tell, so why suffer through them? I left home and came to Leiden because I thought there must be more to life than what I'd seen so far. Then the war started, and for the first time I saw that real evil exists in this world."

"But it always has existed. I see it every day as a policeman. We arrest the criminals if we can, but it's a drop in the sea. What can you and I do to stop evil when it's all over the world?"

"We can fight it. Work to destroy it. Listen, not many soldiers on either side of this war really want to go into battle and risk their lives. But they do it because they believe in the cause they're fighting for. Nazi soldiers fight because they believe in the Third Reich. Allied soldiers fight because they believe in freedom and liberty."

"You aren't a soldier, Ans."

"As a Christian, I'm supposed to be. I go into this battle and risk my life because Jesus gave His life for me. He told us to love each other the way He loved us, which means giving our lives for one another."

"And what good will that do?" He was growing agitated, losing patience. "We can't defeat them. They're too powerful!"

"Jesus said that when we put others ahead of ourselves, the world will see God's love through us."

Erik didn't reply. She wondered what he was thinking. Ans knew she couldn't expect him to grasp so quickly what had taken her years to finally understand. She needed to be patient and give him time. "I love you, Erik," she said. She hoped, for now, that he understood that much.

"And I love you. More than I can ever say with words. I want to shelter you and protect you. I can't bear the thought of anything happening to you."

"I know. But when we're apart, you can trust the God I serve to take care of me."

He drew a deep breath, then sighed and said, "All right." After looking around to see if anyone was watching, he took Ans's face in his hands and kissed her, tenderly at first, then passionately. "Let's just be together and hold each other as often as we can," he murmured when he finished, "so we can forget about everything else for just a little while."

⁓⁓⁓

Two days later, Ans met with Havik outside a pharmacy on Rapenburg Street. They greeted each other as if they had met by chance, then bent their heads together. "Tell Professor Huizenga to go to the train station at 5:10 tomorrow afternoon to meet his 'relatives,' Max and Ina Huizenga. Their cover story is that they were forced to evacuate from Scheveningen."

"How will he recognize them?"

"Max will wear a white boutonniere. Are you still dating your policeman?" The abrupt change in subjects made her pause.

"Yes . . . Yes, we love each other, and—"

"Make sure you tell him that you have refugees from the coast staying with you. We need these people to hide in plain sight, and if you act like you're keeping secrets from him, it will arouse his suspicions."

Ans wanted to repeat that Erik loved her and that she trusted him with her secrets, but she remained silent.

"I understand you're in need of a new housekeeper and a cook," Havik continued as strangers passed them on the street.

"Eloise let her last cook and housekeeper go when our Jewish friends needed to be hidden. We had no idea if they could be trusted."

"You'll receive a new live-in cook and housekeeper in a day or two. I trust you have room for these assistants?"

Ans nodded. "But what if the Gestapo returns to search the town house? They're still looking for our Jewish friends."

"Everyone under your roof will have a regular Dutch ID card. They'll all have legitimate reasons for living there. And now I need to go. We've talked too long."

Eloise and the professor went to the train station the next day to meet their new relatives from Scheveningen. Ans stayed home to cook dinner so it would be ready when they arrived. She'd been doing all the cooking with only a little help from Eloise and was getting tired of it. The Huizengas were probably getting tired of her farm-style soups and stews too. She hoped the new cook that Havik sent really did know how to cook.

"My cousin Max is going to need a place to do his work," Professor Huizenga told them over dinner. "He was a skilled draftsman before the

Nazis fired him for being Jewish, and his skills are now being put to use altering identification cards. He tells me he's very good at signatures."

"Especially Nazi ones," Max said. He and the professor exchanged smiles. Ina and Max were in their late sixties and seemed devoted to each other. Their only son and his family had fled to England before the war, and it had been nearly two years since they'd heard from them.

"Won't Max's work need to be hidden?" Eloise asked. Ans thought she seemed distant from the couple as they ate dinner together, almost as if she was reluctant to get to know them and grow fond of them.

"Naturally," her husband replied. "We'll take a tour of the house after dinner and see about finding a secure place where he can work."

In the end, Max decided to set up his work space in the attic. The buzzer to warn of a Gestapo raid was still in place. The dormer window offered light, and the wooden crate would hide his forgery tools and serve as a desk. Ans taught him how to walk on the narrow rafters as Miriam and Avi had done. As displaced relatives of Professor Huizenga, Max and Ina could settle into one of the third-floor bedrooms, hiding in plain sight. The town house curtains could be opened during the day again.

Ans brought blank identity cards to Max, stolen by the Resistance from various government offices. She traveled by bicycle or train to deliver the newly forged cards to her underground contacts in Amsterdam and Den Haag.

Not long after Max and Ina moved in, the town house's new cook and housekeeper arrived. Sientje and Meta were Jewish sisters-in-law in their early fifties from Amsterdam. Their husbands, who were brothers, had been partners in a small accounting firm and had paid to safely smuggle all of their adult children across the border into Switzerland. The women had gone into hiding just before the first roundups began in Amsterdam and now hoped that their husbands had also found safe refuge. Sientje and Meta gladly agreed to share the servants' quarters behind the town house's kitchen and to take over the cooking and cleaning duties. All of the newcomers seemed to settle in very well.

Ans was preparing to leave to fetch a new batch of stolen ration cards a few days later when she noticed that Eloise hadn't joined the others for breakfast. The professor had left earlier for his job at the bank, so Ans went looking for her. She found her sitting in her sumptuous bedroom, rocking in place and staring out the window. Ans had seen Eloise this way before and knew it meant the beginning of a downward spiral into depression. Ans crossed the room and knelt on the floor beside her. "Talk to me, Eloise."

She didn't reply.

"I know you must be tired after working so hard to get everyone settled. They're going to be safe here. Max is able to do his work, and it's going to make a difference in so many people's lives. You're doing it, Eloise. You're fighting back like you wanted to do."

Eloise still didn't reply as she rocked in place, her elegant hands clenched into fists.

"Won't you tell me what's wrong?"

"We're losing the war," she said, still gazing through the window.

"No, we're not. The Americans have joined the Allies, like they did in the first war."

"I'm going to lose everyone I love again. Miriam and Avi and their baby . . . they're gone. They were like family to me, and they're gone."

"Eloise, listen—"

"You need to leave me too. Aren't you supposed to go meet your contact now?"

"Yes, but I'll be back as soon as I can. And I'll be safe." Even as she said the words, Ans knew she was making a promise she couldn't keep. "Why don't you take some of your medicine before I go?" Ans hated to suggest it, knowing that the drug would put Eloise to sleep and cause the brilliant, vibrant, animated woman she knew and loved to disappear. But at least she wouldn't harm herself.

"Yes . . . perhaps I should take it now. I would like to go to sleep." *And never wake up.* Eloise didn't say the words, but Ans knew she was thinking them.

CHAPTER 36

MARCH 1943

The doll had been an extravagance, but well worth it. "Oh, Mama! Pretty!" Bep had exclaimed when she'd torn away the wrappings to see her birthday present. "Look, Papa! Look, Opa!" She circled the kitchen table showing off her doll and collecting birthday kisses along the way.

According to her birth certificate, Bep was two years old on this wintry March day. Lena had been raising rabbits this winter, hiding them from the Nazis, and had sold three of them in town to pay for the doll. Seeing the joy it brought this child she now thought of as her daughter made Lena glad for the sacrifice, even if it meant less meat in their soup this month. Maaike had sewn a tiny coat for the doll from an old blanket, and Wim had carved a pair of little wooden shoes for her. Papa had saved up enough sugar from his rations for Lena to bake a small cake.

Bep was still hugging her doll as Lena tucked her into bed that night beside her big sister, their tummies full of cinnamon cake. Bep had outgrown her crib and had moved into Maaike's bed, where Ans used to sleep. Friends from church had loaned Lena clothes as Bep had grown from a baby into a toddler, and Lena had cut down and resewn some of Maaike's clothes as well, including a warm winter coat.

"Everyone in bed?" Pieter asked when Lena returned to the kitchen.

"All tucked in. What time will your friends get here?"

"Not for another hour."

"Did you take the rest of the soup out to the barn? Will it be enough for everyone?"

"I think so. We have fewer *onderduikers* this month than in February."

"So I won't need to make such a large pot next time?"

"Likely not."

Lena fetched dried kidney beans from the root cellar, rinsed them, then put them in a bowl to soak overnight. For the past few months, her barn and windmill had housed dozens of furloughed officers from the Dutch army who had gone into hiding after the Nazis redrafted them in January. Only a tiny percentage of them had shown up to register, while the rest had become *onderduikers* along with the thousands of students who had gone under after so many of the universities in the Netherlands had closed.

"Where can all of these men possibly hide?" Lena had asked when the registration had been announced. "Our country is so small and so flat. And it's not like they can escape across any of our borders."

"Heaven knows," Pieter had replied. Now he added more wood to the kitchen stove while they waited for the rest of his small Resistance cell to arrive. With the beans soaking, Lena sat down beside the kerosene lamp to do the mending. The Nazis had imposed rationing on gas and electricity, making it difficult to do chores after dark without using their precious supplies of kerosene.

"One of our *onderduikers* is a former army officer," Pieter said. "He wants to help with the robbery tonight."

Lena managed a small smile. "My husband the burglar. That's something I never imagined you would become when I married you. Are you nervous?" He'd been pacing from the stove, to the kitchen door, to the door that led into the barn—then back to the stove again, peering through the window into the ink-dark night each time he passed it.

He sighed and raked his fingers through his thick hair. "To be honest, I am nervous. But this has to be done. The underground needs those ration cards."

"Everything is becoming more and more dangerous, isn't it?"

"*Ja*. But we have no choice. We have to fight back. You know we do. For the same reasons that I had to train and fight in the army."

"I know," she said, her voice soft. She had accepted her husband's role as an underground soldier, but she didn't have to like it. She put down her mending for a moment. "Are we getting anywhere, Pieter? It seems like the Nazis are everywhere, and more of them than ever in the village. That's why . . ." She didn't want to finish.

"What, Lena?"

She hated telling Pieter how frightened she was, knowing that it wouldn't change his mind, knowing he hated to hurt her. But Lena had no one else she could confide her fears to, and sharing them sometimes helped to lighten her load. "It was one thing for you and your little gang of *knokploegen* to steal a pig or two so the Nazis wouldn't get them. But this . . . this is different."

Last fall, Pieter had banded together with other farmers to steal pigs, one at a time, from their neighbors. Lena had worked all night with the other women to help butcher and clean them. The meat was distributed among several families, who would smoke it, cure it, or make sausage with it, along with their own butchered hogs. The aggrieved farmers, who were in on the thefts, would report them to the authorities, but of course the thieves would never be caught. It meant less meat would go to feed enemy soldiers.

"None of us like doing dangerous work," Pieter said, "but we'll need to get used to it. According to Wolf, we're going to do even more in the months ahead."

"Sabotage?"

Pieter nodded.

Within an hour, his fellow *knokploegen* had all arrived—some on foot, some by bicycle, and some traveling down the canals by boat. They were fellow farmers, men Pieter could trust with his life. The former Dutch officer slipped in from the barn to join them, and they sat around the kitchen table in the dim light of the kerosene lamp, talking quietly. Lena would have offered them tea or coffee if she'd had any. She sat with her mending, thinking how strange it seemed to have celebrated Bep's birthday around this table only a few hours earlier.

"The ration cards arrived at the post office this afternoon," Pieter began. "I've been in the mail-sorting room before, so I'm pretty sure I can find my way around in the dark. It shouldn't be hard to find the packages."

"Have you told the postmaster what we've planned?" one of the men asked. "He's a relative of yours, isn't he?"

Pieter glanced at Lena for a moment. "His wife and Lena are cousins. But no, I've decided not to involve him."

"Why not? He hates the Nazis as much as we do. He'll look the other way."

"He might even help by leaving the door unlocked so we won't make a commotion breaking in."

"I've thought it all through," Pieter said, "and if we don't involve him, he'll be able to report the robbery with a clear conscience. And if the Nazis apply pressure, he won't have any idea who we are."

"Doesn't he live above the post office? What if he hears us and comes down? We don't want anyone to get hurt."

"We'll have to take that chance."

"Pieter's right," the officer said. "These missions should involve as few people as possible. I'm sorry to say, but it isn't safe to trust our own relatives in these times."

"Where will we hide the ration cards afterwards?" someone asked.

"We'll bring them back here."

Lena froze at her husband's words, her mending falling limp in her lap.

"That's a huge risk to take if you're caught with them, Pieter," one of the men said.

"I have a cache where I can hide them. My contact with the Resistance knows where it is. They'll be safe until he picks them up."

"What about random Nazi patrols in this area?" the army officer asked.

"We'll avoid them if we can. The cloudy skies will help tonight. And the snow has all melted, so we won't leave footprints."

"Don't they guard their shipments?" the officer asked. "These robberies have taken place in other post offices."

"We're counting on the fact that we're a sleepy farming village that hasn't caused much trouble," Pieter said.

"Aside from some stolen hogs," one of the men added. Everyone chuckled.

"Well then, are we ready?" the officer asked. He stood as if eager to leave. He slipped his hand into his pocket, and Lena's breath caught when she saw he had a pistol. If Pieter or the others noticed it, they didn't say anything. Lena's heart raced faster.

"I would like to pray before we go," Pieter said. He pulled his chair away from the table, then knelt in front of it with his hands clasped, his elbows resting on the seat. Lena knelt with everyone else. How strange to pray before going off to commit an armed robbery.

"Lord, this is necessary work," Pieter began. "We need those cards to feed desperate people. Please protect us tonight, and if it's Your will, please grant that all will go well and nobody will get hurt." They ended by reciting the Lord's Prayer together. Never before had the words "deliver us from evil" held so much meaning for Lena.

Her head whirled as she stood again. Pieter rarely showed affection in front of other people, but he pulled Lena close and kissed her forehead before leaving. "Be safe," she whispered.

A gust of cold air entered as the door opened and closed behind the men, chilling her. She doused the lamp to save kerosene, even though she knew she would be wide-awake until Pieter returned.

She went upstairs, checking to make sure the children were tucked in tightly beneath their covers. Wim had nearly outgrown his bed, and his stockinged feet stuck out from beneath his blanket. Maaike lay sprawled across the bed as usual, all arms and legs. Pieter had pushed her bed against the wall to keep Bep from falling out, and the little girl was pressed against it, still clutching her doll. Tears filled Lena's eyes, blurring the room. "Lord . . . ," she whispered. "Lord, please . . ." She had no other words.

She pulled a blanket from her bed and carried it downstairs to huddle beneath. The war had taught her to pray like never before, and she dropped to her knees beside the kitchen table while she waited.

Lena was still there several hours later when Pieter slipped in through the back door. She looked up at him, biting her lip as tears of relief fell down her cheeks. "You're still awake?" he asked. He helped her to her feet and into his arms. His coat was cold and wet against her face.

"I've been dozing off and on," she said. "And praying. Where are the others?"

"On their way home. All went well, Lena."

She squeezed him tightly. "Thank God," she murmured. She led the way upstairs, trying not to think about what Pieter might be asked to do the next time. And the next.

CHAPTER 37

Ans rode her bicycle across Leiden to the yellow-brick Bureau van Politie to meet Erik as soon as his shift ended. She waited outside, and her heart did a little dance when he walked through the door, looking so handsome in his uniform. "Did you hear the news?" she asked as they started walking toward his apartment. "They're recalling all former Dutch soldiers, not just the officers."

"Everyone heard. They'll be sent to work in factories."

"Will you be drafted too?"

"No, my work as a police officer is considered essential." He took Ans's bike, wheeling it down the street for her. "Maybe some of the newer police recruits will have to go, but I've been working for the bureau for nearly five years."

They crossed the bridge over the Nieuwe Rijn and took back alleyways lined with bicycles to Erik's street. He leaned her bike against the wall outside his building, and they climbed the steep steps to his one-room apartment on the third floor.

Ans knew how indecent it might look for them to be alone, but there were few places in wartime Leiden where a young couple could go to be together. Eating in restaurants had become too expensive, and Erik felt uncomfortable in Eloise's elegant town house. Besides, the dating rituals appropriate before the war no longer seemed to matter in these uncertain times. Even so, Ans knew that Erik respected her moral principles, so they'd decided to spend an evening or two together each week at his apartment where they would cook dinner, kiss and hug, and talk about all manner of things to take their minds off the war. Erik would walk Ans back to the town house before curfew.

"It looks like our dinner will be meager tonight," he said, showing Ans what was left of his bag of rice. She took it from him and poured it into a small pot, then added water to cook it.

"It's hard to plan meals when you never know what's going to be available from week to week," she replied. She struck a match to start the cookstove. "Hooray! At least we have gas tonight."

"And these are all that's left of my spices from home." He held up the nearly empty containers of Indonesian spices. "I won't be able to get more until the war ends, so I suppose we'll have to eat Dutch food." He glanced at her and smiled. Erik lit the other gas burner, drizzled a tiny amount of oil in the pan, then tossed in vegetables. Oil was becoming scarce too.

"I love your spicy food," Ans said. "I'm going to miss it. And that's another reason to pray that the war ends soon." With so many more Dutchmen now being forced to go underground to escape the labor camps, she was glad that Erik was still beside her. But his exemption as a member of the Nazi Party still bothered her. "What about after the war?" she asked aloud. "What will happen to NSB members when the Nazis lose?"

"You mean *if* they lose. They're very powerful, Ans. And they're deeply entrenched all across Europe."

"Except in Great Britain. They haven't won there yet."

"No, but the British are taking such a pounding from the Luftwaffe that they're certain to give up before long. At least, that's what the Nazi generals are saying."

"Erik, if I didn't believe with all my heart that the Nazis are going to lose, I wouldn't be able to get up in the morning. And if I couldn't keep telling Eloise that we're certain to win, she would give up living." Ans opened the cupboard above the stove and took out two dinner plates. "Besides, we aren't hearing the real news about the war, you know—only what the Nazis want us to hear. And they aren't telling the truth." It was the closest she'd ever come to hinting at the foreign radio broadcasts she and Eloise listened to and the news reports from the underground papers.

"I suppose that's true," he replied.

Again, Ans's thoughts returned to the unsettling prospect of Erik being considered a collaborator and a traitor to his people. "So when the Nazis do lose and the Netherlands is free, what will happen to the people who've joined the NSB and collaborated with the Nazis?"

"I haven't collaborated!" He stopped stirring the vegetables and glared at her. He had never directed his anger at her before, and it shocked her. Then his expression softened and he reached to take her into his arms. "I'm sorry. I didn't mean to shout at you."

"I know." But he hadn't answered her question. Erik had done a lot of things that people in the Resistance would consider collaboration. He'd helped the Nazis put down riots. He'd helped them round up Jews. He'd helped them search for people in hiding. And he hadn't done anything to stand up to the Nazis or try to stop them. The thought chilled her. She shook her head to displace the image. "Is dinner almost ready?" she asked. "I'm starving!"

In May, the Nazis announced that all private radios would be confiscated. Anyone who failed to hand theirs over to the authorities would be arrested. Eloise still hadn't fully recovered from her melancholy, and when she and Ans could no longer listen to foreign news stations and report what was happening beyond the Netherlands, she began to spiral down even further. "There's nothing I can do to fight back," she said.

Ans watched in helpless frustration as Eloise stowed her typewriter in the closet. She hadn't dressed that morning and was still in her bathrobe, her dark hair uncombed. "You can help me turn this back into a bedroom again, Ans. I won't be needing an office."

"Listen, Eloise—"

"My ears are closed to your cheery reassurances, so save your breath." She went back to bed, refusing breakfast.

Ans stopped Professor Huizenga inside the front door the moment he returned from work that afternoon. "I'm worried about Eloise," she told him. "I know I need to stay here with her, but I also need to go to Amsterdam tomorrow to deliver the ID cards Max altered."

"Where is she?"

"She went back to bed today. And she's been crying a lot, grieving the loss of her work with the newspaper, now that our radio is gone." The professor started past Ans toward the stairs, but she stopped him. "Eloise seems to be slipping into melancholy again," she told him. "I wondered . . ." Ans was afraid to overstep her place by voicing her thoughts, but she was desperate to help her friend. "I noticed that Eloise is always stronger when she's doing something to fight back. And I know she fears losing me now that I'm traveling so often. So I wondered . . . what if she came with me on some of my trips? We could visit an art gallery or attend a concert in Amsterdam like we used to do, and it would provide an excuse for my travels."

He moved closer, speaking low. "It's much too dangerous. I want Eloise home, where she's safe."

"But she isn't safe when she's so despondent. You said yourself that she might harm herself. Remember how happy Eloise was when she and I used to go out and do normal things?"

"It upsets her to see the Nazis everywhere. No, Ans, I can't—"

"One of the things I've been asked to do is to document enemy installations as I travel—equipment and military personnel and things like that. The reports make their way to the Allies so they can plan their bombing raids. The Resistance could use Eloise's skills of observation.

She sees details that I easily miss. And she would be fighting back in a very direct way."

"I'll need to think about it."

She saw his reluctance and fear. "She needs something to do, Professor. Please, let her come to Amsterdam with me tomorrow. I know how much you love her and that you want to protect her. Forgive me for being too blunt, but if you hang on to Eloise too tightly, you could end up losing her in the end." When he didn't reply, she let him pass. He would see for himself how low his wife's spirits were. Surely he would want her to return to normal as badly as Ans did.

Neither he nor Eloise joined the others for dinner. Meta carried a tray up to their room. There was very little to do with the radio gone, so Ans went to her room early. The professor knocked on her bedroom door later that evening. He looked worried and tense, the sleeves of his white shirt rolled up, his brow furrowed.

"I asked Eloise if she wanted to go with you tomorrow, and she does." Ans was relieved, but only for a moment. She remembered feeling that she was in over her head when she'd first arrived in Leiden and the professor told her about Eloise's depression. Now, if Eloise traveled with her, Ans would be responsible for her safety outside their home. They would be doing dangerous work against a ruthless enemy. Yet Ans truly believed that this was the best remedy for Eloise's melancholy.

"I love her, too, Professor," she said. "I'll do everything I can to keep her from harm."

The train journey was slow and difficult, taking Ans and Eloise twice as long to get to Amsterdam as it had before the war. The coaches were jammed. At three different stations along the way, Nazi soldiers demanded that Ans and Eloise show their ID cards. Each time Ans presented it, her heart raced out of control. The forged cards she carried would save the lives of dozens of Jewish people who needed them but could cost Ans her life if they were discovered.

The view from the train had been greatly altered as well, in the three years since the war began. The Allies had begun regular bombing raids on shipyards and factories, and Ans saw the damage as they approached Amsterdam. But Eloise had seemed resurrected from the dead from the moment they'd left home, alert and energetic, just as Ans had hoped. She'd shown Eloise the military maps that Havik had given her, along with descriptions and photographs of the military equipment they were looking for. "We need to record any troop movements we see and any fortifications the Nazis are building," she'd told Eloise. They didn't dare take notes, but Eloise had an amazing memory, and Ans knew she was making a mental note of every Nazi installation, radar base, and fortification she saw. They would add them to the map as soon as they returned home and sketch in all the details, including activity at the port in Amsterdam.

They arrived at the Amsterdam Centraal station and Eloise, who was very familiar with the city, led Ans through the maze of streets and canals to the Amsterdam Royal Zoo to meet her contact. The war had left the beautiful zoo grounds nearly deserted, but they still served as a valid excuse for two women to visit the city. Ans breathed easily for the first time since leaving home once the exchange had been made and she no longer carried the forged ID cards. She longed for a bracing cup of coffee but knew how scarce it was these days.

"Let's walk to the Hortus Botanicus on our way back," Eloise said, "and see what those hooligans have done to it."

Ans agreed, happy to see her friend so alive and animated again. The gardens were a short walk from the zoo, and the spring afternoon was sunny and mild. The gardens were also near the Jewish cultural quarter and the huge Portuguese Synagogue, a landmark since the seventeenth century.

But when they got there, they were both stunned to see that all of the Jewish districts in Amsterdam had been cordoned off, creating ghettos. A loudspeaker blared from a van trolling the streets a block away. They stood still to listen as it approached, and Ans's outrage grew with every word that spewed out. All Jews must report to the authorities to be transported to Westerbork, the loudspeakers were saying. All houses would be searched, and any Jews found hiding would be sent to the prison camp at Mauthausen.

Eloise grabbed Ans's arm so tightly she wondered if she would have bruises. "Why are they doing this?" she asked. Ans could only shake her head. It had been one thing to read news of what the Nazis were doing to the Jewish people, but to see proof of it again left her baffled and angry. There was no explanation for such hatred toward innocent men, women, and children. She thought of Miriam's father and their Jewish landlady, and it renewed Ans's determination to do whatever she could to help, in spite of the risks.

Eloise spoke very little as they returned to the train station. Once again, she seemed to be taking note of everything they saw on the trip home. The moment they were inside the town house, she turned to Ans and said, "Tell your contact with the underground that we'll gladly hide more people here. Whole families, even. Herman has lots of distant 'relatives,' doesn't he? And we have a spare bedroom again." Her gaze was intense, her eyes alive with purpose. "And tell them they'd better hurry."

Ans followed Eloise upstairs, watching as she pulled out the military maps and quickly sketched in everything she'd seen. Ans added everything she recalled, as well. "I want to go with you again," Eloise said when they'd finished. "You must help me convince Herman."

"I'll do my best," she said, trying not to smile.

"He thinks I'm like my fine china downstairs, that I need to be protected and kept behind glass, but what good are all of those beautiful things if they never get used? What good is a chest filled with gold that never gets spent? And what good is my life if I selfishly keep it to myself and don't spend it for others?"

Ans hesitated for a moment before asking the next question. "Is that how your parents felt? Is that why they were willing to die working for the Belgian Resistance?"

Eloise frowned as if the question had made her angry, then closed her eyes. "How did you know I was thinking of them today?"

"I didn't. I-I—"

"My parents were good Catholics. They believed in God and in prayer. I used to think, *A lot of good it did them!* They lost everything, including their lives. But I'm starting to see that they didn't lose their lives—they gave them away. You've been doing the same thing, Ans. And I want to do it too."

"I'm not brave, Eloise. I couldn't carry documents that could get me killed if God didn't give me the strength I need."

"I pray for you every time you go out."

Ans stared at Eloise in astonishment. "You do? I thought . . ."

"That I didn't believe in prayer?"

Ans nodded, remembering Eloise's cynical comments about prayer during the Nazi invasion. "Let's just say I've come to believe that prayer can't hurt," she said with a smile. "After all, I have you and Miriam and Avi and their baby to pray for, don't I?"

Tears filled Ans's eyes as she drew Eloise into her arms.

CHAPTER 38

JUNE 1943

Miriam sat at the Ver Beeks' kitchen table, listening as Mr. Ver Beek read from the Psalms as he did every night after dinner. She remembered Avi reading this same psalm to her in their attic hiding place. *". . . hide me in the shadow of your wings from the wicked who are out to destroy me, from my mortal enemies who surround me. . . ."* If she closed her eyes, Miriam could almost hear Avi's deep voice and feel Elisheva nestled in her arms. She wanted to remember and hold them close in her heart for just a brief moment, yet she wanted Mr. Ver Beek to stop. It hurt too much to remember. She feared the pain would kill her when she opened her eyes again and her loved ones were no longer there. After nearly a year, the pain was as fresh as it had been the first day.

The knock on the back door startled everyone. Miriam's instincts screamed, *Run! Hide!* But she couldn't move. Mrs. Ver Beek sprang to her feet, her hand clutching her heart. She was always anxious when someone came to the door, but the look of horror on her face seemed more intense than usual. Miriam followed her gaze to the kitchen door and saw why. She and Mrs. Ver Beek had washed the kitchen curtains earlier that day, and they hadn't dried in time to rehang them. Miriam had been so careful to stay away from the windows when she'd first arrived, but in the months since then, they had all become careless. Now a white-haired woman stood outside, peering in at them through the bare window glass. She gave a little wave.

"She already saw us," Mr. Ver Beek said. "Answer the door."

Miriam couldn't breathe as Mrs. Ver Beek stumbled to the door as if she'd forgotten how to walk. She was honest and blunt, incapable of sugar-coating things, much less telling an outright lie. She opened the door so stiffly and awkwardly the visitor might truly have been from the Gestapo.

"Hello, Gerda," Mrs. Ver Beek said with a nod of her head.

"Good evening. Sorry to interrupt your dinner. The postman put this letter in our box by mistake. I thought I'd just run it over to you."

"Thank you. This . . . this is Christina," she said, gesturing to Miriam. "Gerda lives next door," she told Miriam.

The woman smiled. "Hello, Christina. Nice to meet you. Are you here for a visit?"

Miriam nodded, not daring to speak. It must be obvious to their visitor that the three of them were nervous. Was Gerda just making polite conversation or were her inquiries more sinister? Her smile seemed pleasant enough.

"Would . . . would you like to come in and sit a minute?" Mrs. Ver Beek asked. Everything in her posture and stiff demeanor spoke the opposite—this neighbor wasn't wanted or welcome.

"No thank you. I need to get home."

Mrs. Ver Beek thanked Gerda again and closed the door, leaning against it for a moment. She stumbled back to her place at the table, clutching her heart in one hand, the letter in the other.

"I can't do this, Henk," she said. "I've been terrified all these months, and today . . . I'm sorry, Christina."

Mr. Ver Beek's face was beet red, as if he'd been holding his breath the entire time. "We're both sorry," he said. "We aren't cut out for this . . . being always on edge . . . it's too much."

"You don't need to apologize," Miriam said. "I understand. She gave us a terrible scare. I'm sure the underground can find another place for me to stay."

"If we were younger . . . ," Mrs. Ver Beek said.

"Never mind. I'm grateful to both of you."

Mr. Ver Beek pushed his chair back from the table. "I'll call Dr. Elzinga." And just like that, her time here was over. Miriam had to leave this safe, familiar hiding place. She went upstairs to pack her things.

Mrs. Ver Beek was hastily ironing the kitchen curtains when Miriam came downstairs again. Miriam had time to help with the supper dishes before Dr. Elzinga arrived later that evening.

"Thank you for your kindness—" she began as she prepared to leave with the doctor. She spoke at the same moment as Mrs. Ver Beek.

"I'm sorry—"

"You don't need to be sorry," Miriam said. "I will always be grateful to you for risking your lives for me. Goodbye."

"God go with you, Christina." Mrs. Ver Beek had tears in her eyes, but Miriam knew it wasn't in her nature to embrace her.

The doctor didn't say much as they drove, as if his mind was pre-occupied with countless things. Outside of town, the Dutch countryside was so flat Miriam could see for miles. The roads became narrower and rougher as they drove, the aroma of cows more pungent in the evening air, until at last they pulled to a stop beside a small farmhouse. It needed a new roof, its mismatched tiles composed of several styles and colors. A large barn with a wide, open door was attached to the house. "I'm sorry you had to move," the doctor said. "I know how nice it was for you there."

"You warned me that I might have to move often. At least I was able to stay there for almost a year. They were wonderful people, but I could see how fearful they were."

"Yes . . . well, here we are."

A cow lowed from somewhere inside the barn as Miriam stepped from the car. A wiry, white-haired woman came out to greet them, her skin wrinkled and wind-burned, her hands gnarled as if she'd plowed the rich earth barehanded.

"This is Christina," Dr. Elzinga said. "And this is Mrs. Mulder. She and her husband own this farm where you'll be staying for now."

"Did you have your dinner?" Mrs. Mulder asked.

"Yes, thank you."

"And you?" she asked the doctor.

"I have as well." He tugged on the vest of his three-piece suit as if to emphasize his full stomach. "If you don't need me, I should leave right away."

Mrs. Mulder nodded curtly. The doctor removed Miriam's suitcase from the trunk and handed it to her.

"Come meet the others, then," Mrs. Mulder said as the car drove away. The farmhouse was little more than a cottage, even smaller than the Ver Beeks' modest house. Miriam wondered how many others there were and how they could possibly fit inside such a small home. But Mrs. Mulder led the way through the open barn door, across the pungent, hay-strewn space to a door in the rear that led into the barnyard. Miriam heard grunting sounds that she guessed came from pigs, and then the clucks and squawks of chickens as she neared a low-roofed coop. Mrs. Mulder opened the gate to the fenced-in enclosure, beckoning for Miriam to hurry as a rooster rushed forward, flapping its wings and crowing in displeasure.

Miriam resisted the urge to cover her nose and mouth as they ducked inside the weathered gray coop. Roosting nests lined both sides of the narrow, windowless space. The smell was overpowering. She feared that the "others" Mrs. Mulder had mentioned were the hens and that she would have to bed down with the chickens, but then the woman removed a section of the rear wall of the coop, revealing a hidden room. Four dark-haired women sat on mattresses inside. They looked up anxiously as the door opened and Miriam ducked inside.

"This is Christina," Mrs. Mulder said. "She needs to stay with us for a while. Do you girls need anything while I'm out here?"

"No thank you," one of the women replied.

"Then I'll be putting the chickens to bed now. I'll let you introduce yourselves." The wall closed behind Miriam with a thud, leaving her in semidarkness. She squinted, waiting for her eyes to adjust, fighting the feeling that she was trapped in this tiny space and the walls were closing in. It was no bigger than ten feet square and was a few feet lower than the coop.

"I'm Lies," the woman who'd spoken said. "These are my daughters, Julie and Betsie. And this is Alie."

"How do you do? I'm Miri—I mean, Christina."

The girl named Julie laughed. "We had to get used to our new names too. Have a seat." She patted a space on one of the mattresses on the floor.

A heavy weight began to settle on Miriam's chest as she sank down, squeezing out all of the air. She barely managed to say, "Thank you."

"This place isn't as bad as it seems right now," Alie said. "There's another door back here that we can open during the day to let in some light and air. We can even sit outside during the day if no one comes to the farm."

"But it's better to wait until dark to go outside," Lies said. "The farm is near a busy road and we don't want to take any chances."

"There's nothing but woods behind us," Alie said.

"Even so. It's better to be safe."

Miriam thought she detected tension between the two women and wondered if they would all be at each other's throats eventually, after being crushed together in such a small space. The one named Betsie hadn't spoken.

"The outhouse is behind us, too," Julie added. "And there's a pump for water. Mrs. Mulder brings us food when she feeds the chickens, and even some books to read."

Miriam had no idea how she would be able to eat with such a strong smell invading their room. She glanced behind her at the trapdoor to the coop, where there seemed to be a great deal of commotion. "Is it always this noisy?" Miriam asked. "I grew up in the city . . ."

"You'll get used to their racket," Alie said. "You won't even notice it after a while." But even the low cooing sound the hens made as they finally seemed to settle onto their nests was annoying and unending.

The women seemed delighted to have someone new to talk with, and they shared their stories with Miriam. Lies and her daughters—Julie, who was sixteen, and Betsie, who was fourteen—were from Amsterdam and had gone into hiding during the roundups with the help of her husband's Gentile business partner. Lies's husband and son were also hiding, but she had no idea where. Alie was eighteen, also from Amsterdam, and the daughter of a rabbi. "I'm the oldest, and Abba found a hiding place for me first. I have no idea if my parents or any of my six siblings escaped the roundups. Abba has a special stamp on his papers, which is supposed to give him favored status, but . . ." Her words trailed off. All four women had been in hiding for as long as Miriam had, most of that time here on the Mulders' farm.

Miriam told her story quickly, needing to scrape past the pain. She knew it made her sound unfeeling, but then the others had sounded brusque too as they'd spoken of their families. It was better not to feel any emotion, she'd decided, than to store up the pain until it destroyed her the way Eloise's grief continually threatened to do.

"You must miss your husband and child," Lies said softly. "I know how much I miss mine."

"Yes." Miriam couldn't think about them. Wouldn't think about them. The low drone of airplanes sounded in the distance, growing louder and closer until the planes rumbled heavily above the chicken coop, rattling the walls.

"We hear firefights sometimes," Alie said. "And bombs exploding."

"Have you heard any news of the war?" Lies asked. "Is there any chance of it ending soon so we can have our lives back?"

"I'm not sure. The people I was staying with had to turn in their radio a few months ago. The newspapers are run by the Nazis, and they always claim to be winning." The little room grew darker as they talked and night fell. The chickens seemed to have settled down too, and except for the sound of crickets, the night grew still. Miriam wondered how she would sleep without the rumbling, rustling noises of the city. She heard someone yawn.

"I'm tired," Lies said. "Maybe we should all turn in for the night."

"It's all of us or none of us," Alie said testily. "You'll learn that soon enough."

"How do you see what you're doing in the dark?" Miriam asked.

"We're used to it," Julie said. "We each have our own little space."

"But we can light a candle for you, Christina," Lies said. Miriam heard her rummaging around nearby, and a moment later a match flared, blinding her temporarily. There was the sharp scent of sulfur, then warm candlelight bathed the tiny space. "We keep our things over here during the day," Lies said. She pointed to a crude set of shelves that Miriam hadn't noticed before, made from wooden crates. Four suitcases were stacked neatly inside. Plates and bowls and cutlery lay on top, along with a small basin. A bucket of water stood next to the shelves. "We usually use the outhouse before we undress," Lies said.

Julie pushed open the back door, making the sound of insects louder. She took her sister's arm. "Come on, Betsie. I'll go with you." The girl still hadn't spoken. Miriam knelt and opened her suitcase, unwinding her clothes from around her violin and bow.

"Is that a real violin?" Alie asked. "Do you play it?"

"Yes—that is, I used to play it. I didn't dare at the last place I stayed. The houses were too close together, and we worried that the neighbors would hear me."

"I would love it if you would play something for us," Alie said. "We haven't heard music in ages!"

"I don't think so," Lies said quickly. "Who knows how far the sound might carry in the night?"

"I know I'm not allowed to play," Miriam said. "I was just checking to see if it made the journey safely." They cleared a space for Miriam's suitcase on the shelves, and when Julie and Betsie returned, Alie offered to go to the outhouse with Miriam. As they took the short walk down the dirt path, a memory suddenly flashed through Miriam's mind of her grandmother's beautiful home in Cologne, the way it had been before the Nazis came to power. She remembered the black-and-white marble floor tiles in her bathroom and the deep porcelain bathtub. Her grandmother's maid would fill the tub with warm, rose-scented water for Miriam. But before the memory could erode the iron shell Miriam had erected around her heart, the stench of the outhouse brought her back to reality.

CHAPTER 39

SEPTEMBER 1943

The wet ground tried to suck Lena's wooden clogs from her feet as she and Pieter crossed the cow pasture. They had poled their little wooden boat down the narrow canals to their neighbors' farm, traveling as close to it as they could before tying up. Now they headed across the field, taking the long, indirect route to avoid going near the village, where the Nazis and the Resistance had been active in recent weeks.

"I hope there are other people here to help Mrs. Boertjens so we can finish quickly," Lena said. "I'm nervous about leaving Wim and the girls home alone."

"They'll be fine. The Boertjens family needs our help." They reached the edge of the field, and Pieter held the fence wires apart so Lena could duck between them. Normally Wim would have gone with Pieter to help their neighbors, but Wim had grown to be as tall as his father and looked older than his fifteen years. The Nazis conscripted all men over the age of eighteen now, and Lena and Pieter feared Wim would be snatched up and sent to a work camp.

"Has there been any more news about Mr. Boertjens?" Lena asked as they reached the dirt road and started up it to the farm. "Surely the Nazis will release him to finish his harvest, won't they?"

"He was caught with a hidden radio, Lena. He won't be coming back."

She shuddered, remembering how they'd debated whether or not to hide their own radio when the Nazis had ordered all of them to be turned in last May. More than ever, Lena relied on the underground newspapers that Wolf brought to find out what was happening.

They had walked only a short distance when they heard the rumble of Nazi motorcycles behind them. The sound filled Lena with dread. "What should we do, Pieter?" There was no place to hide in the flat, open countryside. Thank God Wim had stayed home.

"Nothing. Just keep going."

They stepped to the side of the narrow road to give the motorcycles room to pass, but Lena could tell they were slowing. Her heart raced.

"Halt!" one of the soldiers shouted. "Halt where you are!"

The engines roared in Lena's ears as they idled. Heat radiated from the machines. One of the soldiers pointed to Pieter. "You—come with us." He gestured toward the village, the direction the motorcycles had come from. Lena's heart raced faster as the men wheeled their vehicles around.

"What could they possibly want?" Lena whispered. Pieter shook his head. As a farmer, he was exempt from the labor camps. She wondered if they'd caught up with him for working with the underground these past few months.

"Faster," they told Pieter.

They didn't seem interested in Lena, but she gripped Pieter's hand tightly as they hurried toward the village, the motorcycles growling behind them. It was only a ten-minute walk, but Lena's fear mounted with every step she took. She was powerless. And terrified. She tried to pray, but her thoughts galloped and careened like a runaway horse, and all she could manage was a silent, desperate prayer. *Please, God. Please help us!*

They reached the market square and saw six men from the village standing in a line in the street across from the church. The soldiers halted their motorcycles and waved Lena away, pointing for Pieter to go stand with the other men. He squeezed her hand before releasing it.

These were men Lena knew. Her cousin Truus's husband. Two deacons from church. Three area farmers who were their neighbors. They looked pale and frightened, some of the men trembling visibly. Nazi soldiers strode into the square with three more men—the village baker and his elderly father, and one of Wim's schoolteachers—adding them to the line until ten men stood in the row.

Lena clamped her hand over her mouth to stifle a scream. She knew all about Nazi reprisals. If an act of resistance left a Nazi soldier dead, ten townspeople would be executed in revenge.

Panic filled every inch of her. She was going to be sick. She wanted to run forward and throw herself in front of Pieter to protect him, but there was nothing she could do. She was aware of the other men's wives gathering around her, weeping and pleading and hugging each other. Truus ran up beside Lena, screaming, "No, no, no . . . oh, please, God . . . no! Don't let them do this! Please!"

The men were told to kneel. Lena watched Pieter drop to his knees. This couldn't be happening! It couldn't be! They were going to execute Pieter! A Nazi officer stepped forward with a revolver in his hand. He shouted for quiet but the weeping continued. His Dutch was very poor, but everyone understood. An Allied plane had crashed during the night, and a crewman was missing.

"One of you knows where he is. I will shoot, one by one, until you tell me." The officer stepped within a few feet of the men and pointed his gun at the baker.

Terror overwhelmed Lena. Every inch of her trembled and shook. Pieter didn't know anything about the Allied crewman, she was certain of it. She closed her eyes against the horror, sobbing and pleading with God, bracing for the sound of the first gunshot. Instead, above the cries of the other women, she heard a motorcycle approaching. She opened her eyes. The officer had lowered his gun as he waited for the vehicle to halt.

"We found the crew member," she heard the rider say in German. "We've captured him."

"And the people helping him?"

"Yes. Them, too."

The officer turned back to the row of terrified men. "You may go."

Lena's arms went limp and she slipped from Truus's embrace, collapsing to the ground, her legs no longer able to hold her. "Thank You, God . . . thank You!" she sobbed. Then Pieter's arms were around her, holding her tightly as they both wept. She felt his body trembling.

At last they dried their tears and Pieter helped her to her feet. "Do you think you can walk? Should we go to the manse?" he asked.

"Home. I want to go home." Lena wanted to get as far away from the village and the horror of what had just happened as quickly as she could. She needed to see her children and make sure they were safe and hold them tightly. The sight of Pieter kneeling with other men, a Nazi revolver pointed at him, played over and over in her mind like a broken movie reel. She didn't think she would ever erase the image for as long as she lived.

They reached the edge of the village, still holding each other up, and started down the road to their farm. Lena suddenly remembered their wooden boat. "This isn't the way we came, Pieter. What about our boat?"

"I'll go back for it later."

"No! I won't let you! I'll go back—"

"Lena—"

"You need to stay hidden, from now on, where the Nazis can never find you again!"

"I'm not going to hide."

"Pieter, you have to!"

"We must keep fighting back—now more than ever before."

"I can't go through another ordeal like that. They're inhuman! I thought you were going to die!"

His arm tightened around her waist. "I know. I did too. But you know what, Lena? I felt at peace as I knelt there. I thought of that Scripture that says, 'For to me, to live is Christ and to die is gain.' I understood it."

"No . . . I can't lose you!" Lena's tears brimmed and rolled down her face.

"It isn't up to us if we live or die. We're in God's hands. The Nazis can't harm a hair of our heads unless it's His will."

Lena knew he was right. They'd been in the Father's hands since the day they were born. But they'd never been as aware of that truth as they were now, after the horror of this day. "I'm so scared," she said. "For all of us."

"I know. God knows we both are."

CHAPTER 40

It began with a bad cold. All of the women hiding in the tiny chicken coop developed coughs and runny noses that winter, including Miriam. Months had passed since she'd arrived at the Mulders' farm, and as the nights grew colder, Mr. Mulder gave them a small kerosene stove to heat the space. The women used it sparingly, aware that kerosene was difficult to find. Mrs. Mulder brought more blankets and gave them each a pair of mittens and warm woolen socks that the women in her church had knit. But nothing could dispel the constant chill. As the cold, wet winter dragged on endlessly, Miriam couldn't shake her nagging cough. She wondered if she would ever be warm again.

As she'd feared, there were days when being in such close quarters got on everyone's nerves. There also were days when the women managed to laugh as they told stories to each other and read aloud from the books Mrs. Mulder brought. Every once in a while, Mrs. Mulder brought an underground newspaper for them to read, and Miriam wondered if her friends Ans and Eloise had contributed to it. As long as there were no visitors at the farm, Miriam was able to play her muted violin, which caused a great commotion among the chickens but brought smiles of delight to her fellow refugees.

"Has Betsie always been this quiet?" Miriam asked Julie one day when they were alone. "I've noticed she rarely talks."

"Only since we went into hiding," Julie said. "She misses our brother. They were very close. She wanted to go into hiding with him and Abba instead of with Mama and me, but it was impossible."

Miriam's winter cold worsened as the weather grew colder, until the pain in her chest became unbearable. She couldn't sit up or stagger to the outhouse without help. The simple trip there and back exhausted her. She felt as though she was burning up, yet at the same time, she couldn't stop shivering. Sleep brought wild, feverish dreams.

"Christina has developed a very high fever," she heard Lies telling Mrs. Mulder one evening. "I think Dr. Elzinga should come. I fear she may have pneumonia."

Miriam was only vaguely aware of the white-haired doctor kneeling on the mattress in the tiny space, examining her. She tried to talk, but it brought on a spell of coughing and such terrible, searing pain that she curled into a ball, holding her ribs.

"I need to take her to a hospital," he said.

Miriam tried to say goodbye to the other women and to thank the Mulders for helping her, but she couldn't draw enough air to speak without coughing. A heavy boot kicked her in the chest each time she drew a breath. She knew she was very ill, and she longed to see Avi one last time and to hold Elisheva in her arms, to kiss them once more before she died. Avi had begged her to hang on to life and to survive so they could be together again someday, but maybe it was better to let go and slip away from the pain. She would see her loved ones again in the World to Come.

She was aware of Lies helping her crawl out of the shack. Someone carried her to the doctor's car. She was traveling somewhere. Had they remembered to bring her suitcase? And her violin? She couldn't be without her violin! It was all she had left of herself, the last thing that bound her to Avi and Elisheva and to Abba and Mother. She tried to ask about it but couldn't stop coughing. "Shh, just lie still, Christina," the doctor said.

She lay on the back seat of his car beneath a woolen blanket, shivering and listening to slushy snow spray beneath the car's tires. Then she was carried inside and she was warm at last, in a place that was white and smelled of disinfectant. Someone laid her in a white iron bed with white sheets and warm blankets. A hospital? Jewish patients weren't allowed in hospitals. She coughed and coughed and tasted blood. Dr. Elzinga bent over her with his thick, snowy hair and listened to her lungs. He shook his head. Two women in their fifties, dressed in street clothes, brought water and broth and told Miriam to swallow pills for her fever.

Miriam dreamed of her grandmother's house and of playing tag with her cousins in the summertime beside Lake Constance. She dreamed of Avi and Elisheva, and she didn't want to wake up, but the pain from coughing always drove the dreams away. Interwoven among her dreams were loud shouts and cries and moans. Miriam wasn't sure if they were real or not.

One day she awoke and knew the fever was gone. A dull ache replaced the sharp pain in her chest. Her ribs and stomach muscles felt sore as she propped herself up on her elbows to look around. She was in a small room with two hospital beds. The other one was empty. It didn't resemble a regular hospital room but was more like the bedroom of a house that had been converted into an infirmary. Heavy feet tromped up and down the steps outside her door. Floors creaked above her head as people walked around upstairs. The shouts and cries she'd heard in her dreams were real. The door opened, and one of the two women who'd taken care of her came inside, smiling when she saw her. "Are you feeling better, Christina?" It took Miriam a moment to remember that was her name.

"Where am I?"

"You've been very ill. Dr. Elzinga feared we might lose you. Do you think you can eat something?"

"I'll try." The woman left and returned a short time later with a bowl of watery pea soup. She propped pillows behind Miriam's back, then spooned the soup into her mouth. It was warm and delicious, and Miriam remembered being fed this way when she'd been feverish. "Thank you for taking care of me."

"Get some rest now," the woman said before leaving. She hadn't told Miriam her name or where she was. She lay down again and dozed, and when she awoke, Dr. Elzinga was there.

"Christina! Mrs. Woltheim told me your fever had broken. I'm so pleased." He sat on the edge of her bed and listened to her chest, then her back before nodding his head and declaring, "Better. Much, much better."

"Where am I? What hospital is this?"

"It's not a hospital; it's called Meijers House. It's a private institution for residents who are . . . simpleminded. It's run by the two sisters who've been taking care of you. This is their infirmary."

"So I'll have to go back to the farm now that I'm well?" The thought brought panic and a feeling of claustrophobia, even though Lies and Julie and Betsie and Alie were pleasant companions. Mr. and Mrs. Mulder had been kind, the food meager but adequate.

"I've found donors who'll pay for you to remain here for a time," he said, putting his instruments back in his bag.

"Donors? I don't understand."

"Many of my countrymen want to help but aren't able to hide people for various reasons. Their generosity helps others like you to remain in hiding. They'll pay your room and board, for now, as if you were one of the residents. But we aren't entirely certain if the people who come and go here, making deliveries or visiting the residents, can be trusted—including the cook, a cleaning woman, and the laundress who come from town during the day. Until you're fully well and we can find another hiding place, you'll need to pretend you're mentally crippled like the other residents." In her weakened state, she didn't think that would be too difficult.

Miriam moved into the main part of the house when she was finally well enough and began helping with the other residents. Mrs. Woltheim and her sister, Miss Meijers, known to the residents as Miss Hannie and

Miss Willy, were kind, hardworking women who ran Meijers House like their home and treated the residents like their children. "Willy and I grew up in this house," Mrs. Woltheim told Miriam. "My husband left me after our son Frits was born because I refused to send him to an institution. Frits and I moved back here with Willy, who'd never married, and we cared for our parents until they died. When money grew tight and we could no longer afford to pay the bills, we turned Meijers House into a home for other children and adults like my Frits and charged a fee for their care. We'd like to think that it's a home and not a cold institution."

Frits Woltheim was in his late twenties, and like the other two young men, Aart and Jan, he was what physicians called a Mongoloid. Frits yelled whenever he was frustrated or unhappy and was the source of most of the shouting Miriam had heard. Miriam shared a small bedroom with an elderly woman named Miep, who suffered from dementia and sat in a chair, quietly mumbling nonsense all day. Two more women shared another bedroom: Rietje, who was Miriam's age but had the mental abilities of a small child, and Cornelia, who talked to people only she could see and sometimes suffered from paranoid delusions that made her moan and cry out.

Mealtimes were messy and chaotic but eaten together as a family, even though wartime shortages all across the country meant that the soup was watery and the oatmeal was thin. The sisters didn't have a radio and rarely talked of the war or current events, so Miriam had no idea what was happening in the outside world. She might have been living on a secluded island in the middle of the ocean or in an imaginary world like Cornelia's. She felt safe at Meijers House, for the most part, and did her best to avoid interacting with the daytime help. Whenever the other residents' families visited on Sunday afternoons, Miriam would sit alone on the sun porch, imitating Miep, who was lost in the world of dementia.

The sisters had an old-fashioned windup gramophone and often played music in the evenings. Sometimes Miss Willy played the piano. The house was isolated enough from their neighbors that Miriam asked if she could play her violin without the mute after the daily household staff went home.

"That would be lovely," Miss Hannie said. "We adore music."

Everyone enjoyed hearing Miriam play, especially Rietje, who would sit on the floor by Miriam's feet clapping her hands after each piece and saying, "More! Play more, Christina!"

By the time a few months had passed, Rietje had become so attached to Miriam that Miss Willy allowed her to swap bedrooms with Miep so Rietje could be close to her new friend. Miriam had tried to remain aloof from the women at the Mulders' farm, closing herself off from close friendships, but there was something about Rietje, a high-spirited child trapped in a young woman's body, that seeped into a tiny corner of Miriam's heart. They took walks together around the spacious grounds, away from Frits and his friends who liked to tease. Golden-haired Rietje skipped and danced and exclaimed in childlike delight at every ant and worm and bee they encountered. Her antics often brought a rare smile to Miriam's face.

One Sunday afternoon, Rietje's mother and father came to visit. Miriam heard a commotion in the foyer but didn't dare move from her wicker chair on the sun porch to see what was causing it. A moment later, Rietje burst through the French doors exclaiming, "Christina! Christina! Play music!" She was followed by a worried-looking woman and a tall, red-faced man with a stern expression and an emblem of the Dutch Nazi Party on his lapel. Miriam's lungs squeezed. A wave of nausea washed through her as she did her best to stare vacantly past her friend, who was tugging on her arm, saying, "Play your violin! Play music!"

Miss Willy scurried into the room and gently took Riejte's arm. "Come, dear. You know you aren't allowed to bother the other residents."

"I want her to play!" Rietje insisted. She sank to the floor, kicking her feet and throwing one of her rare tantrums. Miss Hannie came running to help, and together they managed to pull Rietje from the room and close the French doors. Miriam continued her blank, vacant stare, fighting nausea, not daring to see if Rietje's father was scrutinizing her and seeing through her facade.

The incident left Miriam badly shaken, even after Rietje stopped crying and Frits stopped adding to the commotion with his shouts. Miss Hannie gave a huge sigh when she came to sit beside Miriam a while later. "They're gone, Christina. Are you all right?"

"Yes . . . How's poor Rietje?"

"Oh, she's fine. She always bounces back quickly, just like a child."

"Did you call Dr. Elzinga? I'll need to be moved, won't I?" The thought of returning to the chicken coop made Miriam want to weep. It meant another change, another loss.

"We won't call him yet, dear. Rietje's father was more concerned with how his monthly fees were being spent than he was with his daughter. The very idea that she's imperfect disgusts him. I don't think he paid any attention to what she was saying."

Miriam felt her stomach do another slow turn. "When I lived in Germany, the Nazis not only hated Jews, but people like Rietje and Frits too. We heard rumors that babies who were born with imperfections were left to die."

Miss Hannie nodded sadly. "My husband felt that way. He was a believer in eugenics."

"I'm so sorry."

"Yes. But I'm sorrier for him. He missed the joy of knowing and loving our Frits."

⁓⁕⁓

On a warm day in March, Miriam looked at the calendar and realized that it was Elisheva's birthday. Tears slipped down her cheeks as she tried to picture her daughter as a curious three-year-old, smiling Avi's beautiful smile, skipping with childish delight the way Rietje did, wearing her shining dark hair in two braids down her back the way Miriam wore hers when she was a girl in Cologne. Her precious baby was another year older. And another year removed from any memory of the father and mother who loved her more than life itself.

"Happy birthday, Elisheva," she whispered. "Happy birthday, my darling girl . . ."

CHAPTER 41

MAY 1944

The apartment in Zoeterwoude, a few miles south of Leiden, was in Ans's territory. She delivered ration cards every month for the people who were hiding there—more than twenty Jews, at last count, including several small children. "The woman who rents the apartment is putting herself and all of those people in great danger," one of Ans's contacts told her. "That apartment is so overcrowded it's certain to draw the attention of her neighbors, especially with so many children living there with an unmarried woman."

"I tell her that every time I deliver her ration cards," Ans replied.

"When you make your next delivery, you must convince the families to separate for everyone's safety. Tell her we know farmers in the countryside who are willing to take small children but not entire families."

Ans's overused bicycle was in need of repairs again, so she walked to the Leiden train station with the hidden ration cards, prepared to make her warnings stern and convincing this time. She was in line to purchase her train ticket when she heard someone calling her name. She turned and saw Erik hurrying toward her. She stepped out of line, smiling as she watched him approach.

"I'm glad I caught you," he said after kissing her cheeks. She wished she could give him a real kiss, but the train station was a public place. Besides, she sensed that something was wrong. Erik was panting as if he'd run a long distance, and he still wore his uniform. He'd been on the night shift again, arresting curfew breakers, and must have come here right after finishing work.

"What's wrong?" she asked.

He didn't reply as he took her hand and led her out of the station. He stopped at a herring cart just outside. "What kind do you want?" he asked, pointing to the fish.

Ans didn't want any, her stomach drawn into a tight knot by Erik's unusual behavior. But she made her choice and waited for Erik to order and pay the vendor. He led her off to one side while they ate, his gaze alert and watchful.

"What's going on, Erik?" she asked after swallowing a few bites. "How did you know I would be here?"

"I asked at the town house. Let's walk a bit." He downed the last of his herring and they crossed the bridge into the old city. She remembered the stolen ration cards hidden in her bag and wondered what he would say if he knew about them. As the crowd hurrying toward the station thinned, Erik leaned close, bending to speak softly into her ear. "I came to warn you not to go anywhere near a certain apartment on Nassaulaan in Zoeterwoude."

Ans went cold all over. How had Erik known it was one of her houses—the one she had been on her way to visit, in fact? Had the police been following her? Was her entire underground cell in danger? If so, she needed to warn them! But no, right now she needed to remain calm and not panic. She needed to play dumb and hide her guilt from Erik. "I don't understand," she said. "Why are you telling me this?"

"The Gestapo knows they're hiding Jews in that apartment. I overheard them talking this morning, saying they're going to raid it soon."

"But I—"

"In the meantime, they're watching it and waiting to arrest anyone who visits. I know you're helping Jews, Ans, so I came to warn you. If you have any involvement at all with that place, don't go near it."

"Erik . . . thank you." She wouldn't say if she was involved or not, but he was certain to notice how badly shaken she was. Not only had she come dangerously close to being caught and arrested herself, but she was terrified for all the people living in that apartment. If only she had learned of the raid sooner. If only she could have convinced the inhabitants to move to safer hiding places. Ans fought hard not to cry, but tears of grief slipped down her cheeks just the same.

Erik pulled a handkerchief from his pocket and handed it to her. "I love you, Ans. I worry about you all the time. I wish . . ." He sighed and didn't finish.

"Where are we going?" she asked as they walked past the Beestenmarkt. She needed to put aside her fear and grief and warn the other people in her cell.

Erik halted and took both of her hands, facing her. "Ans, let's not wait any longer. Let's get married."

"Married? . . . When?"

"Now. Tomorrow. This week. We could go to the registry office and fill out all the paperwork. Then we could be together from now on. You would be safe with me." She saw his love for her and thought of Professor Huizenga's love for Eloise. Both men longed to hide the women they loved behind locked doors and keep them safe from harm. But Ans couldn't live with herself if she went into hiding and stopped helping the underground—any more than Eloise could.

"If we were married, would you ask me to stop?"

"Ans! I want you to stop no matter what! Don't you understand that?"

"I'm not sure I can make that promise."

He released her hands and turned away as if battling his anger. When it was under control, he turned back. "Ans, I'm begging you. If you love me at all—"

"Why not quit the police, Erik, and be an *onderduiker*? I know people who could help you hide."

"And I know how hard the Nazis are working to find all the *onderduikers*." They had reached an impasse. Neither one was willing to concede. "Will you at least think about getting married, Ans? I want to be together."

"So do I, but I'll need a little more time. My parents should be there . . . they've never even met you." In fact, Ans had never told them about Erik. She wasn't sure if her reluctance had more to do with Erik's lack of faith or his involvement with the Nazis. Probably both. "You know how much I long to be with you—"

"Then let's do it. Please, Ans."

She saw a woman hurrying down the street who reminded her of her contact, and she suddenly remembered why Erik had come looking for her in the first place. How many other members of her underground cell were helping the people in that apartment? She couldn't think about marriage right now. She needed to warn everyone about the Gestapo raid.

"I promise I'll think about it, Erik. I should go now."

"Come back to my apartment with me."

"I can't. I'm sorry. I need to tell Eloise I've missed my train." They kissed cheeks again, and Ans rushed away. The underground had a system in place for emergencies like this one. Ans had never used it, but she needed to now. She headed for the busy café on Rapenburg near the university where urgent messages could be left.

"May I use your toilet?" she asked one of the waitresses. The girl pointed to the back. A map of Leiden was tacked to the wall inside the tiny cubicle. There was an envelope with pins and tiny pieces of paper tucked beneath the edge of the commode. She removed one of the pieces of paper and wrote her code name: *Voorn*—the minnow—and *3:00 p.m.* They'd told her the map would be checked several times a day so she could arrange a meeting. Ans pinned the note to the Pieterskerk, a short walk from the town house. Then she flushed the toilet and left.

"I missed the train to Zoeterwoude," she told Eloise when she returned home. "Our travels this afternoon will have to be canceled too." She offered no other explanation, deciding not to say anything about the Gestapo raid until after her meeting with Havik.

He was waiting outside the church when Ans arrived, and he pulled her inside as if they were going there to pray. She hoped Erik or the Gestapo wasn't following her. She quickly told Havik what she'd learned about the apartment in Zoeterwoude and the upcoming raid. He shook his head, punching his hand with his fist.

"We've been trying to warn them. Why wouldn't they listen?"

"Is there any way we can get those people out?"

"It's too late. If your boyfriend knows about it, then the Gestapo is probably inside already, waiting to see who else shows up."

The thought made Ans sick. "I would have delivered ration cards there today if Erik hadn't warned me."

"He knows about your work?" Havik stared at her as if trying to read her mind, his gaze piercing and hawklike, just like his code name.

"Erik knows I'm helping to hide Jews. He doesn't know any of the specifics. He told me about the Gestapo raid because he was afraid I might be involved."

"You have to go into hiding."

"What? . . . Why? I didn't go anywhere near there today."

"Think about it. They'll force the apartment owner to describe the woman who has been coming with ration cards. They'll torture everyone in that apartment for names and descriptions of all the people who come there regularly. They'll follow you to uncover all of your contacts and then their contacts. If you're arrested, they'll torture you until you tell everything you know. All of the people you've hidden will be in jeopardy. That includes your parents and the baby they're hiding and the *onderduikers* we've sent them. Your work here is finished. We need to get you out of Leiden."

"What do I tell the people I work for? And my friends? And Erik?"

"Nothing. You just disappear. We'll give you a new identity card."

"I have a job here. I can't just disappear."

"You must. Don't even go back home."

Ans couldn't think what to do. Everything was happening too fast. Eloise would be so worried about her if she simply vanished that it might send her over the edge. Maybe Ans should accept Erik's marriage proposal. He could protect her, couldn't he? Or might she become a danger to him?

"May I at least go home for my clothes? And so I can explain?"

"You'll be taking a huge risk."

"I know. But I have to. There's a hiding place in the town house where I'll be safe if the Gestapo does come."

Havik exhaled as if resigned to her stubbornness. "Well, while you're there, tell Max and Ina to get ready to leave too."

"Why?"

"He's much too important to the underground to risk his arrest. Someone will come for all three of you before curfew tonight."

Ans waited until the professor returned from work and was with Eloise in their bedroom before telling them that she had to go into hiding. Eloise moaned and sank down on the edge of her bed. "It's just like before. I'm losing everyone."

"The underground is just being extra cautious until this mess at the apartment in Zoeterwoude settles down. Once I know it's safe, I'll come back and we can travel together again." Ans had feared Eloise would break down the way she had after the Leopolds left. But even as Ans watched, she saw Eloise summoning her strength.

"Meta and Sientje are depending on me," she said. "And you can tell the underground to send more people now that Max and Ina are leaving."

"I'll do that." Ans had written a letter to Erik while she'd waited for the professor to come home, explaining that there was an illness in her family and that she had to return to her parents' farm. He probably would see through the lie. He would know she'd been involved with the raided apartment. She couldn't recall ever telling Erik where her parents lived, but she supposed the Gestapo could easily find out if they were after her. She wouldn't really go to the farm, of course, but to whatever safe house the underground chose for her. She handed Eloise the letter.

"Will you please give this to Erik when he comes looking for me? Otherwise, he won't know what happened to me."

"Are you sure he can be trusted?" the professor asked.

"He saved my life today. If he hadn't warned me about the raid, I would have gone to that apartment. I would be in prison right now."

Ans hugged Eloise long and hard when it was time to leave. She hugged the professor, too. She couldn't find words to tell the Huizengas how much she'd grown to love them. How much they'd influenced her life. But Havik arrived, driving a telephone repair van. It was time to go.

Ans picked up her suitcase and hustled out the back door with Max and Ina. "Do you really repair telephones?" she asked Havik as they drove away.

"It's the reason I'm exempt from the labor camps. The Nazis need their telephones."

Ans huddled in the back of the van with her friends, her bones jarring on the bumpy cobblestone streets, wondering about her future, wondering which direction they were driving. She wished she could have said goodbye to Erik—and to lovely Leiden, the place she'd called home for nearly five years. She refused to cry, refused to feel sorry for herself. Max and Ina and all of those wretched people in the apartment in Zoeterwoude faced a future much more precarious than her own.

CHAPTER 42

Lena and Pieter rose before dawn to do their chores and found Wolf sitting in their kitchen. He startled Lena, but only for a moment. She hadn't thought it possible for the young man to get any thinner, but it looked as though he had. "I'm about to cook some porridge," she told him. "Can you stay?"

"I would be grateful." Wolf shivered, and Lena hurried to stoke the fire and warm up the house.

"Take off your wet coat so it can dry by the fire. I'll fetch you a blanket in the meantime." She didn't wait for his reply but ran upstairs to pull one from her bed.

"Any news?" she heard Pieter asking as she came down again.

"Everyone's waiting. The Allied invasion is expected any day, and the Nazis are on high alert. We all are." Wolf hung his coat over the back of his chair. He nodded his thanks to Lena as she gave him the blanket. "I came to ask a favor of you. Both of you." Lena went still, waiting. "We need a safe hiding place for a Jewish couple. He has been an invaluable help to the Resistance, forging ID cards, especially for downed Allied airmen. But he and his wife need a new hiding place. They're an older couple and can't hide outside in the cold. And he will need a place to work."

"I've had an idea for another hiding place that I've been chewing on," Pieter said. "How soon do you need it?"

"Yesterday," Wolf replied. He gave the closest thing to a smile that Lena had ever seen.

"Well, in that case, I'll get started right away."

"I think I know where he can do his work," Lena said. "We built a secret room in the cellar to hide food, behind a row of shelves. You can't tell it's there. It's nearly empty now, after last winter. With a lantern for light, it might make a good work space."

Wolf left before the children got up for school. Lena stood in the open barn door with Bep on her hip, praying as she did every day as she watched Wim and Maaike cycle off on Lena's wreck of a bicycle. The Nazis had confiscated her children's bikes. Lena's rubber tires were long gone and it was especially hard for Wim to pedal on the metal rims with Maaike sitting on the handlebars. Bep waved goodbye, and Lena stifled the urge to shout, "Be careful!" The children had been warned to dive into the ditch alongside the road if they heard planes overhead. One of their schoolmates had been killed by falling shrapnel. Lena would be glad when the school closed for the summer. Trusting her loved ones to God's care had become a daily, sometimes hourly undertaking.

She kissed Bep's cheek and set her down, glad that she could keep one of the children near, and went inside to finish her morning chores. Later, Pieter showed Lena what he had in mind for a hiding place. "We can clean everything out of this storage area," he said, opening the little door to the space beneath the stairs that had become a collection spot for miscellaneous items.

"Sorting through this junk is going to take all day," Lena said. "You'll have to help me find places for everything."

"When it's empty, I'll board up the door and seal it from this side. Then I'll make a secret entrance on the other side of the wall, in the front parlor."

"Isn't the piano on the other side?"

"*Ja.* Come here, I'll show you." Lena picked up Bep, who wanted to explore inside the cluttered, dust-filled space, and carried her as she followed Pieter. "I'll cut a hole in the wall and remove this lower panel on the piano to make a trapdoor."

"Brilliant. But we'd better not do it while little eyes are watching or it won't remain a secret for long."

Lena worked all day to empty the storage area. Her hands and the front of her apron were black with filth by the time she finished. Bep needed a bath after toddling around in the space, touching everything and asking, "What's this?" as she helped Lena. She and Pieter raced against the clock to erase any trace of their work before Wim and Maaike returned home from school. They finished later that night after the children were in bed, cutting a hole in the parlor wall, opening a trapdoor in the bottom panel of the piano, and covering the entire wall with wood where the old door had been.

"I hope all this hammering doesn't wake the children," Lena said.

"If they can sleep through bombers flying overhead every night, they can sleep through anything."

The lower keys on the piano no longer worked when Pieter finished, but the hidden space had enough room for a makeshift mattress stuffed with straw, and some shelves. It was high enough to sit up in but not to stand. Lena furnished it with bedding and candles and some containers and dishes she thought the shadow people might need. She and Pieter had just headed upstairs to catch an hour or two of sleep before dawn when they heard the door from the barn open and close downstairs. They hurried down to find Wolf and a gray-haired couple who appeared exhausted standing in their kitchen.

"You're just in time," Pieter said. "I'll show you the hiding place."

"Let them sit down and have something warm to drink first," Lena said, poking Pieter's side. "I don't have coffee, but I can make some tea with mint from my garden. Will that be all right?" She pulled out bread and cheese to go with it and cut up some withered apples from her root cellar. The couple were introduced as Max and Ina, and they seemed grateful for their new hiding place beneath the stairs.

"They told us it was all right to tell you . . . ," Ina said. "We know your daughter Ans from Leiden."

Lena caught her breath.

"She's very pretty, just like you, Mrs. De Vries," Max added.

"Please, call me Lena."

"And I'm Pieter. How do you know Ans?"

"We've been hiding with the couple she works for in Leiden."

"How is she? I haven't seen her in so long!" Since the night she'd brought Bep to the farm, nearly two years ago. Ans wrote letters from time to time, assuring them she was all right and saying how much she missed them. Lena wrote back, telling her about the farm and how the other children were doing and saying how much she missed her too. Ans would be twenty-four years old soon. A grown woman.

"Ans is good," Max said. "She's a very strong, determined, and confident young woman. But she had to be moved from the town house the same time we did."

Lena went still with fear. "Why? May I ask what happened?"

"Her boyfriend on the police force warned Ans about a Gestapo raid in another safe house."

A stab of pain pierced Lena's heart. Ans hadn't mentioned a boyfriend.

"It was decided that Ina and I should be moved," Max continued, "and that Ans should also go into hiding."

"Do you know where she is?"

"Sorry. We have no idea. And she didn't know that we were coming here."

Lena hated the Nazis for many reasons, but what they were doing to her family was at the top of her list. Lena had often turned to her own mother when she was Ans's age, asking about love and life and marriage. Exchanging letters with Ans simply wasn't the same. And now her precious daughter was hiding somewhere in the Netherlands, probably in danger, cut off from everyone. Cut off from her. The thought broke

Lena's heart. She clenched her hands into fists as her helplessness stirred a powerful rage inside her. If only she could do something to save Ans and protect her—to save and protect all of her children. But how could she lash out against such an overwhelming enemy? How long until she and her family would be safe again? Would they ever be free from Nazi control? Lena had to believe that they would be or she couldn't face another day. She had to believe that she was doing something to fight back by hiding Max and Ina in her home. "We didn't have time to finish your work space, Max," Pieter said. "We thought that fixing you a place to hide was more important."

"We have three children," Lena added, "and we don't want them to know about you. Two of them are in school, and secrets can be a heavy burden for youngsters to carry."

"We understand," Ina assured her.

"I'm sorry the space is so cramped," Lena said when Pieter showed it to them. It was going to be difficult for people their age to crawl through the small, secret panel.

"You don't need to apologize," Max said. "We consider ourselves fortunate to be alive."

<hr/>

By the time Wolf appeared in Lena's kitchen before dawn a week later, the hidden workroom in the cellar was finished, and Max had resumed forging documents during the night. He and Ina were seated at the table with Wolf, eating the food Lena had left for them, when she woke up. "Have you heard the good news?" Wolf asked. "Allied forces have landed in France."

"No, we hadn't heard," Pieter replied. "Tell us more."

"The size of the invasion was monumental, with thousands of warships and airplanes and troops. They had a rough time of it for a while, but they've established a beachhead on the French coast and now they're fighting their way inland. Here, you can read about it." He pulled an underground newspaper from his pack and handed it to Pieter. Lena read the headline over his shoulder.

"We've heard a lot of activity up there," Pieter said, pointing to the sky, "but it's hard to know what's happening without a radio."

"I brought you one," Wolf said, patting his bag.

Lena looked up from the newspaper in alarm. "Radios are still forbidden."

"I'll hide it in the windmill. You're going to need it for the work we'll be doing in the coming weeks."

Lena's stomach lurched. She pulled out a kitchen chair and sat down on it to listen. She didn't want to hear about the dangerous things Pieter would be doing, yet her need to know outweighed her fear.

"Coded messages will be broadcast from Britain telling you when and where weapons will be dropped," Wolf continued.

Pieter leaned close. "How will the drops work?"

"When you hear our plane on the designated night, you'll shine a light into the sky as a signal. Weapons and ammunition will be dropped by parachute, and it will be up to you to hide them in haystacks or manure piles or wherever you can until they're needed."

"I assume we'll have more work to do now that the invasion has come?"

Wolf nodded. "We'll be asking Resistance fighters to do additional acts of sabotage—derailing trains, cutting telephone wires, destroying bridges—whatever it takes to halt the movement of Nazi war materials."

"But there are always reprisals," Lena said. "The Nazis round up men from the nearby communities, and—"

Pieter rested his hand on her shoulder, stopping her. "Wolf knows all about reprisals."

"Once your cell commits an act, you and your men will need to go into hiding. Not here, but out in the woods somewhere. The Germans have been searching for men in hiding. They'll surround a town and search house to house. Any men they find are sent to labor camps. I apologize if I'm scaring you," he said to Lena.

She couldn't reply. She wondered how she could operate the farm by herself with Pieter gone.

"One more thing you should know. If you're caught helping downed Allied airmen, you'll face arrest and execution. And they'll arrest your wife, as well, to discourage you from helping aircrews."

Lena wondered what would happen to her children if she was arrested. She wasn't afraid for herself as much as for them. "That's a huge price to pay," she said.

"Yes, but the alternative is much worse," Pieter said. "If the Nazis win, we'll live beneath their shadow for the rest of our lives."

"I'm heading up to your windmill now to hide the radio if you want to join me," Wolf said, pushing away from the table. "And I left a container of kerosene in your barn."

"Take something with you to eat," Lena said. She rose from the table and rummaged in her pantry, wrapping a few items in a dish towel for him.

"I'm very grateful to you," Wolf said before leaving.

The sky was growing light outside, which meant it was time for Max and Ina to crawl into their hiding space again. Lena needed to rekindle the fire, fix breakfast, and wake the children for school. If only those routine chores could distract her thoughts from what Wolf had just told them. If only the good news of the Allied landing didn't mean that their lives would be in more danger than ever before.

"Are you all right, Lena?" Pieter asked. He'd returned from the windmill to find her shoving wood noisily into the stove and slamming down the lid.

"No. But I will be." She looked up at the man she loved so much. "I know these things have to be done. I know we have to fight for our country. I just wish . . . I just pray that it will all be over quickly."

CHAPTER 43

Miriam was sitting in the parlor at Meijers House with the other residents late one evening, listening to music on the gramophone, when someone knocked on the front door. Miss Willy looked alarmed. Miss Hannie did too, but only for a moment. Her serene smile returned as she rose from her chair. "I'll see who it is."

Miriam moved closer to the hall door so she could hear who it was above the tinny music. She thought she recognized Dr. Elzinga's voice.

"This is Klara and her daughter Tina," he said. "They were hiding with a Dutch family in Haarlem and barely escaped capture by the Gestapo. May they stay with you for a while?"

"The only beds we have are the two in the infirmary," Miss Hannie replied, "but they're welcome to them."

"I know this is an imposition, Mrs. Woltheim, but with the latest razzias, it's difficult to find hiding places."

"What's a razzia?" she asked.

"The Gestapo is going house-to-house, searching for Dutchmen between the ages of eighteen and sixty so they can take them east to labor camps. In the process, they're also finding hidden Jews."

The news opened a well of fear inside Miriam. Where was Avi? Was he safe? Nearly two years had passed since she'd held him and kissed him and said goodbye. They had married four years ago and had been apart for two of those years. Sometimes her marriage seemed like a dream, while her life was a waking nightmare with no dawn in sight. She had to believe that Avi was safe. That Elisheva was living happily on a farm like the Mulders', feeding the chickens and playing with the barn cats. Miriam wouldn't allow herself to imagine anything else.

"They've never searched here," Miss Hannie said, "and Miriam has been hiding with us for four months now."

The music was slowing and becoming off-key as the gramophone wound down. Frits leaped up and gave the crank a few hearty turns, making the needle stumble and skip. "Careful! Don't wind it too tightly," Miss Willy warned.

"I'm not!" Frits shouted. Miriam strained to hear what the doctor was saying above the fuss.

"Have you heard that the Americans have landed in France?" he asked.

"Yes, our housekeeper told us the wonderful news last week," Miss Hannie replied. "They've renewed our hope. We pray they'll get here soon." Miriam's prayer was the same.

"Until they do, Klara and Tina need a new place to hide. My donors will contribute to their support."

"We'll need extra ration cards for them. Food is in very short supply as it is."

"I understand. Someone from the underground will deliver extra cards."

"You're welcome to sleep in the infirmary tonight," Miss Hannie told the women, "but it might be best if we make beds for you in the attic so you can stay up there during the day. We still aren't certain if we can trust the day staff to keep our secrets. Christina has avoided their scrutiny, but it will be harder to explain why we've taken in two new residents when we have no more room."

"We're grateful for any help you can offer us," one of the women said.

"You're wise not to trust anyone who comes in and out of Meijers House, Mrs. Woltheim," the doctor said. "The Nazis pay a bounty for spying on your neighbors and reporting people in hiding." The doctor left again. Miss Hannie returned alone, announcing that it was bedtime.

Early the next morning, before the residents rose and the day help arrived, Miriam helped Klara and her sixteen-year-old daughter, Tina, get settled in the attic. "I think it's cruel to make you live up there all the time," Miss Hannie said, "so you're welcome to join us in the parlor after the cook and housekeeper leave."

"Aren't you afraid one of the residents will let it slip that we have women living in our attic?" Miriam asked.

Miss Hannie smiled. "Who's going to believe them? We'll say they must be talking about the mice in our attic."

Now that the Allies had landed in France, the sound of airplanes thundering overhead went on day and night, along with what Miriam guessed was artillery and machine-gun fire. One night just before bedtime, the explosions were so loud it sounded as if the sky was about to come down on their heads. Flashes lit up the night, accompanying the blasts. When bits of plaster sifted down from the ceiling and the electricity went out, Miss Hannie decided that the best way to keep everyone calm was to light candles, wind up the gramophone, and postpone bedtime for a while, as if they were merely waiting for a thunderstorm to blow over instead of for a battle to end. Rietje clung to Miriam like a frightened child as they sat together on the sofa. Cornelia rocked in place and moaned, a sign that she might be about to have one of her episodes. Frits gave a great shout with each explosion, adding to the noise and agitating the other two boys. His mother's attempts to calm him failed. Only Miep seemed unfazed as she dozed in her chair.

When the worst of the commotion finally tapered off, Miss Willy picked up one of the candlesticks and lit the way upstairs to bed. She was halfway up when there was a loud pounding on the front door.

"We need to hide!" Klara gasped. She and Tina raced upstairs to the attic hatch on the second floor, with Miriam right behind them to help. The pounding continued, but Miss Hannie waited to answer it, giving them more time to put the ladder in place and climb up, difficult to do in the dim candlelight. Miriam signaled that it was safe once the women had pulled up the ladder and closed the hatch. Only Miep and Cornelia could be convinced to go into their darkened bedroom. The other residents refused to listen to Miss Willy and lined up along the upstairs banister, peering down to see what was happening. Frits's shouts added to the commotion.

The moment Miss Hannie opened the door, several men in Nazi uniforms pushed inside, shouting in German. Was this one of their dreaded razzias? Miriam quickly ducked into her bedroom, wishing she'd gone into the attic with the other women. Miss Hannie didn't understand German, which made the angry men shout all the louder. The chaos upset Rietje and she hopped up and down crying, "Tina, hide! Klara, hide!"

Miriam grabbed Rietje's arm and yanked her into the bedroom, holding her tightly to calm her. "Shh, it's all right, Rietje. The men aren't going to hurt us." She managed to quiet her enough to hear one of the soldiers trying to explain in muddled Dutch that a Nazi vehicle and two motorcycles had been wrecked in the bombings. Injured soldiers needed first aid. When she finally understood, Miss Hannie let them be taken into the infirmary while the Nazi in charge demanded to use their telephone.

All the while, Frits shouted from upstairs, "Go away! Go away!"

"If someone doesn't shut him up, I will!" the Nazi shouted back in German. Miriam left her place long enough to drag Frits into the bedroom with her and Rietje and close the door. They were both afraid of the dark, but there was nothing she could do about it.

"If you stop shouting, Frits, I'll let you jump on my bed." He quieted for a moment. It was something he loved to do but wasn't allowed. He took a moment to decide, then grinned and climbed onto the bed and began bouncing. He was making loud thumps, but at least he'd stopped shouting. Rietje climbed onto her own bed and began jumping too. Miriam opened the door again, straining to hear what the officer was saying on the telephone.

Miss Willy had managed to coax the last two residents into their room to get ready for bed, and when she saw Miriam standing in her doorway, she hurried over, carrying a candle. "Can you tell what's going on?" she whispered.

"There's been an accident. Miss Hannie is giving the injured men first aid. The officer just telephoned his headquarters to tell them where he is and to ask someone to come for them."

"So this isn't a razzia?"

"No, I don't think so."

"I should go down and help Hannie. Can you manage the residents by yourself?"

"Of course." Miriam took the candle Willy held out to her. She checked inside Miep's bedroom and saw her sitting on her bed, staring at Cornelia, who was wedged into a corner, mumbling a rapid stream of nonsense. Cornelia would need her medicine to calm down after the men were gone. Miriam went into the boys' room next and found them having a pillow fight, dangerously close to the candle on the dresser. She pulled the pillows out of their hands. "You'd better stop that now and get ready for bed before Miss Willy gets back."

Rietje and Frits were still jumping on the beds when Miriam returned to her room. "If you stop jumping, Frits, and go to your room and sit quietly with the other boys, I'll tell you a story about the goblins that used to live in Holland."

"Me too?" Rietje asked.

"Yes, you too." She chose one of their favorite stories, one she knew by heart after all these months. The flickering candlelight added to the drama. Miriam had just finished when a vehicle pulled up out front. She put her finger to her lips, saying, "Shh . . . ," and hoped Frits would obey. Doors slammed and she heard men's voices outside. The front door opened and heavy boots tromped across the wooden floor.

"They're in there," someone said. "We'll need three stretchers." Miriam held her breath during all the commotion that followed, waiting to see if the Nazis would search the house afterwards. At last, the front door closed for the final time. The vehicle drove away. All was quiet.

"What good boys you are," Miss Willy said when she peeked into the bedroom. "Say good night to Rietje and Christina, now. They need to go to bed too."

As Miriam passed her in the doorway, Miss Willy whispered, "Thank you."

"Cornelia is going to need her medicine," Miriam whispered back.

"I know. Hannie is with her. Good night."

"Good night."

The evening's events left Miriam shaken and drained of strength. The sisters were such kind, compassionate women, caring with dignity and love for the broken souls whom others had rejected. To have their home invaded by the Nazis, even for an hour, seemed an outrage. Yet the sisters had treated the Nazis with kindness as well. Miriam shuddered at the memory of how close her enemies had been to her. The fear that made her stomach ache was going to keep her awake all night.

CHAPTER 44

The hen squawked and tried to peck Ans's hand as she pushed it off the nest to check for eggs. "Ha! I'm faster than you are," she told the disgruntled hen. "I've had years of practice." She ducked out of the coop and carried the basket of eggs into the farmhouse to wash them.

Ans was Bernandina Kamp now, according to her forged ID card, and worked as a maid on a farm much like her parents'. She'd longed to escape from farm life and it now had become her refuge. Jo and Hans Dykstra were in their thirties and, with six children to care for, were grateful for Ans's help washing diapers and dishes, tending chickens, and preparing meals while Jo nursed a colicky baby. Ans guessed that two of the children were Jewish, but she knew better than to ask questions.

The family hid other people besides Ans. *Onderduikers* came and went, and four Jewish boys in their teens helped with the farmwork, then hid in the outbuildings or the thick woods behind the farm whenever the Nazis came. The boys enjoyed telling stories of their close calls. "One time we were shoveling out the cow stalls when the Nazis came and Johan dove into the manure pile to hide. We wouldn't let him near us for days!"

"At least I was smarter than Dries. He nearly drowned after jumping into the canal to hide."

"I had to stay in the water for three hours!" Dries said, laughing. "I was chilled to the bone, but it was better than being caught."

The sound of their laughter and deep voices made Ans homesick for Erik. She thought of him throughout the day and when she lay in her box bed beside the kitchen stove at night, wondering if he would ever forgive her for not quitting her underground work and marrying him when he'd asked. And for disappearing. Sometimes she would daydream about their life together as she scrubbed the workmen's overalls and socks or when she lay staring at the wooden ceiling at night, wondering if there was any hope at all for them after the war ended. If it ever did end.

Summer on the farm meant long days and extra work, but the highlight of Ans's week was when her Resistance contact arrived with the latest underground newspaper. A seed salesman, Leeuw was exempt from Nazi roundups and had a valid reason to travel from farm to farm across the countryside. Ans guessed his code name, Lion, was because of his thick mane of reddish-blond hair.

One rainy summer day, Leeuw delivered the welcome news that the Allies had landed on the Continent.

"We've heard rumors that the Americans had landed," Ans said, "but now we know it's true."

"It's true, my dear. You can read the news for yourself." The newspaper was the one she and Eloise had worked for. Ans saw how vital their work had been, especially after the Nazis confiscated everyone's radios. She wished she could tell Eloise how grateful people all across the country were.

"When do you think it'll be safe for me to return to Leiden?" she asked Leeuw. "It's been two months."

He shook his head, brushing his thick hair from his eyes. "It's still too soon. You must be patient."

"What about letters? You said you would let me know when I could write to Eloise or my parents or my boyfriend."

He continued shaking his head, giving his answer.

"Even if I mailed it from a different town?" she asked. "With no return address?"

"My dear, if they're looking for you and your letter is intercepted, you'll put your loved ones in terrible danger."

August arrived, and with it came hot days of hoeing weeds and sticky nights in her box bed in the kitchen. It felt good to cool off in the canal at the end of a long day, but the farmwork didn't satisfy Ans's need to fight back.

She noticed an increase in Nazi activity nearby and was often awakened at night by the rumble of trucks and heavy vehicles on the back roads. When she walked into town on errands, she saw soldiers everywhere. Something was going on.

She was bringing the milk cans up from the barn after milking one morning when a powerful blast made her dive to the ground and cover her head, nearly spilling the milk. It was followed by a deafening roar as something streaked overhead, soaring high into the sky. The others heard it too and came running outside to look up.

"What kind of weapon was that?" Ans wondered aloud.

Leeuw answered her question when he came a few days later. Ans stood inside the barn with the others to hear about it. "Hitler has a new secret weapon called a V-1 rocket," Leeuw told them. "It doesn't require an airplane to deliver the explosives and can be launched from the ground at any target, any time of day or night. The Allies can't stop these rockets or shoot them down like other enemy aircraft. They have to find out where the launch sites are and target them."

"They launched a rocket nearby," Ans told him. "We heard it the other morning. It sounded very close, east of here."

"That matches the other evidence we have. These rockets will cause a lot of death and destruction before this war is over."

"I want to help," Ans said. "I used to gather military information and sketch maps for the Allies. I know the codes and what to look for. If you let me go back to Leiden—"

He held up his hand, stopping her. He led her away from the others to the laundry tubs she'd abandoned when Leeuw had arrived. "Ans, I need to tell you something," he said when they finally halted. Her heart thudded as she steeled herself for bad news. She wasn't expecting what he told her. "Herman Huizenga and his brother Aalt have been arrested."

"What? . . . That can't be! . . . Please, that must be a mistake! Did they find out he was hiding people?"

"No, something worse. The bank where the Huizenga brothers worked has been funneling money to the underground. They've been underreporting the Jewish assets that the Nazis confiscate and using the money to help Jews in hiding."

Ans admired the professor more than ever, yet she was terrified for him. "What will happen to them?"

"We don't know. They and everyone who worked at the bank are in the prison camp in Amersfoort."

"Was his wife also arrested?"

"No."

"She isn't well. She shouldn't be alone. Are the cook and housekeeper still there?"

"Yes, their cover story is holding up for now. But it isn't safe for anyone else to hide there—or for you to go back. The house might be watched."

Ans groaned, remembering how Erik had been assigned to watch the Leopolds' apartment after they'd gone into hiding. Was he watching the town house? Would he arrest Ans if he saw her there or would he help her again? She closed her eyes and offered a silent, urgent prayer for Herman and Eloise, knowing how distraught they both must be. Eloise's greatest fear was losing the people she loved, and Herman was the only family she had left. Eloise wasn't strong enough to face a loss this great. And Herman must be more concerned for Eloise's well-being than for his own. Ans longed to go to her, yet she understood why it was impossible. Knowing her friends were suffering made her furious.

"Let me go back to work, Leeuw, please! Give me a new territory, someplace where no one knows me."

"It might be too soon, especially after Herman Huizenga's arrest. We don't know if they're still searching for you."

"I have a new identity and forged papers. I can deliver ration cards like I did before and forged IDs and newspapers. I can help you find out where they're launching the rockets and fill in the information on military maps."

"You'll have to walk or ride a bike. Trains are too risky. Too much scrutiny."

"Whatever you need me to do. Please!"

"This wouldn't be because they're overworking you here, would it?" he asked, smiling as he gestured to the pile of dirty overalls beside the laundry tubs.

"This farm can still be my home base. I'll still work hard for the Dykstras when I'm here."

Leeuw twisted a lock of his thick hair, looking Ans over as if wondering how old she was and how strong. "I'll let you know the next time I come."

Leeuw returned a few days later with an assignment—delivering ration books and newspapers. A vigorous bicycle ride from the farm took her to Bodegraven and Woerden or the outskirts of Utrecht. She walked for miles and miles to farms and villages where Jews and *onderduikers* were hiding, and returned to the farm exhausted each night, her feet aching, wondering if this long, endless war would ever be over.

CHAPTER 45

Lena was washing the supper dishes when Pieter pulled her aside. She'd seen him talking to Wolf in the barn earlier and wondered what was going on. "Wim needs to be told everything," Pieter whispered. "Tonight. He's old enough now. You're going to need his help while I'm gone."

"Where are you going?"

He tilted his head toward Maaike, who was drying the dishes. "We'll talk later."

Lena returned to the kitchen after tucking Bep and Maaike into bed, and she knew from the pained expression on Pieter's face that she wasn't going to like what he said. Sixteen-year-old Wim sat at the table with him, his fair hair glowing in the light of the kerosene lamp. Their son was so tall and growing taller every day, his profile so like his grandfather's with his strong, proud nose and chin. "Shall I make mint tea?" she asked.

"Not for me. Sit down, Lena." She sat. Pieter's ominous words *while I'm gone* had been eating a hole in her stomach ever since he'd spoken them earlier.

"Wim, a group of us have been working with the Resistance to fight the Nazis," Pieter began. "Now that the Allies are trying to free the Netherlands, I need to help them."

"Can I go with you?" Wim seemed so eager that Lena had to resist the urge to grab his arm to hold him back. He would hate being treated like a child.

"Not this time," Pieter said. *Not ever!* Lena wanted to shout. "I need you to take over my work here. Your mother and I have been hiding *onderduikers* in the barn and the windmill—"

"I know," Wim said. "I've seen them sometimes, when I couldn't sleep. But I would never tell anyone."

"Good. I know we can trust you, Son. There's also a Jewish couple hiding here in the house. Your mother will introduce you to them after I leave in a few minutes."

His words took another bite out of Lena's stomach. How long had he known he was leaving? Why hadn't he told her sooner?

Lena knew why.

"Can you tell us what you'll be doing?" Lena asked. "And when you'll be back?" Pieter hesitated for such a long moment that Lena reached for his hand. "I know you're trying to protect me, but it's easier for me if I know."

He nodded and drew a deep breath. "The Allies and Nazis are fighting southwest of here, in Noord-Brabant and Gelderland. The Resistance has learned that a Nazi ammunition train is headed there. If we can derail it, Allied planes will blow it up."

Wim made a sound like an exploding bomb. He was grinning, his admiration for his father reflected on his face.

"There will be other jobs after that. I don't know the details yet, but I won't be able to come back or to contact you for a while."

Lena looked away, determined not to cry. "We'll keep everything going, won't we, Wim?"

"Help your mother with the farm and with all of the people in hiding. Keep your sisters safe. They're all depending on us. You'll need to be brave and strong, Wim. And if the Nazis come, I want you to hide with the shadow people. I'll show you all the places."

There would be reprisals after the train derailment. The Nazis had killed a fourteen-year-old boy with one of their firing squads when they couldn't find enough men. She rose when Pieter and Wim did, even though she wasn't going anywhere, and watched them go into the barn. She was standing in the same place when Pieter returned to say goodbye.

"It's no shame to be afraid, Wim," Pieter was saying. "I'm afraid too. But you aren't alone. God will give you the strength you need." Lena knew his words were meant for her, too.

They knelt beside the table so Pieter could pray. They recited the Twenty-third Psalm together when he finished. *"Even though I walk through the darkest valley, I will fear no evil, for you are with me . . ."* Then Pieter kissed them both and left. The house seemed unnaturally quiet.

"I'll show you where Max and Ina are hiding," Lena said. "Max has important work to do. And they'll both be hungry."

With Pieter gone, Lena was reluctant to let her children out of her sight. She needed to run an errand in the village the next day, but it was too dangerous for Wim to be seen, and she was afraid to leave Maaike and Bep behind. In the end, she loaded the girls onto her broken-down bicycle for the trip. She stopped at the manse to see her father before returning home. He sat Maaike and Bep down at his kitchen table and gave them bread with *hagelslag* on top. "I've been saving these chocolate sprinkles just for you," he told them. "Enjoy your little treat while your mama and I talk."

Lena told him about the ammunition train and begged him to pray for them. He hugged her tightly.

"Of course, Lena. We carry such heavy burdens through these endless days."

"Pray for all of us, Papa. The Nazis are going to retaliate after this train is destroyed, and they're becoming more and more vicious. We heard that the Nazis burned five homes to the ground in one village after the local train station was sabotaged. The families had only thirty minutes to get out."

"They tried to win the Dutch people over to their side in the beginning," Papa said, "but they've learned that they can't, and it infuriates them."

"Is this war ever going to end? I hate what it's doing to us, what we're turning into."

"We have to believe that God will triumph in all this suffering. One day the kingdoms of this world will become Christ's Kingdom, and His Kingdom is forever."

Lena heard the distant rumble of approaching aircraft—an entire formation from the sound of it. She would need to wait until it passed before venturing out with her daughters again. Shadows flickered on the floor as the planes flew in front of the sun. Her father noticed them too.

"Every time you see planes flying overhead, let them remind you that we can find refuge in the shadow of His wings."

"I don't understand why God allows this, Papa."

"Keep your eyes on the Cross and the Resurrection. When we remember how much Christ sacrificed for us, we'll know we can trust Him with anything."

They had just finished praying together when there was a tremendous explosion somewhere far in the distance, probably dozens of miles away. Lena felt the hair on her arms and neck rise. The Nazis would make them pay. "I need to go home," she said.

Papa walked her to the door. "You know you can always come to me, Lena, and I'll pray with you. But I may not always be here, and you must—"

"Don't say that! With Pieter gone, I need you! I can't face this alone."

"It may not be up to me. I'm telling you what I tell all of my parishioners. You need to turn to God, not me." It was what Pieter had told her and Wim before he left.

Lena walked up to the windmill that night after the girls were in bed to ask the shadow people if the hidden radio had reported any news of the battles being fought on Dutch soil. "I don't think it's going well for the Allies," one of them told her. "There was a coded message for the Resistance to help with the retreat."

"No . . ." They had drawn such hope from the Allies' presence. How could any of them bear to lose that hope again?

The next day, Lena cycled into town with Maaike and Bep for the Sunday morning worship service. It was still too risky for Wim to be seen. She found consolation in the hymns, comfort in the prayers, and renewed strength from her friends and neighbors who were suffering with her. No one spoke of their fear of an enemy reprisal, but they all knew it was on everyone's mind.

"This war has caused us to face impossible decisions," Papa said in his sermon. "How do we decide which choice to make? Should we tell a lie to protect a Jewish child, for instance? Is it okay to steal from our enemy to feed someone in need?" He paused and gazed out at the congregation. Lena had never noticed how thin he'd become. "Jesus said the most important commandments are to love the Lord your God and love your neighbor. And so, whenever we face a dilemma, we can ask, What is the best way to show our love for God and for our neighbor?"

He paused again and Lena heard the unmistakable sound of Nazi motorcycles approaching. Papa ignored them and continued to preach until they halted outside. The church grew very still. The church door banged open and the congregation turned. Three Nazi soldiers walked inside. The spokesman's Dutch was poor, but everyone understood. They had been dreading this moment since yesterday's explosion.

"A train was destroyed. One man from each town must pay."

Silence.

"Take me." Lena's father stepped from behind the pulpit. "I'll go." He slipped the stole from around his neck as he walked toward the soldiers.

No! Lena tried to cry out but terror clogged her throat. Pastors and priests were exempt from Nazi reprisals. They couldn't take her father!

He reached Lena's pew and handed her his stole. His gaze met hers for a moment as he told her without words that he wasn't afraid. And that he loved her.

No . . . no . . . no! Why didn't someone stop him?

He unfastened his clerical robe as he walked and shrugged it off, laying it over a pew near the door. He seemed so calm. So at peace. Lena pulled Maaike and Bep close, crushing them to herself to shield them.

Dear God, no . . . Please don't let them do this! Please!

They shoved Papa through the door, leaving it open. She heard others weeping. Where was the miracle that would save her father? Angels with flaming swords. Allies dropping by parachute to destroy the Nazis. God had saved Pieter from the firing squad at the last minute.

Oh, God, please, please don't let—

A single gunshot rang out. It reverberated through the building, making Lena's skin crawl. The stench of gunpowder drifted in with it. No one moved or breathed as they sat frozen in shock. The motorcycles started up and drove away.

One of the elders leaped up and rushed outside. Another followed, then another. The first man returned a minute later, gripping the backs of the pews as he stumbled forward as if to keep from falling over. He looked at the waiting congregation—at Lena—and shook his head.

Papa was dead.

CHAPTER 46

By the end of the summer, Ans had done so much walking that her shoes wore out. She had no money for a new pair. She showed Mrs. Dykstra the holes that she'd tried to cover with layers of newspaper. "But now the soles are tearing away from the uppers," Ans said. "Do you know where I can get a new pair?"

"New shoes in wartime? Keep dreaming, Bernandina! But I'll ask at church and see what I can find for you." She came home with a pair of well-worn work boots. They were a little large for Ans but better than the shoes that had fallen apart.

Her travels also allowed Ans to map the Nazis' movements and report on the area where the rockets were being launched. "It's very important to get an estimate of the number of troops and tanks in this region," Leeuw had said. "The Allies are in Belgium, and we're expecting something big in the Netherlands very soon." His words brought Ans hope, renewing her resolve.

The autumn day still held the warmth of summer when Ans rode her bicycle to the towns of Woerden and then Bodegraven to deliver ration cards. She noticed an unusual amount of Nazi activity with troop vehicles and tanks heading toward the southeast. At her last stop in Bodegraven, she asked to use the bathroom and marked down all of the military information in coded symbols on her map, afraid she wouldn't remember them by the time she'd cycled back to the farm. Ans folded the map into a small square and tucked it under the front of her bra. Late in the day, she climbed onto her bicycle to head home.

She was somewhere between Bodegraven and Woerden, riding back roads because of the Nazi activity, when two Nazi soldiers approached, one on a bicycle, the other striding alongside. Her heart ticked faster. There was no chance that they hadn't seen her. Her legs were already weary but she pedaled faster, gazing straight ahead, hoping to race past them. But the one on the bicycle halted and waved his arms at her.

"Hey, hey! Stop!" he said in German. "Where are you going in such a hurry, pretty *Fräulein*?" The other one stepped into her path. Ans had no choice. She braked to a stop but pretended she didn't understand them.

"Here's your chance," the one with the bicycle said to the other soldier. "You can get a bike for yourself."

"It's in pretty bad shape but it beats walking," he replied. He grabbed the handlebars. "I'll take that now, *Liebste*."

Ans hung on tightly, knowing they could do whatever they wanted but hoping they would show mercy. "Please don't take my bike!" she begged in Dutch. "I'm miles and miles from home!"

Whether they understood her or not, they seemed indifferent, chatting about how they'd use the bike on their days off. "Please, I need it to get home. Otherwise I'll never make it there before curfew." Her tears were very real. One of them made a crude comment about Ans in German, and she tried not to blush so they wouldn't know she'd understood. "Please!" she begged. The soldier yanked the bike from her grasp and climbed on.

"Too bad for you, *Liebste*," he replied. Ans knew better than to resist. She watched them ride away, laughing, and was grateful they hadn't done worse to her in this out-of-the-way place. She started walking. It was too far to make it all the way home to the farm before curfew and too dangerous to be out on the open road alone after dark. She tried to recall the last milepost she'd passed and decided she was closer to Woerden than Bodegraven. She could ask for shelter in one of the houses where she delivered ration cards.

The sun flamed low on the horizon by the time she saw church steeples and the blades of the *korenmolen* on the horizon. Her legs were weary, her feet blistered from the oversize shoes. Ans was almost there, heading for her contact's house near the water tower, when a church bell tolled the hour of curfew. She hoped curfew breakers wouldn't be shot on sight.

Ans summoned the last of her strength, jogging through Woerden's back lanes, staying away from the main streets, trying to recall where the bridges were. She remembered the military map she still carried and considered tossing it while she had the chance but decided this new information was much too important.

The outline of the water tower loomed above the rooftops. Almost there. She ducked down a shadowy alley at the same moment that a policeman turned in to the other end. He was unfastening his belt as if he was about to relieve himself. "Hey! Stop right there!" he shouted when he saw her.

Ans's instinct was to turn and run, but running would make her look guilty. Besides, she didn't think her weary, trembling legs would carry her any farther. She held up her hands in surrender.

The Dutch policeman strode toward her, refastening his belt. "What are you doing out past curfew?" He gave her a rough shove, slamming her against a wall. "Can't you tell time? Or are you up to no good?" He had no reason to speak so gruffly or treat her harshly except to instill fear. She wondered if Erik was this cruel when he patrolled Leiden's streets after curfew.

Ans struggled to control her terror long enough to stammer an explanation. "I-I'm a maid . . . on-on a farm. Nazi soldiers stole my bicycle on my way home from Bodegraven. I've been running as fast as I can to get home before curfew, b-but I'm late." She paused to swipe away tears, searching for any signs of pity in his expression. Her stomach ached with fear. "Please, you must believe me, sir. I-I know about curfew but the Nazis stole my bike!"

"Show me your ID card."

Ans groped through her bag. Before she could find it, the policeman snatched the bag from her and searched through it himself, tearing away the lining where she hid the ration cards, feeling inside the space. Thank God she'd made her deliveries. The space was empty.

But she still carried the map. Her stomach writhed as if she'd swallowed live eels.

"Please, I'm only a few minutes late," she begged. She felt trapped, backed against the wall while the policeman stood in front of her, rummaging through her bag.

He studied the napkin that had wrapped her lunch as if it contained hidden messages. He found her forged ID card and examined it closely. Would it pass official scrutiny? He finally looked up.

"Well, Miss Bernandina Kamp, you're under arrest for breaking curfew." He grasped her arm so tightly she winced. Terror turned her stomach inside out.

"I'm going to be sick!" she moaned, and before she could stop herself, Ans bent over and vomited. She tried to turn away but the policeman stood too close, and some of the vomit splattered on his shoes.

He shoved her to the ground. "Wipe it off!" he demanded.

Ans crawled to her knees and pulled a handkerchief from her pocket to wipe his shoes.

"You stink!" he said. "Stand up!" He yanked her to her feet and pushed her forward.

Ans's fear mounted with every step she took toward the police station on the square. They would search her thoroughly. They would find the map. And the terrible things Erik had warned her about would happen.

Lord, help me get rid of this map . . .

Red banners with swastikas fluttered in the evening breeze as she was led up the steps and through the station door. She saw a photograph of

Adolf Hitler on the wall and felt her stomach contents rising. "I'm going to be sick again!"

The policeman dragged her down a hall to a lavatory. He shoved her inside, leaning against the door to watch her.

Ans barely made it to the toilet before vomiting as if her guts were falling out. She knelt in front of it, gasping and spitting. The room had only one dim light, and as she huddled over the bowl, Ans reached beneath her blouse and pulled the folded map out from the front of her bra. When she leaned forward to vomit again, she dropped the map into the toilet, praying that the sound of her retching would make the policeman turn away. She quickly flushed, watching to make sure the map went down, then knelt there until her dry heaves subsided. At last she stood, legs trembling.

"Clean yourself off."

Ans used the tiny sink to splash water on her face and rinse her mouth.

"Let's go."

She felt dizzy and disoriented, her legs rubbery as the policeman dragged her down a long hall, down a set of stairs, down another long hall. He pushed her inside a tiny cell and slammed the door. A key turned in the lock.

Ans collapsed onto the cold floor, weeping. *Thank You, God . . . thank You, thank You!*

CHAPTER 47

The daytime workers at Meijers House brought news that gave Miriam and the others hope. French and American troops had liberated Paris and were advancing through Belgium. But the Nazi military activity in the region surrounding Meijers House was steadily increasing. A line of troop vehicles had rumbled past the house this morning, making Miriam wish she were hiding in the attic with Klara and Tina. But with the housekeeper cleaning the second-floor bedrooms, there had been no opportunity. "May I have a word with you and Miss Willy?" Miriam asked Miss Hannie as they prepared for bed.

"Of course, Christina." Klara and Tina had come downstairs for food and water and hadn't returned to the attic yet. The women all stood in the upstairs hall, their faces shadowy in the candlelight.

"Those military convoys we saw today scared me," Miriam said. "I think . . . I think it would be safer for all of us if I hid in the attic with Klara and Tina."

"I understand, dear," Miss Willy said. "Of course you may. How shall we explain it to Rietje? She's devoted to you."

"I don't know. I'll have to think of something . . ."

"I can give her extra activities during the day to keep her occupied," Miss Hannie said.

"Or maybe I shouldn't come down at all in the evening when Klara and Tina come down," Miriam said.

"No, you have to," Tina said. "You'll go mad up there if you don't come down."

Miriam remembered sharing the tiny space in the chicken coop with Alie and Lies and her girls. It had felt wonderful to step outside sometimes.

"Let's give it some more thought," Miss Hannie said. "We don't have to make all of these decisions right now."

"Do you want to sleep up there tonight?" Miss Willy asked.

"I think I should. The Nazis know you have an infirmary now, and they've been driving past here all day." Miriam knew her fear created difficulties for everyone, but she'd been running and hiding from the Nazis since Kristallnacht, nearly six years ago, and couldn't stop now. Avi had begged her to survive.

"We'll need to pack more food and water for you," Klara said.

"I'll look for some bedding," Miss Hannie said. "It won't do for the housekeeper to ask what happened to the sheets and blankets in your room. We'll tell the day staff that your family took you home."

Miriam awoke the next morning to the sound of Rietje throwing a tantrum after seeing Miriam's empty bed. Miss Willy tried to quiet her with the promise of an extra sprinkle of cinnamon on her porridge while Miss Hannie coaxed Frits to stop shouting. Miriam regretted getting close to the girl instead of keeping her feelings walled off from everyone. It had been a mistake. Miss Willy seemed to be standing right beneath the attic hatch when she shouted above the noise, "If you stop right this minute, I promise that Christina will come back and visit tonight. But she won't come unless you're a good girl." It seemed to work. Rietje's cries tapered off.

It wasn't the safest option, but when Miriam came down the ladder from the attic that evening, she explained that they were playing a new game. "If you don't tell anyone where I'm hiding, I'll play my violin just for you, Rietje, before you go to bed at night." In the meantime, she asked Miss Hannie to contact Dr. Elzinga and tell him that all three of them needed a new hiding place. "Tell him I'll be glad to go back to the Mulders' farm."

Two days later, the messenger who delivered extra ration coupons to Meijers House returned with Dr. Elzinga's reply. It wasn't safe to move anyone at the moment. But there was good news. British paratroopers had landed in the Netherlands near Nijmegen. And American ground forces and tanks had crossed the border from Belgium and had liberated Eindhoven.

"That must be what's causing so much Nazi movement," Miss Hannie said.

"Are those places near here?" Miriam asked.

"Nijmegen is at least fifty miles away, I should think," Miss Hannie replied. Everyone agreed it was good news. But it meant more waiting, and Miriam's nerves felt on edge every moment. She didn't dare to hope.

The next morning, Miriam was in the attic with Klara and Tina when a vehicle pulled to a stop in front of Meijers House. Someone pounded on the front door. Tina carried the ladder to the round attic window at the front of the house, below the roof peak. "Nazis!" she mouthed. Klara motioned for her to get down before she was seen. The three women sat very still, straining to listen. A male voice bellowed in a mixture of German and Dutch, shouting louder when he wasn't making himself understood, as if volume alone could scale the language barrier. Miriam's panic soared when she figured out what he was trying to say. "They want this house," she whispered. "For a hospital, I think."

A confusing jumble of voices and boots along with Frits's shouts came from below. Then footsteps thundered up the stairs, bedroom doors opened and closed. The man continued shouting as he tried to make Miss Hannie understand. "Out! All of these persons must be cleared out! We need hospital beds!"

"But these are our residents' rooms. Where will they sleep?"

"I told you! You must contact their families! Send them to their families!"

"Meijers House is our home." Miss Hannie's voice trembled. "My sister and I and my son live here. Where would we go?"

"If you let us stay," Miss Willy said, "we can help you tend the wounded." Miriam didn't hear the reply as the man moved away and down the stairs.

"Are the Nazis staying?" Klara whispered. Miriam nodded. "We're trapped! What are we going to do? There's no other way out of this attic!" She clutched her daughter close.

"Hannie knows we're up here," Miriam whispered between frantic gasps. Terror had sucked all the air from her lungs, and she struggled to breathe. "She'll find a way to get us out." She had to believe it was true.

But two days passed with no relief in sight. Their food ran out, and they had to ration their water drop by drop. The Nazis weren't leaving. Instead, it sounded as though more men and equipment were moving in while the residents' families were arriving to take them away. Miriam urged Klara and Tina to put their belongings in a back corner behind a pile of discarded furniture, creating a barricade where they could hide if the Nazis inspected the attic.

"What good will that do if we starve to death?" Klara asked. Miriam didn't know.

On the fourth morning, Miriam heard Rietje throwing a tantrum outside her bedroom and guessed that her parents had come for her. "I want Christina!" she screamed. "I don't want to play the hiding game! Tell her to come down!" Miriam's chest squeezed in panic.

"Christina went home to her family," Miss Hannie soothed, "and now you must go home with your papa too."

"No, she's hiding! She's up there, and I want her to come down!"

"There's nobody up there but the mice," Miss Hannie said. "Come, Rietje. It's time to go."

Miriam motioned for Klara and Tina to creep across the attic with her as quietly as they could and hide behind the barricade. Terror filled every inch of her.

"Christina . . . !" Rietje's screams grew farther away but they didn't stop.

Miriam struggled to breathe. Her heart thumped loudly, painfully. They waited for several minutes, then she heard a louder thump as the attic hatch flipped open. "Take a very good look for those mice," a voice from below said in German.

Footsteps creaked across the attic floor. Miriam trembled from head to toe. She couldn't stop her tears. The heavy boots halted beside the barricade. She looked up into the face of a Nazi soldier.

"Out!" he said. "All of you! Out!"

CHAPTER 48

Ans sat on the narrow bunk in the Woerden jail, smelling the stench of vomit on herself, tasting bitter bile. She was alone in the cell only long enough to calm herself, gather her wits, and pray. Then footsteps came down the corridor. A key rattled in the lock. She stood, her stomach still roiling. Maybe her prayers were being answered and they were letting her go.

The cell door opened and she faced a guard who didn't look any friendlier or kinder than the man who'd arrested her. He held her bag, the lining ripped open. He beckoned her forward, prodding her down the hall and up the stairs the way she'd come. One of the special paddy wagons the Gestapo used to transport prisoners waited outside, the engine running, dashing Ans's hopes for a quick, merciful release. The guard pushed her into it.

Night had fallen while she'd been in the cell, the city dark under the blackout, but she recognized the imposing building they halted in front of a few minutes later. Kasteel van Woerden was a Nazi military barracks and Gestapo prison. Ans's legs wobbled as she climbed from the car. Why hadn't she listened to Erik and stayed safe? All his warnings about the terrible things the Gestapo did to Resistance workers flashed through her mind, making her feel sick again. She stumbled up the steps into the lion's den. Then she thought of Miriam and Avi and Elisheva and knew she would do it all over again.

Ans stood before a desk in an office bristling with Gestapo officers, the walls plastered with swastikas and a portrait of Hitler. A clerk questioned her while he filled out forms and stamped papers: name, age, address, occupation. She was Bernandina Kamp, age twenty-two. She worked as a maid on a farm outside of Woerden. The clerk had her ID card and knew all the answers but asked her anyway. "The charges?" he asked Ans's guard.

"Breaking curfew."

A Gestapo officer at a nearby desk looked up and seemed to study Ans when he heard the reply. He pushed back his chair and came to stand behind the clerk. He was in his forties, with light-brown hair and a face that reminded Ans of a fox. "Let me question her when you're finished," he said to the clerk in German.

Ans hadn't had much time to rehearse her story while she'd waited in the first cell, but she knew from her underground training in Leiden how important every detail was. She kept her head lowered, playing the part of a simple farm maid, while the paperwork was completed. The Gestapo officer waited as well, a fox watching his prey. Ans was led to another room when her papers were complete and was told to remove all of her clothes in front of the guards and the waiting Gestapo officer. She wept in spite of her resolve not to. When they finished their thorough, humiliating search, they gave her back her underwear and a shapeless prison gown.

"Come with me, Bernandina," the fox-faced Gestapo officer said in Dutch after she dressed. He led her into a tiny windowless room, no bigger than a closet, and told her to sit down on the only chair. He stood above her. "Why are you breaking curfew, *bitte*?"

"Because I—"

"Ah, ah, ah . . . look at me when you speak, *bitte*."

Ans lifted her face. He would see that her fear was genuine. Would he also see that some of what she was about to tell him were lies? She needed to keep her answers simple and short to convince him that she was a naive, guileless maid. "Because I was riding my bicycle home from an errand in Bodegraven and—"

"What was your errand?"

She gave the reply she'd rehearsed in the jail cell. "Shoes. I needed new shoes." She pointed to her blistered feet and worn-out boots. They hadn't given her time to put them back on after they'd pulled out the laces and searched them thoroughly.

"Where are the new shoes?"

"I didn't buy any."

"So you came to Woerden? To search for shoes after curfew?"

"No, I-I—"

"Wouldn't it make sense to come to Woerden first before going all the way to Bodegraven? They sell shoes here, too."

"It was my day off. I wanted to get away—"

"Tell me why you were out after curfew."

"Two soldiers stopped me and stole my bike. I begged them not to. I knew I couldn't get back to the farm in time, but they—"

"Who owns this farm where you live?"

"The Dykstras. I work there as a maid."

"Yet you came to Woerden instead of going home?"

"I couldn't walk home in the dark."

"Who were you going to stay with?"

"I-I didn't know. We bring milk to a dairy here. They know me. I-I thought maybe with them." That much was also true. The Gestapo could check with the dairyman. Ans had avoided giving any names or addresses of her underground contacts or safe houses. "I would have been home on time if they hadn't stolen my bike!"

She tried to read his expression through her tears but couldn't. He didn't look menacing, but he didn't look kind, either. Then he smiled and her blood ran cold. "That is a very nice story, but you see, Bernandina, I don't believe you."

"But it's true! My bike—"

"Yes, perhaps your bicycle was taken. But I've never heard of a dairy-maid who rides such great distances in the middle of a war unless she is up to something more than buying shoes."

"It was my day off . . ."

"Don't insult me." His smile was gone now. "You are in a great deal of trouble, and I would like to help you because you are very pretty. And because I think you are only a minnow."

Ans shivered at the mention of her code name, Minnow. Was it merely a coincidence, a figure of speech? Or did he know more about her?

"I can help you, Bernandina, but you must help me catch some bigger fish."

"I don't understand—"

"I think you do. Why don't you start by telling me your real name?"

"That is my real name. Some people call me Dina—"

"Is that what your boyfriend calls you?"

"I-I don't have a boyfriend."

"Now, I know that's a lie. A girl as pretty as you must surely have a boyfriend."

"But all the young men my age were taken away—"

"Tell me who you're working for." His tone was becoming harsher, angrier.

"The Dykstras—"

"Who gave you the bicycle and sent you to Bodegraven?" He stepped closer. "What did you really do there? Who did you contact?"

"Nobody! I needed shoes!"

She started to tremble, terrified of the torture Erik had warned about. The room was hot, the coarse prison dress scratchy. She started to cover her face as her tears fell, but the officer shouted at her. "Look at me!"

Ans lowered her hands. Hot tears rolled down her cheeks.

"Tell me where you are from, innocent farm maid. Where is your family?"

Ans had thought this through in the brief time she'd spent in her jail cell. Any answers she gave could be checked—and probably would be. She didn't want to put anyone she loved in danger, so she had decided on a story that couldn't be verified easily and hoped she could fabricate enough details to make it believable.

"The Dutch East Indies. Bandung, on Java. I came to the Netherlands to work as a housemaid, but then the war started and the only work I could find was on a farm." He studied her face. Ans struggled to recall the details Erik had told her about Java, all of the photographs they'd looked at together. She hoped she was a convincing liar.

"What do you miss most about home?" he asked. His cruel smile was back.

"The food," she replied without hesitating. "The wonderful spices." She named some of the dishes Erik had taught her to make, and his smile vanished.

"Stop. I'm going to give you one last chance to help yourself, Bernandina, and then it will be too late. You must stop this game of lies you are playing and tell me the truth about why you went to Bodegraven. Tell me the names of the people you're working for, and I'll see that you're given a nice bed in the prison in Vught and special treatment there. Because you will be going to Vught for breaking curfew, I promise you. Why not make it easier on yourself?"

"I am telling the truth. I work for the Dykstras. I went to buy shoes."

"Then heaven help you, because I can't." He yanked her to her feet and opened the door, then pulled her back into the office. "She wouldn't break," he told one of the other Gestapo men in German.

"Shall I work on her?" the man asked. Ans closed her eyes, praying that she would hold up, that she wouldn't betray anyone.

"For now, her only crime is breaking curfew," the first officer replied. "She had nothing incriminating on her. I had a hunch that she wasn't telling the whole truth, but it was only that. We need to look for cracks in her story first. Put her in a cell."

A guard led her down a corridor in a cellblock that reeked of urine and unwashed bodies and unlocked a door. Her cell was only ten feet by seven feet and already held four women who were asleep on the floor on straw mattresses. They grumbled as they moved aside to make room for Ans. She could smell the bucket in the corner that served as a latrine and stepped carefully over the other women to use it as they settled back to sleep. The only light came from a high window that faced the corridor.

Ans was desperately thirsty. She stepped over the women again to reach a metal water pitcher and tin cups near the door, but the pitcher was empty. The guard hadn't given her a mattress, but Ans knew she wouldn't sleep anyway. She sat down with her back against the wall, wrapped her arms around her bent knees, and tried to pray.

She had much to be thankful for—that her bag had been empty of ration books, that she'd been able to flush the map down the toilet, that she'd known details about Java from Erik. Most of all, she was thankful they hadn't tortured her. But her ordeal wasn't over. Her false ID would be checked, Woerden's dairyman questioned. Thankfully, she had warned the Dykstras that if anything happened to her, they were to say she'd been given the day off. She imagined the Gestapo arriving at their farm and prayed with all her heart that the Jewish boys hidden there wouldn't be discovered.

Ans finally dozed off, still leaning against the cold wall, praying for all the people she loved.

CHAPTER 49

An army truck with a canvas roof pulled up in front of Meijers House. Miriam was shoved into the back of it, clutching her suitcase with her violin inside. After five years of running and hiding, after everything she and Papa and Avi had endured, Miriam's enemies had captured her at last. It had all been for nothing. Avi had begged her to live, to fight to survive. But she'd reached the end of the road. She would never see him or their daughter again.

As she'd waited for the truck to arrive, Miriam heard the Nazis saying that she and Klara and Tina would be taken to Westerbork, then deported to a slave labor camp. Miss Hannie and Miss Willy were being arrested for hiding Jews. Poor, simple Frits, who had no idea what was happening to him and to the only home he'd ever known, would be imprisoned along with them. One of the soldiers had slapped him across the face when he wouldn't stop shouting, and he was still crying hours later.

Klara and Tina seemed dazed as they climbed into the back of the truck with Miriam. Miss Hannie and Miss Willy came in after them, needing help to get over the high fender. Miss Hannie tried to comfort Frits as they huddled together on the hard floor. The truck started up and they began the painful, jolting ride toward the unknown. A soldier with a rifle rode with them, presumably to keep them from leaping out. Miriam watched villages and farmland go past through the canvas flap in the back of the truck until the sun finally set and the sky became too dark to see.

The sisters and Frits were ordered out when the truck finally drew to a halt. Miriam, Klara, and Tina were told to remain inside. Miriam reached for Miss Hannie's hand. "Thank you for helping me. I'm so sorry you're paying such a high price for your kindness."

Miss Hannie squeezed her hand in return. "This isn't your fault, Christina. Lord knows, you're the innocent ones."

Soldiers with guns and bayonets stood guard as the trio climbed out. Dogs barked nearby, scaring Frits. He began to shout, adding to the commotion. Miriam wept for her friends. She wondered if she would ever see them again. An hour passed. Miriam stood while she waited, her backside aching from the hard truck bed.

At last, she heard guards shouting and children crying. The flap opened and the soldiers herded a line of people into the truck—elderly people, children, men and women, all carrying suitcases. Miriam sat down again, knowing she wouldn't be able to stand once the truck began to move. She watched as each person boarded, knowing without being told that they were Jewish, hoping that one of them wouldn't be Avi, thanking God that none of the crying children was Elisheva. As difficult as it had been to let her daughter go, she had done the right thing. The guards pushed people into the truck until there was no more room. Then they pushed more people in. Families sat on their suitcases and on each other's laps.

"Do you know where this truck is going?" an old man seated beside Miriam asked.

"Westerbork, the Dutch prison camp. I heard the Nazis talking about it after they found us hiding."

"They found us, too," he said. He looked weary and defeated, as if he'd lost the will to fight. Papa had looked the same as he'd said goodbye to Miriam.

The truck traveled all night, arriving at Westerbork just after dawn. Miriam's legs ached from being stuffed beneath her for so long. The camp had become huge since Miriam had left with Abba. She'd been filled with hope for a new life in Leiden, filled with wonder and love for Avi. The surrounding heathland that Miriam had stared at for so many months looked the same, but the sprawling camp was a true prison now, with tall barbed-wire fences and seven watchtowers guarded by soldiers with machine guns. Rows and rows of new barracks spread across the grounds.

Miriam stayed close to Klara and Tina as guards marched them forward and forced them to stand in a large, open area in the middle of the camp. They stood waiting for a very long time, not daring to sit down. Miriam's stomach rumbled with hunger and nerves. They had run out of food three days ago in the attic of Meijers House and hadn't eaten since. But worse than her hunger was her thirst.

It took all morning for the truckload of new prisoners to be processed, their names and ages recorded. Miriam's ID card still identified her as Christina Bos, but her accent betrayed her as a German Jew. The knowledge that they'd recaptured one of their own seemed to please her jailers. "All Jews who were discovered in hiding will be housed in the punishment block—a prison within this prison," they were told. "You will be treated as convicts for breaking the law and failing to report for relocation as you were ordered to do. You will be among the first to be deported to the labor camps."

Miriam was assigned to the punishment barracks with Klara and Tina. They had barely spoken to her all day, and she wondered if they blamed her for being discovered. If it hadn't been for Rietje's screams, the Nazis might not have searched the attic. And yet, with no way out, all three of them would have surely starved to death. Would that have been a worse fate than what they now faced?

Miriam carried her suitcase with the violin tucked inside into the crowded barracks and searched for an empty bunk. They were stacked three high and crammed into the barracks so tightly, there was barely space to walk between the rows. The barracks supervisor located a bunk for Miriam in the densely packed middle, up near the rafters where wet laundry draped above her head. She would have no privacy, no way to be alone. "What happens to us now?" she asked the supervisor.

"The deportation train leaves every Tuesday," she replied. "The authorities will give me a list of names from this barracks, and if yours is on it, you leave." Today was Sunday. The train departed in two days.

"Do you know where the train ends up?" Miriam asked.

The woman looked all around for a moment as if worried someone would overhear. "They say we're all going to resettlement camps somewhere in Poland. But nobody ever writes back to tell us they've arrived. They promise they will, but then they board the train when their names are called and we never hear from them again." Her words made Miriam shudder. She'd heard nothing from Papa or any of her relatives in Cologne.

"Has anyone ever tried to escape?" she asked. She was thinking of Avi and how he'd escaped from Westerbork once before. If they had captured him and brought him here, perhaps he might have escaped a second time.

"A few have tried it. But every time someone attempts to escape, ten other people from that barracks are deported in retaliation." Avi would never endanger his fellow prisoners that way.

Prisoners in the other barracks labored in a workshop where they made shoes or in a scrapyard where aircraft wrecks were disassembled for parts. Prisoners in the punishment block wouldn't be in camp long enough to work.

The food that evening tasted wonderful to Miriam, the first she'd eaten in three days. She remembered the Sabbath dinners with Abba and Avi and how thankful and hopeful they'd felt as they'd recited the traditional blessings and prayers. Now Miriam knew this was the end for her. She would never see Avi and Elisheva again. If they survived, they would have no way of learning what had happened to her.

That night, after lights-out, Miriam sat up on her bunk, her head brushing the rafters, and took out her violin. It was the only thing that remained of herself and of the life she'd once lived, and she wanted to play it one last time. She played it muted at first, expecting people to shout at her to be quiet, but no one did. Instead, she heard murmured thanks and requests to play more. Miriam removed the mute and poured all of her sorrow into every note. She had the fleeting thought that if Avi were here, he would hear the Tchaikovsky violin concerto and know it was her. Yet she prayed that he wasn't, that he was asleep somewhere safe. At last, she put the violin away and tried to sleep.

A voice in the dark asked her to play again the following night after lights-out. Miriam knew it would be the last chance she would ever have before tomorrow's train carried her into the unknown, so she poured her heart and soul into the music once again. She was in the middle of the Brahms lullaby she used to play for Elisheva when the outside door burst open. A light shattered the darkness, shining all around until it spotted her on her bunk. Miriam shielded her eyes. There was no place to hide.

"Who are you?" a voice behind the light asked.

"Christina Bos."

"Get your things and come with me."

CHAPTER 50

Lena's grief was bottomless. Not only was her father gone, but the brutality and senselessness of his death made it impossible to accept. She held tightly to Bep's and Maaike's hands as she watched men bury him beside her mother in the churchyard. Friends had offered to take the girls during the funeral, but Lena needed them beside her to remind her why she must remain strong. At three and a half, Bep didn't know what had happened except that Opa had walked out of the church and hadn't come back. Maaike wept inconsolably. She'd heard the shot that killed her grandfather. Now she had withdrawn into herself, no longer a happy ten-year-old. Lena didn't know how to explain to Maaike why Opa had volunteered to die or why the soldiers would kill a man who had done nothing wrong. The world was upside down.

Wim grieved at home, alone, unable to attend his grandfather's funeral. It wasn't safe for him to be out. Lena had no way to contact Ans to tell her that Opa had died, since Max and Ina had told her Ans, too, had gone into hiding.

Lena heard the muffled tears of the people around her as the elder officiating at Papa's grave site read Jesus' words. "'My command is this:

Love each other as I have loved you. Greater love has no one than this: to lay down one's life for one's friends.'"

After the service, the women offered a small lunch in the empty manse. No one seemed able to eat. Then Lena climbed onto her bicycle with her two girls and pedaled home.

She stood in her bedroom later that night, gazing out the darkened window, unable to sleep. High above, shadowy airplanes blotted out the moon and stars as they moved across the sky, and she remembered Papa's words about finding refuge in the shadow of God's wings. It didn't seem real that he was gone. Below in her kitchen, the shadow people made soft rustling sounds in the dark. Lena was accustomed to them by now. But when she heard footsteps coming up the stairs, she turned. Pieter stood in the doorway. She ran to him, clinging to him, unable to stop weeping. His body shook with sobs as well.

She finally pulled back to look up into his beloved face. "Is it safe for you to be here?"

"I heard about your father. I had to come."

"He's dead . . . Papa's dead . . . ," she sobbed. "He volunteered to die! He offered his life so that no one else would be killed."

"I'm so sorry that you and the girls had to witness that."

They lay down on the bed together until nearly dawn, sharing their love, telling each other all of the things that the chores of daily life never allowed enough time to say. Pieter left again before dawn. When the sun rose and Lena's grief returned, she wondered if she'd only dreamed that Pieter had come.

CHAPTER 51

Miriam shielded her eyes against the light shining in her face. "Get your things and come with me," the guard said. Miriam struggled to breathe, her chest aching, constricting, as she hurried to fetch her suitcase from beneath her bunk. Her fingers trembled as she quickly packed her violin and bow inside it. The barracks had fallen still as if no one dared to move or breathe. She sensed her fellow prisoners watching her in the darkness as she shuffled through the rows of bunks to the door where the guard with the light stood waiting.

"Thank you," she heard someone whisper as she brushed past. Then another voice and another. *"Thank you." "Thank you for your music."* The whispers multiplied in the darkness, bringing tears to Miriam's eyes.

She emerged into an icy rain and was led past rows of darkened buildings. They crossed the assembly square in the center of camp to a row of barracks on the other side. Rain dripped from Miriam's hair and down her back, making her shiver. She feared the coming punishment for daring to play her violin after lights-out—perhaps a beating or solitary confinement. The guard led her inside another barracks much like the one she'd just left. Women murmured their complaints as he shone his light all around. He pointed to an empty bunk with his light.

"That's yours. Stay here until someone comes for you tomorrow."

She climbed up, clutching her suitcase.

"Why did they bring you here?" a voice from the bed below hers asked.

"I-I was playing my violin . . ."

"That was you?" another voice asked. "It was beautiful."

"Thank you." Miriam had never imagined that the sound would carry so far. She pulled the thin blanket around her to warm up, but her shivering stemmed as much from fear as the cold. She would have the long night to worry about what would happen to her in the morning.

A sense of doom and foreboding filled the entire barracks the next day, and Miriam quickly remembered why. The deportation train arrived today. A hush fell over the women as the head of the barracks stood in the doorway to read the list of names. Miriam sagged with relief when her name wasn't on it. But she still didn't know what punishment she faced.

"Get ready for the journey," the matron told the people on the list. The same scene was playing out in the other barracks, with children crying and people weeping as they bid each other goodbye. Those whose names hadn't been called were ordered to remain inside until the train departed. The women on the bunks surrounding Miriam's sat with heads bowed. She sensed their relief. Miriam stood by the window to get a better glimpse of the fate she would one day face, watching the turmoil outside as hundreds of deportees assembled in the square with their suitcases. She tried to see if Klara and Tina were among them, but there were too many people. They formed lines after roll call, and the camp police marched them to the waiting train. Miriam was stunned to see that it wasn't a passenger train.

"Those are boxcars!" she said aloud. The wide doors on the windowless cars stood open, and she watched in horror as people of all ages were herded inside. She hadn't realized she'd spoken aloud until a woman watching alongside her spoke.

"One of the men I work with saw inside those boxcars. There's no place to sit down except the bare floor. There's one barrel for a toilet and another for water. No food, no heat, and no air in the summer."

"They'll ride like that all the way to Poland?"

"Yes, and who knows what they'll find there." The woman looked at her. "You're new here, aren't you?"

"I arrived two days ago."

"Well, let me tell you about this place. Every week that your name isn't called gives you one more week to hope that you won't end up in those cars. But the hope doesn't last very long. As soon as this train leaves, the agony over who will be next begins all over again." How could people endure this unrelenting suspense, their fate hanging in the balance week after week? It might drive sane people mad.

"Perhaps it would be better to have your name called and get it over with," Miriam said.

"I've been here for two months," the woman said. "I've watched this horror show eight times now. It never gets any easier."

Miriam had to turn away as parents with small children and babies climbed into the railcars. She shuddered, thanking God that she hadn't kept Elisheva with her. Letting her go had been one of the hardest things she'd ever done, but enduring this with her now-three-year-old daughter would have broken Miriam's heart.

By eleven o'clock, the doors to the boxcars had been slammed shut and locked. The train departed into the unknown, and prisoners were allowed to go to their work assignments. Miriam sat alone in the barracks, her stomach churning as she waited to see what would happen to her. She hadn't eaten breakfast, fearing it wouldn't stay down.

An hour later, a man in his fifties knocked on the barracks door, then let himself inside. He wasn't wearing a guard's uniform but appeared to be a fellow prisoner. "Are you the one who was playing the violin last night?" he asked. He spoke Dutch with a German accent.

"Yes." Miriam's heart raced wildly.

"My name is Ernst Lubbers," he said, offering his hand. "And you are . . . ?"

She hesitated, unsure whether to give her real name or her false one. But Herr Lubbers had a kind face and was clearly Jewish with his dark, curly hair and beard. "I'm Miriam Leopold." It felt good to say her real name.

"You've had professional training, I could tell," he said, switching to German. "You performed with sensitivity and skill. Where are you from?"

"Cologne. My mother and uncle and some of my other family members are musicians."

"We need you for our orchestra."

Miriam blinked. "Your *orchestra*?" She couldn't have been more surprised if he'd said they needed her for the zoo.

"The camp *Kommandant* decided that the prisoners would be much happier here if he organized some entertainment for us in the evenings. He ordered all of the musicians to form an orchestra. We now perform a variety of music—everything from cabaret to classical pieces. Even a ballet. We could use another violinist."

Miriam could only stare at him in amazement. She wasn't going to be punished. She was being invited to perform with other musicians.

"I'm the manager and conductor," Herr Lubbers continued. "If you decide to join us, you'll be given a regular work assignment like the rest of us, but also time off for rehearsals when we have an event coming up." When she still couldn't reply, he added, "I understand you were in the punishment block?"

"Yes, the Nazis found me in hiding."

"Well, you're out of there now. You'll live in this barracks with some of the other musicians. And you'll be exempt from deportation for the time being. So what do you say? Would you like to join us?"

"Yes! Thank you!" The tears she'd held back all morning rolled down her face.

"We have a rehearsal this evening after supper. I'll see you then."

When he was gone, Miriam sank down on the nearest bunk, weak with wonder and relief. Music had been part of her life for as long as she could remember, bringing her joy, challenging her, giving her a purpose. She had brought her violin with her when she'd fled Germany because she couldn't imagine her life without it. Then, miraculously, her music had drawn Avi to her. It had soothed baby Elisheva to sleep. And it had provided a way for Miriam to express all of her sorrow and fear and grief. And now, most assuredly, her music had saved her life.

CHAPTER 52

Boots tramped down the prison corridor. Ans and the other women in her cell went still when the steps halted outside their door. The key rattled in the lock. The door was solid wood, so there was no way to know who the guard was coming for until it opened.

"Bernandina Kamp," he said.

Ans went cold as she struggled to her feet. The fox-faced Gestapo officer stood beside the guard, his brass buttons and belt buckle gleaming. It was the first time she had been out of her cell in Kasteel van Woerden in two days. A tremor of fear shivered through her as she walked the long corridor and up a flight of stairs to the windowless room where the officer had interrogated her before. This time he made her stand in front of him.

Lord, help me . . . Please help me . . .

"Look at me, Bernandina." His voice could have turned water into ice. Ans forced herself to meet his gaze, determined not to let it waver. It was all right to let her fear show, she told herself. An innocent dairymaid would naturally be terrified. His narrowed eyes bored into hers. "We know you work as a courier for the Resistance, so do not deny it." Ans shook her head, her throat too tight to speak. Did he really know or was he bluffing? "It will be much better for you if you tell me everything. I really do not want to hurt you."

"But I am telling you the truth." Before she could blink, the officer lifted his hand and slapped her face.

"Don't lie to me!" She staggered backwards, clutching her stinging cheek. He pushed her hand down and forced her to look at him again. "You won't like the prison camp at Vught. You'll suffer there. Perhaps you'll even die. Do you want to die, Bernandina?"

"No."

Terror flooded through her. Then, unbidden, the words Ans had been made to memorize in catechism class swirled softly through her mind: *"I am not my own, but I belong, body and soul, in life and in death, to my faithful Savior, Jesus Christ. . . ."*

"I can arrange favored treatment for you in prison—better food, a warm blanket, special favors from the guards. Favored prisoners do not die."

". . . He watches over me in such a way that without the will of my heavenly Father, not a hair can fall from my head . . ."

"Tell me the truth right now, Bernandina, and I'll make certain you are favored."

She swallowed. "I am telling the truth."

". . . He also assures me of eternal life and makes me sincerely willing and ready, henceforth, to live unto Him. . . ."

"I don't believe you." He lifted his hand as if he might slap her again, and she flinched. A tear rolled down Ans's cheek.

"Why won't you believe me?"

He glared at her for a long moment before saying, "I have a few questions about your home in Java." Ans's stomach rolled, and she looked down at the floor. He reached to lift her chin. "You will look at me when you answer." Someone must have coached him, because his questions poked at details about her home and her family as if seeking a thread he could pull to unravel her lies. Ans stared into his lean face as she described everything Erik had told her, adding as much detail as she could recall. His expression gave nothing away. Ans had no idea if he was finding errors in her stories or not. The interrogation seemed to last for hours until her legs grew weary and her fear overflowed in tears.

At last he paused, bending until his face was very close to hers. "Do you hope to return to Bandung one day? To your family?"

"Yes . . . but I haven't heard from them since the Japanese overran the island."

"Well, if you wish to see your home and your family, then you will need to think harder about cooperating with me. Do you understand?"

She nodded, not daring to move away from him. Her heart beat faster when he yanked open the door and called for a guard.

Please, Lord . . .

She was very surprised when the guard led her back to her cell and pushed her inside. She slumped onto the floor, covering her face with her hands, weeping with relief. She silently thanked God for the memorized words that had come to mind, giving her peace when she'd needed it. Erik had saved her life again, this time with stories of his homeland.

"What happened? Did they rough you up?"

Ans looked up to see who'd spoken. A new woman her own age had been assigned to the overcrowded cell while she'd been gone, replacing the middle-aged woman accused of selling meat on the black market.

"I haven't had my hearing yet," the stranger said. "Tell me what they did so I can be ready for them."

"They accused me of lying, but I'm telling the truth. My bicycle was stolen and I was late for curfew—that's all!"

The young woman sat down beside her as if they were old friends. "I hear they torture you until you tell the truth."

"It is the truth!" Ans had been warned back in Leiden not to befriend anyone if she was ever arrested because the Nazis often planted spies in prison cells. This friendly woman's abrupt arrival made Ans suspicious. She'd spoken only superficially with the other women sharing her cell, but they all had a core of tensely coiled fear that this talkative one lacked.

"My name's Trix. What's yours?"

"Bernandina . . . but if you don't mind, I don't feel much like talking right now."

"You might feel better if you told me all your troubles and had a good cry—"

"Shut up and leave her alone," one of the others said. Ans looked up at her gratefully. The nosy cellmate retreated.

The guard returned for Ans the next day, leading her through the labyrinthine hallways until she stood before a Nazi judge for her hearing. The fox-faced Gestapo officer was her accuser. "This is your last chance to tell the truth so I can help you," he told Ans.

"But I did tell you the truth."

The judge beckoned for the officer to come forward to speak privately in German. "I think she's a courier for the Resistance, but I have no proof," the officer told the judge. "She claims to be a farm maid, but she seems too bright and well-spoken."

"Does she have the hands of a farm maid? Tell her to show me her hands." The Gestapo officer ordered Ans to hold out her hands. She pretended to be baffled and held them up as if in surrender. The officer yanked them down and pushed them in front of the judge so he could examine them. For the first time in her life, Ans was grateful for red-chapped washerwoman's hands.

"They're the hands of a maid," the judge said. "Was she carrying contraband?"

"No, but she admitted that she'd been to Bodegraven, so she might have delivered it before her bicycle was commandeered." Ans objected to the word *commandeered*. Her bike had been stolen, plain and simple. But she didn't dare react.

"Ask her how to milk a cow," the judge said. Again, the Gestapo officer translated the request into Dutch, and again Ans tried to appear baffled, as if there were no mystery to milking a cow. She described the process, including a warning to watch out for the cow's rear hooves.

"You have to squeeze and pull . . . Here, I'll show you." She grabbed her accuser's hand, using his fingers as teats to demonstrate the gentle squeeze-pull motion that drew out the milk.

"Such a clever girl," he muttered in German, his fox eyes narrowed. "A little too clever for a dairymaid, I think."

"I only learned how to milk after I came to this country," she told the judge. "I wanted to be a housemaid, but the only work I could find was on a farm." The Gestapo officer didn't translate what she'd said.

"She appears genuine, then?" the judge asked in German. The officer shrugged as if reluctant to give up. Ans stared at the floor, unwilling to let them see her relief. She jumped when the judge slammed down his gavel.

"Bernandina Kamp, I find you guilty of breaking curfew and sentence you to a term in the prison camp in Vught."

"What did he say?" Ans asked her accuser. He didn't reply.

They made Ans change back into her own clothes and drove her to the prison in Vught that night, stuffed in the back of a canvas-covered truck with two dozen other female prisoners. She recognized her former cellmate accused of black marketeering, but Trix, the talkative one, wasn't there. It was still dark, with just a sliver of light in the east, when the truck halted on a narrow, rutted road in the woods. The guards ordered the women to get out, and for a horrifying moment, Ans wondered if they were going to be executed in this lonely, deserted place. She'd heard rumors of such things happening. But the soldiers told the women to start walking, prodded forward by bayonets. Anyone who stumbled in the darkness was struck by a rifle butt until she stood again.

At last Ans saw guard towers ahead, silhouetted against the slowly brightening sky. Spiky rows of barbed wire stretched between them. Dogs barked and snarled in the distance. The prison camp looked enormous, sprawled across a flat, sandy area and surrounded by woods. "At least they didn't send us to Germany," the woman beside Ans whispered.

They were marched through two sets of gates and into a windowless reception hall. "Undress! Undress!" someone shouted. Ans removed her clothes, dropping them to the floor to stand naked and shivering with the other women while prison guards and laughing soldiers watched. "Do not think of escaping," the women were told. "The fences have electricity. The guards in the towers have machine guns. And beyond the fence is a minefield." They let Ans keep her underwear and sweater and issued her a striped prison gown.

Guards called out their names and assigned each woman to a barracks and a work detail. "Bernandina Kamp, since you are a scrub maid, you will clean the latrine floor every day, then proceed to the camp laundry to wash the guards' clothing." It was a special punishment from the Gestapo officer. He'd had the final laugh.

CHAPTER 53

It was Tuesday morning again. The lists of names would be read today. Despairing souls would assemble in the camp square in the cold, drizzling rain, then shuffle to the railcars. The train would depart as it did every week. Miriam had been assured that she was exempt. Yet she'd awakened this morning with the same sickening dread she'd felt every week since arriving at Westerbork, wondering which people from her barracks or from the camp kitchen where she worked would be missing after today.

She stood in the barracks doorway after the names were read, forcing herself to watch the painful ordeal in the camp square, silently reciting the psalm that had become her unending refrain: *"Have mercy on me, my God, have mercy on me, for in you I take refuge. I will take refuge in the shadow of your wings until the disaster has passed."* Then she closed her eyes against the sight of children clinging to their parents and elderly couples holding each other's hands as the roll call was taken. She prayed for God to have mercy on the souls who would leave here today.

Miriam had returned to the punishment block to search for her friends Klara and Tina from Meijers House, but no one seemed to know or remember them. She'd asked several of her fellow musicians from the orchestra if they'd ever met Avraham Leopold—or Andries Bakker, his false identity. No one had. Nor did they remember her father or Mrs. Spielman. Miriam understood the reluctance most people felt to befriend their fellow prisoners. It made the endless, seemingly random goodbyes too painful.

She often thought about the women from the Mulders' farm—Lies and her daughters, Julie and Betsie, and the rabbi's daughter, Alie—wondering if they were still safe in their dark, cramped chicken coop. She grieved over the unknown fate of Miss Hannie, Miss Willy, and Frits. So many good Dutch people like the sisters and the Ver Beeks and the Mulders and Dr. Elzinga and Eloise and Ans had risked their lives for her and her fellow Jews.

Miriam didn't recognize anyone among the one thousand people standing out in the square this morning, most with their heads bowed and shoulders hunched against the icy rain. She moved away from the door as the guards herded the deportees to the train so she wouldn't hear the wooden doors slam shut or the iron bar lock into place to seal them inside. The ground rumbled as the train steamed away.

Later, Miriam thought of Mrs. Spielman again as she peeled potatoes in the kitchen, remembering how the kind woman had taught her to cook and bake. Miriam was grateful for the simple skills she'd learned from her, but it pained her to imagine her landlady and Abba hearing their names called, climbing into the boxcars.

The potatoes were small and soft and shriveled, making them difficult to peel. Miriam didn't want to waste any bits of potato by paring off peels that were too thick, yet she'd learned that all the peels and scraps would be boiled for broth. Her workday at Westerbork lasted from seven in the morning until noon, and then from two until seven, with evenings and Sundays free. Except on Tuesdays, of course. On that day, all the prisoners remained in their barracks until after the train departed. Working in the camp kitchen was tedious and meant standing for much of the day, but the other prisoners had assured Miriam that the assignment was easy compared to working in the shoe factory or scrapyard.

That evening, Miriam rehearsed with the camp musicians for the concert on Sunday, her first. Performing with them was like nothing she'd ever experienced. Many orchestra members were seasoned professionals, and it was a privilege and a challenge to work with them. She thought it a terrible waste of talent to ban musicians from the great concert halls of Europe because they were Jewish.

The sheet music was another challenge, copied by hand and cobbled together, often arranged by the musicians themselves from memory. Some pieces were new works, composed in the camp. Many people shared the same part, with extra sections written on scraps of paper. In places where the notation thinned or parts were missing, the conductor told the players what he wanted and relied on them to fill it in. Miriam felt lost at first and afraid to play by ear without music. The other violinists encouraged her to try, "for our audience's sake."

On the day of the performance, Miriam vibrated with nerves and excitement as she took her place on stage to warm up. The audience was enormous, as if every prisoner in camp had come. Minutes before the concert began, the front row filled with Nazi soldiers, including an official in the uniform of the dreaded SS. "Who is that man?" Miriam whispered to the violinist beside her.

"That's Obersturmführer Gemmeker, the camp *Kommandant*." Miriam's lungs squeezed like a fist. "Are you all right?" the violinist asked.

"No . . . I can't . . ." Miriam rose and staggered off the stage, nearly bowling into the conductor. He grabbed her to steady her, halting her flight.

"Miriam, what's wrong? Is it stage fright? Listen, you don't need to—"

"It isn't that," she said, her lungs wheezing. "The *Kommandant* . . . and the Nazis . . . I didn't know they would be here! I can't play for them!"

He led her to a chair and made her sit. She was afraid he would be angry with her, but he seemed more worried than angry. "If you don't perform, they'll call your name on Tuesday."

Her stomach rolled. She drew a few breaths, still struggling for air.

"My music comes from my soul. I can't . . . I can't bare my soul to them. They've already taken every other part of me. This is all I have left!"

He looked at her for a long moment, pity and sorrow in his dark eyes. "You're not performing for them. You're offering your talent as a gift to your fellow prisoners. This camp is such a dark, despairing place. Our music helps restore memories of happier times and brings an hour or two of joy, a smile, hope."

"But it's false hope. The Nazis' presence reminds us that we're prisoners and that there is no hope!"

He crouched in front of her. "You're wrong, Miriam. You've seen the propaganda that the Nazis spew out about us, saying that we're an inferior race, portraying us as less than human. When faced with their cruel treatment here day after day, we begin to believe those lies and lose our dignity as human beings. But each time our orchestra performs, each time beautiful, glorious music flows from our instruments and from our God-given abilities, we're slapping the Nazis in the face, proving that they're wrong about us. They may treat us like animals, but animals don't work together the way an orchestra does to create sound and beauty. The beaten-down souls in our audience sit up a little straighter when they hear us perform, because they are reminded of the beauty that's inside each of them. You're baring your soul, Miriam, to help restore their dignity."

The pain in Miriam's chest began to ease. She remembered how her music had encouraged Avi when they'd been in this place together. Abba said that Mother's music had drawn him closer to God.

The conductor helped Miriam to her feet. "Play for our fellow Jews, Miriam. Our lives may be ending soon, but let's pour out the last of our strength in praise and music, not in tears."

She was able to draw a deep breath as she walked onto the stage and sat down. The conductor raised his baton. Miriam began to play, imagining that Avi was sitting in the audience with Elisheva on his lap, finding hope in each note she played. She imagined Abba and Mrs. Spielman sitting beside him, along with Mother and her aunts and uncles and her cousin Saul. She imagined Lies, Julie, Betsie, and Alie sitting with Klara and Tina. And with Miss Hannie, Miss Willy and Rietje and Frits—all the residents of Meijers House, who'd been declared inferior. As the music soared, they could all escape the indignities of living in chicken coops and attics and prison barracks and reclaim their humanity. She played for them and for the sorrowful souls who would be forced to climb into the boxcars in a few days. *You were created in God's image,* she told them with every note she played. *And so was I.*

On the following Tuesday morning, the head of Miriam's barracks called for everyone's attention. A wave of anxiety spread through the barracks. The matron cleared her throat. "There will be no deportations this week. Report to your work assignments immediately."

Above the buzz of astonished murmurs, someone dared to ask, "Why? Why were they canceled?"

The faintest hint of a smile brightened the matron's face. She was a prisoner like the rest of them. "There are rumors that all the railroad workers in the nation have gone on strike."

CHAPTER 54

Lena endured another long month without her husband, without her father, trying to scale the great mountain of her grief, slipping back into the valley of death's shadow continually. Sunday church services were no longer the same, the memory of the Nazis' violence still fresh and raw on everyone's hearts. But the congregation continued to meet, offering strength to one another. Lena picked up Wim's and Maaike's school lessons each Sunday, unwilling to allow Maaike to go into town alone to attend school, terrified to let Wim be seen. Lena could tell he was growing restless, tired of living in the shadows. She'd heard of other mothers who'd disguised their sons in women's clothing, but Wim had laughed at the idea, then shook his head firmly when she suggested it. They both wondered how much longer they'd be forced to live this way.

"I'm taking the cows out to graze in the pasture today," Wim told Lena at breakfast one morning. "There's still a little grass out there, and we need to save the feed for winter." He was taller than Pieter now, with Pieter's large, strong hands.

"Do you think that's wise?" Lena asked. "The cows are terrified of the low-flying planes. And I heard that cows have been killed by falling shrapnel."

"They need to eat or their milk will dry up."

"I can take the herd out."

"I need to get out and walk, Mama. Please."

She couldn't deny him such a simple thing. Lena guessed that he wanted to feel the fall sunshine on his head more than he wanted the cows to find grass. Ever since Wim was a child, the sun would bleach his thick blond hair nearly white during the summer months. Now it was the color of ashes after hiding indoors for so long. Lena stood in the open barn door with the milk cans, watching Wim stride across the field with the cows. "Not too far," she whispered. "That's far enough . . ." Wim kept going.

When she heard engines approaching, Lena looked up. The sky was clear. The vehicle was speeding closer. "Wim!" she screamed. "Wim, come back!" He didn't seem to hear her. She started to run toward the pasture, calling his name. Then she remembered that Maaike and Bep were inside the house alone. If this was a Nazi vehicle—and who else had gasoline these days?—she couldn't leave her girls here by themselves. "Wim!" she screamed again. "Wim, hide!"

He finally turned to her. But the truck was close now. Lena could see it. Wim wouldn't have time to run all the way back to the barn. Whoever was in the truck would surely see him standing in the middle of the flat field. He might be able to make it to one of the irrigation ditches in time if he crouched low. *Oh, God, please!* she begged. *Please don't let them see Wim!* She had prayed for her father, too, and God hadn't listened. But He had to answer her prayer this time—He had to! Swastikas fluttered from the truck's antennae. Lena turned away from the field and moved into the barn so they would have to follow her there to speak with her.

The truck pulled to a halt and the soldier in the passenger seat jumped down, armed with a rifle and bayonet. He would use it to stab all the haystacks, searching for men in hiding. A second soldier jumped out of the back, also armed. Then a third.

"Where is your son?" the soldier asked in German. "We know you have a son."

Oh, God . . .

Lena set down the milk cans so they wouldn't slip from her shaking hands. Which of her neighbors had told them about Wim? She held her palms out, shaking her head, pretending not to understand. "Your son!" he said in Dutch. One of the soldiers went into the barn. The second one started to follow him, then something caught his eye in the distant pasture.

"Over there!" he shouted. He pointed to Wim, who was trying to crawl toward the ditch. "Halt! Halt right there or I'll shoot!"

Lena closed her eyes. *Oh, God . . . oh, God . . . oh, God . . .* She heard the door to the kitchen open and saw Maaike and Bep peeking out. She shook her head at them and they disappeared inside.

It seemed to take forever for the soldiers to cross the field and haul Wim back with them. And yet it took only an instant. "No! You can't take him!" Lena screamed. "He's only sixteen!" One of the soldiers blocked Lena's path to keep her from going to him. "Please! No!" she begged.

They parted the canvas flap and Lena saw that the back of the truck was filled with young men Wim's age. "Get in," they told him. He looked at Lena, his face white with fear.

"No!" she screamed. Everything in Lena wanted to run forward and save her son. But she couldn't. The soldier pushed Wim's shoulder, and he climbed on board.

A moment later, the truck was gone. They had taken her son! Why hadn't Wim stayed inside where it was safe? They'd been so careful all these months. Why hadn't she walked the cows out to the pasture instead of him?

Lena sank down in the doorway of the barn, rocking in place, screaming and wailing with grief. "God, why? How could You let this happen?" There was no answer.

Lena hadn't slept well in days, waiting for her contact to come, hoping and praying that he would know what had happened to Wim. She was sitting with Ina at the kitchen table after midnight when Wolf slipped through the door from the barn to join them.

"Do you have any news of my son?" she asked, rising from her chair.

"Your son?" He glanced around the darkened kitchen as if Wim were playing a game and might leap out of the shadows.

"The Nazis took him away."

"I'm sorry . . . I'm so sorry . . ." He sank onto a chair as if burdened by the news.

"They put him in a truck full of young men. Do you know where they were taking them? To a factory in the East, do you think? The Allies are bombing those Nazi factories, and . . ." She couldn't finish.

"I don't think so. We've heard that they're pulling men off the streets, even men with work exemptions, to help dig anti-tank trenches and build bunkers. The work is hard, but it's in the Nazis' best interests to keep their laborers fed and healthy."

"Will you please try to find out for me?" Before Wolf could reply, Max crept up the stairs from the root cellar with the newest batch of forged ID cards. He exchanged them for the stolen cards and photographs that Wolf had brought, and the men talked about their work for a few minutes. Lena gave Wolf a bowl of the soup she'd made for dinner, then got out a stack of bowls and spoons so he could distribute the rest to the shadow people. When he finished speaking with Max, Wolf turned to Lena again.

"I can't promise that I'll be able to find your son. The Nazis have been on high alert as the Allies make progress toward Germany. They make sure no one gets too close. Besides, the Nazis have abducted so many men, it'll be difficult to find your son among them. I'm sorry."

"He's just a boy!"

Wolf closed his eyes for a long moment as if searching for words to console her. He always came at night, and Lena wondered what he looked like in daylight. He opened his eyes again and met her gaze. "Lena, I've gotten to know you and your husband well these past few years. I've seen your strength and your faith, and I know that your son has learned to be strong from the two of you. He'll be able to endure whatever he has to."

"It's the worst feeling in the world not to know where he is or what's happening to him. I'd rather learn the truth so I can begin to accept it—like I've had to do with my father."

"I was very sorry to hear about your father. He was a brave man, and he helped us a great deal."

Lena pulled a handkerchief from her pocket and wiped her eyes. "And my daughter Ans? Do you know anything about her? Max and Ina told me she had to go into hiding the same time they did."

Wolf concentrated on his soup as if he hadn't heard her.

Fear slithered through Lena. He knew something. "Ans works with your Resistance cell, Wolf. Someone along your chain of contacts must know where she is and what's happened to her."

Wolf still didn't speak.

She gripped his arm, stopping him from eating. "If you know something, please tell me. Don't imagine that you're sparing me by holding back."

"I understand." He laid down his spoon, then paused for such a long time that Lena wanted to scream. At last he sighed and looked up at her. "Ans is one of our best couriers. But she was late for curfew after her bicycle was stolen, and she was arrested. Nothing incriminating was found on her, and she didn't give away any of her contacts. But she was sent to the Nazi prison in Vught."

Lena leaned against Wolf's chair as she tried to absorb this information. Her beautiful, vibrant daughter—a prisoner.

"Your family has paid a huge price for your country's sake."

"We're not doing it out of patriotism," Lena said sharply. "It's because of our faith in Christ. Are you a Christian, Wolf?"

He gave a humorless laugh. "I may be before the war is over. So many people I work with have told me the same thing—that they're risking their lives because of their faith." He slowly rose to his feet. He was so thin his clothes might have belonged to someone else. "I need to go. I'm sorry I haven't been much help to you. If it's any consolation, the Allies are winning the war." He took the food Lena had prepared for the shadow people and left.

Lena said good night to Max and Ina and went upstairs to bed. She already knew she wouldn't sleep. The news that Ans was in a Nazi prison had shattered her. Two of her children were in the enemy's hands, and she worried that her husband might be too. It was hard not to imagine the worst for all of them. In the past, she would have gone to the manse in the morning and asked her father to pray for Ans and Wim and Pieter, but he was gone. Lena remembered his words quite clearly: *"I may not always be here."* It was as if he'd known what was coming. Before the war, Lena's life had been full and rich and complete. Now she was being slowly emptied out.

CHAPTER 55

Guards stood outside Ans's long wooden barracks. The only windows were up near the rafters where no one could see out. Rows and rows of metal bunks, stacked three high, filled most of the building. A few wooden tables and benches for meals stood along one side, although there weren't nearly enough for all 175 women who lived in Ans's barracks. The bathroom had only ten toilets, with no doors or partitions between them for privacy. With so many women sick with diarrhea, including Ans at times, the latrine was not only humiliating but revolting.

Each day was numbingly the same. Guards woke them at 5:45 a.m. for roll call. After a breakfast of bread and margarine, most of the women were sent to work in the rope factory. Lunch consisted of thin, watery soup with an occasional vegetable floating in it. Supper was bread and margarine again. Every once in a while, the Red Cross arrived to serve a hearty soup. Ans looked forward to it as if it were a feast. She soon lost weight on the meager diet, becoming so thin her underwear wouldn't stay up. She could count all of her ribs. Several other women in her barracks grew ill and died.

Ans scrubbed the floor of the latrine on her hands and knees every morning, the stench making her gag. Then she reported to the laundry, where she soaped and scrubbed and rinsed and wrung the guards' heavy clothing until the skin on her hands cracked and bled. Day after weary day, her hope drained away like the gray wash water swirling down the drain. At night, shivering on her bunk, despair seeped through to her soul like the cold wind that leaked through the cracks in the barracks walls and around the windows.

On some days, Ans chatted with the other laundry workers to help pass the time, but most days, they all fell into silence, their grief too heavy to voice, their sorrow too painful to speak of. Ans scrolled through her memories to keep her mind occupied, and most of them were happy ones. But as the days dragged on and the weather grew frigid, regret for the mistakes and poor choices she'd made began to color all of her memories. She couldn't think of her mama without regretting that she'd fought with her. If only she had another chance to make it up to her. She longed to tell Mama how much she loved her, how much she missed hearing her sing while she worked. The farm life Ans had rejected had been ideal in so many ways—she'd been well-fed and nurtured, surrounded by a family who loved her and each other. Yet she'd rebelled against the rules and a life of faith, longing for something more. What that was, Ans couldn't say. She had been foolish—so foolish.

She wished she could thank her parents and grandparents for their patient Bible teaching and for insisting that she memorize the catechism. Those words had been in her mind and heart when she'd needed them, giving her peace and calm. She remembered doubting God's goodness when her grandmother became sick and died. It had been her first experience with grief. Ans hadn't known that death would soon surround her every day.

Ans prayed for her loved ones at night when she couldn't sleep and while she scrubbed floors and clothes during the day. Not knowing what was happening to them was torture. She thought of Miriam and Avi and baby Elisheva, praying that they'd remain safe and well hidden. She prayed often for Eloise and Herman, wondering if Eloise had sunk into despair after Herman's arrest. He must be so worried about her. Was he even alive or had he been executed for his crime? Ans prayed and prayed as she wrung out the clothes, begging God for mercy.

Most painful of all were her thoughts of Erik. Would he ever forgive her? He'd begged her to stop working for the underground, warning her that she might be arrested. She should have listened. How he must hate her for not marrying him when she'd had the chance. And for disappearing. Ans comforted herself in the freezing nights by remembering the warmth of Erik's arms. She would close her eyes and recall his kisses. They had enjoyed walking and talking together, cooking spicy meals and laughing—how she'd delighted in making quiet, serious Erik laugh. He was her first love, her only love. But then she would recall her fumbling attempts to share her faith with him and wish she'd done a better job. Erik didn't know how to pray—for her or for the war to end. He couldn't find comfort in trusting God.

What would become of the two of them after the war? Could they ever be as happy as Mama and Papa, who worked together in a life they both loved? Or as her grandparents had been, serving the church? Would they ever be as unselfishly devoted to each other as Eloise and Herman? Or Avi and Miriam? Could she and Erik truly look forward to a life together after the very different choices they'd made, the opposite directions they'd taken?

On some days Ans's thoughts were as bleak and cold as the gray winter skies, her tears dampening the cement floor as she scoured the latrine. She heard planes droning overhead and the distant rumble of explosions, and she grieved for her once-beautiful country, now being trampled and scarred and forever changed. And she would never be the same, either. She had failed the people she loved—her parents by leaving her faith and her home. Eloise, by deserting her. Professor Huizenga had relied on Ans to watch over his wife, and she'd failed him, too. And Erik. If she had truly loved him, she would have done what he'd asked. Yet that would have meant abandoning Avi and Miriam and Elisheva.

Ans's thoughts swirled while her regrets piled higher and higher. Had she also disappointed God? Was He punishing her for walking away from Him? Ans had rediscovered her faith and had worked to serve Him by saving people, and now she was here, slowly dying in prison. And who would ever know what had happened to Ans de Vries? It would be Bernandina Kamp who had lived and died in Vught Prison.

As the rain turned to thick, slushy snow that soaked through Ans's shoes, despair like she'd never known before filled every inch of her. She began to cry as she lay shivering on her bunk one night, unable to stop. *If You're there, Lord—if You can even hear me—please, please help me.*

The barracks was silent except for the soft breathing of the women around her. God seemed far away. And then a shaft of silvery moonlight suddenly shone down on Ans's bunk from one of the high, narrow windows. She looked up and saw the winter clouds slowly thinning like frost melting from window glass to reveal a glorious full moon. It filled the wooden window frame, bathing the room with light. She remembered marveling at a moon like this one with her grandmother a few nights before she died. Oma had compared her life to the phases of the moon, growing fuller and brighter with purpose, then gradually diminishing until it disappeared in darkness. *"But watch the sky, darling Ans. The moon isn't gone at all. It shines eternally, like our life in Christ."* Oma had accepted her death as God's will without questions or bitterness, even though Ans had not. *"We can trust His promise of eternal life,"* Oma had said. *"It's more wonderful than we can even imagine."*

". . . He watches over me in such a way that without the will of my heavenly Father, not a hair can fall from my head . . ."

If that was true, then God must want Ans to be here, in Vught Prison. Not as a punishment, but for reasons only He could see, just as He'd had reasons for taking Oma to heaven. But what could they possibly be? As the moon bathed the barracks in light, another Scripture sprang to mind. *"You are the light of the world. . . . Let your light shine before others . . ."*

Ans thought of the women in her barracks and the laundry. What if she tried to help them battle despair the way she'd once helped Eloise? Instead of withdrawing inside herself and wallowing in self-pity, what if Ans reached out to them, offering encouragement and hope? She had worked with the underground because she'd wanted to serve God—and now He'd placed her in this prison. Could she serve Him here with joy? Without bitterness?

". . . He also assures me of eternal life and makes me sincerely willing and ready, henceforth, to live unto Him. . . ."

Ans wiped her tears as a deep peace flooded through her, like the moonlight that filled the room, chasing the shadows.

CHAPTER 56

Winter arrived early, bringing bitter-cold weather. The nation's rail-roads had been ordered by the exiled queen and her government to go on strike, making supplies of food and coal impossible to get. Fence posts and trees began to disappear as Lena and her desperate neighbors struggled to stay warm. The *onderduikers* all moved into the barn, where the heat from the animals helped keep them warm. Lena brought the girls into bed with her at night, piling on all of their blankets. The potatoes and cabbage and other food stored in her root cellar was dwindling fast, and she didn't know what they would eat when it ran out. The rabbits she'd raised for the stewpot were as scrawny as the people eating them. The underground provided her with extra ration stamps, but the shelves in the village stores were nearly empty. It was hard not to sink into despair, but Lena knew there were always people worse off than she was. She still had milk and eggs and butter on the farm.

"Thousands of people are starving to death in the big cities," Wolf told Lena on one of his visits. "And that's not an exaggeration. There's no food to be found at any price. Our countrymen are suffering more this winter than in all the months of war put together."

Lena was washing the supper dishes one evening, with Maaike and Bep drying them, when there was a knock on the front door. No one used the front door. And she hadn't heard a vehicle approaching. "Stay here," she told the girls. She dried her hands on her apron and went to answer it. The knock sounded a second time before Lena reached the door, and she decided to peer through the curtains on her front window first. Three huddled figures stood on her doorstep, two of them small enough to be children. She quickly opened the door. "Come in," she said before they could speak. "Our house is chilly but it's warmer than outside."

The woman, wrapped in several layers of clothing, hesitated before gently prodding the bundled children through the door. "Thank you. You're very kind. My sons are hungry. Please . . ."

"This way," Lena said. "It's warmer in the kitchen." The lamp gave enough light for her to see that the trio looked bone weary. "Have a seat. I'm Lena de Vries, and these are my daughters Maaike and Bep."

"I'm Janneke." The boys pulled off their wool hats, the static making their fair hair stand on end. Lena guessed the woman to be in her thirties, the boys around Maaike's age. It was clear from their gaunt faces and hollow eyes that they were starving. "Get three bowls and spoons," she told Maaike. "Bep, can you fetch the bread, please? And the butter." Lena had made pea soup for supper, and she put what was left of it on the stove to warm. "Where are you from, Janneke?"

"Den Haag."

"You walked all this way? That's quite a distance."

"We had to. There's no food anywhere in the city. I couldn't let my boys starve. Some of my neighbors have died."

"I understand. I would do the same for my children." Lena watched them gobble down the food. She had hoped to serve the leftovers to her family and the shadow people again, but she filled their bowls a second time, praying that a kind stranger was feeding Wim and Ans and Pieter tonight. Janneke stopped her boys from taking a second slice of bread.

"We'll take it to Oma," she told them. She looked up at Lena as if fearful of a reprimand. "Please . . . may I take this for my mother? She isn't well, and I promised her we'd bring something."

"Yes, of course. Let the boys have another slice, and I'll pack some bread and a bit of cheese for your mother."

Tears rolled down Janneke's face. "I didn't want to bring my boys. I knew the trip would be hard for them. But there are so many other beggars on the roads, and I was afraid of being robbed if I was by myself. Even desperate people think twice before stealing from children."

"I can't imagine facing such impossible choices," Lena said. She'd thought her hatred for the Nazis couldn't possibly grow any stronger, but the plight of these desperate travelers deepened it.

Janneke stood when she finished eating and prodded her weary sons to their feet. "You have been so kind, Lena. We won't impose on you any longer. May God bless you for your generosity."

"You can't go back out in the cold. Stay the night, please. My son's bedroom upstairs is empty."

"You would take in strangers?"

"You would do the same if you were in my place. Come. You look tired."

"Mama?" Maaike whispered later in the dark when they were all in bed. "If we give away all of our food, won't we run out?" In truth, Lena feared the same thing. But the war had given her no choice but to place everything in God's hands and trust Him. She'd also learned that trusting Him wasn't a onetime decision but a daily one. She sat up so she could see her daughter's face better.

"Maaike, Jesus said, 'Give, and it will be given to you . . . pressed down, shaken together and running over.' He's teaching us to trust Him. I know how hard that lesson is, believe me. But as we were feeding those poor travelers tonight, I prayed that someone else was feeding your papa and Wim and Ans for us."

"Is that how it works?"

"Yes, dear one. I think that's how it works."

More people came to Lena's door in the weeks that followed,

desperate people who had walked from Den Haag or Leiden or even from Amsterdam. They wore layers of clothes for warmth, rags and pieces of carpet tied around their feet. They were starving, begging for food, willing to trade anything they had for a piece of bread or a cup of milk or an egg. Some stood at a distance and sent their children to her door. "Hunger trippers" people called them, risking capture by the Nazis or being robbed by their fellow beggars for a bite of food. Lena was now cooking the sugar beets meant for the animals. *"Give us this day our daily bread"* became her fervent prayer.

At times, she felt as though she were feeding the world. But Lena couldn't turn anyone away. For as long as the Lord provided, she would share what she had.

CHAPTER 57

FEBRUARY 1945

Ans sang the hymn that had been her grandmother's favorite as she scrubbed the latrine floor. She sang for the women in the barracks who were too sick to report for work, and for the woman sitting on the toilet, too ill to keep the food she ate from running straight through her. Some of the invalids hummed along with Ans. "We look forward to your songs every morning," many of them told her. Most of the guards looked the other way when Ans took time away from scrubbing to pray with someone. At Christmas, she had coaxed the women to sing carols. She and another woman fashioned a crèche from scraps of wood and cloth and retold the story of Christ's birth. In saving others from despair, Ans realized that she also had saved herself.

She was in the middle of the second verse when a guard opened the outside door, bringing in a gust of wintry wind. "Which one of you is Bernandina Kamp?"

Ans sat upright on her knees. "I am."

"Get your belongings and come with me."

"What about my bucket and scrub brush?"

"Leave them."

Ans quickly scooped up the rags she used to cushion her knees from the hard floor and stuffed them beneath her sweater. Someone else would snatch them up to pad their clothing for extra warmth if she left them behind. She hurried to her bunk and gathered the toothbrush and comb she'd received from the Red Cross, along with the other items she'd collected over the months. She had arrived at the prison with nothing.

Cold, damp air struck her as she walked outside. The guard who prodded her across the prison grounds wore a long woolen greatcoat and leather boots. Ans wore only a sweater. She didn't need to be encouraged to hurry. The guard led her to the administration building, where she'd been forced to strip on the first day, then left her standing for more than an hour while the clerks behind the desks ignored her. At least the building was warm. She tried not to imagine what punishment she might face for singing and praying with her fellow inmates. She feared solitary confinement most of all.

At last, one of the clerks called her name and motioned her forward. "According to our records, you've served your sentence for breaking curfew," he said. "You're being released." Ans grabbed on to the edge of the desk to steady herself. He shoved her bag into her hands with the blouse and slacks she'd been wearing when she'd been arrested in Woerden and said, "Get changed." She knew better than to ask for privacy and quickly slipped off her prison gown. Her body was so thin and malnourished, she almost hoped the guards would stare and that they would feel ashamed. Her clothes still stank of vomit from the night she'd been arrested.

Ans couldn't imagine freedom. She hadn't dared to imagine it. But unless this was a cruel joke, she was about to walk out of Vught Prison a free woman. She wished she could run back to the laundry and say goodbye to the women she'd worked with and then stop to encourage her friends in the barracks to remain strong. Would her release give them hope that their freedom would come soon—or would it fill them with despair at being left behind? Either way, the prison authorities weren't going to give her a chance to go back.

When she was dressed, one of the guards escorted her through the front door and out through the prison's double gates. They slammed shut behind her. She was free! Ans couldn't comprehend it. Tears filled her eyes. She gazed around at the beautiful woods and heard the birds singing. She was weak and cold and hungry, but she thanked God for her freedom as she stumbled down the long driveway from the main gate. When she reached the road, Ans had no idea which direction to turn. She tried to recall the day she'd arrived at Vught in the early morning hours and decided to turn left. But where should she go? Back to the Dykstras' farm? To the town house in Leiden? To her parents' farm? All three places were at least fifty miles away, and she knew she wasn't strong enough to walk that far. She had no money for a train ticket. Even so, she kept walking, stopping every few minutes to rest her weakened leg muscles and pull up her baggy slacks. If she collapsed, she would freeze to death on the road.

Eventually the trees thinned. She passed frozen fields and saw church steeples on the horizon. After walking another fifteen minutes, Ans staggered into a town. A sign above a shuttered bakery told her she was in Vught. Next to the bakery, like an answer to a prayer she hadn't uttered, was a Red Cross post. A woman hurried to greet Ans as she stumbled through the door, no longer able to feel her frozen toes. "You must have come from the prison," the woman said.

"Yes . . ." She felt dizzy. She was going to collapse. The woman caught her just in time and helped her to a chair. She wrapped a blanket around her shoulders.

"Let's get you something to eat. What's your name?"

"Ans de Vries." She spoke without thinking, then remembered she was Bernandina Kamp now. She didn't care, glad to be herself in this moment.

The soup with beans and carrots was warm and delicious. Ans tried not to wolf it down. "Slowly, dear. Don't eat too much or it will come up again. Your stomach has surely shrunk by now."

"Everything about me has shrunk," Ans said, trying to laugh. Tears of joy and relief hovered close to the surface of her laughter. She was still shivering.

"I'm sorry it isn't warmer in here, Ans, but there are fuel shortages all over the country because of the rail strike. Food shortages too."

"It feels wonderful."

"Where is home for you?"

The question stopped her. She was afraid to say too much to this kind stranger or talk about her work with the Resistance. The Nazis still might be searching for her under her real name, and if she went home, she feared they would hurt her parents—and discover Elisheva. "I was living in Leiden when the war started," she finally said.

"I think we can help you get to Leiden if that's where you'd like to go. Until recently, we always provided rail tickets to paroled prisoners, but train travel is impossible right now. Our relief vans travel to the various jails and prisons around the country, so we might be able to shuttle you from place to place and eventually get you to Leiden."

"Thank you. I would be very grateful." She would find a way to get home to her farm from there, but first she needed to make sure Eloise was all right. Ans's greatest fear was that Eloise had sunk so deep into despair after her husband was arrested that she would try to harm herself.

"But before you go," the woman continued, "you should know that many, many people are starving in the western part of our country, especially in cities like Amsterdam and Leiden. The Nazis were so furious when all of the railroad workers went on strike as our queen asked them to do that they stopped distributing food in order to punish us. The Nazis have also destroyed many of our harbors to prevent the Allies from using them, and that means there are no food shipments by sea, either. Our Red Cross has organized soup kitchens in the cities, but we're running low on food ourselves."

"It's a good thing I learned to get by without much food in prison," Ans said. She pulled the waistband of her slacks out to show how huge they were. The woman looked away.

It took nearly a week of shuttling from place to place, but eventually Ans said goodbye to her Red Cross hosts outside Leiden's train station and walked across the bridge into the old city. The train station had suffered bomb damage, and the city's buildings and streets looked tired and beaten down—as did the people she passed. The Red Cross had fed

Ans along the way and she'd regained some of her strength. They'd also given her a secondhand winter coat.

She took a detour past the café where the Resistance once relayed messages, hoping to contact Havik again, but the café was closed and shuttered. She drew a deep breath, steeling herself for the worst, and hurried to the Huizengas' town house on the Witte Singel, walking around to the rear and knocking on the kitchen door. She had no idea what she would find.

Ans was relieved when Meta, the Jewish housekeeper, opened the door a crack and peered out. It meant that the Nazis hadn't arrested her and Sientje.

But Meta didn't seem to recognize Ans. "Yes? May I help you?" she asked.

"Meta, it's me—Ans. I'm back. Is . . . is Eloise here?"

The door swung wide and Meta threw her arms around her. "Oh, my goodness! It is you! I thought you were another beggar asking for food. Come in, come in! Eloise will be thrilled that you're here!"

Eloise is here.

The town house's kitchen was filled with strangers, all huddled around the range, all wearing coats. A large pot of something that didn't smell particularly good simmered on the stove. Ans was glad to see Meta's sister-in-law, Sientje, holding Mrs. Spielman's cat on her lap, but she didn't recognize anyone else. "Everybody, this is Ans!" Meta announced. "She's home at last!"

"Eloise told us all about you," one of the women said. Someone was chopping something in another room. And she heard a ball bouncing.

"Is Eloise here? I want to see her."

"I'll take you to her," Meta said. They stepped around the gathered people, passing two boys in overcoats bouncing a ball back and forth in the frigid dining room. And there was Eloise! She stood in the foyer, supervising a boy of twelve or thirteen as he chopped one of the spindles off the bannister. Most of the other spindles were also missing. So was the door to the front closet. "Eloise, look!" Meta shouted. "Ans is home!"

Eloise turned, and Ans was relieved to see how well she looked. She was much thinner, and the white streak in her dark hair had widened and spread since Ans had last seen her, but her eyes sparkled with excitement as she hurried toward her.

"Ans? . . . Is it really you . . . or just your shadow?"

"It's me!" They fell into each other's arms.

"I can't believe you're really here," Eloise said. She ran her hands down Ans's arms as if to convince herself she was real. "We heard you were in prison."

"I was, but they released me a few days ago."

"Thank God! That gives us all hope that maybe Herman and the others will be released too. You can stop chopping now," she told the boy when the spindle finally broke free. "That's enough wood for today. Besides, I believe in miracles now that Ans is here, so maybe we'll have another miracle and the weather will warm up, or the war will end before our town house is chopped into pieces. How are you, Ans? And don't say 'fine.' I can see that you've suffered. Come sit in the parlor with me so we can talk. I would offer you tea, but . . . well, there isn't any."

She was the same Eloise that Ans knew and loved, talking rapidly and without pause, gesturing with her fluttery hands. There were more strangers in the parlor too, including a young woman holding a baby, both heavily bundled against the chill. "Everyone . . . this is Ans," Eloise announced. "She's . . . well, she's like a daughter to me, and she's home!"

There were dozens of questions Ans wanted to ask as everyone chimed in to welcome her, but she knew Eloise would answer them in time. At last, she and Eloise were able to sit down at the little table where they'd had tea on Ans's first day. It seemed like a hundred years ago. "How are you, Eloise? And—" she leaned closer to whisper—"who are all these people?"

"I'm as good as can be expected, with good days and bad days. Today is a wonderful day now that you're home."

"And the people . . . ?"

"They're the families of Herman and Aalt's bank employees. When the Nazis arrested them, they also arrested the men who worked with them. Many of their wives and children had no way to support themselves and no place to go, so I invited them to live here. We've become our own little family. So you see, Ans? I'm still fighting back."

"Yes, I do see."

"I took them in because they're important to Herman and his brother, so they've become important to me. And after that, I couldn't break down or withdraw from the world, no matter how hard it was, at times, not to give up. To abandon them would be selfish of me." Ans wanted to ask how Eloise could afford to support them all, but as she gazed around, she noticed how ravaged the once-lovely town house looked and how many of Eloise's treasures were missing—the Meissen china, the sterling silver, valuable paintings. She remembered Eloise's words on the day they'd traveled to Amsterdam and saw the Nazis rounding up Jews: *"What good is a chest filled with gold that never gets spent? And what good is my life if I selfishly keep it to myself and don't spend it for others?"*

"Now that you're back, you can help us search for food every day. It's becoming quite a challenge, believe me, and the others are getting discouraged, but I know you, Ans. You don't let anything discourage you. We've learned to make do without fuel and electricity, but it's impossible to get by without food."

"How many people live here?"

"I don't know. Besides the bank families? I've lost count because it varies. I can't ignore people who are freezing and starving and begging in the street, can I?"

"Listen, if I go home to the farm, I can bring some food back. I want to see my family and let them know I'm all right and—" Eloise winced, sending a shaft of fear through Ans's heart. "What? Do you know something about my family?"

"No, I don't. I'm sorry. It's isn't that. It's just that it's going to be impossible for you to go anywhere because of all the roadblocks and Nazi activity."

"I know—it was hard for the Red Cross to get me here, but—"

"No one under the age of forty is allowed to travel. The Nazis will arrest you on sight if you're caught. And the countryside is very dangerous these days because of the hunger trippers. People are so desperate they defy the law and go to the country to hunt for food. Robbers lie in wait to steal from them on their way back."

Ans longed to go home in spite of the danger. But before she could argue further, Eloise reached across the table to take both of her hands. "Please don't leave me again, Ans. I would be sick with worry for you out there. And I could use your help."

Ans looked down at Eloise's elegant hands, gripping hers. The beautiful rings she'd always worn were gone. "Of course I'll help. Tell me what to do."

"We're eating whatever we can find these days. A horse dropped dead in the street last week and there was practically a stampede to carve it up. Mrs. Spielman's cat wouldn't last five minutes out there. People call cats 'roof rabbits' and eat them as fast as they can catch them."

Ans smiled. "And what is Mrs. Spielman's cat eating these days?"

"She's a very capable mouser, it turns out. She does well for herself. Meanwhile, I'm selling or swapping anything I can find to buy food. Rabbits cost thirty guilders each at the butcher's last week, and they barely had any meat on their bones. They set up mobile soup kitchens around town from time to time, if we can get there before the soup runs out. And you'll love this—they passed out pamphlets with instructions for cooking tulip bulbs. One recipe said to fry them, but we haven't seen cooking oil in years, so the only choice was to boil them. Meta dug up all of my bulbs, but they tasted 'like a slap in the face,' as the old Dutch expression goes. Not that rabbit or horse tastes any better."

"I'll be another mouth to feed."

"True, but I'm guessing you'll know how to skin a squirrel if we manage to catch one." Eloise smiled, then leaned forward, serious again. "The Nazis now pay ten guilders for reporting a Jew in hiding. Can you believe there are people so desperate that they'd trade a person's life for ten measly guilders?"

"I often wonder how Miriam and Avi are. And Elisheva."

"God knows, I pray for them every day." Eloise sighed and ran a hand through her hair. It was no longer perfectly cut and styled, but Eloise was still a beautiful woman.

"Have you seen Erik?" Ans asked. "He's been on my mind for days as I made my way home, and I can't wait to see him. I'm so afraid he's angry with me for disappearing."

"He came by the day after you left, and I gave him your letter. He returned the following day asking for directions to your parents' farm. I could honestly tell him that I didn't know."

"Did he seem angry?"

"Frustrated, I think."

"I need to go see him after I wash and change my clothes. I know I look horrible at the moment—"

"There's no hot water, but we can warm some for you on the stove. But, Ans . . . do you think it's wise to see him?"

"What do you mean? We love each other. He warned me about the Gestapo raid and saved my life."

"You've been apart for nearly a year. He may have changed his mind about you since then. And . . . and he works for the enemy."

"I know. And I've seen my share of cruel policemen and prison guards. But Erik isn't like them."

"I hope you're right."

It felt wonderful to bathe and change into fresh clothes. But the mirror told Ans why Meta hadn't recognized her. Her skin was gray, her blonde hair thin and limp. Dark circles rimmed her eyes like bruises. She had the figure of a ten-year-old girl. She wondered if Erik would be repulsed.

The walk to his apartment across town tired her out. The trek up his stairs left her breathless. But the joy she felt when Erik opened the door and pulled her into his arms was worth all the pain of getting there. "Ans! You're skin and bones!" he said after holding her tightly and kissing her.

"I've dreamed of your kisses for months. I can't believe we're finally together again!"

"Come in, come in," he said, opening the door wider. Erik seemed exactly the same, as if he hadn't suffered from wartime hunger like everyone else—a privilege for Dutch Nazi Party members, she guessed.

"Are you all right, Ans? When did you get back?"

"Today."

"From your parents' farm? You're so thin!" She didn't want to lie to him, but a niggle of doubt made her afraid to trust him after so much time. What if Eloise was right and he had changed?

"I . . . I've been in Vught Prison."

"Ans! I begged you to stop fighting the Nazis! I knew something like this would happen!" His anger surprised her.

"That isn't why I was arrested. I was on my way back to the farm when two Nazi soldiers stole my bicycle. I had to walk a very long way, and it made me late. The police arrested me for breaking curfew." He stared at her without speaking, and she couldn't tell if he was shocked or if he didn't believe her. "Will it jeopardize your job to be seen with a convicted felon?" she asked, trying to make light of it.

He pulled her close and held her again without answering. Erik seemed different after all these months. He'd always been alert and on guard, but now that alertness made him seem restless and jittery, like a mouse watching for a cat. He seemed happy to see Ans, but at the same time, he seemed to be holding back as they chatted, as if she'd hurt him and he was afraid to get close to her again. She knew that a measure of trust between them had been broken. After a few minutes, she saw him glance at the clock. He was in his uniform, and there was a suitcase open on his bed and piles of folded clothes.

"Are you going somewhere or did you just get home?" she asked, gesturing to the suitcase.

"I'm being sent away on a special detail."

"For how long?"

"I'm not sure. Will you be at the town house when I get back? May I come to see you?"

"Absolutely!" They kissed again and clung to each other, but somehow, being with Erik wasn't the way Ans had remembered—or how she had long dreamed it would be.

CHAPTER 58

Lena stood in the doorway to her cousin's apartment above the post office, trying to unroll the flimsy newspaper after hiding it inside the handlebars of her bicycle. "Here, I brought you the latest news, Truus. It's good, for once. The Nazis can't last much longer."

"Come upstairs," Truus begged. "We haven't had a chance to sit and talk in such a long time."

"It will have to be quick. My girls are with me, and we need to get home before the next bombing raid starts. I try to time our trips into town to avoid the worst of them."

"I admire your courage," Truus said as she led the way upstairs. "Riding out in the open countryside leaves you so exposed." She gestured to the kitchen table, and Lena sat down, pulling Bep onto her lap. Maaike didn't want to sit but went to the window that faced Papa's church across the square. "All I have is ersatz coffee," Truus said, "but at least there's gas today." She lit the burner under the coffeepot, then placed cups and saucers on the table. "Remember the days when we drank real coffee together, with pastries from the bakery? Something buttery and flaky?"

Lena smiled. "I would be happy with just the coffee nowadays. With maybe a tiny pinch of sugar."

"We have to keep believing that better days are coming and that every-thing will be the same as it used to be, soon." Her words bothered Lena.

"The war may end, but I wonder if any of us will ever be the same. And I wonder if we'll be changed for the better or for the worse."

Truus gave a little frown. "What do you mean?"

"Are you the same person you were before the war?"

"I should hope so!" Truus had always been a practical, down-to-earth woman, never one to ponder her own motives or look too deeply into her own heart. It would never occur to her to question God or examine her own faith too closely. But the war had changed Lena. Her faith had been shaken, challenged, destroyed, and rebuilt into something completely different. It was stronger—she was stronger—and yet she knew her faith was more frag-ile than ever, reduced to a childlike trust in the face of circumstances she was helpless to control. Surrendering control, which she'd learned had been a mere illusion all along, had altered her relationship with God forever.

"Well, I hope I'm not the same," Lena said. She waited until Truus filled their cups and sat down before leaning closer, still trying to probe her cousin's faith. "What went through your mind when your husband knelt in that lineup, facing execution?"

Truus looked away. "I've tried hard to forget that day, so please don't remind me of it. Besides, he was saved in the end."

"But what if he hadn't been saved? What would you have said to God then?"

"I don't know. And I never will know, because he didn't die. And neither did your husband, so can we please talk about something else?"

Lena took a sip of the hot, bitter liquid, conceding to Truus's wishes. Pieter was still out fighting the Nazis somewhere. For all Lena knew, he might be dead, and she might be forced to answer her own question.

A Nazi motorcycle rumbled up the street outside. Maaike drew away from the window as if trying to hide behind the curtain. "She's so jumpy and fearful," Lena said softly. "The Nazis stole her childhood. She and Bep can't even remember a time when there were no planes overhead or firefights and explosions during the night."

"I can barely remember, myself," Truus said. As Bep played with the doll she carried everywhere, pretending to feed her imaginary food, Truus seemed to be studying Bep's face as if trying to find a family resemblance. "She's a beautiful child. Are you and Pieter going to raise her as your own after the war, or will Ans take her back?"

Lena's arms tightened around Bep. She'd grown to love this child as her own. She knew there was a chance that Bep's parents were still alive and would return for her after the war. For their sake and for Bep's, she prayed that they would survive. But that meant Lena would have to give her up, and she knew a piece of her heart would tear away when she did. Once again, the magnitude of the pain and suffering the Nazis had inflicted on the world—and on her—nearly overwhelmed Lena. She stroked Bep's dark hair. Truus was waiting for her reply. "I'm not sure," she finally said.

The rumbling motorcycle and painful memories had stirred the ashes of Lena's hatred, reigniting the flames. Because of the Nazis, Bep had been separated from her family, just as Lena had been. Because of them, Lena's life and Bep's life would never be the same. "I hate them," she said, spitting out the words like poison. "I hate what they've done to us and to our country. I hope the Allies show them no mercy when they win."

Truus drank her coffee. "Is there still no news of Ans or the rest of your family?"

Lena shook her head. "That's what I hate them for the most—for taking the people I love away from me." Lena had visited her father's grave before coming here, and as she'd gazed at the scarred earth, she'd prayed that there wouldn't be any new graves beside Papa's when the war ended.

"I think everyone in town feels the same way you do about the Nazis."

They finished their coffee. Lena slid Bep off her lap and stood. "I should go. Thanks for the coffee."

She was almost home, with Bep riding on the handlebars and Maaike on the rear fender, when she saw a Nazi soldier standing in the middle of the road. She slowed. He stood alone, without a vehicle, gazing at the new spring grass in her pasture. The sight of her enemy so close to her home filled Lena with a hatred too deep to contain. Every Nazi she encountered, including this one, might be the one who'd killed her father.

Maaike saw him too and said, "Mama, stop! Turn around! We need to get away from him! Hurry!"

Lena braked to a halt, wondering if she should turn around.

"Who is that, Mama?" Bep asked.

"It's a Nazi!" Maaike hissed.

The soldier faced away from them about twenty yards distant. He hadn't noticed they were behind him yet. Lena's heart raced as she debated how to get her daughters around him safely. The fields were too wet to cut across, especially with the bicycle, and besides, he would still see them. She was too weary to cycle all the way back into town. Should she pedal quickly past him? Who knew what he would do? Shoot at them? She helped the girls off the bicycle and gave it to Maaike to hold. "Stay here," she said. "If I wave at you, get on it and pedal home with Bep as fast as you can, understand?"

"Mama, no! What are you going to do?"

"I'm just going to see what he wants. I'm counting on you to be brave, Maaike."

"I'm scared!"

"I know. I am too. But what do we always do when we're afraid?"

"Pray," she whispered.

"Good girl." Lena walked toward the man, her rage building with every step. She couldn't imagine what he was doing here, but she wouldn't let her enemies take one more thing from her. If only she had a weapon. She would kill him as swiftly and ruthlessly as one of them had killed her father. This soldier didn't deserve to live. None of them did. "What do you want?" she shouted as her hatred overflowed. He turned as if startled and gazed at her in surprise. "You're on my property! The town is that way," she said, pointing. He would see her daughters cowering in the road.

He lifted his hands, palms out. "I'm sorry. I don't understand Dutch."

"Why are you here on my farm?" she shouted, speaking Dutch anyway. "Why are you in my country? You've taken nearly everything I have and everyone I love! Can't you see how much we hate you?"

He shook his head and held out his hands again. He might not have understood her words, but he couldn't mistake her anger. "I'm sorry if I've done something to make you upset," he said in German. "I'll leave now. I just . . . I just wanted to smell the fields in springtime . . . to remind myself of home."

His words and the sorrow in his voice threw Lena off-balance. He looked young, surely not even twenty years old.

"I received a letter from my sister back home," he continued. "She told me that my mother has died. I couldn't remember her face or her smile, so I thought . . . I thought if I smelled the farm, it would remind me of home . . . and I would be able to picture her." Tears glistened in his eyes.

He could be Wim, missing his mother, his home.

"Jesus commanded us to love our enemies," Papa had said in one of his sermons. *"He prayed, 'Father, forgive them,' even as His enemies nailed Him to the cross."*

Papa had died loving others more than himself. Lena still remembered the calm, peaceful look on his face as he'd gazed at her for the last time. And as she remembered, something deep inside her burst and drained away, easing the unbearable weight she'd carried for so long. She stepped closer to the young soldier and met his gaze.

"I'm sorry I yelled at you," she said in German.

His eyes widened in surprise.

"And I'm very sorry about your mother. I'm sure she missed you very much. It's hard to be separated from the people we love, isn't it?"

He nodded and wiped his eyes.

"I have a son who is just a bit younger than you. He's away from home too, and I think of him constantly."

"I don't think I'll live to see my home again. They're trying to hide the truth from us, but I know we're losing the war." He sighed and looked out at the pasture for a moment. "Is this your farm?" he asked, gesturing to the fields and the house and barn in the distance.

"It is."

"I'm sorry if I trespassed."

Forgive us our trespasses, as we forgive those who trespass against us. "I forgive you," she whispered, her heart squeezing.

"I'll leave now. I . . . I only wanted to walk into the countryside . . . so I could imagine that I was home."

Lena thought of her own children, longing for home, and her eyes filled. "Is it . . . ? Would it be all right if I hugged you? Maybe you could imagine that I'm your mother, for just a moment, and I could imagine you're my son."

He went forward into her arms. She felt a sob shudder through his body. Lena's tears flowed as well. "Oh, God, end this war," she prayed. "Bring this young man and all of the people we love back home again."

At last he pulled away and wiped his eyes. "I must go," he said. "Thank you for your prayer. And for . . . for not hating me."

"I hope you make it home."

"I hope your son does too."

He turned and quickly strode toward town. Lena saw Maaike cringe and pull away as he walked past her. Lena felt drained as she returned to where the girls were waiting. "Come on, let's go home."

Maaike didn't move. "You hugged a Nazi soldier! Why?"

"He was just a boy, like Wim. He misses his mother."

"He could be the soldier who killed Opa!"

Lena rested her hands on Maaike's shoulders. "Opa offered his life so that no one else from the village would be killed. He wasn't afraid to die. He wanted to show us that we don't have to be afraid to die either." She tried to wrap her arms around Maaike, but she pulled away.

"Why are the Nazis here in our country? I hate them all!"

Lena winced, knowing Maaike had learned to hate from her. She had shouted those very words just minutes ago. "I know I've said the same things and felt the same way you do, Maaike, but it was wrong of me to hate. Very wrong. God used that young soldier just now to remind me that if we want to be like Jesus, we can't hate others—even our enemies."

The bicycle clattered to the ground as Maaike went into Lena's arms. "I want Opa! And Papa and Ans and Wim!" she wailed.

Lena stood in the middle of the road with her daughter, rocking her in her embrace. "I do too, my sweet child . . . I do too . . ."

CHAPTER 59

Ans woke from a restless sleep as the roar of a V-1 rocket blasted off somewhere outside of Den Haag, a dozen miles away. A brilliant flash lit up the room as the rocket streaked across the sky, then the sound faded into the distance. Some of those rockets never made it to their targets in Britain but exploded in the Netherlands. She sat up carefully, trying not to awaken Eloise or the ten other people sleeping in the town house's kitchen, and made her way to the stove to stoke the fire. Hunger made everyone lethargic, and they slept on, accustomed to the noise of war. Planes flew overhead continuously, with some formations lasting as long as an hour. Windows rattled from the heavy loads and roaring engines. Ans and her companions fell asleep at night to the sound of firefights, the clatter of antiaircraft guns, the fatal sputter of injured planes, and "fireworks" lighting up the sky.

With the stove rekindled, Ans measured water and oats and put a pot of porridge on to cook. Eloise had bartered a pair of emerald earrings for the sack of oats, once intended for horses. The butchered animals wouldn't need it. "Was it only four years ago," Eloise had asked at last evening's meal, "when we all ate as much as we wanted? How times have changed when these few morsels make us happy!" They had divided four eggs and four slices of bread among twelve people—and shared each leftover crumb, as well. As sparse as the meal had been, they had bowed their heads and thanked God for it. Thousands of their countrymen had starved to death. There was no wood for coffins, no men to dig graves.

The aroma of cooking porridge awakened the others. Eloise and Meta were spooning it into bowls when the doorbell rang. Ans hurried to answer it and was surprised to see Erik, home from wherever the Nazis had sent him. "You're back! Do you want to come in?" She longed to embrace him but hesitated. He looked troubled and wasn't smiling.

"Can you come for a walk with me? I need to ask you something."

"Of course. Let me tell Eloise where I'm going." Ans was already wearing her coat and needed only to put on a hat and mittens to be ready. They started toward the park, and she knew something was wrong when he didn't reach for her hand or wrap his arm around her shoulders. She made him halt before reaching the bridge. "Erik, tell me what's wrong."

He stared down at the ground for a long moment, then glanced all around before looking at her. "I don't want to do the Nazis' dirty work anymore." He kept his voice low as if afraid of being overheard. "Can you . . . ? Will you help me go into hiding? You told me once that you knew people—the ones who helped your Jewish friends disappear. I want to disappear too."

For a terrible, interminable moment, Ans couldn't reply. As her heart raced out of control, she was horrified to realize that she didn't know whether to trust him or not. This was Erik, the man she loved, asking her for help. Yet the Resistance had warned her to trust no one. She remembered the young woman she'd suspected of being planted in her jail cell. Traitors were paid well for helping the Nazis. But then she pushed all those thoughts aside. Erik loved her, and she loved him. Why did she hesitate?

"I know you were in contact with the underground," Erik continued when she didn't reply. "I saw you delivering their newspapers, remember?" Yes, she remembered, and he had made her promise to stop. "And then, after I told you about the Gestapo raid in Zoeterwoude, you disappeared from Leiden. I figured you were involved in that. Why else would you leave?" He reached for her hand, gripping it tightly. "Please, Ans! Ask your friends to help me!"

She began to shiver. "Even . . . even if I used to know some people . . . ," she said, her teeth chattering, "I-I've been gone for nearly a year. For all I know, they've all been arrested."

"If you love me, please help me. We want a life and a future together, don't we?"

Ans didn't know where the panic she felt was coming from, but she struggled to get past it, to gather her thoughts, to decide what to do. The café where she used to leave messages for Havik had closed. She could hide Erik in Eloise's town house or on her parents' farm, but did she dare risk endangering them?

"I-I'll try to think of something. But . . . but I'll need some time. Can you come back to the town house tomorrow?"

"Please hurry, Ans. I may not have much time!"

She turned and sprinted home without looking back. She was breathless after running the short distance, her legs trembling, her empty stomach rumbling. "Back already?" Eloise asked when Ans found her in the kitchen. "That was quick. We saved you some oatmeal."

"I need to talk to you. I-I . . ."

Eloise grabbed one of the blankets from the makeshift pallets on the floor and wrapped it around Ans's shoulders. "You're shaking like a leaf! Let's go up to my bedroom. It's freezing up there, too, but we'll have privacy." Ans wanted to weep when she saw what had become of Eloise's elegant, fairy tale–like bedroom. The wooden bed frame, the bench for her dressing table, and even the picture frames on the walls had all been chopped up for firewood. Eloise made Ans sit on the slipper chair by the window, and then she knelt on the floor in front of her. "What happened?"

"Erik asked for my help. He wants to go into hiding. He doesn't want to work for the Nazis anymore."

"Are you sure he isn't setting a trap?"

Ans's tears started to fall as she faced the reason for her panic. "No. No, I'm not . . ."

"Ah, no wonder you're so upset. You love him but you don't know if you can trust him."

Ans began to sob. "I-I don't know what to do!"

Eloise leaned forward and drew her into an embrace. She held her and let her tears fall before pulling back again and handing Ans a lace handkerchief. "What I need to tell you, Ans, may be very difficult for you to hear. Please understand that I'm saying it because I love you." Ans nodded, wiping her eyes. "Your boyfriend has worked for the Nazis for five years. He's a member of the Dutch Nazi Party. What better way to win their favor than to expose a Resistance cell and take credit for their arrest? If we offered to hide him here or on your parents' farm, imagine the reward he'd receive for turning in hidden Jews like Meta and Sientje and Elisheva."

"I know . . ."

"But even if it isn't a trap, why does he want to go into hiding now? Is it because the Allies are winning and he may face punishment for working with the Nazis?" She paused as if to let Ans digest her words. "Why did he remain on the police force and join the NSB? Why didn't he become an *onderduiker* a long time ago?"

Ans struggled to remember. "They would have sent him to a work camp if he refused. He wanted to stay so he could do good as a policeman. He could protect people from the Nazis."

"And has he done that? Did he work with the Resistance behind the scenes, sharing information with them? I've heard of police officers in other cities who helped prisoners escape. The Resistance wanted to free Herman and the others from the Leiden jail, but there weren't any sympathetic policemen we could trust. No, Ans. Erik did everything the

Nazis told him to do. When they started rounding up Jews, he helped them do it."

"He could have arrested me when he caught me with the underground newspapers—"

"Instead, he tried to control you. He made you promise to stop doing the work that your heart told you to do."

"He saved my life when he warned me about the raid in Zoeterwoude."

"If you had been arrested, he would have been under suspicion too, as your boyfriend. He was saving you but also himself. He didn't care about the people in that apartment. And did he show any compassion for Avi and Miriam? Did he offer to help them because they were your friends? No. He wanted you to stop saving Jews and working for the underground because he didn't want to lose you."

"He loves me."

"Perhaps that's true . . . but he loves himself even more. Instead of going to a work camp, he became a Nazi." She reached to take Ans's hands. "Listen, I understand Erik because I acted just like him in the first war. He wanted to be safe and avoid suffering. Cowards think only of themselves. They're selfish. My parents and my brother took enormous risks to free our country, risks that cost them their lives. I ran away and saved myself. And now in this war, Erik saved himself while everyone else we love took enormous risks to rescue others and to fight the Nazis. The war is coming to an end now, and Erik is still trying to save himself, trying to escape being punished for collaborating with the enemy."

Ans closed her eyes and wept as the truth of what Eloise said pierced her heart. But could she turn her back on the man she loved?

"Herman knew how I'd behaved in the first war," Eloise continued. "He knew I'd been a coward, but he loved me and married me in spite of it. And you may still want to marry Erik. Maybe he'll beg Avi and Miriam and Professor Jacobs to forgive him for his indifference, and maybe they will. With your help, Erik may eventually ask God for forgiveness too. But you've seen the damage that selfishness and cowardice and guilt have done to my soul. You've seen the price I've paid—and dear Herman has paid it along with me. Herman may already be dead because of his great love and courage. I only hope that this time, in this war, I've done enough."

"You have," Ans whispered. "You've sacrificed more than enough. You're the most courageous woman I've ever known."

Eloise released her hands and looked away as if uncomfortable with praise. "I've no doubt that you'll marry someday, Ans. You'll make a wonderful wife and mother. You're strong and compassionate and courageous—and capable of becoming so much more than Erik Brouwer's wife."

"He's coming for my answer tomorrow. I don't know what to tell him."

Eloise looked at her again. "Search your heart. I think you do know."

Ans spent all day and most of the night weeping and praying, reliving every wonderful moment she and Erik had spent together—and all of the dark, disappointing ones. When she opened the door the next morning and stepped outside to talk with him, she was trembling from head to toe.

"Did you find someone to help me hide?" he asked.

She drew a shaky breath. "Even if I still knew people in the underground, they would never agree to help you because you didn't help them when they needed it. You worked for our enemy. You chose the Nazis' side when you decided to stay on the police force. You joined the Dutch Nazi Party and attended their rallies. You made your choice. You can't expect the underground to help you now."

"Please! Let me hide here with you!"

"This isn't my home. There are a dozen of us living here, families whose husbands and fathers are in a Nazi prison for helping Jews. We're chopping up the furniture and woodwork to stay warm. We're eating horse food and tulip bulbs to stay alive. I can't ask these poor souls to take pity on you." She paused. "I can't help you, Erik. I'm sorry."

"I thought you loved me!"

"I thought so too."

CHAPTER 60

It was still night when the tremor of vehicles and voices roused Miriam from sleep. Everyone in the barracks heard it too, and questions whispered through the darkness. "What's going on? What are the Nazis doing?" Miriam and most of the others were too afraid to open the door and venture outside. The darkness, inside and out, magnified her fear.

As the uproar continued, the barracks supervisor peered cautiously through the window, then said, "There's no guard outside. He's not at his post." The supervisor and two others decided to take a chance. They opened the door and disappeared into the night. They returned minutes later, barely able to keep from shouting the news. "The Nazis are packing up! It looks like they're leaving! There are no guards anywhere, even in the towers!"

"Will we have to go with them?" someone asked.

"I don't see how they could take all of us unless there's a train coming."

"If there is a train, we're all done for. They pack a thousand people at a time on those trains, and there are fewer than nine hundred of us left."

The thought made Miriam's lungs squeeze. *"Have mercy on me, my God, have mercy on me, for in you I take refuge. I will take refuge in the shadow of your wings until the disaster has passed. . . .*" She recited the verses silently while she and the others waited. She'd lost track of the number of times she'd been forced to wait through endless minutes and hours of dread this way, her life, her hope, dangling by a thread. She struggled to breathe, listening for the rumble of the train. Gradually it became apparent that the Nazis and their vehicles were in fact leaving, yet no one had ordered the prisoners to collect their things or stand for roll call in the center of the camp. The train didn't come.

The sun rose, bringing light and hope as shafts of sunlight streamed through the grimy windows. The commotion outside had faded into the distance with the departing vehicles. More prisoners slipped outside, and Miriam heard shouts from all over the camp. "They're gone! They're gone! The Nazis are gone!" She joined the rush of women leaping down from their bunks and streaming through the door into the chilly April morning, shivering with cold and joy.

"We're free to go?" someone asked.

"They left the main gate wide-open!"

The shouts and cheers could probably be heard for miles. Yet after all these years of being hunted and hounded and demeaned and imprisoned, Miriam was afraid to believe she was finally free. She went in search of the orchestra director, Ernst Lubbers, and found that several other musicians had done the same, gathering around him for advice. "What do you think we should do, Ernst? Are you leaving?"

"I think I'll wait and see. For my wife's sake." Frau Lubbers was a flautist who seemed as ethereal as the sound of her flute. It was a tribute to Ernst's love that she'd survived persecution this long. "There's food and shelter here," Ernst said. "And who knows what we'll find out there. As far as we know, the Netherlands is still at war."

"What if the Nazis return? Won't we be sorry we didn't run while we had the chance?"

"Undoubtedly. Listen, I can't speak for anyone else or advise you what to do. We each must decide for ourselves."

Miriam knew she wouldn't survive on her own. Avi had faced myriad obstacles when he'd escaped Westerbork and walked across the country to Leiden. And that was before five years of war and bombings and Nazi occupation. Some of her fellow prisoners were already hurrying down the road to Assen with their loved ones and suitcases, but like a caged bird, she was afraid to fly through the open door.

She knew how helpless and dependent she'd been these past years— on Abba and his student and the German guides who'd helped them leave Cologne. On the Dutch people who'd fed and housed them with the other refugees here at Westerbork. On Ans and Eloise after she and Avi fled the Nazi roundups. And on Dr. Elzinga and his underground network who'd risked their lives to hide her and care for her. She hadn't survived this long by her own strength and wits, but because of the courage and love of others. Miriam had tried to wall herself off from people, afraid to get too close, afraid of experiencing the blinding pain she'd felt after losing Avi and Elisheva. Trusting was a risk. Loving was a risk. Now she owed a debt to love in return. She made up her mind to return to the camp kitchen and resume her work duties. In a few hours or a few days, perhaps she and a group of fellow prisoners would band together and decide on a plan. But for now, everyone needed to eat. She was surprised to find that nearly all of the others had chosen to work as well.

Shortly before noon, as pots of soup simmered on the stove, they heard the unmistakable sound of heavy vehicles approaching. Everyone in the kitchen froze. The woman working alongside Miriam collapsed to the floor with a moan of despair. "They're back; they're back! Oh, why didn't we run while we had the chance!"

Miriam tried to help her to her feet in spite of her own longing to run and hide. The others had all rushed to the door. "Come, let's see if it is the Nazis before we panic," Miriam said. "Maybe someone has come to rescue us."

Before they reached the door, shouts of joy resounded outside. "It's the Canadians! Canadian soldiers!"

The woman clung to Miriam, laughing and weeping at the same time. "We're free! Really and truly free!" Miriam couldn't comprehend it.

The prisoners swarmed the Canadian troops and their vehicles, applauding, cheering, begging for news. "Is the war over? Have the Allies defeated the Nazis?"

The Canadian commander stood on the fender of his vehicle, his hands raised to call for silence as an interpreter came forward. "The war isn't over yet. Parts of the western provinces, the cities of Amsterdam, Rotterdam, and Den Haag, still haven't been liberated. But the Nazis are on the run. It won't be long until they're finally defeated." Miriam was afraid to believe it, afraid to hope. "Anyone who wants to leave this camp may certainly do so," the commander continued. "But I recommend you wait here until all of the hostilities cease. After that, we'll figure out how to get you back home."

Home. To Leiden. To her family.

Dutch Red Cross workers arrived the next day, bringing more news. Miriam and the others hungered for it even more than for food. She was sitting in the warm sunshine outside the dining hall with Ernst Lubbers and a group from the orchestra, discussing the railroad strike that had halted the deportations from Westerbork, when one of the Red Cross workers made a comment about the trains' destinations in the East. "You're among the lucky ones who didn't end up in Poland in those horrible concentration camps. The others . . . May God rest their souls . . ." Her words brought silence as if everyone had stopped breathing.

"What do you mean?" Ernst asked an eternity later. The worker hesitated, her hand over her mouth as if she'd said more than she should have. Ernst sat forward, pleading with her. "We've had no news in months—years. Please, tell us what you know so we can face whatever it is."

"I'm so sorry. I shouldn't have said anything. It might be better to wait and hear about it with people you love."

"Most of us don't know what has become of the people we love! Tell us!" He was demanding, not asking. Part of Miriam wanted to run out onto the heath and keep running rather than hear the truth about where Abba and so many of her loved ones had gone. But the anxiety she saw on her friends' faces made her decide to stay and face the news with them.

The worker spoke quickly now, as if unloading an unbearable burden. "Our Soviet allies have liberated the labor camps in Poland. They discovered that the Nazis have been sending people to their deaths, killing women and children and the elderly the same day they arrived on the trains. Thousands more starved or died of diseases in the camps. From what I've heard, Westerbork is a paradise compared to the other camps. I'm so sorry."

"You mean they've been killing all of the Jews who were deported from the Netherlands?" Ernst asked.

The worker's eyes filled with tears. "Not only from here . . . The Nazis deported and executed Jews from every country, including their own. Austria, Romania, Hungary, Belgium, France . . ." She couldn't finish.

"This can't be true," someone murmured. "That would be millions of people."

The Red Cross worker lowered her face, tears falling onto her lap. "I'm so sorry."

Miriam pictured her family's home in Cologne and the Jewish streets and neighborhoods surrounding it. Thousands of Jews had lived there, worked there. Hundreds had attended the synagogue in Leiden. Tens of thousands lived in Amsterdam. Had the Nazis killed all of them? It seemed impossible. And for what reason?

Abba. Avi. Elisheva . . . Mother. Aunt Louisa and Uncle David. Aunt Shoshanna and Uncle Nathan. Saul and her other cousins . . . Mrs. Spielman and her family . . . the families of the women she'd hidden with . . . Impossible.

If Miriam had survived and Avi and Elisheva hadn't . . . then what? Miriam didn't know. She would have to wait. And pray. And try not to lose hope.

CHAPTER 61

MAY 1945

Lena dug her fingers into the soil of her garden, lifting a damp clump of it, rubbing it between her fingers. The May sunshine had warmed it sufficiently. Today she would begin to plant. She picked up the pitchfork to turn the soil. In the distance, their fruit trees blossomed in a frothy display of beauty that never failed to awe her. A new season of planting and waiting, a new season of hope was beginning.

Farming the land year after year should have prepared Lena to trust God. Every seed she'd planted had been an act of faith. Every day and week and month spent waiting and praying for sunshine and rain and a good harvest required trust. She couldn't do anything to make the plants grow. Nor could she do anything to ensure her family's safety, their future. They were in God's hands.

Liberation had come. Her country was free. She'd returned from the village yesterday with the good news, the joyous sound of church bells still clamoring in her ears. Lena had spent most of that long-awaited day celebrating with her shadow people, helping them get ready to go back to their homes, their families. Perhaps her loved ones had spent yesterday doing the same.

She thrust the pitchfork into the ground, pushing it deep into the earth with her foot, then lifted it to turn the soil. She remembered asking God to teach her how to release Ans into His hands when she'd left home for Leiden. Now, as Lena watched Maaike and Bep search for worms in the newly tilled soil, squealing as they held the soft, squirming creatures in their hands, she realized how well God had answered that prayer. The war had forced her to release not only Ans, but Wim and Pieter, too. Bep had been a daily reminder of another mother's decision to trust the Almighty. The only thing Lena could do was pray—and she had never ceased praying.

The barn door creaked open behind her. Lena turned, thinking it was the wind.

It was Pieter.

She dropped the pitchfork and ran into his arms, her wooden clogs flying off her feet in her haste. He held her so tightly her ribs ached, but she would never let him go again. Never.

"Papa! Papa, you're home!" Maaike shouted. She and Bep dropped their worms and ran to him, calling, "Papa! Papa!" Lena released him so they could hug him too. He looked dirty and ragged and bone weary— and wonderful! She caressed his whiskered cheek, brushed his hair from his eyes, and kissed him. And kissed him. Pieter was alive and whole and well—and home! *Thank God, thank God, thank God.*

They went inside and Pieter sank onto a kitchen chair as if his legs could no longer hold him. "I must have walked a hundred miles to get here," he said. "It was so late when I arrived that I didn't want to come into the house and frighten you, so I slept in the barn."

"Are you hungry? We don't have much, but I'm sure I can find something. I gave almost everything to the shadow people."

"Is there any milk? I would love a glass of milk." Lena poured him one and watched him guzzle it down. Her tears of joy were still falling. "Best milk I ever had," he said.

"Oh, Papa!" Bep laughed. "It's just milk!" She tugged his hand, dancing with delight until he lifted her to his knee and kissed her forehead. He gazed at Bep for a long moment, then looked up at Lena.

"Any word . . . ?" He was asking about Bep's parents. Lena shook her head. "And Ans?" he asked. "Have you heard from her?"

A knot of sorrow choked Lena, making it impossible to reply. The news of Ans's imprisonment had been difficult for her to hear, and she hated to spoil Pieter's joy by sharing it. But she had to.

"Wolf told me she was arrested and sent to Vught . . ." She swallowed and reached for his hand. "And . . . the Nazis took Wim, too."

The color drained from his face. "When?"

"Months ago. Wolf said they were grabbing men off the streets to dig trenches and build earthworks."

"We'll find them, Lena. If we have to spend the rest of our lives searching, we'll bring them home." He squeezed her hand, then released it.

They talked while Pieter ate the last of the watery bean soup Lena had warmed. He insisted that the stale rinds of bread—all that was left of the loaf—were the most delicious he'd ever tasted. Lena didn't want to let Pieter out of her sight and neither did the girls, but she saw how weary he was. "You look as though you could use a bath and a shave and a long nap. I think we have hot water today."

He pulled himself to his feet, leaning against the table, and gathered Lena in his arms again. "I love you," he whispered. "I love you so much!"

After he'd bathed and changed his clothes, Pieter went into the barn to tend his cows while Lena looked for something to fix for their dinner. She was searching through the cupboard when she heard Pieter shouting, "Lena! Lena, come here! Quick!" She left the sack of withered apples on the kitchen table and hurried out to the barn. Pieter stood in the open doorway, pointing down the road. "Look! It's Wim!"

Lena ran to her son, stumbling forward, her legs unable to carry her fast enough, and embraced him with all the joy and love she'd felt on the day he was born. He was so tall! She'd forgotten how tall he was. Had he grown taller while he'd been away? His fair hair was long and ragged and

needed to be cut. His chin felt stubbly when she kissed it. Pieter would have to teach him to shave. She was holding Wim at last! It didn't seem real. Her husband was home and now her son. *Thank God, thank God!*

Lena laughed when Wim also asked for a glass of milk. She poured him one, remembering that he'd been caring for the cows when the Nazis took him. Unlike Pieter, who didn't want to talk about the past few months, Wim told his story as if it had been an adventure. "We weren't treated badly," he said. "But when the Nazis heard that the Canadians were coming, they just left us in the camp and drove away. The Canadians fed us and told us we could all go home, but we didn't even know where we were. They had to draw us a map!" He chuckled before adding, "I guess I should have paid more attention in geography class."

"Were you scared?" Maaike asked. "I would be."

"When they shoved me into the back of that truck and we drove away . . . and I had no idea where . . ." He paused, gathering himself. "*Ja*, I was scared. I prayed the Lord's Prayer, over and over, because those were the only words that came to mind. And it helped."

Lena gazed at this boy, soon to be a man, and her heart swelled with love and pride.

"The work got so hard that sometimes I thought I was going to drop . . . and they would beat us if we stopped working . . . so I started saying the Twenty-third Psalm, too. The others heard me mumbling all day and started calling me Dominie—but I knew they meant it in a good way. We were all young, all scared. I wasn't the oldest, but I was the tallest." He smiled, then took another gulp of milk. "After a while, the others started asking me to pray for them, too. They sort of depended on me. I knew I had to stay strong and ask God to keep me going because I didn't want to let the others down. I thought of Opa so often. Things he said in his sermons . . . I remembered how he'd held all the people in his church together."

"Yes . . . he did do that," Lena murmured.

Wim looked up at her. "Do you think I could really be one someday?" he asked.

Lena caught her breath. "A dominie? Of course you could, Wim! You'd make a wonderful pastor." Maybe God would use the ordeal of the war and Wim's capture—the very things Lena had wanted to protect him from—to show her son a glimpse of his future.

"You wouldn't mind?" Wim asked, turning to Pieter. "If I didn't take over the farm, I mean?"

"Mind! Wim, your mama and I would burst with pride!"

CHAPTER 62

The Allies had arrived in Leiden. Ans dragged Eloise and everyone else in the town house—including Sientje and Meta, who hadn't dared to go outside in three years—over to the city center to welcome them. Eloise's household had food again, thanks to parcels the Allies air-dropped into starving cities for five straight days. Ans could hear the noise of the celebration long before she got close enough to see the Canadian soldiers for herself. "They're here . . . they're really here," she murmured. Liberation! Freedom! What glorious words! She and Eloise had made it through the war. They had survived.

Dozens of young women ran to the soldiers, hugging and kissing them. Children climbed onto their army vehicles. The citizens of Leiden looked thin and dirty and hungry, their clothes worn, yet they laughed and cheered and waved flags, happy to be alive. And free. Ans hoped she never took freedom for granted again.

Eloise gave Ans a nudge as they watched the celebration. "Such handsome fellows, these Canadians, hmm? What do you think?"

Ans smiled and nudged her back. She hadn't noticed. She'd been scanning the faces in the crowd, wondering if she would see Erik, wondering how he was and what he would do now that the war was over. Continue as a policeman? Return to Java? She also wondered how long it would take to get over him.

"I'm tired," Eloise said after a while. "Let's go home." They told the others they were leaving and walked home to the town house. There was nothing to do now but wait to hear from Professor Huizenga. Ans knew he was on Eloise's mind every waking moment and when she lay in bed at night, unable to sleep. She had asked Ans to sleep in her bedroom with her and she'd agreed, afraid to leave Eloise alone. Caring for the people who'd taken refuge with her had kept Eloise strong so far, but Ans didn't think she would survive the loss of her husband. Ans could never keep Eloise from despair without Herman. She prayed that she would know what to do if he didn't return.

Three days later, victory in Europe was declared. The Nazis had surrendered. When the trains started running again, Meta and Sientje decided to return to Amsterdam to search for their families. Ans stood with them on the windy train platform to say goodbye. "The Nazis confiscated everything we owned before we went into hiding," Meta said. "We need to start the process of getting everything back."

"You've shown such courage," Ans said as she hugged them. "Professor Huizenga will be so grateful to you for helping Eloise when he couldn't be here."

"The Huizengas saved our lives. We're family now."

Eloise had excused herself from going to the train station, saying she hated goodbyes. Ans found her sitting alone by the window in her ravaged bedroom when she returned. "Did the ladies get off all right?" Eloise asked.

Ans sat down on the floor beside her, leaning against the frameless bed. "Yes. I was sorry to see them go. But they promised to visit."

"You need to go home to your family, Ans. They must be so worried about you." Ans had tried in vain to reach the farm by telephone. The nation was still in chaos after the liberation, and apparently telephone service hadn't been restored to the village. She'd posted a letter, but who knew when it would arrive.

"I'm not leaving you, Eloise."

Two of the families from the bank had also moved out, and with each goodbye, Eloise had begun the long, slow journey into melancholy like a cart rolling downhill, picking up speed as it went. Ans was reminded of how they'd waited to hear from Professor Huizenga in the hours after the Nazi invasion. She hadn't known then how best to help her, but experience had taught Ans ways to block Eloise's descent and keep her from crashing at the bottom.

"I'm going to volunteer with the Red Cross here in Leiden," Ans told her the morning after Meta and Sientje left for Amsterdam. They were sitting in the kitchen, eating tasteless porridge. "Come with me, Eloise. They could use all the help they can get." A plea for help had appeared in the newspaper, now free from Nazi control. There had also been articles and photographs detailing the Nazi atrocities in the con- centration camps. She and Eloise had both wept when they'd seen them. Surely it couldn't be true. How could such things happen in a civilized world? Miriam and Avi and Professor Jacobs were on their minds and in their hearts.

"I don't think I would be much help to the Red Cross," Eloise replied. "I was trained as a journalist, not a nurse."

"There are dozens of things you could do, like handing out food in the soup kitchen or helping displaced people reunite with their families. You could help those who've lost everything find a reason to go on. You know what that's like, Eloise. I know you do."

"And what if I don't have a reason to go on, myself?"

Ans didn't reply. She wouldn't offer false hope and empty words. The uphill road for Eloise was too steep. And they were both too weary. At last Ans sighed and said, "Just walk over there with me this morning. We don't have to stay and help if you don't want to, but the walk will do us good."

Eloise agreed, and after finishing breakfast, they got ready to go. Ans opened the front door and was startled to see an old gray-haired beggar with stooped shoulders and ragged clothing standing in front of the house. He had a wreck of a bicycle with him, and he was staring at the muddy flower beds that should be blooming with beautiful tulips, as if wondering where they'd gone. Eloise came through the door behind her. She recognized the beggar first.

"*Herman!*"

He dropped the bicycle and they held each other tightly, weeping, touching each other's faces, murmuring their love for each other, their joy. Ans watched, thanking God through her tears.

"Aren't you going to let me inside?" the professor finally asked.

"Oh, Herman! I need to explain something first. I need to tell you what I've done to your beautiful home. We needed fuel, you see, to stay warm, and so the furniture and woodwork is gone. Up in smoke. But what else could I do?" Ans was overjoyed to see her friend's fluttering hands and hear her breathless, gushing voice as she soared uphill on wings. "And food—there wasn't any food, and no money to buy it, and there were so many people depending on me, so I had to sell some of our lovely things and—"

He put his fingers over her lips to stop her. "I don't care about any of that. Just you." Eloise hugged him again and then led him inside. His gaze was on her the entire time, blind to everything else. Ans decided to move the professor's bicycle to a safer place and give them privacy, and as she was wheeling it around to the rear of the town house, she had a sudden thought. She could go home! She could ride his bicycle home to see her family!

She left early the next morning, just after the sun rose on what promised to be a beautiful Sunday morning. She pedaled so fast in her eagerness that she arrived in the village while everyone was still in church. The sanctuary was packed with people, every pew taken, so she stood in the rear to wait until the service ended.

As she listened, the past came rushing back to her—the discontent she'd once felt in church, her restlessness and longing for something

LYNN AUSTIN · 383

different. And with those memories came a flood of guilt. How arrogant she'd been to say that the church didn't make a difference in people's lives. She'd had no idea how God was working in their minds and hearts. She'd chafed at sitting here week after week, but the words and songs had worked their way deep inside her just the same, and she'd found them rooted there when she'd needed them so desperately. All along, this congregation, her parents, and her grandparents had been helping Ans nurture a relationship with God.

Opa wasn't in his usual place behind the pulpit. Ans didn't see him anywhere. One of the church elders stood in his place to offer the closing prayer and benediction. But Mama and Papa were in their usual pew, with Wim and Maaike and little Elisheva. *Thank God, thank God.*

The congregation crowded into the aisles afterwards, and tears filled Ans's eyes as she watched her parents talking with people, smiling and laughing. She couldn't get to them through the crush of people, so she would have to wait. But then her mother happened to look back and saw Ans standing in the rear of the church. She gave a cry of joy that startled the people around her, and she began pushing her way down the crowded aisle, elbowing people out of her way. She reached Ans at last and pulled her into her arms, holding her tightly, rocking her. There was no need for either of them to say a word.

Papa and the others hurried to her as well after people saw what was happening and cleared the way. He wrapped his strong arms around Ans, lifting her from the ground. "You're as light as a feather! Welcome home! Welcome home!" The farm was home, and this church was too. Wim and Maaike each wanted a hug, but Elisheva held back. Ans was a stranger to her.

"How big she's grown," Ans murmured as she fingered Elisheva's dark braid. She was as beautiful as her mother, with Miriam's delicate features, her dark hair and eyes. But Elisheva had Avi's smile.

Please, God . . .

"Let's go home," Papa said. He took Ans's hand, plowing a path for her through the curious crowd, then out of the church and down the front steps.

"Where's Opa?" Ans asked. "Why isn't he here?"

Papa halted and drew her into his arms again. "He's in heaven, Ans . . . with Oma."

"What? . . . No! . . . Oh no! . . . What happened?" She pulled back and turned to Mama, begging her without words to say it wasn't true.

"An ammunition train was destroyed and the Nazis came for reprisals. They were about to choose someone from our village . . . Opa offered himself."

The joy Ans had felt a moment ago was swept away by grief. None of them spoke as they walked through the cemetery to his grave. She saw the rawness of their grief as well. His grave beside Oma's made his death real to Ans but no less painful. The Nazis had been angels of death, sweeping thousands, millions of innocent people to their graves.

"Don't hate them," Mama said as if reading Ans's mind. "They'll win if we hate them."

Papa put his arm around her shoulder. "Let's go home." Wim loaded her bicycle onto the truck, and they drove down the familiar road to the farm, all six of them crowded into the cab. "So . . . all my children made it through the war," Papa said.

"Yes. We all made it," Ans replied.

"Thank God. Thank God."

After lunch, Ans sat in the front room with her mother and sisters, trying to catch up on all they'd missed in the years since they'd seen each other. The room seemed smaller to Ans than when she was a child, but the warmth of her memories and the love she felt from her mother, seated beside her, could have heated the entire farmhouse. Maaike and Bep sat side by side on the piano bench, the little one concentrating as if learning to play was of utmost importance. "She loves music," Mama said. "She always has."

"I see that. But what's wrong with our piano? It sounds terrible."

Mama smiled. "I'll show you when they're finished."

"When I was in prison," Ans said, "I longed to see you and tell you how sorry I was for fighting with you. And for leaving the church."

"None of that matters. You're here now, and all is forgotten."

"There were so many other things I wanted to tell you. I met someone before the war. Erik and I fell in love, and I thought we would spend our lives together."

"Did he die?" Mama asked, her voice soft.

"No. But it would have been no less painful if he had. He was a policeman in Leiden, and when the Nazis came, he worked for them. At first he thought he was simply adjusting to new commanders. He didn't want to be sent to a work camp, and he thought he could still be a good policeman. But the Nazis kept demanding more and more, and he gave in. He helped them round up Jews like Elisheva's parents and grandfather. He helped raid homes where Jews were hiding and arrested everyone. He stood by while Nazis tortured people. In the end, it broke my heart to realize that Erik had collaborated with the Nazis because he was selfish. He didn't care about others. He only wanted to save himself."

"I'm so sorry, Ans. You've suffered so much."

"We all have, Mama." Her words rested heavily in the room.

After a while Mama asked, "Have you thought about your future plans now that the Nazis have surrendered?"

"I think I'll need time to get used to freedom first." Ans smiled. "When I moved to Leiden, I was so naive. I didn't know anything about myself or what I wanted to do with my life. The war has taught me so much about God and people—and about myself. I know those experiences have shaped me and changed me . . . I'm just not quite sure what it all means for my future yet."

"Before you left home and we were arguing so much, I went to Opa for advice. He told me that your stubbornness and your strong will might be your greatest asset one day. I see now how right he was."

Ans laughed and hugged her mama. "Have you heard anything from Elisheva's parents?" Mama asked.

A wellspring of sorrow opened in Ans's heart at the thought of Miriam and Avi. "No, but I haven't lost hope."

"I've been showing her the photographs of her family." She gestured to the album on the table next to Ans. "I've been trying to prepare her . . . but for what, I don't know. It's going to be hard to let her go. One more loss to grieve. She's my beloved daughter—but she isn't."

"It will be hard for her, too. You're the only mother she remembers." Ans reached for the photograph album and opened it, leafing through the pages. She found the letter Miriam had written to Lena and the one she'd addressed to Elisheva. "Have you read this to her?" Ans asked.

"No. Not yet."

"Maybe it's time."

Mama drew a deep breath as if for courage, then nodded. "Bep, honey, come here for a minute. I want us to read this letter together." The girl played a few more notes, then slid off the bench to sit on Lena's lap, leaning comfortably against her shoulder. "It's from your mother, the one you had before you came to us. Remember how the baby rabbits grew inside their mama? Well, you grew inside this mother that way."

"I knew your mother," Ans said. "I remember when you were still in her tummy, and I saw you when you were first born. They named you Elisheva—it means 'God's promise.' Your mother and father loved you very, very much. They were so sad when they couldn't take care of you anymore. I'm the one who brought you here to stay with this mama and papa for a while."

Lena opened the envelope and pulled out Miriam's letter.

"Darling Elisheva,

From the moment you were born, you've been our joy, our life. Saying goodbye and letting you go is the hardest thing I've ever had to do. But there is no other way for your father and me to save you. The only chance you'll have to be safe, to live, and to grow and become a woman someday is to release you into another mother's loving arms. You're much too young to understand these dark times

and the painful choices we are forced to make. Many good, loving
people are giving their lives to free the world from the evil that is
causing our separation. People have risked their lives to save our
family, and I pray that we can find a way to thank them.

If we meet each other again, dear Elisheva, the day will be as
joyous as the day you were born. If we don't see each other again
until the World to Come, please remember your father and me
from the photographs in this album and know that we love you
with our very life and with our every breath.

May God be with you, my beloved child.

Your loving mama"

Lena refolded the letter and tucked it into the envelope. "Will I see
that mama and papa again?" Bep asked.

An arrow of pain pierced Ans's heart. "We're not sure yet," she replied.

"Can I finish my lesson now, Mama?"

"Yes. You're doing so well, Bep." She returned to her seat on the
piano bench and began practicing again.

"Bep's mother has been such an inspiration to me these past three
years," Lena said. "She showed me how to place the people I love into
God's hands. I've learned from her courage."

"So have I, Mama. I need to go back to Leiden tomorrow and wait
for her parents. If they're alive, that's where they'll go. Then I'll bring
them here."

CHAPTER 63

Everyone in Westerbork rejoiced when the Nazis surrendered. The war in Europe was finally over. Miriam would be able to travel across the country to Leiden, although the Canadian soldiers warned that the devastation would make the journey difficult. The Nazis had blown up bridges and dikes and flooded large areas of the country. Their demolition squads had destroyed the docks in Amsterdam and Rotterdam, leaving a wasteland in their wake as they'd retreated. Miriam relived her long journey from Cologne as she crossed the Netherlands in the overcrowded railcar. She'd fled across the border at night with Abba six years ago, and after several months in Westerbork, they'd made this journey to Leiden together, filled with hope for the future. How lovely the Dutch countryside and quaint villages had seemed. But now the view from the train was very different. She might have been traveling across a different country.

Burned-out tanks and demolished vehicles littered the landscape. Every city they passed through had bombed-out buildings and gaping craters in the roads and fields. Allied soldiers swarmed everywhere with their guns and tanks and army vehicles. The Canadian soldiers had been right about the chaos, but after dozens of frustrating delays and detours,

Miriam finally arrived, exhausted, at the Leiden train station. It had also suffered damage. She hurried through the old city to the town house, crossing bridges and canals, dodging rubble, carrying her suitcase with her violin tucked inside. With every step she took, she offered a prayer that she would find Avi and Elisheva and that they would all be together again.

Ans answered the front door. She took one look at Miriam and burst into tears. "Miriam! Thank God, thank God!" Miriam had held herself together all this way, but now a tremor started deep inside her that threatened to loosen all her bones and muscles.

"Avi . . . ? Elisheva . . . ?" she stammered.

"Elisheva is at the farm, well and happy and safe. I was just there."

Miriam melted with relief, collapsing onto the front stoop before Ans could catch her. "My baby! My baby survived! Thank God . . . !"

"We haven't heard from Avi yet, but Eloise contacted Dr. Elzinga and we're trying to find him. Let me help you up. You need to come inside." She struggled to lift Miriam to her feet.

"I need to see Elisheva!"

"I understand. But you're trembling all over. You can barely stand. Come inside. Eloise will be overjoyed to see you."

The town house was nearly unrecognizable, battered by the war, but it still held memories of so many emotions for Miriam. Relief after arriving here with Abba. Joy in the days spent in her wedding suite with Avi. Terror as she and Avi and Elisheva hid from the Gestapo. And sorrow at their parting nearly three years ago. But their precious daughter was alive! Miriam's prayers had been answered.

Eloise understood Miriam's longing to see Elisheva right away. "For goodness' sake, Ans, take her to her child! Don't make her wait."

"I will; I will! But she needs to sit down and eat something. You need to get your strength back, Miriam." Ans drew a map for Avi with directions to her parents' farm. He could ride the professor's bicycle there when he came. If he came.

"I'll tell him the moment he arrives," Eloise promised.

He'll come. Avi will come, Miriam told herself as she returned to the train station with Ans for another journey. *Please, God* . . .

"Can you tell me about the past three years?" Ans asked when they were seated on the train. "How you survived?"

"I will one day. But not yet."

"I understand. I can barely talk about the war either."

"I'm so glad that you and Eloise are all right. I know your work with the underground put you in terrible danger. You're so thin, Ans."

"I spent time in Vught Prison. I was delivering ration books and was arrested for breaking curfew. But it's all in the past now. The war is over and all is well."

"Professor Huizenga looked so different. I hardly knew him."

"He suffered terribly in the Amersfoort prison camp. His brother was executed. They paid a huge price for the work they did at the bank, but they saved thousands of lives."

"I can never repay you for helping us or your parents for hiding Elisheva. So many good, kind people risked their lives for us. I would like to find out about the sisters who owned the last house where I hid. The Nazis arrested them along with me, but we were separated when I was sent to Westerbork."

"Oh, Miriam! You were in that horrible place?"

"My violin saved me. I played in the camp orchestra, so I was exempt from the transports. Otherwise . . . I heard about the concentration camps . . ."

"And now we have a chance to start all over again."

"I know that I'll never have the life I grew up with in Cologne or even the one I had in Leiden with Abba and Avi. My future is going to look very different from what I imagined."

"That's true for all of us, I think." The train was moving too slowly, starting and stopping so many times that Miriam wanted to scream. She needed to keep talking or she would go crazy.

"You had a boyfriend . . . will you marry him now?" she asked Ans.

"I broke up with Erik. I couldn't accept what he did, helping the

Nazis, joining the Nazi Party. Professor Huizenga says that all of the NSB members are being captured and sent to Westerbork. I suppose that means Erik, too."

"I don't wish that place on anyone."

"The professor said he hopes there will be justice, not revenge."

"I know that evil people exist in this world, but there are good ones, too. Whatever happens . . . if Elisheva and I are the only ones who've survived, I want to raise her to be one of the good ones."

They arrived at another station and waited to transfer to a different train. After an eternity, they arrived in the small village near Ans's farm. She and Miriam were both too weary to walk the final miles, so Miriam waited some more while Ans begged a ride from someone she knew in town.

Miriam began trembling again when they halted outside the farmhouse, an earthquake deep in her soul. Ans waved at the two men standing in the barn doorway. "That's my papa and my brother, Wim." She thanked the driver and helped Miriam from the truck. Miriam longed to run, but her legs could barely hold her. "This is Bep's mother, Miriam Leopold," Ans told her father.

"Bep's playing out back. I'll take you to her." Ans and her father had to hold Miriam up as they walked through the barn and outside again. She saw a woman working in the garden and two girls playing nearby. The beautiful child with the long dark braids was her daughter.

"Bep, Lena, come here," Ans's father called.

"You must be Miriam. I'm Lena," the woman said. "I'm so happy to see you!" Lena had tears in her eyes. Elisheva was holding the other girl's hand as they walked over. Miriam knelt down to face her daughter.

"Elisheva . . . ," she breathed. She ached to hold her, but Elisheva didn't remember her.

Lena rested her hand on Elisheva's back. "Bep, honey . . . this is your mother, from the photograph album. She's here!"

"May I give you a hug?" Miriam asked. Her daughter looked up at Lena, and in a heartbeat, Lena knelt down and enfolded both of them in her arms, holding Elisheva between them so she wouldn't be afraid. Her little body was warm and sweaty and alive. Miriam could feel her heartbeat. She inhaled the scent of the wind in her hair. Until the day she died, Miriam would never forget the exquisite joy of this moment.

With Lena's patient help, Elisheva warmed up to Miriam in the hours that followed. Bep showed her the doll she'd received for a present and the clothes her sister Maaike had sewn for it. "What's your doll's name?" Miriam asked.

"Nollie. She sleeps with me."

Miriam held Elisheva's hand as she and her brother, Wim, gave a tour of the farm and all the animals. Miriam couldn't take her eyes off her child. She especially loved hearing her laugh. She had Avi's wonderful smile. He would always be with Miriam in their daughter's smile.

Miriam slept on a mattress in Elisheva's bedroom that night to be near her. And so she could gaze at her in the moonlight and watch her sleep. She was alive. She was real. They were together again. Miriam helped her dress in the morning and brushed and braided her hair. Each simple act was a gift.

After breakfast, Miriam took out her violin to play for her daughter. She'd been trembling too greatly throughout the first day to even attempt it. "This is a lullaby I used to play for you when you were a baby. It was your favorite." Miriam lifted the instrument that was so much a part of her and played from the wellspring of love in her soul. Elisheva didn't move as she listened, her dark eyes shining. *She remembers. Her heart remembers.*

"Play more!" she said, clapping her hands when Miriam finished. Rietje and the residents of Meijers House had done the same. Music had power to heal. Miriam had felt dead inside for so long, but music provided the bridge back to living. She played everything she knew by heart, losing track of time as she filled in all the years that had been lost. At last she stopped, exhausted in body and soul, aware of where she was again. Her beloved daughter was still sitting with rapt attention.

"She has always loved music," Lena said. "In the first months she was here and missing you so terribly, singing to her was the only way to soothe her to sleep."

Lena loves her too, Miriam realized. And she was grateful.

Suddenly Ans's brother began shouting from outside, "Ans! Mama! Everyone, come here!" Miriam hurried outside with the others. Her heart stopped when she saw what the fuss was about.

Avi!

He was climbing off Professor Huizenga's decrepit bicycle, letting it fall to the ground, running forward to embrace her. Neither of them could stand. They fell to their knees, wrapped in each other's arms. How she'd dreamed of this day, fearing in her darkest moments that it would never come. Avi was alive! He was alive! Their daughter was alive! And for the very first time in many years, Miriam heard the song of the wind in the trees and the birds singing praises to God.

EPILOGUE

FALL 1945

Lena stuck a fork into one of the potatoes bubbling in a pot on the stove. Almost done. She was grateful to have food to cook again, her root cellar full after a good fall harvest. She crossed to the sink, glancing out the window as she passed it, watching for Ans. Avraham and Wim were returning from the cow pasture with Bep riding on her abba's shoulders. She was comfortable with him now, after these past few months together. They had all laughed when Avi had shown them that he could milk a cow. "I learned how while hiding out on a farm like this one," he'd said proudly. How good it was to see their family reunited and thriving again.

"I finished setting the table," Maaike said. "May I go outside and watch for Ans?"

Lena smoothed Maaike's fair hair from her face. "Yes, you may. And be sure to let me know when she gets here."

"I will." Maaike dashed off through the door. Lena thanked God that her daughter was becoming less anxious, her nightmares fading into the past. It had been Wim who'd helped Maaike chase away her fears, assuring her as they walked to school and back every day that the Nazis were gone for good.

The beautiful strains of Miriam's violin drifted down from upstairs as Lena worked. She would miss hearing Miriam play. Her music had blessed all of them as they'd shed the last layers of gloom from the war. Pieter had invited the Leopolds to live with them while they regained their strength and decided what came next. Truus and the other gossiping villagers now knew the truth about Bep. Ans's reputation had been vindicated. These past months with her parents had given Bep a chance to get to know them again—and Lena's family had time to say goodbye to her.

Bep was fascinated with Miriam's violin and comfortable sitting on her lap in the evenings as Avi read from the Psalms. They were leaving soon, and Lena would miss them all—but especially little Bep. She was Lena's beloved daughter, and yet Lena couldn't hang on to her any more than she could hang on to her other children. The time would come when she would release all of them into God's capable hands. Miriam had taught her that.

The potatoes were done. Lena had cooked them with apples, and she mashed them together now to serve with the meatballs that were staying warm in the oven. It was one of Ans's favorite meals.

"She's here! She's here! Ans is here!" Maaike called from outside.

Lena smiled to herself. Ans had left home a strong-willed teenager and had suffered much during the war, enduring trials that Lena never would have wished on her beautiful daughter. But Ans had allowed God to use hardship and suffering to transform her into a strong woman of faith. Lena hurried through the door to welcome her home. Ans had regained the weight she'd lost in prison and looked wonderfully healthy again.

"Are you hungry?" Lena asked after hugging her tightly. "You must be after your long bicycle ride. Come inside and eat."

"Look at Ans's new bicycle, Mama," Maaike said.

"It's not brand-new," Ans said, laughing. "I got it at a sale of bicycles that were confiscated during the war. Maybe you can get one too."

Pieter came out of the barn to greet Ans as well. And Avi and Wim were back from the field with Bep. "The food is all ready," Lena told everyone. "Wash up so we can eat." She crouched down in front of Bep after Avi lowered her from his shoulders. "Will you do something for me? Run upstairs and tell your mother that it's time to eat. She's practicing her violin." Bep skipped into the house and up the stairs.

When they were all seated around the lunch table, Pieter bowed his head to thank God for the food. "And thank You for bringing all of these loved ones safely through the war." He repeated those words every time he prayed. Lena never tired of thanking God too.

"Amen," she said. "Now start passing the food."

"I'm bursting to tell everyone my good news," Ans said as she loaded her plate. Lena looked at her, waiting. "I've decided to go to university. Classes start next week."

"That's wonderful!" Pieter said, voicing Lena's thoughts. "What will you study?"

"I'm not sure yet. Maybe journalism? I remember how much we relied on newspapers during the war. Eloise thinks I should study medicine."

"How are the Huizengas?" Miriam asked. "Will you still live with them?"

"Yes, they want me to stay. Professor Huizenga is up to his ears with his work at the university. And Eloise is volunteering with the Red Cross in Amsterdam twice a week, helping displaced persons."

"So she's doing well?" Miriam asked.

"Very well. Eloise has enough energy to do the work of ten people."

"We have news too," Avi said. "We might be neighbors in Leiden soon. I'm going to finish my engineering degree at the university."

"That's great!" Ans said.

"And we'll still be close enough to come home to the farm," Miriam added, "so Elisheva can visit her other mama and papa."

Tears filled Lena's eyes each time she thought of letting Bep go. Her arms would feel so empty without her. How she loved this precious child!

"And her sister and brother, too," Maaike added.

"Our other news isn't so happy," Avi said. "I've been traveling to Amsterdam every week to see what I can find out about our families. Records from all the camps are slowly being released, so I've been searching for names. And I learned that Miriam may be entitled to her family's assets in Cologne."

"Yes, but let's not spoil this wonderful meal and grand occasion," Miriam said.

Lena already knew what Avraham had learned. His family in Berlin and Miriam's family in Cologne had all perished. Miriam's father, Professor Jacobs, had died as well. Lena had mourned with them these past weeks, still grieving the loss of her own father. The pain never went away entirely, but time had made it easier to carry, and the waves of grief came less often.

"Do you have a place to live in Leiden?" Ans asked. "I'm sure Eloise would let you stay with us. She'll be so excited to see you and Elisheva."

"We're eager to see her too," Avi said. "I met Mrs. Spielman's grandson when I was in Amsterdam—Mrs. Spielman was our landlady in Leiden. He was searching the records too and learned that his grandmother was gone. But he knew who Miriam and I were, and he offered to let us live in our old apartment as caretakers. He plans to list the other apartment for rent."

"I wonder if Noah felt this way after the flood," Ans said. "There's so much destruction everywhere and so much rebuilding to do as we start all over again. But the world is still a beautiful place."

"And we have much to be thankful for," Miriam added. "I realize now that when we were in hiding, we were never hidden from God."

"Even so," Lena said, "it must be very difficult for you and Avi to begin again. Pieter and I still have our home and our farm. I admire your courage to move forward after losing everything."

"We don't understand why God allowed this to happen to our people," Avi said. "But we won't turn away from Him in our grief and disappointment. We'll bring our questions to Him. Miriam's father once told me that his favorite students were the ones who weren't afraid to ask questions. He thought God must feel the same way. I believe it will draw us closer to Him as we wait for His answers."

"One of my questions," Miriam said softly, "is why we were spared when so many, many others weren't."

"Only God knows," Avi said. "But Miriam and I and Elisheva owe a huge debt to all of you. And to so many other courageous people who risked their lives for us. I don't know how we will ever repay you."

"The best way to repay us," Pieter said, "is to do the same thing—show kindness and generosity to others."

"And by refusing to hate," Lena added. "I hope none of us ever forgets that hatred and greed were how this terrible war began."

Lena would always be grateful for that lesson. And for learning to trust the sovereignty and goodness of God even when tragedy and hardship overwhelmed her. She knew now that God had directed her family in the past and was here with them today. None of them knew the future, but they could trust Him with that, too.

"Who would like seconds?" she asked. "Eat hearty, everyone! There's plenty more."

DON'T MISS

The Wish Book Christmas

❧

Coming from

LYNN
AUSTIN

Fall 2021

Turn the page for a sneak peek!

CHAPTER 1

DECEMBER 1951

Christmas was coming. Eve Dawson saw signs of it all around her Connecticut town as she walked home from work. Pine boughs and wreaths decorated front doors. Christmas lights and tempting gift displays adorned shopwindows. Even the snow blanketing lawns and rooftops and sitting in puffy mounds on all of the bushes looked festive. Yes, Christmas was coming, and with it, the anxiety of trying to squeeze a few extra dollars from her tight budget to buy presents for her five-year-old son, Harry.

The afternoon was growing dark as she hurried along. The shortened December days meant it was barely light when she left for work in the morning and nearly dark when she returned home. Harry would be watching for her from the picture window, eager to show her something he'd made in kindergarten or to describe the latest exploits of his TV heroes, the Lone Ranger and Tonto. Eve remembered watching for her mum the same way, waiting outside Granny Maud's cottage for the first glimpse of Mum coming up the road. At least Eve's job in the typing pool allowed her to return home to Harry every day and tuck him into bed at night. When Eve was Harry's age, her mum, who'd also been a single mother, had worked as a live-in servant at Wellingford Hall and was only able to see Eve once a week.

A hunched figure hurried up the sidewalk toward Eve—Mrs. Herder, bundled against the cold and the gently falling snow, walking her dog. Eve smiled at the older woman as they passed. "Hello. Lovely evening, isn't it?"

"If you like snow." Her words were muffled by the thick scarf wrapped around her neck and chin. Mrs. Herder continued past, her rambunctious yellow Labrador stopping to sniff at mailbox posts one minute, then tugging on his lead the next. They seemed a mismatched pair, the young dog too large and energetic for the small, white-haired woman who reminded Eve of her granny.

Eve quickened her steps, gazing at the houses she passed, wishing she had a home of her own for her and her son. What would that be like? Lights glowed from behind her neighbors' windows, revealing glimpses of their lives, as if peering at distant television screens. She knew very little about her neighbors, including Mrs. Herder, even though she passed the older woman and her dog nearly every day. Eve only assumed her name was Herder because it was printed on her mailbox out front. The older woman lived in an historic house with a wide front porch that stood at the very edge of Eve's neighborhood of new, postwar bungalows. Mrs. Herder still displayed a gold star in her window six years after the war had ended, as if she didn't want anyone to forget that she had lost a loved one. The star stirred memories of Alfie Clarkson, Eve's first love, who had also died in the war. Alfie and Mum and Granny—Eve wished she could hang gold stars somewhere to tell the world how much she missed them.

She turned to watch Mrs. Herder and her dog walk up the steps and enter their house and felt a wave of homesickness for the little English village of Wellingford, where she'd grown up. Her neighbors had known each other's names and had watched out for each other, their brick and stone cottages sitting shoulder to shoulder as if closing ranks against the outside world, not separated by private lawns and picket fences as they were here in America. The cottage in the village that she'd shared with Granny, and the nearby woods where she'd loved to roam, were the only true homes Eve could recall. But she had needed a new start for herself and Harry after the war, in a place where no one knew the shame of Harry's birth. While she wasn't proud of the way she had maneuvered that fresh start, things had turned out better than she deserved, for both her and her son. They lived with Eve's widowed friend, Audrey Barrett, paying rent every month, and the four of them had become a family of sorts. But if Eve could wish for any gift this Christmas, it would be a home of her own.

Harry wasn't in his usual place, watching for Eve from the front window as she walked up the driveway to Audrey's little bungalow. She went inside through the kitchen door, stomping snow off her boots. She pulled off her hat, then smoothed down her hair. "It's snowing again," she told Audrey.

"The boys will be happy about that." Audrey stood at the kitchen stove, mashing a pot of potatoes into gooey submission. "Personally, I don't much like driving in snow."

"We drove our ambulances on some rather slippery roads during the war, remember?"

"At breakneck speed. With bombs falling. But it had to be done."

Eve hung up her coat and followed the happy sound of Harry's voice as he played with Audrey's son, Bobby. She found them sprawled on the rug in the living room, paging through a brightly colored catalogue. The boys were the same age and nearly the same size and might have been twins in their corduroy pants and plaid flannel shirts, except that Harry had ginger hair—a redhead, the Americans would say—and was friendly and talkative and boisterous. Bobby had inherited his father's ebony hair and his mother's shy reserve.

"What has you so charmed that you can't even say hello to your mum?" Eve asked.

"Hi, Mommy." Eve sighed inwardly at her son's American accent and wording. It was her own fault, since she had brought him to the States as an infant. Bobby, having been here for a year and a half, was starting to adopt the same type of speech, but at least he still called Audrey "Mummy."

Harry barely glanced up, as if he might miss something if he looked away for too long. "We're picking out all the toys we want Santa to bring us from the Christmas Wish Book." He pointed to the page, saying, "I want that airplane. Oooh, and that submarine, too! And I want this army truck and this tank and this motorcycle . . . We could play army, right, Bobby?"

"That would be fun!" Bobby laid his hand on the page for a moment as if claiming territory. "I want *all* of the trucks on this page—and especially this motorbus!"

Harry waited until his friend lifted his hand, then flipped to the next page. "I want this pickup truck. Look, it has lights that really light up! And wow, look at this steam shovel! We could dig holes with it!"

"I want one," Bobby said. "This army jeep has real lights, too!"

Eve squatted beside the boys for a better look as they continued turning pages, gleefully pointing to fire engines and bulldozers and police cars. "It looks to me like you're asking for every toy in the book."

"Not the *girls'* stuff," Harry said, making a face. "We don't want *dolls*!"

"Or baby toys," Bobby added. "Just all of the boys' toys on all of these pages." Eve watched them flip through a few more pages, chorusing, "I want this and this . . ."

She frowned. "There isn't room in this house for all of those toys. And besides, you have so many playthings already."

"But they're *old* toys, Mommy. These are *new* toys. We're going to ask Santa for all of these new toys when we see him at the parade tonight."

"The parade? That's tonight?"

"Yep. Did you forget, Mommy?"

"I may have, yes. I had a busy day at work." A mind-numbing day, actually. One that was exactly like the day before it and the one before that, clacking out letters in a windowless office as part of a typing pool. After paying her rent and a portion of the debt she felt she owed Audrey, Eve would be lucky to have enough money left over to buy one toy for Harry, let alone an entire catalogue full of them.

Audrey poked her head around the corner from the kitchen. "Dinner is ready. Wash up, please."

Eve stood and walked toward Audrey. "Where did they get the catalogue?"

"It's called the Wish Book, Mommy," Harry called to her.

"I think it came about a month ago, but I found it again when I straightened up this morning. They've been glued to it all afternoon." The boys stood to wash their hands, carrying the catalogue to the bathroom with them.

"Look at that, Bobby!" she heard Harry saying as they went. "It's a whole service station, with gasoline pumps and cars and everything!"

"I want one!"

"That Wish Book seems to have opened a Pandora's box of greedy longing," Eve told Audrey with a sigh. She would never be able to buy even a quarter of those toys for her son.

When they finally sat down at the kitchen table, Harry bolted his food in record time. "Hurry, Mommy, hurry!" he begged. "We're gonna miss the Santa Claus Parade."

Eve continued to eat at a leisurely pace. "Don't worry. We have plenty of time."

"Do you have to go away tonight, Mummy?" Bobby asked Audrey. The worried look on his face was exactly like his mother's. Audrey had been a worrier for as long as Eve had known her, which was most of their thirty-two years. They had met as twelve-year-olds in the woods surrounding Wellingford Hall, where Eve's mother served as lady's maid to Audrey's mother, the wealthy and aristocratic Lady Rosamunde.

"No, my classes are all finished for the semester," Audrey replied.

"Don't you remember how anxious your mum was when she was

studying for her exams last week?" Eve asked. "We barely got a full sentence out of her."

"My final marks came in the mail today," Audrey said quietly.

"Well, are you going to show us or were they a disaster?"

Audrey smiled her shy, Audrey smile, dipping her head a little as if bowing before royalty. "They weren't bad."

"Let me guess—you earned top marks in both classes, am I right?"

"Yes."

"Good job, you! We'll have to celebrate."

After eating, they stacked the supper dishes in the sink to save for later and bundled up for the short drive into town for the parade. On the way there, Eve heard the boys whispering in the back seat and she swiveled around from the passenger seat to look. They had the catalogue open and were pointing and murmuring, "I want a gun and holster set like that!"

"We can pretend we're the Lone Ranger!"

"You brought the Wish Book with you? To a parade?" she asked in astonishment. The boys stared at her as if she'd asked a silly question.

"Did they really?" Audrey asked, glancing in the rearview mirror. "You've been studying it all afternoon, Bobby."

"I know, Mummy, but I might forget to tell Santa something I really, really want."

"We're gonna just *show* him everything instead," Harry added.

"You cannot sit on Santa's lap with the entire Sears Wish Book in your greedy little hands," Eve said.

"Why not?"

"Please, Mummy?"

"Well, for one thing, Santa Claus brings toys to a lot of other children besides you two," Eve said, "and the things you're asking for would fill his entire sled."

"He can make lots of trips, Mommy. He has all night."

Eve glanced at Audrey and saw her trying to hide a smile.

"Besides," Harry continued, "Santa only brings toys if you're good, and there are lots of kids at school who aren't being good."

"They'll get coal in their stockings," Bobby said solemnly.

Audrey found a parking spot near the village square, and as the boys tumbled out of the back seat, Eve spotted the catalogue peeking out from beneath Harry's jacket. "The Wish Book stays in the car," she said, yanking it out and tossing it onto the seat.

"But, Mommy . . ."

She shut the car door. "If you can't remember everything on the list, maybe it's because your list is too long."

A huge Christmas tree stood in the picturesque town square, waiting for the mayor to throw the switch and light it up at the end of the parade.

"When are we going to get a Christmas tree?" Harry asked.

"Maybe this weekend. We'll cut one down from Uncle Tom's farm like we did last year, remember?"

Audrey's late husband's childhood friend Tom Vandenberg had been like a father to both of the boys, and he also held a special place in Eve's heart. In fact, he'd hinted more than once that he'd like to marry her and be more than just a father figure in Harry's life.

Beneath the village Christmas tree was a throne for Santa and a roped-off section where the children could form a queue to talk with him. Eve took Harry's hand in hers as they headed down the town's main street, wading through the crowd of pedestrians, searching for a place to stand along the parade route.

The quaint Connecticut town had been decorated with Christmas lights that twinkled against the snow, and the store windows were beautifully staged to tempt shoppers. Eve paused to look at a display of the latest aluminum kitchen appliances and coffeepots for modern housewives, along with aluminum ladders, Thermos bottles, and saws for their husbands. These were items that belonged in a home—a real home with a mother and father and children.

She closed her eyes, fighting off the familiar emptiness when she considered her and Audrey's makeshift family. At least Audrey had a respectable reason for being a single mum. And Eve should be thankful that her friend had invited Eve and Harry to share her home. She had lived off Audrey's insurance money and her husband's inheritance for nearly four years, living in Audrey's house, driving her car. And although Audrey wasn't demanding a penny of it, Eve was determined to pay it all back.

"Wow! Look at that airplane, Bobby!" Harry pointed to a large propeller plane, also made from aluminum, dangling behind the store window from a wire. "Was there a big airplane like that in the Wish Book?"

"I don't think so. I want it!"

"Me, too. We'll tell Santa tonight. What's the name of this store, Mommy? We need to tell Santa where he can buy it."

"Santa will know," Eve said, tugging his hand. "Come on."

No matter how far they walked, the sidewalks were so crowded with families and children standing three- and four-deep to watch the parade that Eve couldn't find a place where all of them could stand. The cadence of drums sounded in the distance. The parade was about to begin.

Harry hopped up and down in frustration. "I can't see! I can't see!"

"Mummy, look," Bobby said. "They have daddies to help them." He pointed to the families in front of them, and Eve saw that many of the fathers had lifted their small children onto their shoulders or held them in their arms so they could see. Eve and Audrey were both petite, and besides, the boys were too heavy to hold for the entire parade.

"I need a daddy so I can see," Harry told Eve. "Everyone else has one."

"It's not fair," Bobby pouted.

"Oh, dear," Eve murmured. She met Audrey's worried gaze.

The next moment, Harry dropped Eve's hand and ran up to a well-dressed gentleman who was just coming out of the department store. He carried a brightly wrapped box tied with a silver bow. "Will you be our daddy?" Harry asked him.

"*Harry!*" Eve gasped, horrified.

"Mine, too! Mine, too!" Bobby echoed, running to the man.

A tide of heat rushed to Eve's face as she hurried over to apologize to the gentleman and yank her son away. But before she could utter a sound, the man crouched down to talk to the boys. "Hello, Harry and Bobby. Are you here to see Santa Claus?" Eve recognized him then. Mr. Hamilton was the leader of their Boys' Club at church. But she was still horribly embarrassed. And judging by her friend's expression, Audrey was too.

"Yeah. We were going to show Santa all the toys we wanted in the Wish Book," Harry told him, "but Mommy made us leave it in the car."

"I hope I can remember everything." Bobby wore his fretful look again.

Mr. Hamilton smiled. "I'm sure you'll remember the important things." He was probably in his midthirties and movie-star handsome. When millions of American GIs had landed in England during the war, Eve and Audrey and all the other women used to comment on how handsome the American men were—and here was another one, not wearing a uniform but a very expensive-looking overcoat, fedora, and cashmere scarf.

He stood again as the high school marching band approached playing "Jingle Bells."

"It's starting! The parade is starting!" Harry said, hopping up and down. "And we don't have a daddy!"

Mr. Hamilton gave Audrey and Eve a questioning look, as if not understanding.

"To boost them up," Eve said quickly, gesturing to the families around them.

"I see. I'll be glad to help." He handed his package to Audrey and crouched again, then lifted up both boys, one in each arm. Mr. Hamilton was a big man, tall and broad-shouldered, as solid as a Frigidaire. He looked as though he could easily manage two boys.

"But . . . I'm sure Mr. Hamilton needs to get home to his family and—" Audrey began.

"I don't mind at all," he said with a smile.

"Well . . . thank you. You can put them down whenever you get tired," Eve said.

Fire engines rolled past, red lights flashing. Prancing horses carried

Roy Rogers and Hopalong Cassidy look-alikes shooting cap pistols. The mayor waved from inside a Model A Ford strung with fairy lights. Local business owners towed homemade floats with Christmas decorations and pretty high school girls singing carols. Santa's elves gave out candy canes to the children along the way. Then Santa Claus himself arrived, his sleigh pulled by a shiny new John Deere tractor.

"Hey! Where are all his reindeer?" Harry asked.

"Maybe they're resting up for their big night," Mr. Hamilton replied.

"They'll need a long rest after pulling a sled filled with all the toys you boys want," Eve said. She and Audrey thanked Mr. Hamilton profusely when the parade ended and he had set the boys down on the sidewalk again. He tipped his hat to them and retrieved his package from Audrey.

"My pleasure, ladies. I hope you have a very merry Christmas—and that you boys get everything you want from that Wish Book."

"Not a chance," Eve mumbled. They followed the rest of the crowd back to the village square, applauding when the mayor flipped the switch and the towering Christmas tree lit up.

The queue of children waiting to sit on Santa's lap seemed miles long, and Eve was weary. The cold had seeped through her boots, chilling her toes. "It's going to take hours for you boys to have your turn," she moaned. "And then another hour to recite the unabridged version of the Wish Book to him."

"I have an idea," Audrey said. "Why don't you write letters to Santa instead? That way, you can take your time, and you won't forget anything." Audrey's cheeks were as red as apples, and she was shivering. The boys seemed oblivious to the cold.

"But I can't write yet, Mummy. Just my name."

"I'll help you. I promise."

"That's a great idea," Eve said. "Let's go home."

"He's only Santa's helper, anyway," she heard Harry telling Bobby as they trudged back to the car. "The real Santa lives at the North Pole and has lots and lots of toys to make."

⚜

Harry got into a tug-of-war with Bobby at bedtime, arguing over which of them would get to sleep with the Wish Book under his pillow. "It isn't going under either one of your pillows," Audrey said, taking it away. "It's not as though you've lost a tooth and are waiting for the tooth fairy." She set the book on their dresser for the night.

"But, Mummy . . . ," Bobby whined.

"Didn't you see all of those other children at the parade tonight?" Eve asked. "Santa has to bring presents to all of them, too. He can't bring you every single toy in the Wish Book."

"We'll ask Nana and Granddad for the rest," Eve heard Harry say as she switched off the light. "They always buy lots and lots of presents." Eve started to argue but knew it was true. She looked at Audrey helplessly.

Eve went into the kitchen with Audrey afterwards, talking while they washed and dried the dishes. "I had only been in America for a few months last Christmas," Audrey said as she rinsed suds off a plate, "and I wasn't familiar with all of the Christmas traditions. But I do remember that my in-laws gave Bobby a great many toys, and it did seem a bit too much. I guess I was so overwhelmed by the love Robert's parents showed Bobby and me that I didn't want to speak up about all the toys."

"I'm quite sure Nana Barrett will repeat her performance this Christmas. She does it every year." Eve and Harry had spent every Christmas with the Barretts since Harry was a baby, and while she still felt uncomfortable with the extravagant generosity, she had come to expect it. Harry, of course, didn't have any problem with it at all. Until last year, Eve had allowed the Barretts to believe she and Harry were their daughter-in-law and grandson, and it was only by God's grace that they still wanted to maintain a close relationship with Eve after she confessed her deception.

"Even if the Barretts can afford every toy in the Wish Book," Audrey said, "I don't want Bobby to grow up craving so many things—or expecting to get them. It isn't right."

Eve wiped a plate dry and put it in the cupboard. "I remember being grateful for just a few simple gifts at Christmas when I was their age. I would hang my stocking on my bedpost for Father Christmas to fill, and in the morning, I'd find a little doll or a toy on top . . . maybe an orange and some candy. Granny would knit new mittens or a hat for me. I learned later that Mum had saved up for months to buy me those things. She always had to work on Christmas Day, but we could spend Boxing Day together." Eve wondered if her mum had felt the same sense of loss at missing out on her child's life because of her need to work.

"I remember how our gardener would cut armloads of greens and holly branches," Audrey said, her hands submerged in the soapy dishwater. "Wellingford Hall looked and smelled so splendid. There would be a huge tree and presents to unwrap, chosen by my tutor, Miss Blake, I'm sure. Not by my parents. And we always had Christmas crackers to pop open at the table. But best of all, Alfie would be home from boarding school for a few weeks."

They worked in silence for a few moments, Audrey scrubbing a pot with a Brillo pad. Eve supposed they were both remembering Audrey's older brother, Alfie, and how much they had both loved him. "During the war," Audrey said, "we were grateful if we got through Christmas without being startled out of our beds in the middle of the night by air-raid sirens, remember?"

"Oh yes. And I remember how the American GIs would hold sprigs of mistletoe over our heads at the Christmas dances so they could steal a kiss."

Audrey fell silent again, and Eve knew she was thinking of her husband, Robert. "I want Harry to have lovely memories of Christmas, but I don't think getting every toy in the Wish Book is going to accomplish it. Besides, I can't spend wads of money on presents with my budget."

"My brother felt entitled to anything and everything he ever wished for, and it ruined him in the end. I don't want that to happen to Bobby. Is there some way we can teach them not to want so much?" Audrey handed Eve the pot to dry and pulled the stopper from the sink.

"I don't know. I'll have to think about it. But I agree. They need to learn that Christmas is more than getting every toy they could ever wish for."

A Note from the Author

Chasing Shadows was not an easy novel to write. My goal in writing each of my books is to proclaim God's love and bring hope to readers. Telling the story of life in the Netherlands during World War II meant that I had to take readers to some very dark places. I pray that in doing so, I also showed how faithfully Jesus walks beside us through those dark valleys.

I have grown to dearly love the Netherlands and its people after visiting several times on book tours, and I've always wanted to make it the setting for one of my books. I had a little knowledge of how much the Dutch people suffered during the war after reading two autobiographies years ago—*The Hiding Place* by Corrie ten Boom and *Things We Couldn't Say* by Diet Eman. I can't begin to put into words the profound effect these books and these two women had on my faith. Both Corrie and Diet were Christians—living normal lives, falling in love, and making plans for the future—until the surprise Nazi invasion of their neutral nation on May 10, 1940. Both women's faith in God proved strong and dynamic when put to the test. Their lives challenged me to question the vitality of my own faith if I were to be tested in such an overwhelming way.

Many of the incidents in this story are based on true accounts of courageous Dutch Christians who lived through the Nazi occupation. Ernst Lubbers is based on the real-life musician Max Ehrlich, a popular actor and theater director who staged musical productions while imprisoned in Westerbork. He died in Auschwitz in 1944.

In reading historical accounts of the Dutch experience, I was surprised and amazed to hear secular historians give credit to the church and to people of faith for withstanding the darkness. The Nazis considered the Dutch their Aryan brothers and hoped to incorporate them into the Reich. But Dutch Christians answered to God above all and refused to give in to the Nazis' evil demands—even at the cost of their lives.

I pray that we'll never have to endure what Christians in the Netherlands did. But it's my hope that *Chasing Shadows* will lead readers to take a closer look at their own faith, as I did after reading *The Hiding Place* years ago. I remember wanting a faith like Corrie and her family had and like Diet Eman and her fiancé had. I pray that this novel will inspire you to pursue a closer walk with God and lead to a commitment to serve His Kingdom with whatever gifts He has given you.

God bless you all!
Lynn

Acknowledgments

Giving birth to a book has many similarities to giving birth to a child. Each novel begins as a tiny seed of an idea, then slowly develops and grows over time until that joyful and sometimes-painful moment when the new "baby" is finally ready to meet the world. And giving birth to either a baby or a novel is something I could never do alone. I'm grateful for this chance to thank the many, many people who have helped me give birth to *Chasing Shadows*.

My husband, Ken, is always vitally important in my writing just as he was, of course, with our actual children. He's my first reader, plowing through my half-finished chapters and unresolved plot ideas and listening to me ramble on and on about what might or might not happen. Ever since that long-ago day when I first said, "I think I want to try writing a book," Ken has been my most enthusiastic cheerleader. He never stopped believing in me, even when I sometimes stopped believing in myself.

Our son Benjamin, who earned his doctoral degree at Leiden University, was an invaluable help in writing this book, teaching me all about that lovely city and showing me (and my characters) how to get around. We also bicycled out of Leiden into the Dutch countryside one memorable day to where Lena and Pieter's imaginary farm would be located.

My longtime friends and fellow writers Jane Rubietta and Cleo

Lampos have been vitally important to every book I have written. We have been meeting and critiquing each other's work for more than twenty-six years, before any of us was ever published, and I'm quite certain that I couldn't write a book without them.

My nonwriting friends Ed and Cathy Pruim and Paul and Jacki Kleinheksel are also irreplaceable and essential to my writing process. They allow me to air my frustrations, they pray with me, and they offer me spiritual insights and down-to-earth advice whenever I need it. I'm so grateful to all of these friends for keeping me grounded—and for getting me out of my office to go biking and have fun! I'm also grateful to Paul and Jacki for introducing me to Dutch friends who were willing to share their war stories with me, especially Mary DeBlaay, Jennie Vander Maarl, and Toni Vanluinen.

Christine Bierma is my assistant who is so much more than my assistant! She brought me into the twenty-first century with web pages and blogs and social media and all of that other technology that I still don't fully understand. She's the midwife who helps me launch each new book by acting as coach and cheerleader for my amazing launch team. Christine is a partner to me in every way, and I would not want to launch a book without her and her online business, Launch Right.

My publishing partners at Tyndale House have guided and shaped this book into a finished product. Stephanie Broene has been alongside me from the beginning stages and throughout the rewriting, cover design, and marketing processes. I so appreciate her insight and partnership. My editor, Kathy Olson, has patiently guided me through a new way of doing edits and has made it fun and painless. She also made this a much better book. I have loved working with Andrea Garcia and the marketing team, and with Katie Dodillet and the publicity team. You all excel at what you do. So does my amazing literary agent, Natasha Kern. The publishing world is changing so quickly and so dramatically that my writing career would be lost at sea without Natasha's knowledge and expertise. But more than that, she offered valuable input into this story and gave me encouragement and advice when I needed it most.

I'm indebted to my many friends from Kok/Voorhoeve Publishing in the Netherlands for first introducing me to their beautiful country. They've shown me so many wonderful places on my book tours, taught me about their country's history, and introduced me to the wonderful Dutch people. They helped provide the background and setting for this novel, including a very moving visit to the Westerbork prison camp. I'm grateful to all my Dutch friends who shared their families' stories of life in the Netherlands during that terrible war.

A warm, heartfelt thank-you to all of you. I wish you God's richest blessings. *Chasing Shadows* would not be the same book without you.

Discussion Questions

1. The three main characters in *Chasing Shadows*—Lena, Miriam, and Ans—are all in different seasons of life and have different outlooks on the world. Which character did you most closely identify with? Which one was the hardest for you to relate to? How did each woman grow and change as a result of her experiences during the war?

2. In the prologue, we read that Lena "used to believe that the enemy of faith was doubt." But by the end of the war, "she'd learned that faith's destroyer was fear." Do you agree with this conclusion? Read Hebrews 11. Did these heroes of faith battle doubt or fear or both?

3. A recurring theme in Miriam's story is the power of music. Do you have a similar appreciation for music? What form does it take in your life—playing an instrument, singing, listening to favorite artists or genres? Why do you think music can be such a powerful force? How does it help Miriam, both physically and emotionally?

4. Ans tells Erik that she answers to a higher authority than the Nazis. If God asks her to disobey the authorities (what's known as civil disobedience), she says she has to obey God, even at the risk of her own life. How do you feel about civil disobedience? What are some other examples from history that come to mind? Are there any moral issues you feel strongly enough about to risk disobeying the law?

5. In one of Erik and Ans's conversations about right and wrong, Erik asks, "What can you and I do to stop evil when it's all over the world?" Have you ever felt overwhelmed by the evil in the world? How have you found ways to make a difference? What advice would you give a friend who has the same outlook as Erik?

6. Miriam's father tells her and Avi that his best university students were the ones who asked questions. He says, "I think God likes it when we ask questions." Do you agree? Can you think of examples from the Bible that point to this being true? How might this idea of questioning God change your prayer life?

7. After Pieter escapes death from a Nazi firing squad, he tells Lena, "I felt at peace as I knelt there. I thought of that Scripture that says, 'For to me, to live is Christ and to die is gain.' I understood it." The Scripture he quotes is Philippians 1:21, written by the apostle Paul. What do you know about Paul's life that might have led him to make this declaration? How does it apply to Pieter's life? Is this an assertion that you feel able to make? Why or why not?

8. Ans and her grandfather discuss whether it's okay to lie for a good cause. He brings up the example of the Jewish midwives lying to Pharaoh in order to save Jewish babies and says, "There's a difference between lying to save yourself and for your selfish ends—to get yourself out of trouble or make yourself look good—and lying to save another person's life. A huge difference." Can you think of other examples from the Bible where someone lied for a "good" reason? How do you feel about passages like these?

9. Eloise speaks words that inspire Ans and which Eloise goes on to live out: "What good is my life if I selfishly keep it to myself and don't spend it for others?" How does this reflect a biblical worldview? What are some ways you have been challenged to spend your life for others? What do you find difficult about doing this?

10. *Chasing Shadows* deals a lot with impossible choices—trying to decide between two or more options, none of which are really good or right. Miriam and Avi are faced with the impossible choice of whether to separate and entrust their precious baby to strangers, just in hopes of surviving. Have you ever needed to make a decision that had no right answer? Do you think you would make the same choice they made?

11. Lena's pastor-father tells his congregation, "Jesus said the most important commandments are to love the Lord your God and love your neighbor. And so, whenever we face a dilemma, we can ask, What is the best way to show our love for God and for our neighbor?" How do various characters in the book choose to show their love for God and neighbor?

12. After Pieter is deployed, Lena tells her father she's "never understood why [God] doesn't answer our prayers if He loves us." How does her father respond? When you've faced a challenging circumstance and it feels like your pleas are falling on deaf ears, what comforts you?

13. After being invited to join the prison camp orchestra, why does Miriam falter before her first performance? What does Luke 9:23 say about the life of a believer in Christ? Is it too much to ask Miriam to go on with the show?

14. As the war nears its end, Lena has an interesting conversation with her cousin Truus in which Lena tries to share how she's changed and how her faith has grown. Truus responds, "Can we please talk about something else?" Do you like to share and analyze like Lena, or would you rather put the past behind you and focus on the future like Truus? Is one way better than the other?

15. When we go through a major event—whether it's a personal battle like an illness or the loss of a loved one, or something more widespread like a world war—does it make sense that we would come out the other side changed? In what ways have you experienced change after big upheavals?

About the Author

Lynn Austin has sold more than one and a half million copies of her books worldwide. A former teacher who now writes and speaks full-time, she has won eight Christy Awards for her historical fiction and was one of the first inductees into the Christy Award Hall of Fame. One of her novels, *Hidden Places*, was made into a Hallmark Channel Original Movie. Lynn and her husband have three grown children and make their home in western Michigan. Visit her online at lynnaustin.org.

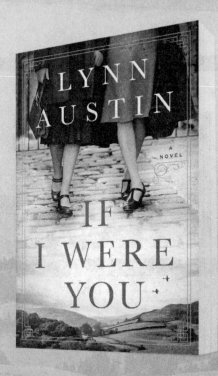

CONNECT WITH LYNN ONLINE AT

lynnaustin.org

OR FOLLOW HER ON: